IRE OF WAR

A Devil's Trials Novel

Stephanie Gluck

This one is for Dylan.
Thanks for letting me pepper you with questions!

&

For Mr. Puff, always

Also, by Stephanie Gluck:

THE DEVIL'S TRIALS
Feast of Samael
Heist of Haures
Ire of War

THE FOUR REALMS
Death's Stalker

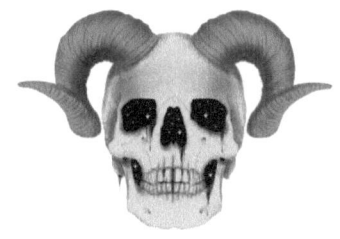

Chapter One

We had escaped the underbelly of Envy's city unharmed. If we didn't count the cracks to our psyche, which webbed delicately from the fissures Gluttony had created, leaving us on the precipice of crumbling.

I was barely keeping myself together.

We ran from the sunset, staggering away from the last vestiges of light as it disappeared behind us. The crone told us to move east, and Niklaus Heira led the way without hesitation. He marched forward, clinging to the woman we had stolen from Envy's collection, not sparing a single backwards glance for the brother left behind.

I wondered if the cracks in his soul collapsed deeper into his heart for the family he had lost. If they had, he showed no sign of it affecting him.

The Envylands were cold and miserable. With the evening came the chill of the rain, relentless, leaving me soaked. Outside the city, in the shroud of the falling darkness and cover of the night, the harpies hunted us and picked away at the weakest first.

Their screams rolled in from the distance, a hunting ground far from us. The first one swiped at a young man with their dark talons, shredding his skin and bone. I couldn't deny the threat. The harpy tore viciously into his torso as it slammed into the man. They rolled onto the wet path, a collision of flesh, blood, and leathery wings.

A bloodcurdling shriek pierced the air, and we scattered, Nash's nails digging into my skin as he wrenched me off the road. The challengers hid in the long prickly grass as the harpy reared back, shrieking as it beat the man. It ripped into his body. The sound of tearing flesh and his bones cracking kept me afraid, another experience that would haunt of the rest of my waking hours.

I curled between Nash Wickham and Finley Nightingale, trembling and tense as I waited for it to end.

Wet, squelching, feasting noises quietened the screeching from the attack. When it fell silent, I craned my neck to see if the monster had left us alone. The beast stood, poised over remnants of the man. Its sightless eyes were wide, head cocked to one side as if listening intently, lingering, and waiting for one of us to move the wrong way. It opened its mouth, a cry pierced out, a shrill howl of death from the midst of its chest, before it stretched those large leatherlike wings.

A gust of wind shifted the grass around us as the harpy straightened and prepared to take flight. My heart thundered in my chest, waiting for the inevitability of another attack, but the harpy's muscles bunched as it crouched again, scooped up the remains, and leapt into the skies.

Between the cold and my paralysing fear, shudders wracked my body until Nash wrapped me in his arms tightly, the warmth of his body slowing the panic overwhelming me.

"Shhh," he whispered. "We can't attract attention, Tav."

"I know," I said from behind the fingers covering my lips.

He coughed twice in my ear, and I wanted to shush him back. His coughing felt louder than my laboured breathing.

We waited until the coast appeared clear and someone else found the courage to creep back onto the road first. It was a new form of torture to watch them, half sure it would attack them at any moment. Finley and Nash stood slowly, chin tilted, as they looked at the sky for any sign of danger.

"Seems okay now," Finley grunted.

Nash nodded, and along with the other competitors, we rose. The grass rustled around us, sticks snapping and gravel crunching below our feet.

The scream of warning wasn't enough, not for everyone to duck, weave, and hide again. Those too slow would become the hunted.

Finley slammed me into the ground in his haste to get away, my teeth tearing through my upper lip, blood pooling in my mouth as the gravel scraped my skin. We rolled onto the grass, and he landed on top of me, knocking the air from my lungs and leaving me gasping. We lay in the dirt, nose-to-nose, in silenced terror as the feasting harpy echoed.

Finley's dark eyes were wide, darting around with unconcealed fright. His umber skin paled. Darkness and light flickered in his eyes, haunted like mine, while the harpies feasted on the unlucky.

Their cries of anguish hushed with death as the wild harpies took their time tearing them to ribbons.

It seemed we hadn't eluded the terrors of Invidia at the end of the trial and that our journey to the Wrathlands would be slow, especially if the demons of the night hunted us the moment the sun slipped behind the mountains.

Silence fell across the plains, a post-death eerie stillness surrounding us, as even the animals mourned the loss of the life.

Finley gripped the rough grass, holding onto it for dear life.

His muscles tensed against me as he prepared to change position. I thought back to the harpy that had taken Monika and eviscerated her body like paper in the rain. Fear seized me. He would be next if he shifted the slightest amount.

"Wait," I said.

Finley stilled on my command. I felt like an angel when he obeyed my commands without hesitation. A small thrill lit me up from within.

His dark gaze lingered on my face, studying my expression. "What?"

"Don't move," I said. "They're still out there."

His lips tilted into a slow, patronising smile. "Octavia, darling . . ."

"Don't you *darling* me." I lifted my head, bumping my forehead to his in chastisement. "Just listen."

Finley blinked, his freckled nose wrinkling. "Why should I?"

"They're blind," I blurted. "Don't move."

"Huh?" His face scrunched in confusion.

"You asked me a question once." I stared at him, trying to portray everything I wanted to say into my narrowed glare. "About how to survive a harpy? You stay still, and you stay quiet, Fin. That's the only way to survive."

"Because they're blind . . . ?" he repeated.

A grim smile twisted across my face. "Yes. They're listening to us. They'll hear you move."

He paused for a beat, considering the wisdom of my words. "Shut up, then," Finley hissed.

We stayed in the long grass at the edge of the path for hours.

Finley braced on top of me until his muscles grew tired, and his weight dropped on me uncomfortably—he's heavier than he looks. A stick poked the small of my back, like it was skewering me, but we didn't move, too afraid of the demons.

We drifted into a restless sleep, Finley's breath tickling my neck. His weight was almost unbearable. Uncomfortable as I felt,

I couldn't avoid the pull of my bone-deep fatigue, and when his weight rolled off me, I found sleep until the first rays of sunrise appeared over the hill.

Whispers drifted around us as the others woke, carrying in the wind, and the competitors rose with the new day. Wary, damaged, but still soldiering on.

I cautiously lifted a hand and prodded Finley's ribs. He was lying on my arm, which had turned numb. Nothing happened. I slid my hand up his side, eliciting a shudder, before I jammed my fingers into the soft side of his cheek. He grunted.

"Fin?" I said. "Finley?"

His long dark lashes fluttered before revealing his sleep-groggy oak-brown eyes. He blinked, and I could almost see the wheels turning in his head as he tried to figure out what was happening. "Mmm?" He flashed his tonsils at me as he yawned.

"Get off me," I demanded, shoving his shoulders. "Now."

"Oh." Finley scrambled up, groaning as he stretched, his joints popping. He rubbed his hands through his curls, dislodging stray pieces of grass. He waved in my face. "Need a hand?"

I muttered a "thank you" before he had wrenched me up onto my feet, nearly pulling my shoulder from its socket. The force of it sent me stumbling forward until we collided again.

Finley steadied me, a small grin teasing at the corner of his lips. "You always want to be touching, don't you?"

My face scrunched up. "Bite me."

He snapped his teeth at me in a fake bite and laughed. "You wish."

It was only then, standing in front of him in my still-damp dress, the cold of the morning clinging to my skin, I realised I had dropped the vial given to me by the crone. A flash of hot panic ran through my body and chased away the morning chill. I pushed Finley and his teasing words from my mind, then dropped to my knees again, searching through the grass for it.

"Uhhh," Finley hesitated, watching me. "Searching for your

sanity down there?"

"You're so helpful!" I snapped.

I was too worried about the strange gift I had been ordered to deliver to deal with his jokes. Grass prickled against my skin, and the longer it took to find, the more I worried, an intricate knot twisting in the pit of my stomach. I didn't know what the vial contained or why it needed to be delivered for the crone, but I had a lingering suspicion that if I didn't do what she asked, bad fortune would await me. Not that all my fortune wasn't bad enough.

"What's she doing?" Nash asked Finley.

"I actually think she's finally cracked . . ." he answered, the humour in his voice clear.

My chin jerked, and I shot them a glare from beneath my lashes, wishing I could zap them with a single thought. "Dropped a vial."

"A vial of what?" Nash asked.

"That doesn't matter," I huffed, unwilling to admit I didn't know what it contained and why it was so important. "I just need it."

Neither of them helped me, watching as I crawled through the grass in search of it.

The earth was rough under my hands, small stones pressing into my flesh, and I ignored everything else as my panic built and crested into sharp, bitter nausea.

Nash heaved a sigh somewhere to my left and finally started helping, dropping to his knees in an area I had already examined.

What could have been hours later—and may have only been three minutes—his blonde head appeared in my line of sight.

"This?" He opened his hand to reveal the little glass bottle, and my racing heart settled a notch. "What is it?"

"Thank you!" I snatched at it.

It was a fat, spheric vial half filled with a soft mauve liquid. It fit snugly into the palm of my hand, and I gripped it, wishing I had a secret pouch or another way to secure it in this ridiculous dress of Margot's.

We shuffled into the middle of the road with everyone else, and he sank his hands into his trouser pockets.

His elbow bumped my side, and he jerked his chin at my clenched hand. "What is it?"

"What's what?" I asked.

Nash scoffed. "The vial, Tav."

"Oh." I glanced down at my blanched knuckles. "I don't know."

"What do you mean, you don't know?"

"The crone gave it to me," I blurted. "I didn't catch what she said was inside it."

Nash inhaled sharply. His fingers curled around my wrist, the grip harsh and urgent, strong enough that I almost dropped it again. "Is that a good idea?" His tone indicated it wasn't. "Trusting the crone and anything she gives you?"

Blowing out a small breath, I glanced at him from the corner of my eye. "It's not for me."

"I think that might be worse," he muttered, the muscles in his forearms tensing. "Is she sending you to kill someone?"

"No!"

My denial was sharp and bitter, but I didn't know if it was true. I could carry death across the Wrathlands in search of General Inaina, and I would never know. It wouldn't surprise me if Eadlin had more enemies than friends.

"Of course not! Look, if it wasn't for the crone, I wouldn't be standing here, Nash. I almost died in that castle. You understand? As much as I hate it, sometimes, I need to settle a debt or two."

He huffed, and a troubled expression rolled across his features. His normally bright eyes raked over me in brisk assessment, as if he were looking for the injuries that might have killed me in Envy's castle.

I wondered if he could see the young girl's blood on my

hands, the mark of a murderer. Or if I looked like a drowned rat in someone else's fancy dress, cold and wrung out to the point of exhaustion. Broken into pieces and barely holding it together.

"Fine." Nash shifted, sounding unhappy with my answer. He pulled his sweater on and shoved it in my direction. The material held the heat of his body. He tugged the sleeves of his shirt back down to his wrists. "Put that on, or you'll die of a chill."

"Yes, Mum," I teased, tugging the warm clothing on.

It smelled of dirt, chalk, and Nash, warmer than I could have imagined. Best of all, it had pockets to stow the vial away. Out of sight, so it wouldn't ignite more questions.

"You're a brat."

"Guys?" Finley wrapped an arm around our shoulders and leaned his weight down on us until we staggered to the side. "We're falling behind. I don't want to be in the back of the pack after last night. The stragglers become dinner."

Sure enough, when I glanced up, the other competitors were stretched down the road. They had made the best of the daylight hours and trekked to the east.

I stared past them, at the endless path. A third trial seemed impossible before it had even begun. Not even conquering it but facing the Angel of Wrath, who could be the worst yet.

The journey to the challenge with no food, supplies, or plan would be the death of us all.

Finley nudged us forward, and I finally moved, dragging my feet down the never-ending road. When he agreed with our pace, he let go of us, clasping his hands behind his back and whistling a tune. Soon, I hummed it beneath my breath, cursing him for bringing it up at all, as it replayed in my head.

We walked until my feet were numb, until the group seemed to slow, and murmurs rippled about taking a break, the exhaustion seeming to be a consensus.

"How many did we lose in the attack?" Nash asked suddenly, and his voice carried across the quiet plains.

It brought a jarring end to Finley's song, and with it, we all stopped and huddled, stronger as a group. The sombre subject and harsh reality of our circumstances brought most of us together; a few outliers huddled on their own.

I shrugged.

A woman turned and glanced back with red-rimmed eyes. "Four," she croaked, fresh tears pooling in her gaze. "What if they hunt us the entire way there? We might all die like Lenny, feasted on my devil's minions."

Her question was haunting. She was right. We wouldn't survive if the harpies followed us night by night, picking us off one by one.

With no answer to her question, I twisted my fingers together, my eyes downcast.

A rejection came from towards the front.

"No, they won't." It was Margot who proclaimed it with assured confidence. "After the first couple of days, they won't come looking for us. Not if we make good pace."

When she turned and strode through the crowd, others moved out of her way.

A flicker of envy curled in my stomach at her command of others. I realised it hadn't all been the influence of the angel. A part of me was bitter over the way people turned to look and listen.

Margot Galatea was the type to command attention. From the way she looked, her albinism rare across Kaida, and the command of her voice. A woman used to getting what she wanted when she wanted it.

"How do you know?"

I wasn't sure why I spoke up, only that my envy had curled into a firm desire to challenge her and to steal the attention, since everyone always looked at someone like her before they looked at me. My contrary question attracted attention.

They turned to study me. I lifted my chin and continued. "I thought you had never left Invidia?"

She smiled and blinked rapidly, her blue eyes narrowing at me. "Of course, I've left the city. I'm not that sheltered. I left with Envy . . ."

Those standing close shuffled further away. Awareness rippled across the competitors that Margot dallied with angels and might have even sicced Envy after them. Their curiosity looked to have turned wary, inducing snide satisfaction within me.

Margot was not as popular as she first seemed.

"But—"

"The harpies only ever followed so far," she said. "They prefer to hunt around the city. When we wanted to travel at night, we used fire to scare them off."

"Fire?" someone asked.

She smiled. "Of course. Even the harpies fear fire. They're not invincible."

I folded my arms across my chest, strangely doubtful about this information.

The guards in the city had used noise to distract the creatures, to slay one of them but not fire. It took me a second to figure out why.

"That's ridiculous," I said, scoffing.

Margot stalked closer and stood in front of me. Her tight smile never reached her eyes and left her face.

Finley stepped back from me, creating space between himself and potential conflict, in case association with me would become dangerous.

"What was that?" she asked, her tone dangerously smooth.

"What's one thing that's happened every day that we've been in the Envylands? In Invidia and even today?" I asked, raising my hands in indication.

The attention of other competitors burned into my skin, but I forced myself not to shrink away from it. Not with making Margot look bad.

Her icy-blue eyes narrowed on me, lips thinning as her smile

10

dropped.

"It's rained!" someone called out.

A smile stretched across my lips. I advanced a step on Margot, and she shifted backwards. "That's right. How do you propose we fight them with fire when the rain puts out every flame we light? Are you a dragon in disguise, Margot?"

If her translucent skin could have paled, I imagined it would have.

Margot's nostrils flared, and irritation flashed across her face. She never had to hide her emotions before, not as the Queen of Envy's castle reigning supreme. And, in the wilds with us, it left her exposed like an open book, with each thought displayed across her face for all to read.

"Envy always—"

"Envy isn't here," I snapped. "You didn't want to stay with him, remember? We swapped Mikhael for you."

My tone solidified it was a poor swap, and when I said it, she flinched back a step.

A sadness in her face forged the first flicker of guilt in my stomach. It could have convinced me that Margot cared for Mikhael, as her lower lip wobbled, her face solemn. I knew he would have never passed that trial, even if he had never met Margot. Although Mikhael Heira had seemed better than his brother, he had never been kind, either. His personality faults aside, it was easier to turn my envy into accusation and lay the blame squarely at Margot's feet.

If she hadn't convinced Mikhael to risk everything to steal her, if she hadn't blackmailed me into helping and stolen a promise from Niklaus to protect her, then we had more of a chance he would have been here. It was slim but still a fragment of hope.

"What do we do, then?" someone asked.

The question roused me from the emotions rolling through me, heady and sickening. It felt like even more of them were looking at me. My brain seemed to screech to a halt because I couldn't save them or come up with plans to help others succeed. My advice was good for nothing, and aside from coming from a select few, a group that had shrunk significantly since the start of the trials, I cared little about whether anyone else lived. Their best choice, in my eyes, was for their lives to forfeit so I could live. That wasn't the answer they wanted, the reality that they wanted.

Finley nudged me, his pointy elbow jabbing my ribs. "We do what you said . . ."

I sucked in a sharp breath, glancing at him nervously. "Remind me what I said again?"

He stepped forward. A charming smile fixed in place as he flipped his dark curls out of his eyes.

Tension in the group dropped as their attention shifted to what he had to say. Something about his smile seemed to relax them. Finley Nightingale had a natural charm. People liked him, I realised. He was safe, happy, and they could trust his words. He carried fewer sharp edges than I did, forged from less trauma.

"Well," Finley started, "the harpies are blind, right? So, they use their other senses to hunt us down, their ears. The second attack only came as we started being noisy again. We led them right to us."

Murmurs of agreement rose amongst the group.

I listened on, my blood running hot and cold with a strange possessiveness as Finley took my earlier advice and spun it into softer words that could bring hope to the ragtag competitors.

It felt like he was stealing from me, and I wanted to hate him for it, but his delivery was a lot more elegant than I could ever offer.

"When the sun goes down," he continued, "we hide. We find safe, obscured places, and we stay quiet. If they use their ears to find us, they should pass us by if we're silent enough . . . The biggest game of hide-and-seek in our lives."

"You're right!" someone called out, others cheering in agreement. Energy in the group rose as they latched onto his idea.

"That's the best plan we have! If what blondie said is right, in a few days, they won't follow us."

"We've just got to hide! Even if we need to do it every night," Kyra Willett shouted.

"Staying quiet is easy!" a voice cried from my left.

Someone else jumped in. "I bet—"

We moved again, traipsing down the road, after Niklaus grumbled his sentiments that we needed to make more progress and to find water as soon as possible or that hiding wouldn't save a thing.

Competitors swarmed Finley, who pulled him in close to talk about the monsters. He laughed with them, grinning broadly.

I dropped towards the rear of the group to stay out of their way, thinking about the looming threat. I was thirsty and half starved, sure I wasn't alone in my growing needs.

But the bigger threat was the monsters, and so many of the others seemed relieved because we could manage them. Finley Nightingale had easily become their hero, and it suited him.

"You okay?" Nash asked an hour later, twirling chalk between his fingers.

I grunted, unable to stop the impending feeling of doom surging through my entire body. Finley made our survival sound achievable, as if the harpies didn't have four other senses and that we didn't smell like humans, unwashed and drenched in the stench of our own sweat and fear.

The surrounding crowd seemed to relax, brightening with a little more hope of surviving. We needed to see what the night would bring, and I wouldn't be the one to crush their anticipation of a good outcome.

It was hope and hope alone carrying more magic than all the angels and demons together.

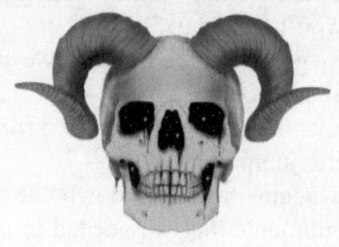

Chapter Two

We veered off the path and towards safety long before the sun set, venturing into the trees to hunt animals and appease our growing hunger. Searching for pools of rainwater to quench our thirst. Between us, all were enough skills to keep us fed, although not everyone seemed keen to share. It never seemed like enough.

Stretched across the competitors and even with a belly of food, I remained hungry. With every drink, I was only thirstier.

When the sun set, it was time for us to hide. I thought the roar of my stomach as it demanded more, more, more would be enough to attract the harpies. I tried not to think about it, not as we scattered in different directions with the promise to reconvene on the road at first light. There were too many of us to stay together and not attract attention, and the dire question of how many would return haunted me. I clutched Nash's hand. He squeezed my fingers gently as we raced through the trees, stumbling over fallen branches, the night plummeting around us faster than expected.

Branches and leaves cracked and snapped beneath our feet, a symphony following us through the undergrowth. If the demons of the night were awake, we may as well have been screaming at them to come and play.

It took too much time to decide where to hide. We slowed as Nash stopped to pluck berries from bushes and rifle through the undergrowth. Juices stained his fingertips and smeared at his lips, a macabre lipstick in the dead of the night.

"Come on!" I tugged at his arm, desperate to find a hiding place but also not to stray too far from the road. If we couldn't find our way back in the morning, they would leave us behind. Nobody would wait long.

"All right, all right." He snatched at the last of them and hurried along, his presence at my back comforting as the first piercing screams ripped through the still night.

We circled until settling on the twisted roots of an old, gnarled tree. It wasn't the best hiding place and did little to protect us from the drizzling rain, but the roots rose high enough to create nooks to shield us from the harpies. All we needed to do was stay as quiet as humanly possible.

I pressed myself firmly against the tree, my clothing catching the rough, wet bark, pulling as I slid to the ground.

Nash curled in beside me, shifting to bury his face in his shirt as he coughed, stifling the sound. He sniffled as he righted himself, pulling his knees to his chest and curling into a tight ball.

Since I'd taken his warmest layer, I knew he had to be cold, but I didn't want to give it back and freeze. So, I huddled close, offering my meagre warmth, as he shivered.

"Open your hand," he whispered, and I offered him my palm. Nash tipped half his fistful of bruised blackberries into my hand and then turned over the husky shells of wood he had found, settling them on the ground.

15

"What's that for?" I whispered as quietly as I could.

"A drink." He slumped back against the tree, his voice loud enough to make me cringe. "May as well catch the rain if we can, and it might make a really terrible cup."

A soft giggle, half hysterical from the hopelessness of our situation, rose, unbidden, to my lips.

He pressed a long finger against my mouth. "Shh. The nights are going to be long."

When I glanced up to the treetops, I knew he was right.

The darkness was heavier, and the foreboding feeling of doom in my stomach intensified. If Margot was right, and the harpies didn't hunt too far out from the city, we just had to survive a night or two and then we would march across the Envylands with only food, water, and enduring one another as our biggest problems.

Having so few stressors would be nothing short of a dream after weeks on end of being in a permanently tense state.

Drifting in and out of a state of sleep, never truly resting, I had never imagined hours would pass so slowly. Every noise in the woods made me jumpy, the soft crow of nocturnal birds, the snapping of sticks or rustling of leaves in the distance. Every time the noises rippled through the night, my pulse jumped, and I thought it was death closing in around us. True rest felt virtually impossible, especially when Nash kept twisting in close, burying his mouth against my shoulder and coughing until he was out of breath.

With no other way to occupy my time, I ate the berries. They were strange, bumpy beneath my tongue, tart and unripe.

Before long, my belly ached. I shouldn't have trusted them, trusted anything that grew in the Envylands. I wrapped my arms around my cramping stomach, willing the nausea to settle.

Nash had fallen asleep, snoring softly against my shoulder, and my legs cramped, demanding a change in my tightly wound position, but I couldn't move. Not for my fear of making too much noise but for not waking Nash, who looked haunted by the dark shadows beneath his eyes.

We both needed sleep, with meagre pickings for meals and another long day of walking ahead. We wouldn't manage without energy, and if I couldn't sleep, it was better to leave him undisturbed.

Slumber claimed me eventually, when my eyes were so heavy that they couldn't stay open. I'd moved past the discomfort of my soaked clothing, the way my hair stuck to the back of my neck and the bark prickled my skin, but I dreamt of the forest as haunted in sleep as I had been awake, restless and afraid.

Awareness hurled into me with the intuitive feeling I was being watched. Hair on the back of my neck stood on end, and my body tensed as I tried to shake the fogginess of sleep. I grappled to orientate myself and get a sense of my surroundings, realising too late how foolish it was for us to both sleep at once.

It was still dark, but the rain had stopped, leaving behind the distinct smell of fresh, wet foliage.

Shifting my attention, I looked for any sign of the harpies looming above us, that could have been hovering in the thick canopy of the trees, waiting to pick their teeth with our bones.

They were not the problem, though. A new danger had approached in the night, unexpected and unwanted. My heart thumped behind my ribs.

"Nash," I whispered.

He shifted, grumbling in his sleep, but he didn't wake. He curled in tighter against my side, his arm wrapping around my stomach as his cheek rubbed my shoulder.

I moved my hand to his arm and pinched his skin hard enough to bruise, twisting for good measure, as I'd once done to wake my brothers, who slept like the dead with exhaustion.

"Ow!" he cried, flinching away.

"Quiet," I chastised. "You need to get up."

"What's happened?" Nash asked, eyes still shut.

My attention didn't waver. I couldn't look at him as I stared ahead, watchful but not meeting the eye of the new predator stalking towards us.

"Nash, look up and to the left, slowly."

It was a beast, the biggest hound I had ever seen. Large as a full-grown man, bigger than my father. It sat on its haunches, shaking the last vestiges of the rain from its short sleek midnight-black fur. Luminescent yellow eyes watched us both with acute interest. It crouched low, its whiplike tail erect. Jowls shook before its lips curled back, flashing rows of sharp teeth, and a snarl rippled through the air, unsettling the birds, and turning my blood cold.

It was a warning that transcended language.

I trembled. I had seen dogs before, mangy, thin things that roamed the streets in Ilrea, stealing scraps and fighting each other for the next morsel, but I had never seen a creature quite like this one. It was inky like the black night, glistening where beads of rain clung to its coat. Its eyes were enormous, glued to us, dawning a strange intelligence. Its pointed ears cocked towards us, listening carefully.

"Is that . . . ?" Nash had woken properly, and he tensed beside me. "That's a . . ."

Instinctually, I wanted to make myself as small as possible and become less of a threat or a meal for the gigantic beast. I hadn't considered the other beasts hunting the forest, not when the harpies had been my full focus.

I should have known that other dangerous creatures lurked in the Envylands. The entire continent seemed full of things that would delight in tearing us apart.

Nash shifted, drawing the beast's attention with the movement, and I clung to his shirt in a desperate attempt to make him stop. It stalked closer, huge paws indenting the soft, wet dirt. It tensed, ready for us.

"Don't, Nash. Maybe if we don't seem like a threat, it'll

leave," I babbled.

My mind pulsed as rapid as my heartbeat.

"No." Nash stood. "It's a hellhound, Octavia. They don't leave their prey alive. They don't decide they have better things to do."

I didn't know what that was. Although most of the stories of my childhood proved true, especially the terrors weaved within them, I'd never heard of a hellhound. I didn't know if there was lore about these beasts or ways to defeat them.

Nash raised a hand towards the beast and edged forward, murmuring soft, placating sounds. The hellhound growled and snapped its sharp teeth at his outstretched hand. Nash recoiled, and my heart skipped an entire beat.

Slowly, never taking my eyes off the hellhound, I crouched beside him, my muscles aching and protesting after hours of being balled up. I could do little to escape, with the large roots of the tree crowding us in on either side and the hellhound stalking closer. My perfect hiding space, once protective, had become a relative prison.

Nash crouched lower and reached for one of the bowed pieces of wood that had been collecting raindrops while we slept. He lifted it carefully with both hands, watching the hound as he moved, whose growl seemed to shake the leaves and rattle my bones.

"You want a drink now?!" I asked, sounding near hysterical as the words came out strangled.

Nash scoffed, reminding me he was not the happy, softer man that he was at the start of our journey, full of life, colour, and imagination.

We had split up for a month in Invidia, and I didn't know what he had endured to survive, but there was no denying it had left him a little rougher at the edges, sharper in his smile. *A little more like me*, I thought, thinking of the life I had taken, the sins I had committed in the devil's name.

We all did what was necessary to survive these trials, and I couldn't blame him for the actions that had changed him. No more than I would allow myself to drown in guilt. Both would eat us alive, and I needed Nash more than I had first thought.

The idea of his death worried me. I wanted him to survive with me more than anything. Out of everyone, I thought he truly deserved the riches and luxury of Eternis, the only soul that had come into this competition untainted.

"Hold still," he demanded.

I tensed to stay in place, since I had no better plan. Nash and his drink were the only things standing between me and the beast's sharp teeth.

I exhaled slowly. "What are you going to do?"

"Don't distract me." Nash's hands trembled enough for the water to spill.

"I'm n—"

He hushed me, and I sighed, battling a flare of annoyance as he kept me in the dark. The muscles of Nash's back rippled as he tensed. The man and the hellhound stared at one another, the blonde meeting the beast's eyes, daring it to strike.

"When I do this," Nash said, "you run. Back to the road as fast as you can."

"But the harpies?"

"Just run, Octavia. As fast as you can."

It was choosing between one danger and another, but Nash had already chosen his path without consulting me. I had to trust he had another plan for the next danger or that the sun was rising fast to chase away the demons. It was hard to trust at all, but the hellhound's presence was encouragement enough.

I muttered a soft noise of agreement. It was what he had been waiting to hear, and Nash Wickham moved jarringly quick. Water splashed right into the hellhound's piercing yellow eyes before he threw the piece of wood at the beast.

Before it hit him, I scrambled over the tree roots and away

from the hellhound. Splinters digging into my skin, painful, but not enough to stop me as fear propelled me forward.

I crashed through the forest, the desire to survive driving me to follow his command to run until my lungs burned and my pace slowed.

Graced with longer legs, Nash caught up to me, and he urged me onwards.

My feet caught on roots, and I stumbled.

Nash growled like the hellhound itself when he turned back for me, reaching for my wrist to pull me forward.

"Don't stop!" he cried.

Behind us, an eerie, otherworldly howl rose through the woodlands. It echoed into the night, both a call and a command.

In the distance, scattered across the land, more hounds howled back. A haunting song.

Just barely over my own heaving breaths and the rushing blood in my ears, I could hear the snapping of the hellhound's teeth and the power of its body as it crashed through the thicket, chasing us down.

"Nash."

His name was a whine in the back of my throat as I tried to find my footing.

Adrenaline had kept me going, but the fatigue weighed heavily on my body, my lungs tight as they demanded more oxygen. I couldn't keep this up for much longer. I was better fed than I'd ever been, but I was still not fit enough to survive.

"Move, Octavia," Nash demanded. "Run!"

Above us, the harpies screeched, their dark wings blocking the stars as they encircled us.

My heart turned to stone, with paralysing fear. I didn't know which danger I could have preferred, the harpies' talons and desire to consume human flesh or the hellhounds' sharp teeth and . . . Well, come to think of it, they would probably eat me, too.

We couldn't win.

"I said *move!*" Nash bellowed. He shoved me forward as hard as he could.

I stumbled, but his push set me off again as I fled through the forest, wishing I could run as quick as my heart thrummed in my chest and ears, preparing me for the end.

'Left,' Samael purred.

On faith alone, without questioning I could trust his word, I followed Samael's command and veered sharply to the left, flinging myself around the next tree.

Nash let out a yelp as he struggled to follow me, unprepared for the sudden change of direction.

I pushed myself forward, hoping that the devil invading my mind would save me once again.

'Turn right this time.'

Once more, I trusted him and twisted to the right, barely managing to get over the tree that had fallen across the path. My thighs burned, my saliva bitter in my mouth.

The harpies screamed more than once, chorusing above us. Nash blathered swear words, brightly coloured curses flowing with each breath.

"Octavia!" he bellowed, "where are you going—"

An agonising scream rang out.

I faltered, almost tripping over my feet, and twisted on the spot to turn back for him.

"Nash," I called softly, too softly.

'Octavia,' Samael growled in warning, *'leave him. Do not go back there. Keep running.'*

The desire to obey the devil was immense, his command strong, the trust overwhelming. My trust should have lain with the devil, who had helped me so many times before, who kept me sane in the darkest of my moments; but I couldn't bring myself to turn away from my friend.

Nash Wickham screamed again, a sound I felt in my soul,

and before I could second-guess it, I was retracing my steps at a run. Racing back for him.

'Foolish girl,' Samael chided.

He wasn't wrong; I rounded the tree and found Nash kicking out at the hellhound. Sharp teeth had latched onto his arm.

I crouched out of view, hand wrapping around a heavy rock by my foot. I acted before I could think on it. Giving it too much thought would've had me scampering back to the safety Samael had promised.

My arm drew back, and I threw the rock as hard as I could. It bounced off the side of the wolf's head. It was sheer luck instead of good aim, and to my surprise, its grip loosened, and Nash scrambled backwards.

The beast's narrowed yellow eyes settled on me, a new target.

My stomach flipped as the hellhound growled a promise of death. It shifted on its haunches, preparing to leap at me, a strange peace flowing through me. I hoped Nash survived because I knew I wouldn't, not once the strong, vicious creature leapt for me. It slammed into me, the huge furry body knocking me to the ground.

My head smacked the ground hard enough to leave me dizzy, and I cried out in pain, a scream of pure terror. The hellhound pinned me to the ground, my ribs cracking beneath it, pain slicing through my body. The beast snapped its teeth in my face, the promise of violence in that yellow glare.

I thought it would enjoy eating me alive.

This time, I didn't close my eyes to avoid death, witness to the exact moment two of my fears collided.

The harpy didn't scream in warning this time. It simply slammed into the growling hellhound and knocked it free of my body, talons scraping my skin as it moved, slicing open shallow cuts that instantly welled with blood.

Both creatures went flying to the side, crashing through the undergrowth, as the harpy slashed at the hellhound. Its tail crashed against the trees, and the hellhound snapped back, teeth sinking into the cursed creature's leg.

They were so intent on each other they seemed to have forgotten us, neither hunting us specifically. We were easy prey, and they would take one another if they could.

Nash crawled behind me and shifted, helping me up off the ground.

My body ached, pain shooting through me each time I breathed too deeply, cuts across my chest weeping with blood.

Nash cradled his arm, his blood dripping to the ground. The clear imprint of the hellhound's bite gouged into his muscle.

We moved as quietly as possible, slowed by our injuries, not wanting to attract the fighting beasts' attention.

"Come on," Nash muttered, the pain clear in his voice.

We slipped through the forest, slower and quieter than before, unwilling to risk attracting any more predators, especially having trailed fresh blood.

My head flared with sharp pain. With each step, blood trickled down my front, where the harpy's talons had clipped me on their way into the hound. My body hurt with every step, but a quick look told me it wouldn't be the worst of my scars. It had survived worse things.

"Devils, Nash, your arm." I gasped when I caught a decent look at his forearm's exposed flesh. "Do you need to stop?"

He dripped with blood, and from the look on his face, it was painful, his arm tenderly cradled against his wrong. Nash grunted, rejecting the idea, and kept moving through the woods, refusing to respond when I brought it up again.

'Keep going straight,' Samael said, tone clipped and unimpressed.

It surprised me he had come back to talk to me, but he stubbornly said nothing to justify my action, although I had the ridiculous urge to apologise to the devil for disobeying his orders.

I corrected our path without explaining, and Nash followed

24

without asking; both of us were too tired and sore to hash it out.

When we stumbled back out into the worn road that wove through the Envylands, the sun was rising, marking us for the new day and safer times.

Its sight brought to me to near hysterical tears as I finally processed what had happened to us.

Rain fell again, fat droplets soaking us, washing away the stain of blood, the horrors of the night before.

Nash turned, wrapping his good arm around me and squeezing tight. I clung to him, as if he could float, and I was close to drowning.

"We're safe," he said.

'No,' Samael snapped with a snide snarl. *'You're just lucky.'*

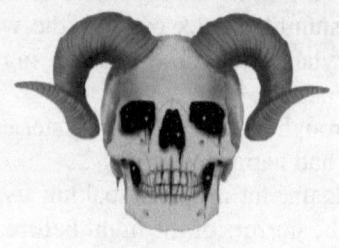

Chapter Three

We weren't the only competitors to return from the woods with injuries. The first hour of the day raced by as we compiled the supplies for tending to the worst of the wounds, deep, life-threatening gashes, and gouges, just as destructive as the beasts themselves.

Nash and I were luckier than others, although we hadn't been the only ones to face off against a hellhound.

Wild tales of them littered the road as we walked, becoming grander and more dangerous with every retelling, the beasts fit for a nightmare.

"How are you feeling?" I asked Nash just after midday, glancing at his wrapped arm. We faced hours of travel ahead of us, and he had grimaced with pain.

"Tired."

"Me too," I admitted. "And I'm nervous."

"Of what?" Nash asked. "After all that we've faced!"

"Another night like last night, I guess. I wish it could stay morning until we reach the Wrathlands, a never-ending day."

He hugged me, one-armed and stiff in the movement, but I appreciated the gesture. "We'll survive, Tav. We always do, right?"

I just had to hope he was right, especially since, for things we didn't want to do, time seemed to move faster to bring it close.

The sun seemed to sink much faster than it had risen, and there was a little less hope among us and fewer brave faces as we faced our third night in the Envylands.

By morning, Margot was smug with the proof she had been right all along. We hadn't heard a single harpy stalking the night to find us, the darkness absent of their screeches, although some competitors said they heard the howls of the hellhounds again.

Margot's knowledge was something she didn't let us forget, and she brought it up at least three times before lunch to anyone who would listen—at least until Niklaus barked at her that everyone was sick of the sound of her grating voice. His teeth grit and eyes flashed to show he was tired of her already.

She looked affronted, her expression souring, when not a single person stepped up to defend her honour. For the rest of the day, she was stonily silent, and I decided I would not want to be Niklaus when Margot extracted her revenge for that comment.

She was surely a woman who would seek revenge.

We wound into the woods, the cover of trees inescapable. By the fourth day, I was coughing as much as Nash, my throat sore, a sickness developing from the repetitive cycle of being sodden from the rain and drying out in the moments of reprieve and sunshine.

The sounds of a river drew us close, and as a group, we decided to rest there for the night, our self-appointed hunters disappearing in search of something we could eat.

Others tried to build a fire while the rain had subsided, and I did absolutely nothing to contribute to the group, feeling damp and useless.

Instead, I shed Nash's sweater, wrung it out, and knelt by the riverside, gasping as the water flowed over cuts on my legs and staring through the glassy surface.

My distorted reflection stared back at me. It was me, but it wasn't me. I could pretend that my reflection had more strength and more heart than I did, enough to carry her through this competition. My reflection was a woman who could survive, and I was merely a shadow of that, struggling endlessly.

I was alive only because it amused the devil to keep me that way, and I couldn't help but fear what would happen when Samael stopped wanting to chat with me. When he became bored with the trial or found someone more interesting, which was how it always happened.

Friends came and went, as they found someone who interested them more, someone a little softer, much more put together, fun.

Samael would, one day, leave me, too. I was not fool enough to think I could maintain the devil's attention for too long.

Distorting my reflection, I splashed the water, destroying the pretty story I had created in my mind with grim satisfaction. I scrubbed my grime-covered fingers, rubbing off blood and dirt as best I could before I cupped my hands and drank from the depths of the river. As if I had never had fresh water before, as if thirst were my curse, and I could never quench it. I drank until my belly was full to the point of pain, and after days without enough, this water tasted sweeter than the cursed river in Gula.

Wearily, I returned to the campsite, where the crackling flames dried me out properly. I sat too close to the fire, watching the thick grey smoke as it rose into the canopy of trees.

Nash huddled on one side of me, leaning heavily against my shoulder, and a familiar face sat on the other side.

"Aureen?" I whispered.

"What?" she asked, turning to look at me, the light flitting across her dark oak skin. She narrowed her eyes at me as if it surprised her I was here *alive*.

Her long hair swung free of its usual tight ponytail and tumbled around her face, softening the way she looked; her eyes still held a haunted edge.

It was strange to see her without her sister, Kyra, pressed to her side, shielded by her body.

"Are you okay?" I asked.

One of her dark brows rose, a sleek, condescending movement.

"Why do you care?"

I inhaled sharply, surprised at the venom in her question. "Uhh . . ."

"That's what I thought." She stuck her nose up, sneering before turning her attention back to the fire.

My face screwed up, heat flaring across the bridge of my nose as I muttered, "I guess you're right. I don't care."

Turning away from her was harder than I expected, only because I was mourning something that had never happened. I had hoped to find friends in the group challenge in Invidia. I might have if Monika had survived to walk with us, but the remaining two members of my group, Aureen and Kyra Willett, wanted nothing to do with me. It seemed as if they would prefer to think I didn't exist at all. It hurt, even though we'd never been close.

It was hazardous to make friends in a game like The Devil's Trials. When the aim of the game was not only to survive yourself and your circumstances but beat cryptic challenges set by deadly angels who wanted nothing more than to see us fail.

In the first trial, facing the Angel of Gluttony, I had made a friend, and an angel had ripped out her still-beating heart.

The trial had been a challenge to stop indulging, and she had not found the willpower to withstand it and win. Part of me couldn't blame her for it, either. Ophelia Bell had lived for the indulgences in life and had been a happier woman than I for it.

The second trial, the Angel of Envy, was unexpected, too. I'd thought we were just stealing our way to success, taking what others had coveted, because Envy was coveting what others had. It was a trial of kindness more than anything, for kindness tempered Envy, even if it couldn't remove it. It was a trial I should have failed. My actions weren't kind, although the crone had claimed that ending the unwarranted suffering of an imprisoned woman was merciful and kind.

I suspected I only passed because of the vial she wanted me to deliver, because I was the only competitor of whom Eadlin, the twice-cursed crone, had any sway. She could manipulate me in the third trial if she helped me through the second.

Monika, I thought, would have passed, in the same way that we might have become friends, but a harpy had torn her to shreds, and she had died in my lap without the dignity of a funeral. Her family would never know how she had passed. She was kinder than me in her own way.

It stood to reason that making friends didn't seem like the wisest move—at least not for me—but I couldn't help feeling a desire to connect with others.

'You have me, Little One.'

Samael intruded my thoughts.

I sighed and lifted my attention back to the patterns in the smoke, squinting as if I could make out a face for him there. "You're talking to me again?"

A bite laced my tone.

Samael chuckled, a lazy sound, as if he were indulging me. *'I never leave for long.'*

My paranoia from earlier heightened from my already-frayed nerves, and I gulped, whispering softly so nobody would think I was half mad. "Why do you talk to me at all?"

'Do I need a reason? I am Samael, the Devil of Kaida. I explain myself to no one.'

"I just don't understand it." I fidgeted with the torn edge to my dress. "There's at least two hundred more interesting people still alive in this trial."

'Is that so?'

"So, why am I so interesting to you?"

'Octavia Nox, are you fishing for compliments?'

Despite myself, my cheeks flushed with warmth, my sight dropping to the flames, as if they would hide it as I quickly muttered, "No."

The devil laughed in my ear. *'I think you are . . .'*

"Well," I bit out, "everyone likes a compliment. Even me."

'Well . . .' He mocked my tone, the devil haunting me, the voice inside my head. *"When you can believe you're interesting, I'll tell you why you are, Little One."*

"Oh, come on . . ." I huffed, exasperated with his answer.

He didn't reply.

I waited, but he stayed silent, sometimes there, sometimes gone, and I felt like I spent much of my time waiting for him to reappear.

In the quiet that followed our conversation, I wondered if I was just imagining him, wishing so hard to be special that I had created a figment to ease the desire. But real or not, in his absence, I felt more alone than I had before.

I heaved a sigh and turned to nudge Nash gently. He raised a finger, signalling for me to wait, as he held an animated conversation with the man on his other side. I envied how easy it was for him to make connections and engage with other people. It was a skill that had always escaped me.

When Nash turned to me over five minutes later, I swallowed down the lump of loneliness in my throat and forced a smile for him. "We should find somewhere to sleep."

His head tilted up as he studied the treetops, squinting as if he could see the night sky beyond them. I watched the way his Adam's apple shifted when he swallowed, and he nodded slowly. "You're right."

At his agreement, I shifted, clambering to my feet and dusting myself off. The feeling of someone watching me weighed heavily on me.

When I glanced around the firepit, I caught Niklaus Heira studying me from the other side of the flames. My lips pursed, and I raised an eyebrow in question. His gaze darkened, chin lifting, as his full lips shifted to mouth something at me.

My tongue ran over my lower lip as I watched his mouth, but before I could decipher his meaning, Margot caught my attention instead.

She pressed into his side, her stark white hair unbound and tumbling across his shoulder. The stress of the road had caught up to her, marring her delicate features, creating dark circles beneath her eyes. She almost looked like a damsel in distress worthy of protection.

When I caught her eye, easily done with the way she glared at me, I could think only of her skill in manipulating us to get here at all, her threats from within the safety of the castle she had called home. A blunt reminder she was a deadly snake, the living emblem of the Angel of Envy.

I stalked away before Niklaus or Margot could say anything, telling myself I would try harder to avoid them in the future. Both were more trouble than they were worth.

Nash was slow to follow but caught up, saying nothing—my only genuine friend in these trials, so it was worth waiting.

We found a place to sleep, and for one of the first nights in a long time, we slept safely, albeit lightly, before a new day dawned, and we continued our walk to the Wrathlands.

A week passed in this manner before we started getting agitated with each other, restless and rude. Fights broke out, small pockets of competitors breaking away on their own when we rested each night but coming back to the thick of it as we marched on in search of the next trial.

I stuck as close to Nash as possible, trusting his judgement of the other competitors, even over my fatigue-tainted perception.

When others riled me, namely Niklaus, who had taken to falling to walk beside us, peppering me with comments until I snapped, Nash helped me return to a state of calm, talking about meaningless subjects until my blood boiled a little slower.

Two more days passed before the path forked ahead of us, and we needed to decide where to go. Our group had thinned to seventy odd people, the rest stretched far ahead and behind us. We dithered at the fork in the road, peering into the darkness that led both ways.

I hung to the side as the strongest of the personalities debated the best choice at the front of the group, namely Niklaus and Aureen. Rocking on my heels, I waited for a whisper in my ear, trusting Samael would not let me make the wrong choice. He was silent, and it filled me with the strange discomfort of invasion knowing he was there, watching through my eyes. So, I shuffled towards one path, taking three steps along it, before the devil cleared his throat.

'*Uh, uh, uh,*' he admonished, like a mother clucking her tongue at naughty babies.

I couldn't help the smile splitting across my face; elated victory left my heart pounding in my chest, the small feeling I had manipulated him towards my goals for the first time.

My next big problem was that I didn't know how to offer opinion with the rest of the group. I wasn't trusted amongst the competitors, not seen as brave, wise, or resourceful. It would be ridiculous to shout that we needed to go right because the devil had told me so. They would scoff in my face.

Samael laughed as if he knew my predicament, as if struggles with how to proceed with the information he'd given amused him.

I dithered about it for a good five minutes. All while their arguments grew, the advocates for each path firmly believing they were right and trying to list the reasons they should decide.

Finally, I reached for Nash. "This way!" I announced as brightly as I could manage, looping my arm through his before dragging him down the right-hand path.

It took a few moments before his brain registered what we were doing, and Nash dug in his heels to bring us to a halt, easily finding the muscle to keep me from moving.

"What are you doing, Tav?"

"Going the *right* way."

"You don't know this is the right way." He glanced back to the group, and following his line of sight, I saw Finley had started following us down the path. "We should wait for the others, make a group decision."

I bit my tongue to refrain from telling him about Samael, although I wanted to brag about how the devil cared enough to save my life time and time again, but I forced myself to shrug flippantly.

"We don't know which is the right way, and we never will. They're not making knowledgeable arguments. They're working off their gut feelings. We can't stand around all day. As long as we're together, we'll make it, I promise."

He didn't look convinced, and the doubt in his expression left me feeling hollow.

Nash was the only person who I cared about coming with me, or I would have walked off on my own. That was how sure I was Samael would tell me the truth and not lead me astray, but because Nash did matter to me, I fought to give him a reason to follow.

"Either way," I said slowly, as if I were patiently reasoning with him, "the Envylands must end. They don't go on forever, so let's just follow this path and see how we go. It's a fifty-fifty chance, and I like those odds."

"All right." He sighed after a beat of hesitation.

I like to think he agreed because he knew I'm a woman aware of her odds, but he probably just wanted to get on with it.

Finley caught up with us, his signature crooked grin fixed firmly in place. He flicked a curl from his face and spoke as if he'd been with us all along. "Ready to keep moving?"

At least one of them wouldn't argue.

We set off without waiting for the others, and I paused when Niklaus Heira's angry voice boomed down the path. A whip strike of words. "Where are you going?"

I turned and glanced over my shoulder at him.

He stood at the fork in the road, his arms folded across his chest, chin raised in demand. A muscle on his left cheek thrummed with agitation.

I narrowed my eyes at him and considered not answering at all, but I knew that the cheery, flippant wave I gave him would annoy him much more.

"I'm going to Ira," I called back to him in a sing-song voice. His face clouded over. "Are you coming or not?!"

Turning my back on him left me with a sense of bright satisfaction, and this time, when we moved, others joined. Our group of three expanded, as most of the competitors took the chance on the right path, and I prayed Samael had not lied to me and sent us in the way of further danger for his amusement.

Two hours passed before the woods thinned, and we stumbled out into grassy slopes. Shadows of buildings loomed in the distance, beckoning our tired bodies forward, the first hint of civilisation we had seen in almost two weeks.

"Is that the Wrathlands?!" came a hopeful cry from the back of the group.

"No," someone else said, scoffing as we drew close. "That village is flying banners of green."

Nervousness roiled in my stomach. I wasn't sure we would

be welcome in an Envy village after being cast from Invidia and forced to walk, but it seemed to be the only path forward, unless we wanted to battle the trees to cut around it.

"Who cares?!"

Helina sounded too close to me for comfort, the sharpness and familiarity of her voice leaving me tense. "They'll have real food! Actual beds!"

A collective shriek of agreement rose to her comment, and despite the tiredness plaguing us all, we moved much faster towards the outskirts of the little village, stumbling past the low wall that might have been a half-hearted attempt to keep the woodland beasties out. They'd venture into the little village, a plague of ragtag humans seeking food and warmth.

A well-dressed man met us in the middle of the square. His shirt had ironed creases, hinting at unfitting wealth that match the patchwork buildings. It reminded me of home. Ilrea was a forgotten village in the Pridelands, and this was just a little village, lost to time in the Envylands.

The man cleared his throat, watching us carefully.

"Welcome, competitors!" He spread his arms wide, the pitch of his voice higher than expected, carving away the serious edge to him. "To the village of Zerut. I am the devil's chancellor, and we're honoured to have you visit. May I ask how long you'll be staying?"

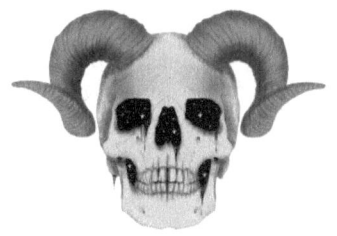

Chapter Four

The answer to his question turned out to be a three-day stay in Zerut. That was how long it took for the village and its people to revolt against our presence. Or how long it took for the Wastelands' Rebellion to join us. They had left us undisturbed for the first two days, allowing us to relax and recuperate.

The chancellor had us housed amongst various families who couldn't quite fit us all, which left us sleeping on the floors to avoid the rain. It forced them to feed us from their own rations, but we never whispered a word of complaint. The biggest luxury for me had been when someone found an alternative to the slinky, scaled dress I had been wearing since the end of the last trial. Ill-fitting men's pants had never felt so comfortable, despite their itchy material.

By the second night, we weren't the only recent visitors in town. Men slinked in just as the sun fell behind the treetops. They moved into the tavern, taking the last two available rooms with a flash of silver coin, and squeezing six burly men inside of them. It didn't take them long to hunt down the trial competitors.

I was wrapped up in my own preoccupations, which was to say I'd swiftly and quietly removed a purse of coins from beneath a loose floorboard in my host's house, emptied it, and replaced it with small stones.

After, I took myself out around the town in search of a game of cards, anything to quench my thirst for a bet and ease the anxiety piquing in my body. Knowing the opportunity was close left me fidgety.

Finding somewhere to play proved hard when Nash stuck close to me, where his presence was reassuring when I had nothing to do.

It felt stifling.

I thought he would judge my choices, even if he didn't know my history. He didn't seem like a gambling man. The easiest path was to convince him to come to the tavern for a meal, and I thought I could lose him in the thick of the people—given his easily chatty nature—find a game, and slip back before anyone missed me.

Nash didn't question the money, not when I pulled it from where I had hidden it. Wrapped securely in a torn scrap of fabric from the discarded dress, hidden in my boot, where it pinched my toes.

I suppose Nash had to have seen that I had hidden my coins in my shoes often enough that he wouldn't care when I loosened the laces, pulled out a few pieces of silver, and offered to buy him dinner, hoping a quick grin sold the idea.

The tavern was full, so we perched on stools at the bar, which left us with a view of everyone. A bitter turnip soup was the nightly meal, and they handed us a tart pint of ale before we even asked.

The server snatched the coins without a word and turned

back to the other patrons, leaving us to our food and thoughts.

Nash ate quickly, as if he might not see another hot meal again, and I followed suit, a hard habit to break since the Gluttony trial, the need to stay satiated.

The ale went down slower. It tasted awful, but I didn't say a word about it, having witnessed one man's complaint, where the server dumped his whole glass out on the floor for his troubles.

"It's terrible," Nash said, parroting my thoughts.

"Waste not, want not." I stated my mother's favourite saying from whenever her children had complained about dinner. "Besides, you can't say that I bought it for you as a gift."

He chuckled into the glass but kept drinking. When our mugs were dry, he bought a second round. I didn't ask why, since we knew we disliked it and because I would have spent a lot of money to stay where we sat at the end of the bar, close to a roaring fire keeping the chills at bay.

Nash and I had both been coughing up chunks of phlegm for days, sniffling the snot in our noses, so the warm heart of the tavern was bliss, easing the pressure in my chest.

"We could just stay here forever," I murmured, twisting on the stool to stare out at the patrons.

Nash did the same, leaning back against the bar and tipping his chin.

"If only," he sighed.

"Feels a bit like home, right?"

"No taverns at home," Nash grunted. "The Envylands are a little richer than us."

He was right. Their houses, although worn and overcrowded, was of better quality than ours, and the day had proven that the people also seemed happier.

My heart ached for the home I had left behind, one I thought I would never see again, with a bitterness I hadn't expected. It would have been easier if I could have left Ilrea and my family behind, to not have thought of them at all, but they lingered in my thoughts, haunting me.

The second glass left my head a little cloudier. It took me a while before spotting what I wanted. The little table at the back of the tavern sat overcrowded but had a bright energy, filled with the cheer of success.

I drew in a deep breath, attention not straying, while I lamented about home with Nash Wickham.

When chairs cleared, and I'd plucked up enough courage to face any judgement from my friend, I shifted to face him. "Hey, Nash?"

"Yeah?"

"There's a game happening over there." I pointed to the table.

He craned his head, his brows knitting together. "Looks like it."

I sucked in a breath, irritated at how difficult it felt to ask. "Do you want to play?"

"A card game?" He hesitated, fingernail tapping the side of his glass. "I don't know that I'm good at it."

I bit the inside of my lip, not daring to count it as a victory just yet. "You don't have to be good," I cajoled softly. "I've got a few spare coins from Invidia, you know, if you want me to spot you. Just be a bit of fun to relax for the night. It's been a hard time out there. We deserve to relax, have a little fun . . ." I turned to face him, eyes wide and lips parted.

He glanced from the table to my face and back again before shrugging. "Devils, why not? You don't need to loan me anything, Tav. I've got a few devil's coins to spot myself if I need."

My stomach twisted, heart racing, when he admitted he had been carrying gold all along.

We brushed past the newcomers and moved to the back of the room to fill spare chairs, my attention flickering over the layout of the cards.

It was a card game I was familiar with, so I quickly launched into whispering the rules to Nash, explaining the value of each card, the dealer, and how it all unfolded.

He had a good bout of beginners' luck, and he brightened with the wins, a broad smile tugging at his lips and a flush rushing to his cheeks, until he became more like the Nash I'd started out with.

For that reason, I told myself it was a good choice, even after my coins slipped through my fingers like raindrops, intangible before long, true of my normal luck.

We easily wasted hours playing, and I lost a small fortune, nearly all I had—stolen, along with my few precious coins.

Nash stopped playing long before I did, pocketing a few extra coins for himself, able to recognise his limits and enjoying watching the games as they unfolded. He found his fun in scrutinising the carefully blank faces of the other players.

By the end of the night, it was just us, the jolly dealer, and another player, who bowed out when I reached into my boot and could only pull free the Wrath coppers.

The dealer glanced at them dismissively and grunted as he tried to work out how to be polite.

"I know, I know," I huffed. "You don't take those here. Wrath coppers have never been so useless."

It looked as if my game was officially over.

The dealer congratulated us on a good play—although I suspected it was a comment more meant for Nash than me—and quickly packed up his things. He left us alone at the table without a coin or card forgotten.

"Should we get going?" Nash asked. "It's emptying, and there's no fun left."

When I glanced over my shoulder, I could see he was right. The bartender was wiping down the bar, the server giving tables the same hasty treatment. A few lonely patrons nursed their drinks, not the sort I wanted to deal with. "Sure."

As we shifted to rise from the table, three men joined us.

They slid into the chairs without asking, without hesitating.

"Going so soon?" one asked in a firm tone.

I paused.

Nash watched the man over my head, his lips pursed and eyes downcast. I couldn't tell what direction he wanted to take this intrusion.

"Yes," Nash admitted. "We're about to walk home."

"No, no, no," the man refuted loudly, his thick fist pounding on the table. "How about we buy you two a round of drinks, then?"

I swallowed roughly, suspicion tickling the length of my spine, yet I couldn't read Nash. "Why?"

"We want to know about the trials," he said simply, the mocking hint in his voice implying I was thick not to think about it.

"Oh," I said, glancing to my wrist.

The two shining tattoos and the iridescent cuff of the devil meant I couldn't hide being a competitor in his trials, even if I wanted. I'd become so used to it I'd almost forgotten it completely. I was instantly identifiable.

"Come on," one man said as another waved down the server. "Tell us a story, lovie."

A shudder ran down my spine at the nickname, a soft touch of disgruntlement from Samael that left me momentarily disorientated.

Nash set his chair down with a solid thump and glared at the man. "What do you want to know?"

The man regarded him for a moment. He was rough and looked as gruff and unruly as his voice sounded. He looked to be nearing sixty years alive, although I was never good at guessing ages.

"How are you lot feeling, then? They are tough, those trials. I remember the last time the community went through them, eh?

Barely anyone survived, as good as I can tell."

Nash's eyes narrowed, but it cut his retort when the server unloaded a tray of drinks on the table. She stuck out her hand for payment, and one man slapped coins into it with a wink that had her upper lip curling back. Even I heard the scoff of disgust from the back of her throat.

"We're tired," Nash admitted, shattering the silence. "The trials are hard. So, we'll have to decline these drinks and be going to bed." His hand wrapped around my upper arm, signalling with enough pressure that we should get up.

"But we've just paid for your drinks. You wouldn't want to be rude, eh?"

"That's not my problem."

Nash was firm.

I stood beside him, willing to follow his lead.

"Wait!" The oldest of the three men parked his elbows on the table and leaned towards us, watching us closely. "We have a proposal for ya. We've been talking to all the challengers, and I think ya'll want to us out, 'eh, boy? Make a smart choice. Now."

Nash straightened like he had a spine of iron. He glanced in my direction, but I didn't know the signal he was searching for or what to tell him. I didn't know what these men would have for us, unless it was a free pass through the next trial, something I didn't believe any of us could manage.

"Your life will be easier if you take our proposal. I guarantee ya'll not have to fight for it, but ya'll fight for a cause instead. You'll have some real passion behind ya because you know what it's like out there, how the devil manipulates us for his own fancy. Look at these sick games he's put ya through . . ."

A shudder ran down my spine as I revolted against the spoken ideals of Samael being manipulative and cruel.

Nash pinched my skin, and he looked at the three men with new regard. "Continue . . ." He sighed.

The old man looked pleased; a broad, smug grin stretched

across his face like a smarmy frog. "We're from a faction of the Wastelands' Rebellion," he announced.

All three men pounded their fists twice over their hearts in a strange salute.

I stepped backwards, pushing Nash back with me, creating space between their ideas and the danger they carried.

'No, Little One,' Samael whispered in my ear. *'Stay close. Let me listen to what this wise man has to say.'*

I didn't know what to make of Samael borrowing my ears to eavesdrop, and my chest ached as I tipped my chin and dropped back into the chair.

Nash huffed with surprise but moved to stand behind my chair, gripping the furniture.

Since Samael was listening, I thought I better ask questions, eager to please. "What's the Wastelands Rebellion?"

Although I'd heard of it briefly during my time with Envy's collection, I'd never bothered prying.

The old man nodded at my drink. So, to appease him, I wrapped my hands around the cold, metal mug. When I lifted it to my lips, I pretended to take a sip, unable to tolerate another mouthful of the brew.

He watched me intently and nodded at Nash to take a drink.

It took a moment before Nash reached past my head for his mug, lifting it from the table, action enough for the old man to explain.

"Right," he said gruffly. "We're a group or more multiple groups, eh? There are patches of wasteland across Kaida that are forgotten by the more sinful population. We'll take anyone who doesn't want to play by the devil's damned rules anymore."

"Oh?" I murmured. "What do you want with us, then?"

The old man grinned, and his smile was missing one or two of his yellowed teeth, an unpleasant sight. "Well, young miss, we think there ain't many people who wouldn't want to join our cause more than those of you the devil has wrung out to dry himself. His challengers, left to die at the hand of his sins."

Nash spoke over my head.

"By wrung out to dry, you mean what?"

The old man's face crumpled in confusion, but it didn't take long for him to collect himself.

"Well, he's thrown ya into this thing, hasn't he? Enticed you to sign up with pretty promises and then thrown ya in the ring with no help and literal angels to face down. Men"—he paused and gestured at me—"and lassies, we're not made to stand against these angels. We're not built to withstand their powers. And here's the damned devil, letting ya get pummelled by their influence. He's letting it break ya down, and what's he doing to help?"

Silence followed his question.

A lump had formed in my throat. I wanted to tell them how the devil had saved my life time and time again. I wanted to give Samael the credit for leading us here, and it was difficult to stop the words from rolling off the end of my tongue.

"Nothing," Nash said.

I craned my neck to look back at him, offended by his statement on behalf of Samael. "The devil's done nothing to help me. And you're right—it's shattering us. We're in bits."

With my fingers, I drummed the side of the metal mug, feeling pleased Samael spoke only to me—or, at least if he spoke to Nash, he didn't offer the same aid he did when I faced trouble. He didn't pull him through the trials by the skin of his teeth.

The man leaned forward, heavily pressing the table as it creaked beneath his weight. He flashed that crooked grin again. "We have a plan, and we could use ya resilience, kids. We could use folks who know what we're up against, know a sinner more than we do."

My heart lodged in my throat, beating steadily in the wrong place.

"What sort of plan?" I asked.

45

"Well, lassie"—he tapped the side of his stubby nose with his fat finger—"top secret, but if ya lot join us, we'll get ya clued in real fast, eh? All ya need to know is us humans. We'll be getting our own against the devil. We'll be reclaiming back Kaida, and ya help would be invaluable to the course."

"Ah," I said softly, biting my lip.

'Interesting,' Samael whispered. *'Ask how you join, Little One.'*

I desperately wanted to ask him why he would want me to join instead of continuing with the trials and winning my way to him, but I didn't know how to communicate with Samael without speaking aloud.

"How . . ." The words stuck in my throat for a second. They felt treacherous to voice. "How do we join the rebellion?"

Nash lay his cool fingers against the back of my neck, an unexpected contact, not saying a word. I didn't know if it was a to warn me or reassure me of the path I was taking. Not for the first time in my life did I wish I could peer into mens' heads to sort their tangled thoughts.

The old man's chest puffed up. "Ya come with us tomorrow morning, behind this tavern, before the sun rises. And we'll take ya to our faction headquarters, test ya, and get ya inducted. Easy as that, eh?"

I nodded slowly.

Samael was uncomfortably silent, so I twisted in my seat to look back at Nash.

His face was carefully blank. I swallowed roughly, unable to get direction from either of them.

"Okay, well, we should go if we want some sleep. Uh . . ." Nash helped me get my chair back, and I stood slowly. "Thanks?"

The gruff old man followed suit and stuck out his hand to shake. "Chester."

A stiff smile pulled at the edges of my lips, and I refrained from the commitment the handshake would bring. Tucking my hands into my pockets, I backed into Nash, who grasped my shoulders.

"Let's go," he murmured firmly.

"Okay."

We may as well have been running from hellhounds again at our speed. Nash directed me out the door and through the winding paths of the village, searching for the house in which we had been staying. We slipped through the front door and down the darkened halls. It wasn't until we lay on the lumpy, shared mattress that Nash spoke, his voice rough in the quiet of the early morning.

"You aren't thinking about it, are you?"

"Hmm?" I mumbled.

"Leaving the trials. I mean, to join the rebellion."

Even though he was whispering, it felt like the entire house could hear him.

I curled into a tighter ball and wished Samael would tell me what he wanted me to do. "No. I was just curious, you know, to see what they can offer us."

Nash grunted.

"Not much," I added.

I felt the shift of his head against the mattress as he nodded in the dark, curling around me carefully. "Just more false promises, don't you think? The devil promises an eternity of luxury, and these guys promise a revolution of a lifetime."

"I guess so."

"The chances of getting either are so slim."

He sounded miserable, and it was sobering that we likely wouldn't survive any of the options laid out in our future, all because we'd dared to venture away from home.

Ilrea was boring but safe, aside from old men with sharp knives.

"Don't say that!" I whispered.

"Why not?" Nash asked. "It's the truth."

The reality of it felt heavy, compressing me like a weighted

47

blanket, crushing my ribs and constricting each breath.

Pressing my face into the thin pillow, I closed my eyes to block out the overwhelming intensity of it. "Because we need to have hope."

"Hope?" Nash curled around me.

I imagined I was anchoring him as much as he did to me. Two people keeping one another going when the darkness became too much.

"Yeah, Nash. If we stop believing we can win, then it's all for nothing. You have someone to fight for. Remember that!"

He nodded, his hair tickling my neck as he buried his face in my shoulders. "You're right."

"Get some sleep. Tomorrow's a new day."

It didn't take long for his breathing to even out.

I wished I felt as confident about holding onto hope as I sounded when I spoke to him. It felt like grains of sand slipping through my fingers, impossible to keep. But for Nash Wickham, I could pretend. It was easier to hide lost smiles in the cover of the dark.

Owners of the house roused us from sleep early in the morning. They leaned low over our bodies, and the stark alarm on their faces set my heart racing. They were pale with familiar terror. Even half claimed by sleep, with my head pounding in protest at too little rest, I could see their tension, the nervousness in them.

"What's wrong?" Nash asked as he jolted upright.

"You need to go to the square," the woman whispered, her thin lips pinched, brows drawn close. "Quickly! The chancellor has come around looking for you a lot."

The urgency in her voice alerted us, an underlying note of worry striking a chord deep in my chest.

I scrambled for my socks and boots, then tugged them on and

tucked the laces behind the tongue. I was still pulling Nash's sweater over my head when we stumbled back out into the street, our few worldly possessions weighing down our pockets.

The early morning was miserable, rain that wept with poor fortunes and quickly chilled me until my teeth chattered.

We neared the square, and I wished I had time to wash so I didn't smell like the lingering stench of a tavern.

The Chancellor of Zerut stood tall, his arms folded across his chest. His eyes held a vacant edge, as if he were listening to a tune nobody else could hear.

I wondered if Samael spoke to his chosen representatives the same way he communicated with me, in a soft whisper against the shell of my ear, the tenderness against the very essence of my soul. I wondered what Samael had told him and if that was the reason for the look of betrayal flashing across his face, his lips thinning into an unimpressed line.

My anxiety spiked, an invisible force suffocating my windpipe, exacerbating as we waited for the last competitors to arrive. Confused and sleepy, I huddled into the square, shivering in the morning air.

His throat cleared, pulling the crowd's attention in his direction, proving he was not a man who needed to yell to gain the spotlight. The chancellor stretched, cracking his knuckles one by one, drawing my attention to the thick gold rings on his fingers, spoils of the devil.

One day, I hoped, Samael would spoil me that way.

"It has come to my attention," the chancellor said, "that your arrival has drawn unsavoury characters to Zerut. These men claim to be the face of a rebellion that threatens to ruin the very structure of our lives, and they have some to tempt you to their cause. I must warn you that theirs is a path with certain death."

Our group felt too still, an implied proof that many of us had spoken to the rebellion last night.

Hot spikes of irrational fear trickled down my spine, the

worry I was about to be punished, even though I had only entertained the men on the devil's own instruction. The heat chased away the morning chill.

"I can't stop those of your group who have already abandoned you for certain death, leaving you behind as the run rose," the chancellor announced grimly. I glanced around to see if any familiar faces were missing. "But I can forewarn you, it is not the right path, no matter how upset or worn out you may feel right now. The Devil's Trials are a challenge of privilege. You *can* persevere, if you only you learn to trust yourself at your very core, in your humanity. You may feel exhausted and unhappy. You may feel it has been dangerous and tough, but the devil wants to see you succeed. I promise you that much. The reward will be worth it."

Whispers shifted through the crowd, and the severity of the chancellor's expression slipped away.

I was close enough to see the pity in his eyes, and my stomach twisted at the sight of it. It left me on edge.

"What's coming next?" I asked, and although I had intended to murmur it for Samael to answer, it was loud enough for Finley Nightingale to pipe up.

"Nothing good," he said ominously.

Samael didn't disagree. He didn't say a word, although I could feel his presence, the invasive shift in my mind, which left the hair on the back of my neck on edge.

The chancellor rolled his shoulders, straightening his posture, then turned to point at the path that led from the square. "Regardless of what's coming and how you will handle it, I must ask you all to leave Zerut immediately. We cannot condone having these men in our streets posing a danger to our citizens. When our town guards tried to remove them, they reacted with violence, and I will not risk my people. You are what attracts them, and so you must continue to your trial of Wrath."

A collective groan swept across the square.

50

It felt like our rest wasn't long enough, the weariness still heavy in my bones.

Glancing at Nash, who shrugged, I followed the group, dragging my feet.

We were all but out of the square when the chancellor spoke one last time, offering us one last sentiment.

"Good luck."

He sounded as if he knew we would need it.

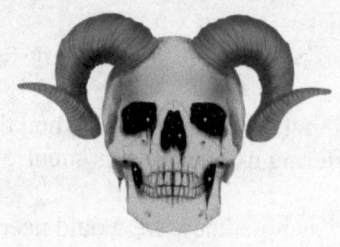

Chapter Five

The path wasn't long, and we stood in the thick of more Envyland woods.

It felt easier to spend a day walking, since we had filled our bellies and rested a little, but the constant conversation about the rebellion, whispers of what they had offered and who had abandoned us, disrupted the journey. Whether they had been worth joining, whether it was the right path to take, and whether they would follow us to the border of the Envylands as we ventured into territories at war.

Paranoia became my fast friend, as I couldn't shake the feeling that they would follow us and try to recruit more of us to their cause—by force, if necessary—as much danger lay on our tail as it did on the path ahead of us.

In the middle of the night, after I scraped up my limbs trying to climb a large tree and get away from the dangers of the ground, I realised the paranoia was not all my own.

Samael would occasionally murmur in my mind, whispering about rebellions and foolish plans.

As I sat on the thickest of branches, hugging the rough bark of the tree trunk, I wondered if the flighty feeling of danger was his as well.

Was the devil panicking? Was I drowning in his emotion? Did the devil really fear these men? My Samael, who didn't seem to fear anyone? Who laughed at the idea that the angels could be more dangerous than him? Surely not.

I was distracted by the fear of falling from the tree and snapping my bones on impact while I slept—or falling and becoming dinner for the hellhounds that howled in the night. Their hunting song haunted me, and with every mournful call to the moon, I startled out of slumber and sat, tense, waiting, scared, until I couldn't avoid my fatigue any longer and drifted off again. It was an exhausting and repetitive routine that wore me through.

For the next three days, we repeated the sequence of walking the long road and scaling the trees at night for safety. That was how long it took us to stumble through the overgrown forest, which seemed to grow darker and more intimidating before it lightened and thinned out, leading us to wide-open plains again. The rain let up as well, a relief, almost—to be out of the woods— until my brain truly processed what I saw.

We were approaching the ruins of a town, the rough, abandoned burial grounds of long-forgotten life. Buildings had long since crumbled, and the reedy, sharp grass of the Envylands had overgrown the remains. Humans once living there, forgotten.

The rebellion should have met us here, I thought, in the quiet moment when realisation dawned. We were just as forgettable as these people, and our own villages could be decimated just as easily and left behind. It would have been more impactful than a meeting at a tavern, a proposal over a mug of brew. Their offer would have held me over the bones of our brethren. It would have left me on the verge of joining.

My mournful feelings were unshakeable as we passed through that village. By nightfall, we found another one, another village, just as forgotten, building and man crumbling away.

It was here that the group, as a majority, decided we would camp out for the night. Rubble and structures provided more coverage than we had otherwise seen.

Dinner was meagre, brief, and sombre, before we scattered in different directions to hide, each on their own again.

Nash and I moved west, ducking into a half-fallen building reeking so strongly of decay I thought I couldn't stomach the roasted rat we'd eaten for dinner.

Pulling the sweater up over my nose, I buried myself in the corner against the rocks and the rubble, hoping the stench meant I'd be hard to find in the night.

Nash settled in the opposite corner, coughing into his elbow, turning to me under the silent agreement we would watch each other's backs, knowing sleep would claim us before long.

The village screamed with a wind that tore through the buildings, howling as it barrelled around us. The earth mourned for the men and women disintegrating beneath our feet.

It kept me awake, even as Nash nodded into his chest, and I imagined ghosts would walk across the rubble, visions of the long dead men and women.

"Samael?" I whispered. "Samael? Samael? Samael?"

His name became a prayer that kept me awake and, hopefully, alive.

'Yes, Little One?'

"What happened here?"

'War.'

"Between Envy and Wrath?" I recalled the comments in Envy's castle about how the troubles with Wrath had been consuming him and, by extension, the city itself. "Why do they hate each other so much?"

Samael was silent for a beat, long enough for another wild

54

wind to barrel through, kicking loose rocks.

In the distance, more of the town crumbled beneath the forces of nature with a loud crash.

'The war that flattened this town was not of the sins making. It's born of the constant war between man and magic.'

"Magic isn't real."

Denial rolled off my tongue before I could stop it. I instantly wanted to take it back, especially as Samael laughed.

'Really? For all the things you've seen since leaving your village, the angels and harpies, the erklangs and hellhounds, you still think magic doesn't exist?'

"I didn't mean it like that."

'Then, how did you mean it?'

"Magic is . . ." I didn't have the right words to explain it, the thoughts in my brain not lifting from my tongue. Frustration rolled through me at my inability to express it. "Magic is the work of miracles. Amazing things happen, and life flourishes and becomes the best thing ever. Magic is hope and power and . . ."

'That sounds like a tall story, Little One.'

I huffed but said nothing, realising he hadn't answered my other question.

He was giving away no clue to the war we were entering between Envy and Wrath, to the trouble we would face.

'Magic is not so black and white. It will never be so simple. Magic came with us from the old world. It is power like nothing humanity had felt before, so of course you struggled against it, struggled to adapt. Think of how the angels fly, the way they take your humanity and twist it into knots until you're living and breathing the sin of their design. Thriving and crumbling in both their curses and their blessings. That is magic, Octavia. Magic keeps the rain falling in the Envylands and the never-ending blue skies of the Lustlands. Magic keeps us alive, but there is always a cost. It poisons man. Humanity was not made to contain magic. Your bodies are fragile, your minds complex. Some believe they

can handle it, Little One. That man will rise and harness the magic we brought to you. They believe they can use it to reclaim their place in the world but never forget that magic is a toxin to humankind. You are not built for it, truly. If you were, this world would be a revolution.'

"So . . ." My breathing felt too loud in the face of this new information, discomforting concepts I wished to never know. "So, we're all just doomed to die? We're going to be poisoned by your magic?"

'Everyone dies, Little One.'

"Except your immortals."

He offered us that as the ultimate prize, the way to thwart death and thrive.

'Sometimes, even those who may live forever tire of life.'

He wasn't wrong, but it didn't make it any easier of a truth to handle.

I fidgeted with the sharp edge of a rock, and it sliced across the pad of my finger. A shallow cut beading up with blood, just enough to remind me I was alive.

"And if I win The Devil's Trials, do I become able to harness magic?"

'With my blessing, you will become immortal. It is a promise of my trials. But you will never be magical. You will still be human at heart.'

I wanted that, to live where others had already died. I wanted to live fully and do anything I wanted for an eternity, to live without worry and make choices without risk.

"Could I . . . If I were immortal, when I win, could I bless others?"

Samael laughed, a half cruel sound, and I knew it was a foolish question.

'I will bless you, Little One. You, who is so lucky and tenacious, but that doesn't give you the right to bless others—that is the right of angels alone.'

Something heavy weighed in the pit of my stomach, tears burning in the corner of my eyes.

"So, blessed to live forever and doomed to be alone."

'You won't be alone, Little One.'

I closed my eyes, shut him out, and wished for sleep, but those words were inescapable, especially when he stated them with irrefutable confidence.

"I'm always alone. This is the loneliest I have ever been."

'Lies,' Samael purred. *'You have me.'*

The musk of ash and fire roused me into consciousness, along with a burning in the back of my throat, a sting in my lungs.

Nash and I scrambled from our hiding place, coughing against the thick black smoke invading the air and curling down my windpipe. I failed to take his hand, and we ducked, running from the rising heat as fast as we could.

"What the fuck . . ." Nash coughed.

Grass was on fire in both directions, herding us back into the middle of the road and out of the city itself.

A group of ragtag and dirtied faces followed us down the road, not flinching from the lit reeds and smoking grass, as they advanced on us with torches in hand. The world glowed orange and burned bright.

"What do you want?!" someone screamed.

We shuffled back, fleeing the smoke.

Someone else screamed, "What do you want with us?!"

A burly man stepped forward and pulled down the cloth wrapped around his face. It was the man from the bar, and I tensed as I recognised him—Chester. The way Nash pinched me told me he recognised him, too.

The rebellion had followed us, and Samael was not completely paranoid after all.

"Come with us," Chester barked. "I know there were more of ya tempted to join us. Now is the time. Did ya not see this village? Come with us or die with them!"

A body slammed into my shoulder, a purposeful hit. It sent me staggering to the side, my hands scrabbling at their soft cloak for purchase to stay upright.

"Niklaus says to keep moving," a familiar voice hissed in my ear, the prim, proper tones of Margot Galatea.

She clasped my wrists with her soft hands, and I could have laughed that Margot had me in figurative shackles again. "He says they'll attack us and that you need to get to the back of the group."

"Why?"

"What?" Margot scoffed. "You are daft, Octavia, aren't you? Listen to what I'm saying."

"No, I mean . . . why are you telling me?"

Margot rolled her clear blue eyes, turning her head for a glance back to the tattooed man, who stood ahead of us. Once again, he placed himself between danger and those who would rather not face it, a shield of flesh and blood.

She leaned in close, her hair tickling my skin. "Because he asked me to, and that should be reason enough for you to move. Niklaus wants you both out of the line of fire."

I wanted to argue it, push back against his bossy demands, his assumption that I wanted him to save me, but I nodded, knowing that it was my best choice.

When I glanced up, it was apparent that Nash and Finley had been listening. They pressed close to me, and we pushed through the crowd of competitors, moving firmly towards the back of the group.

Margot clung to me, as if I was, once more, her only chance of surviving—or the person she would throw into the path of danger ahead of herself.

We were far enough away that, when the fight broke out, we weren't at risk, but the cries of anger and swinging fists kept us in place.

People screamed in terror and rage, the heat of the fires building, until I was slick with threat, suffocating on the smoke and praying for rain.

Still clamped to my arm, Margot twisted her body, taking me with her to watch Niklaus and Chester square off.

"You want us to join you after you dare try to burn us in our sleep?" Niklaus roared.

A roughness inflated his cry, sharp, broken edges and desperation in his voice.

His clenched fist caught the old man square in the jaw, who stumbled back, spitting blood onto the ground.

"It wasn't us." Chester spread his arms wide, a declaration of his innocence. "The devil set ya all right. We're ya rescuers, boy!" He screeched as if we couldn't see the flames at the end of their torches, as if we hadn't heard his threats to die with the village.

'Lies!' Samael hissed in my ear.

I screamed the word before I could stop myself.

People turned to me.

Slapping my mouth with my free hand, I wished I could force the word back into my chest.

Niklaus's eyes narrowed on us, and I had the distinct feeling we weren't as far away as he would have liked. Worse yet, I was drawing attention to us.

Chester spat another mouthful of blood onto the path and straightened. "What's that, girlie?"

"I said that's a lie."

My voice didn't carry this time without the devil's conviction. His words had knocked the fight from my chest.

When Chester stepped forward, I shuffled back, keeping the distance between us. "The devil wouldn't burn us. The chancellor was right. He wants to see us through it. Without us, there's no game for him."

I didn't know the others would listen to what I said. I was no prophet or voice of reason, not a wise or trusted woman. The weight of their attention left me weary, and I rocked back another step.

"Ya don't believe that, do ya?" Chester called, refuting my statement with such confidence that, for a moment, even I questioned the truth of my words.

It took a moment to find my voice, and Samael offered no encouragement.

"Yes," I snapped. "Even if we're just tools for his entertainment, he will want a longer game than this. He wouldn't burn us when we sleep if he can watch us bend beneath the power of his angels instead."

It resonated with me as the truth, one I might not have wanted to acknowledge before. I could be a pawn in Samael's plan, and I would die for it, but he would keep it going to amuse himself. It could not be easy to be so ancient and so bored with the life you had. Pitiful, powerless humans were dying from his magic all the same, so his trials would provide an entertainment for him, a way to see how we truly faced off against magic.

'Is that what you really think of me, Little One?'

It was tough, but I ignored him and raised my chin at the stocky leader of the rebellion instead.

Margot pinched my arm, a warning to move, and I forced a smile on my lips, stiff but present, flashing a feigned confidence.

"If you'll excuse me"—I backed away another step, dragging Margot with me—"I have a trial to complete, and you're wasting my time."

Turning my back on them was a dangerous choice, but I walked away without looking back. Nash, Finley, and Margot were by my side, my heart pounding wildly in my chest, and I knew some of the other competitors would make different choices. They would defect to the rebellion.

Niklaus stalked to our side, pulling Margot away from me and settling himself between us. Blood dripped from his tattooed knuckles, disapproval radiating from him.

Other competitors joined our march from the conflict.

Smoke billowed at our backs, the heat disappearing as we left behind those who didn't have the strength to leave.

We walked out of one battle and right into another.

We were close to the Envylands' and the Wrathlands' borders. They should have known we were close, purely from the violent frustration sparking within me from the confrontation and how the rain had thinned, with our clothes drying properly for the first time in the weeks of walking.

Samael had said rain always washed the Envylands, and most of the morning had been dry as a bone. Nothing had fallen to diffuse the fires.

Overlooking the signs was foolish, but I was not the only one caught by surprise when we stumbled along the path with black snakeskin-patterned tents in the distance.

My stomach twisted at the sight, and I instinctively recoiled.

The insignia of Envy promised trouble.

Our group came to a halt as recognition rippled across the competitors.

I looked to Margot, whose translucent skin had turned a pallid shade of green, knuckles blanching as she gripped her hood and pulled it over her face.

Envy could have been in there, waiting to collect the treasure I had helped steal. He could have slaughtered us all for hiding her within the ranks, a woman to which he had laid claim.

Margot pressed against Niklaus's side, and his arm slung lazily around her shoulders, chin raised arrogantly as he pushed forward, as if he didn't believe a lick of danger lay ahead of us.

"We . . ." I couldn't find the words as his other arm wrapped around my shoulder, dragging me with them. "We need to hide?"

"Hide where?" Finley asked. "Those tents look like they go on forever, and there's nothing here."

He was right. The hills had flattened, and the grass was dying down, no longer rain-fed and lush green but stiff and yellowing underfoot.

If we had walked up to the Envy base camp, we wouldn't have been far from the Wrathlands' border and our destination. It also meant that what we sought was beyond them, and we would have to bypass them on our way there.

"What do we do?" Margot asked.

My eyes, along with others, swung towards Niklaus Heira.

Son to a chancellor, familiar with power and privilege, he was one of few with the skills to step into place as our misfit leader.

His throat bobbed, distorting the tattoos etched into his skin. He didn't look nervous, as excitement glimmered in his green eyes.

"We go around," he stated.

"What if there is no way around?" someone challenged.

"Then, we go through them." He rolled his shoulders and stood taller.

His attention never wavered from the tents, and I remembered his brother had been sentenced to work as Envy's general in the front lines. Mikhael could very well be here already.

"That's just asking for death!" someone cried.

Niklaus pinned the loudmouthed competitor beneath his wild green stare, and the wiry man shrank back, his chin dropping to his chest. "So is standing still."

He had a point, as reluctant as I was to admit Niklaus could hold a decent idea. If we did nothing, we were sitting ducks. If we marched right in, we might survive.

Nobody moved.

I didn't want to be the first of us to walk into the camp. The mere sight of Envy's flags left my stomach in knots, and I imagined I wasn't the only one.

After we stood in idle indecision for a good fifteen minutes, Niklaus pulled us off the side of the road and called for volunteers to find a way around the battle camp. Only two people were brave enough to come forward. We huddled in the grass, scared and in wait, as they disappeared down the path. It took hours for them to come back, and even then, only one of them returned.

She staggered along the path, a deep cut carved along her cheek, dripping with blood. It splashed against her collarbones and stained her fingers, with which she tried in vain to hold her skin together as she wept in pain.

Niklaus was on his feet the moment he saw her approaching, running down the path and barely catching her as her legs gave way, and she crumpled to the ground. He swung her up against his chest, cradled her, and backed off the road.

I was one of the few who followed him, white-knuckling the crone's vial, acrid adrenaline burning my tongue.

The woman sobbed against Niklaus, and through her whimpering, I could barely understand her words.

"C-Commander Mi-Mikhael Heira invites you into th-the c-camp." She drew in a deep breath. "Any refusals to h-his h-hospitality will be c-considered engaging in w-war. We h-have until m-mid-afternoon to c-comply."

Her words were weighted.

I stared at the side of Niklaus's head, but aside from the tight lock of his jaw, he said nothing. He shifted his grip to adjust the way he held her. His gaze swept over my head and landed on my man at my shoulder, Nash. I missed what passed between them before he nodded tersely.

"Get everyone together," Niklaus commanded of the lankier man.

At some point, he had decided to trust Nash Wickham; they had bonded in my absence.

Nash twisted away from me and walked back to the group

with Niklaus's beckoning on his lips, all while I stared at our supposed leader, his face tight and unreadable.

Unexpectedly, it hurt more that he didn't trust me to voice his command, but I told myself I didn't care. I didn't need or want Niklaus paying me any more attention.

I folded my arms across my middle and stared past him at the snake-crested flags until the rest of the group caught up; a twist in my gut told me this meeting between the brothers couldn't go well.

"We've been invited to enter. So, we'll walk right through them. Hold your heads high. We've done nothing wrong." Niklaus spoke like the commander of his own army. A band of misfits and broken souls. "Be alert and be careful. Don't trust the people you knew before, the forfeits—they won't be the same." Niklaus turned and carried our wounded scout right into the heart of his brother's territory on that warning.

His final warning became fantastic advice but poorly heeded.

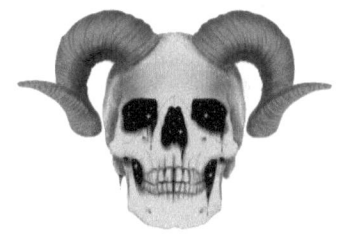

Chapter Six

Soldiers examined us as we walked through their base camp, tense and waiting for the possibility of our attack, their armour clanking as they shifted positions.

A soldier in a gleaming scaled breastplate led us around the first of the winding tents, and the camp expanded much further—an entire village of black-and-green canvas. We would never have been able to get around it, since braving their camp had always been the only option.

"This way," the soldier shouted, then turned to the left, his pace quickening.

His hand sat on the pommel of his sword; his knuckles blanched with the ferocity of his grip. He was leading us to the biggest of the tents, this one unpatterned but intimidating with its sheer size. Whole homes in Ilrea would have fit inside it.

Carefully, I kept to the middle of the group, wanting to go unnoticed, but Margot stayed irritatingly close, always by my side, no matter how often I tried to escape.

She would be the reason I couldn't fade into obscurity because, although Niklaus would be the first to enter and face his brother, it was surely Margot Galatea he would look for in a crowd.

The soldier didn't slow as we swarmed around the tent, filling the free space around it.

There were too many of us to have been silent to have ever gone unnoticed. We were fools to think this was an avoidable confrontation.

The soldier didn't allow us a moment to breathe when we stilled but simply swept the side of the tent open.

Mikhael Heira strode out, tall and proud in his scaled armour, his green eyes narrowing on us. His face looked thinner, cheekbones sharper, his hair ruffled in the wind.

Mikhael's presence was one I couldn't ignore, a world away from the man of Ilrea, a ruler in his own right.

Margot whimpered at the sight of him.

It looked as if Mikhael Heira of Ilrea had left us since his forfeit.

His eyes glowed a brighter green, imbued by Envy himself, but he didn't falter. He studied us in a beat of silence, the group he had left behind, although he hardly looked like he had been in our shoes. He had been washed and groomed and looked as if he had never traipsed through the hardship of the trials.

Sleek armour fitted his body, his chest plate decorated with the fiery-green akelda we had hunted for an entire month. His cuffs, boots, and the hilt of his sword woven with serpents. A sly smirk twisted on his full lips, his eyes settling on the one he wanted.

The woman pressed against my side, and his stare did not waver from Margot, soaking her in.

He was the poster boy of Envy's army, the commander to lead them to victory, so that they could settle the ever-violent envy in their hearts and claim what the Wrathlings held.

"Niklaus." He all but spat his brother's name, not bothering to look at him. "We've been expecting you. Took you long enough."

Even at a distance, I could see how Niklaus tensed, the muscles in his back rippling.

He murmured words too soft to carry on the dry breeze and slowly lowered the girl in his arms to the ground.

She groaned loudly, and Nash slipped quietly to their side to help her keep steady. When her knees buckled, he sat beside her on the ground, burying her head in his shoulder.

"Mikhael," Niklaus replied firmly.

The commander's lips stretched into a wide serpentine smile. He reminded me of the antagonistic young angel that ruled him.

I dropped my eyes, studying the toes of my boots instead. When Margot slipped her fingers through mine and held tight, I didn't protest, only wondered if she could see it, too—the way he had turned into a front man for Envy's goals, mimicking the slight movements of the angel himself, with Mikhael shadowed beneath.

"Come inside, brother," Mikhael said. He watched Margot closely, and when I glanced up, he had frowned, a crease deepening between his brows. "Everyone else may relax with my soldiers. Eat, drink, and be merry. The devil requires that no harm will come to you from us on your way to the Wrathlands. Lord Envy graciously abides by his promise not to hunt you down until after you enter your next trial."

For a moment, I thought he meant us, too, and, foolishly, the tension in my body melted away.

Margot and I could head to a firepit, eat hot food and drink fresh water, while the Heira brothers fought it out. Then we would walk on, safe and sound, leaving Mikhael to his new lot in life.

"Octavia."

At the sound of my name, I tensed as if struck.

"Bring Margot inside with us."

My heart sank to my boots, and Margot inhaled sharply.

Mikhael didn't wait for us but disappeared into the tent with his brother hot on his heels, both already hissing at each other.

The expectation that we would follow was clear, into the tent that could swallow us whole.

"He's different," Margot stated when neither of us moved. "He reminds me of . . . *Him*."

She was right. It was undeniable, and I didn't know if I liked this new version of Mikhael, who was twisted by Envy and trying to be angelic.

Before, I would have looked to him for leadership, comfortable with his place and power amongst our ranks, his sense of justice. But he had an edge of danger to the man I couldn't trust.

"Yeah, well . . ." I shoved my hands in my pockets, rough edges of my nails biting into my palms as I debated turning to run. "I bet he's still an asshole when he doesn't get what he wants." I nudged her gently. "We better go in there."

My head jerked to show that Margot Galatea would be braving the tent first, and I would follow.

No amount of false courage sent me willingly into danger.

Her icy eyes narrowed, nose flaring with unhappiness, but Margot didn't protest as she lifted her chin and strode inside.

I considered abandoning her—not for the first time since we had the misfortune of meeting, but Mikhael called my name again, a sleek command, like the crack of a whip against the ground. It left no room for disagreement.

He was an asshole, bossing me around as if he owned me.

I steeled myself, clenching my jaw, finding my nerve, before I stepped inside his war tent as if it were the battlegrounds.

"Oh, mighty Commander . . ." Snark might not have been the best tone to take as I walked inside, but it felt good to get it off my chest. "You called?"

They glanced towards me, identical expressions showing

they were both unimpressed by my attitude.

Margot wavered, standing between the two brothers, one placating hand extended towards them.

The last place I wanted to be was in the middle of their drama, so I turned slowly and inspected the tent instead. I tried not to be impressed by the rich dark colours and warmth of Mikhael's war tent. He'd lined the ground with rich furs accenting the walls, with a green so dark it reminded me of the leaves in the Gulan forests. It was cosy, almost warm. A large table spanned one side, covered in maps, with little red-and-green markers scattered across it.

I shuffled closer and peered at it. The words meant nothing, but I wasn't stupid enough to miss the symbolism of each piece—the players in his deadly game.

"Bigger than I thought," I commented.

Everyone ignored me, of course.

'That's what she said,' Samael purred in my ear.

I snickered, validated by the devil's response, which cooled the sting of rejection from the lack of acknowledgement.

I didn't want to impress them, not truly. The Heira brothers and Margot Galatea hailed from a different world to me, a place softened by privilege and emboldened by expectations. But being outright ignored was always hard to swallow; even I had some pride.

"Were you telling the truth, Mikhael?" Niklaus asked through his clenched teeth, his arms folded tight across his chest. "We're all guaranteed safe passage to the Wrathlands' border?"

Mikhael sighed heavily, as if he carried the weight of a world on his shoulders, weighed down by the gems on his chest plate.

When he spoke, he was clearly looking to antagonise his brother, his words dripping with implied idiocy.

"I said as much, didn't I?"

Niklaus's mouth pulled down at the corner, a muscle twitching in his cheek, his green gaze darkening. "What do you want, then?"

"Margot, of course," Mikhael said.

The woman sucked in a sharp breath again, too loud in the silence following his claim. Her pale face pinched, and for the first time in weeks, her haughtiness cracked through her uncertainty and fear.

"*What?!*" she demanded of Mikhael, turning to him, a pale finger prodding the breastplate over his heart. "I'm not a possession for you to claim!"

"We got what we wanted, my sweet. You're free of Invidia."

Mikhael's words were soft, but even with the sharp edges dulled for Margot, he still didn't seem himself.

He captured her hand, his gloved fingers stroking over her knuckles. "You can stay with me. I'm the commander, the most powerful man in this camp. I'll protect you here. I'll give you everything you could ever want."

It was a fanciful idea, one I had heard many times wrapped in different packages. The devil, the sins, the rebellion, and an array of others liked to claim they could give everyone everything they wanted, but nobody ever stopped to ask what exactly that might entail.

I shuffled to the side quietly, wanting to be as far away from this tent and the conversation happening within as I could.

Niklaus glanced at me when I moved, his thick brows drawing together and green eyes flashing in warning not to do anything stupid.

A red flush swept across Margot's cheeks, bright and indignant. It lit her up, a fire burning from within, offering heat to her reply.

"You want me to go from being caged in *his* city to caged in yours? Another pretty bird on display."

Mikhael's jaw sharpened.

When he caught my eye, his narrowed with accusation, and I looked down.

My influence didn't have Margot refusing him. I didn't want to know or influence her at all. In fact, I would have preferred she forgot I existed.

"You wanted us to be together, Margot!" He focused on her again, gripping her hand tighter. "You said it wasn't fair if we weren't together!"

"That was before!"

Panic rang as clear in her words as it did on her face; her glance flitted around the tent as if assessing the exits in her new cage.

"Before what?!" Mikhael shifted, using the bulk of his body to cut Niklaus and me out of the conversation. "Before you were free? Is that really all you wanted of me? A quick kiss and a ticket out of Invidia!"

Margot closed the space between them, and her pale hand caressed his stubble-roughened cheek. A heavy sadness etched across her face, as if she were preparing to break her own heart in two.

"Before you were Envy's . . ." she whispered, devastation plain on her face. "I don't like this version of you, Mikhael."

He frowned. "I'm still me."

"Really?" Margot asked. Strands of white hair fell across her face when she shook her head. "*My Mikhael* was softly determined and thoughtful. He led others for the safety of everyone, not the power it offered him. He knew their weaknesses but never exploited them. *My Mikhael* wasn't so arrogant as to walk us through his camp like he had his own collection. On display for his soldiers to laugh at, to view. *My Mikhael* . . ."

"Enough!" Mikhael snapped.

His intense demand made me flinch.

Mikhael's fingers had wound into Margot's hair, the braid at the back of her head looping around his fist. He tugged her head backwards, forcing her to look him in the eye.

Pain pinched Margot's face, but to her credit, she didn't avert her eyes and stared him down.

She had years of practice bending for Envy—manipulated and shattered at the whim of an angel. I imagined that, in comparison, Mikhael's arrogance was nothing.

"I'm still me," Mikhael croaked, sounding like he was convincing himself more than Margot. "I'm still the man who fell for you. I'm still the man who loves you."

"Fell for me?" Margot whispered back. "How dare you say that when I'm the one who's breaking, Mikhael?"

"I gave up everything for your freedom, Margot." His throat bobbed as he swallowed, his voice thick with emotion. "Will you not give up seeing the Wrathlands and stay—for me?"

"It's not about seeing the Wrathlands!"

Mikhael blinked, confusion marring his handsome face. His grip in her hair loosened a touch, enough that her shoulders relaxed. "What's it about? Explain it to me, Margot, because I don't understand."

"Even if you are the man I met, even if this is all just a ploy to survive"—she struggled back a step, and Mikhael relented in his grip, allowing her to move—"I can't stay here. In *his* war camps, where he could visit on a whim. What do you think Envy will do if he finds me here? I'm not safe!"

"I . . ."

Niklaus nudged me. I hadn't realised he'd drawn so close, and we turned to study the maps on the table, trying to block out the painfully obvious fact that Mikhael hadn't even considered he would be placing her in Envy's way again. Trying to ignore their emotions.

"He'll break me, Mikhael. Tear me into tiny irreparable pieces that we won't be able to put back together," Margot cried, tears slipping down her face. "And he'll make you watch as he does it. He'll give you a piece or two, scraps to play with, but I'll never be the same."

Their silence was deafening. I was acutely aware of my

heartbeat.

Niklaus nudged me again, a pointed jab of his elbow into my ribs.

I grit my teeth because I knew what he wanted—I wasn't stupid. He wanted me to interject. He couldn't do it, not without Mikhael believing he was trying to steal Margot away, but I was just the village idiot to them. Everyone would think I was a fool if I said what I wanted. I was the woman who danced with angels and barely survived to see the next day.

Staring hard at all those green pieces, symbols of battle, I thought about what I had said to Nash about hope. I wondered if Mikhael had held hope that Margot would stay with him, his own piece of Envy's treasure to hold forever. He wanted what the angel had coveted. I wondered if Margot hoped to return to the village where her quaint old cottage had once existed. She wanted the memory of safety. Did we all hold foolish dreams in the name of hope?

"She's right," I said.

Before I could stop them, the words flew out.

I turned to face them and squared my shoulders with a confidence I didn't truly feel. *Stupid Niklaus, asking this of me.* He owed me more than he knew, especially as Mikhael skewered me with a look.

"Margot isn't safe here."

If glares were incendiary, Mikhael would have lit me up on the spot.

I didn't flinch back from his glare, a sign I was no longer the woman who would have fled any form of confrontation in Ilrea.

"Stay out of it," Mikhael warned, drawing himself up to his full height. He was impressive in his snugly fit armour flashing soft green light, a man with shadows of emotion for everyone except his beloved. "This has nothing to do with you."

"You called me in here," I argued.

"What?" he snapped.

"You called me in here." I stepped closer to them. "In fact, you involved me in all of this, Mikhael Heira. You told Margot about me, the woman so desperate to live she would save her from Envy. You begged me to help you get her out. You stood inside of this tent and called me inside. You beckoned me into your mess, so I think I get an opinion, don't you?"

I could almost hear his teeth gnashing.

One more step forward, and I reached for Margot, my fingers anchoring in her dirty dress sleeve. I yanked her back to my side.

Mikhael let her go, a good sign. Niklaus crowded at our back.

"If you really love her, you'll want to keep her safe," I argued, although I knew nothing of love—not really. It was a story built for hope, not an experience I had lived. "You're not safe for her, Mikhael Heira. You're forfeit to the angel who made her life hell, who turned her into the shell of the woman she should be. If you love her, you'll let her go. You'll want better for Margot."

It was a pretty sentiment, although I wasn't sure where I had heard it before. I only hoped those stolen words would resonate in his thick Heira skull and that Mikhael would understand.

Margot, on my right, looked close to breaking down; her entire body trembled, tears running thick and fast down her cheeks as she sniffled.

"What's fair is us both having what we need, Mikhael."

If I had said those words, it would have been throwing them in his face, but Margot's soft, broken voice was just a reminder for him.

"You need to survive Envy and this war, and I need to feel safe. I won't feel safe until I'm as far from the Envylands as I can get."

Mikhael growled. "How far is that?"

"Not until I'm home," Margot muttered.

"Where's home, Margot?" Mikhael asked, sounding broken. "I thought it would be with me."

74

"The Greedlands." She pulled free of my grip, stepped forward, and pressed her pale lips against his mouth roughly. A passionate kiss and a mournful goodbye. "Come find me when the war is won."

His arms wound around her body, constricting her as if he could pull Margot Galatea into his very soul and protect her by burying her deep in his beating heart. Mikhael kissed her back so deeply, so passionately, that I thought he might truly be there, beneath the façade of the commander, a man who loved a woman enough to sacrifice himself.

"Go on, then," Mikhael commanded when he released Margot, pain shuddering across his face. "Leave me."

"I *will* see you again," Margot promised, even as I wrenched her backwards, desperate to leave the tent before Mikhael changed his mind.

Niklaus stayed still, but his brother ignored him, only having eyes for his love, as I snatched her away and she cried, "I will see you again!"

"*I know*, Margot."

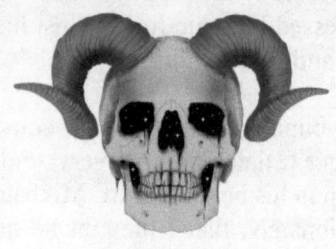

Chapter Seven

Mikhael allowed us a few hours of rest, camped in the dirt around his soldier's tents.

I spent half the time tense with worry that his word wasn't worth it.

At midday, as the sun sank behind grey clouds, he exiled us to our last day of walking.

"Our soldiers will cease battle today. Rest will be our luxury, and the energy we find will renew our battle until the Wrathlings bow before us," Mikhael announced, standing tall in the middle of camp. A peaceful smile played on his lips, and his soldiers were hanging from each word. "The devil's competitors will walk alone across the plains to meet the forsaken Wrathlings and will meet no harm from us—by word of the devil, by word of our Lord Envy." He paused, his focus sweeping over the mixture of soldiers and competitors. "Tomorrow, my men, we kill anyone who lingers behind. We will show them no mercy as they face our venom, and we win this war!"

He jerked his chin at the man beside him, who sprinted through the camps, set to deliver the message of relaxation to the rest of camp, ensuring no black-and-green soldiers would follow us along the plains and run us through. Skewered by sword would be an uneventful end to these tumultuous trials. The soldiers who gathered cheered loudly, slapping one another on the back. They dissipated quickly with murmurs of returning to bed.

I desperately wished I could sleep another day away, too.

Mikhael turned back to his brother, his sly smile stretching wide as he gestured to the battlefield beyond the camp.

Empty plains of dry land where Envy and Wrath went head-to-head.

I couldn't see the Wrathlands, only the way the sun spilled across the dirt, warm and inviting compared to the rain we had endured.

"Head east, brother," Mikhael commanded, as if Niklaus was just another of his soldiers.

Niklaus nodded, his lips pressed together tersely. He turned his back on his blood and lifted the injured competitor off her feet, securing her against his chest. He strode away, heading east with paced, determined steps.

My eyes never veered from his muscled back as the competitors wordlessly followed his lead.

I glanced back as we exited the camp to where Mikhael stood tall, his arms folded across his chest, envy plainly splashed across his features. How had I never seen it before? The way he looked at his brother as if wishing they were one and not two.

It was then and only then I realised Niklaus had silently used us to make a point. Mikhael held an army at his command, but we followed Niklaus's leadership without direction, following him in blind faith. I was sure this hurt his brother more than anything else.

It took most of the day to traipse across the battlefield. We walked long past the moment of my toes going numb, an ache running deep through my legs. Dead soldiers' bodies were abandoned, and we skirted around corpses stripped of armour, who were left for the large birds of prey to pick at their bones. It showed the young, arrogant angel's careless disregard for the people who battled in his name.

The odour of blood and rotting flesh intensified as we moved into the warmer climate. This wasteland, tucked between two warring territories, had chased away the rain, and the sun became a relentless goddess above us. The longer I walked, the more my skin burned beneath her visage. The air was dry, heat crackling in my lungs with every inhale, an aching thirst leaving my throat raw.

We didn't slow, Mikhael's warning enough to force us to march past the point of tiredness. We had a single day's grace before we joined the feast of the birds.

An invisible border seemed to separate the Wrathlands from the Envylands, and I couldn't have pinpointed when we crossed it. The lands looked dead, slaughtered by the war itself, so nothing demarcated the soft greenery of Envy fading into the baked, dusty lands of Wrath.

We walked blindly to the east, and in the next, darkness appeared in the distance.

Marching soldiers appeared without warning and approached quicker than expected. We had fallen cautiously still at the sight of them. A dark body of shrieking war calls, marked by flags supporting the red lion. They swooped across the land, slowing to a halt in front of us, an intimidating wall of supple leather and chain mail. The angry symbol of Wrath stamped across their chests, red strands woven into their hair and striped across their faces.

They were tall, unflinching, and bore down on us aggressively.

Amongst the competitors, I was not the only one to step back.

I wondered if the death promised from the Envy battalions was not, in fact, a better option than facing these soldiers prepared for rage and war.

"Who are you?" a woman barked. From the midst of the group, she strode forward.

Dry winds whipped at her hair, a braided smoke-grey threaded with enough red strands to cause my stomach to flip.

Aieke had said that each strand represented a kill, and I couldn't even count the amount in this woman's hair.

She held an implied level of authority as the soldiers parted to carve her path.

As a group, our competitors shuffled together.

Moving close to Nash, I pressed against his side, his presence reassuring in the face of new danger.

We had nowhere to go, and the day's heat was unbearable, even as the sun had slipped away. Beads of sweat trickled down my spine, my shirt clinging to my body uncomfortably. I waited for Niklaus to speak for us.

Someone else took his place. Aureen Willett shook her head, a flick of her wrist sending her long dark ponytail over her shoulder. Her chin raised high in pride.

"We're competitors." She proved, in that moment, that she was the bravest of us all. "Competitors in The Devil's Trials. We have faced Gluttony, Envy, and, now, we seek safe passage to Ira to begin our Wrath trial."

The words felt heavy as they lingered between us and the red army. Their expressions were inscrutable from behind the leather masks shrouding them from the eyes down.

The grey-haired soldier was silent for so long I thought she would reject us. I couldn't blame them; I would have distrusted anyone who wandered from behind enemy lines. If Envy had been intelligent, he would have sent his forfeits with us, who would pretend to be competitors set to slaughter his enemy from the inside.

The violent thought surprised me, and I shivered, wrapping my arms around my midsection, squeezing tight.

"I am General Inaina, Commander of the Fourteenth Wrath Battalion." She tapped her clenched fist to her chest, right at the lion's maw. "You may all follow me."

Her words carried on the wind, and my heart raced. I fumbled around the pockets of the pants I had gained in Zerut until I touched the cool glass of the crone's vial. General Inaina's name was seared in my mind since leaving Invidia, although I had half believed she was fictional and that old Eadlin had sent me chasing stories with a pocketful of treasured rat piss for her own amusement. But the general was real, and it sparked a burning hope for answers in my chest. I just had to find a moment to get her alone and deliver the crone's gift.

General Inaina was an intimidating woman, taller than many of her soldiers, leather armour moulding against her muscular body. Her hair may have been charcoal-coloured but had since faded to the grey of ash and smoke, threaded with pieces of fine red string and braided into a tight, heavy rope hanging along her lower back. The heat of the sun had tanned her skin. Callouses peppered her hands. Her dark eyes flashed with wary intelligence, the rest of her face hidden by her mask.

Her eyes narrowed just enough to give me the impression that she found us lacking, and she wasn't wrong. She marched away, her soldiers falling into step with ease, and I followed with the crowd. We trailed the fourteenth battalion; a staggering mess compared to their tight-knit unit.

The sun disappeared, sinking behind us, and darkness brought the soft relief of shade, a reprieve from the harsh burn.

Their camp appeared in the distance, missing one moment, there the next. It started with the same smattering of tents built of black linen that had faded beneath the sun. Red flags of their sins flew high. It sprawled further than I could see, but in the distance, solid structures rose from the middle of camp.

The war had raged for so long that the Wrathlings had built a town to base themselves within, as if to show they truly belonged here, fighting for their side. Towering dark-bricked buildings surrounded us, covered with sun-baked terra-cotta roof tiles. They cast shadows across the tents, creating an air of intimidation.

My heart sank as I realised there were more soldiers here than Envy had on his side. As they moved, the soldiers peeled away. We remained in the march, led by the proud general. The light of dancing flames flickered around us, barks of laughter breaking through the tension.

Walking beside Nash, I stared out at the soldiers by their tents. They stared back at us. Dark eyes full of judgement, they shuffled and watched as they led us around the winding paths and towards the brick-and-tile centre of the army.

I turned my focus back to the General Inaina.

It was tempting to run forward and press the vial into her hand. I wanted to disappear, but my curiosity had become too much, eager like my thrumming heart. Having had carried this message for weeks now, I tucked it in my pocket, and I wanted to know what it meant—mostly if Eadlin had played me for a fool.

"Something feels wrong," Nash murmured.

Finley, on my other side, grunted in agreement.

"What do you mean?" I asked quietly.

He shifted, twisting to glance over at a crackling fire and the bodies strewn around it. The soldiers lazed as if we weren't bothering them, more focused on their meals. "I think they were expecting us."

"What?" I asked with a choked laugh. "Of course. Sam asked for us to have safe passage through Envy's camp. Why not here as well . . ."

"Sam?" Finley's dark brows rose, his voice sharp. "Who in the devil's name is Sam?!"

"The devil," I blurted. "I meant to say Samael and got

distracted partway through."

Finley blinked but seemed to accept my lie.

Nash, however, let out a slightly aggravated sigh. "It's more than that . . ."

"Like what?" I asked.

"I can't explain it."

"We'll be okay."

It was a false reassurance.

I didn't know if we would be fine. Probably not, especially now that Nash had voiced unease; it tickled my nerves as well.

We passed through a wooden arch between the tall buildings.

A low, threatening growl rolled through the evening. Instinctively, I moved away from the now-familiar sound and slammed into Finley, who also scrambled.

When the general paused and glanced over her shoulder at us, we had fallen back, creating a wide arc of space between where she stood and where we cowered.

"What is it?" she asked, sounding bored.

The growl rolled through the quiet street again, the deep, throaty warning of the hellhounds.

My chest ached. I wanted to run far away.

The hellhound padded into the street, illuminated by the light thrown from the lanterns on the front of the buildings. It looked wild, eyes shining, teeth bared, its dark muzzle secured with a strap of red leather.

General Inaina laughed, a throaty sign. "Continue."

At the command, the hellhound crouched, muscles in its hind legs tensing to pounce.

Fear was acrid, and I studied my fellow competitors to see who would be the first to follow the command. It would never be me.

"We do not tolerate cowardice here."

Her announcement was too casual, but the words left me shivering as I recognised it as a warning.

I was sure that the armies of Wrath slaughtered those they didn't find the tolerance for or who failed to meet their expectations.

The hellhound was a test.

Niklaus shifted to step forward, but Aureen gripped her sister's wrist and shoved her in front of him in a sharp, jerky movement.

Kyra stumbled, barely keeping her balance, face tight with fear when she glanced back. When she straightened, spine stiff, her fingers trembled by her sides.

"Go on," her sister urged.

Aureen put her sister into a position of power, effectively raising her to the eyes of the general.

The hellhound snarled, and the sound rattled my bones.

Kyra's chest expanded with a deep breath, and she flipped her braids over her shoulder. They swung against her back, and by the time they settled, she seemed to have centred herself. With her chin raised, she looked past the snarling beast and to the general.

Inaina watched with her arms folded across her leather breastplate, her feet planted and dark eyes unreadable.

Kyra Willett didn't stop to look at the beast once she moved. She marched past it, as if it didn't exist.

The muzzled hellhound snapped at her heels.

I flinched, but Kyra kept walking until she stood nose-to-nose with the Wrathling general.

"Shall we go?" she asked. Only a touch of breathlessness belied her fear. "I don't want to be wasting your time, General."

The soldier's thin dark brows lifted, her arms relaxing until she stood at ease. "Congratulations, child. You will be the first to have the honour of meeting Wrath."

General Inaina turned and marched away without another word.

Kyra followed, hot on her heels, until she strolled by her side, her long legs keeping pace with the soldier.

They didn't wait for us, but Aureen, then Niklaus, Helina, and many others were quick to bypass the hellhound, less intimidated that the fine-boned, fragile Kyra had passed the test.

I lingered back, Nash and Finley moving ahead of me. Soon, I was the last one left to face the hellhound, and it turned its gleaming yellowed glower on me with ease. The growl rolling from its belly should have had me shaking in my boots. I wasn't fool enough to think that muzzled danger, avoided by others, was not still a threat to me.

Unlike the others, I watched the beast as I passed, taking slow, measured steps to skirt around it.

It grumbled as I drew too close, its scorn flashing, and I paused a step away. Too close to the beast because bound teeth wouldn't save me from sharp claws.

"What if . . ." I murmured.

'Don't be a fool,' Samael hissed.

Ignoring Samael, I inched a fraction closer to the beast. "What if I unmuzzled you?"

The hellhound cocked its head, as if it could understand my words. Yellow eyes narrowed, and its lips drew back as I reached towards it. It snapped at my fingers, fighting against the red leather, and I flinched backwards. The hellhound stalked towards me, encouraged by my fear, and I forced myself to move, scrambling behind Nash.

The beast leapt after me, whining when a chain yanked it back.

A laugh pulled from my chest, and I shook my head. "See," I told Samael smugly. "I was never in danger."

'Merely lucky,' Samael scoffed.

I felt he'd said that a lot. His lack of confidence wasn't reassuring, but I didn't have time to think about me, having fallen so far behind.

"What took you so long?" Nash asked sharply.

I blinked. "Did you see the giant hellhound standing in the way?"

"The one we all walked right past without getting hurt . . ." Finley piped up.

"Yeah, well, I had to tie my shoe, obviously." I shoved him lightly, and he staggered dramatically, gasping as if I'd hurt him. He righted himself and slung a heavy arm around my shoulder, laughing. "Were you scared?"

The question lingered between us as we approached the back of the group outside the tallest of the brick buildings. Two more of the beasts were tied on either side of the doorway, watching us wearily.

"I'd be a fool if I wasn't . . ." I snapped, irritation at his tone making my skin crawl.

"Watch out, then!" he cried as we edged past the set of hellhounds and through the large arching red doorway.

We followed the other competitors down a long hallway, clustering at the end where General Inaina stood in front of scarlet doors, arms folded across her chest.

"What's happening?" Nash asked.

A girl in front of us twisted to speak in a whisper, her expression panicked. "Wrath's in there."

It shouldn't have been surprising that the angel might have been here, especially not because the general had announced Kyra would be the first to meet him.

But I'd thought we would have days more travelling to reach Ira, that would we complete the next challenge in the capital city of the Wrathlands, just as we had for the sins that had come before.

'Do not make the mistake of thinking that Wrath is like Envy or Gluttony.' Samael spoke to me idly. *'Each sin is uniquely dangerous, Little One.'*

"I know that." I sniffed.

'Do you?'

"I—"

"Who are you talking to?" Finley asked.

My face heated. "Nobody!" I bit out.

'Oh, I'm nobody now . . .'

Again, I ignored Samael, shuffling forward each time the line moved. Nash and Finley disappeared ahead of me, leaving me the only competitor standing in the hall—just me and General Inaina, who watched me closely out of the corner of her eye.

"I . . ." My throat seemed to dry up and stick, capturing words before they could leave. "I . . ."

"What?"

The general's voice was a cracking whip, encouraging me to act.

I reached into my pocket for the smooth glass vial, still half amazed it had survived this long, and thrust it in her direction. It rolled in my palm for a moment, and her dark eyes widened, her brows rising with surprise.

"The crone, I mean, Eadlin. She told me to give you this . . ."

General Inaina snatched it the moment Eadlin's name had slipped from my lips. She had stowed it away before I finished rambling.

I waited for her to say something, anything, but she stared me down.

"Uhhh," I hedged.

"You may go in." General Inaina tapped on the red door, and it creaked open.

"What was in the vial?" I asked impulsively. "Why do you need it?"

The general ignored my question and nodded at the door again.

I wished I could see the lower half of her face, catch any sign of what she was thinking in her expression, but her eyes were blank.

"You may go in."

I wanted to stall, to demand answers of General Inaina and find out what I had delivered. After all, I had kept it safe for days, even when my curiosity burned with the desire to crack the vial's wax seal and test the contents, even in the moments I had believed it all to be a hoax. I had no resolution. It was simply no longer mine.

General Inaina's stare burned a hole in the side of my head.

I could feel her judgement and impatience as she waited for me to move. Tension radiated from the soldier.

I heaved a sigh, chest tight, as I pressed a palm to the red door, shoving my way through. The door bounced off the wall, swinging back towards me.

Before I could second-guess my choices, I stepped through the closing entryway, receiving my first real look at the Angel of Wrath.

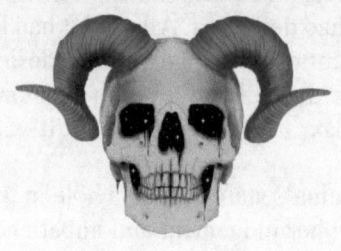

Chapter Eight

"You're a woman?!" I gasped.

The Angel of Wrath stood across the room. She had turned just enough that I could see the distinctly feminine curves to her body. Despite the whispers in Envy's castle of his sister, I'd still believed Wrath would present male, just like the last three sins I had met. I'd thought of another male, hot-headed and cruel.

Wrath looked surprisingly like her soldiers, having adapted to ethnicities of her lands. Her inky hair threaded with worn red strands had been braided and wrapped around her head tightly, a diadem of kills. A crown of death. Her skin baked golden by the sun, showing that the angel didn't cower behind castle walls or in the lap of luxury, distinctly different to Envy.

She was short, I realised, as she dropped to the ground in front of me. Her wings offered extra height as they arched strongly behind her, but Wrath stood just shorter than me, as compact as she was muscular. Her wings rustled, snapping in tight against her back now that she was close, protected but sheathed like a sword. They were a weapon to be unsheathed and not a glorious asset to be displayed in the way Envy had utilised his. I imagined she was fast when she soared through the air.

When the angel turned fully, I realised I was only half wrong. A cruel, sharp edge curled on Wrath's smile. A godly power that I feared as I drowned in the overwhelming feeling that she could crush me in the blink of an eye.

My chest felt tight, bound by a corset of my anxiety, but I fought to keep my head up.

"You've kept me waiting, human." So much animosity came from that statement that I cringed away, rocking back on my heels as Wrath hissed. "I wait for nobody."

"And yet, you waited for me . . ." I blurted.

My hands slapped my lips, a desperate attempt to revoke my snappy statement, incensed by my hot anger from the angel speaking down to me.

Wrath stiffened, her wings intimidating, stretching out wide, before she stalked in my direction. Her leather boots made no sound as she walked, and I realised she was hovering, stalking through the air towards me. It gave her more height to stare down at me.

My stomach quivered, but I kept my eyes locked onto her.

I would have bet all the coin in the world that Wrath used her wings like she used her anger, in a deadly manner. It amazed me that the angel stalked the front lines of battle, her energy pulsing across the barren lands, leaving us all with a restless thirst to act.

The angel's energy pulsed through the room, creating a weight on my chest, as if she were encasing me in the same heavy armour she wore.

My jaw aching from grinding my teeth, I was irritable, pulse racing.

The corner of Wrath's mouth quirked up, as if she could hear every frantic heartbeat.

"You live only because I will see you die for those words in my challenge, human."

Her haughty tone set me on edge. My fists clenched, the jagged point of my nails biting into my palms.

"I won't die in your trial." I proclaimed, keeping my voice steady.

Her sleek black brow rose. "Such confidence. You hail from the Pridelands, I'd suspect."

Wrath wasn't wrong, but it stroked my already-irritated nerves that she had guessed my heritage.

Her sharp smile widened, as if this was all a game to the ancient being.

When I swallowed around the dryness in my throat, I couldn't stop the bite in my words.

"I passed Gluttony and Envy. You won't be much harder to beat."

A laugh rolled from her throat, a deep sound that I imagined had become a death rattle within this war.

It unsettled me and incited my instinct, the pure humanity, into a quivering desire to flee.

"Foolish child," Wrath murmured. She stepped away, as if I were nothing to her.

It felt like a slap to the face, more of an insult than her words.

The angel stalked to a table, and from it, she picked up a dented goblet and a golden envelope. When she turned, she held it out to me.

My stomach twisted again—this time, with nerves. It was, unmistakably, another test, useless for me. I couldn't read the contents of that envelope if I wanted to, the lettering within as foreign as the customs of the Wrathlands.

Stiffly, I planted my feet, folding my arms over my chest. I wasn't sure if I took the stance to look aggressive or to hold myself together because I trembled, surely about to fall to pieces.

"Keep it," I told the angel in an attitude I was sure would get me killed.

The golden envelope dropped from her fingers and to the floor.

I didn't move, and Wrath watched me closely, her scrutiny burning my skin. A strange light bloomed in her eyes. Where Pride was golden honey, Gluttony's was a violent shade of violet, and Envy was the green of his precious akelda. Wrath's eyes seemed almost flat. A black void of nothing but rage, so much that it lacked the swirl of tempering emotions from feeling nothing more than bloodthirsty anger.

When I didn't move for the envelope, Wrath approached me again. Her muddied boots stepped on the golden paper as she walked, destroying it. It showed how much she cared for my trial, my future, and my life.

"Don't you want to know what you'll be facing here?" Wrath's hand shot out, strong fingers weaving into my hair in a tight grip. I winced as pain seared my scalp. "Would you go into the Wrath trial foolishly blind, human?"

The ferocity of her words and the way her power flared left me nauseous. My hands shook with the suppressed desire to claw her eyes out for touching me, the anger so abrupt my body felt off balance.

"Tell me, then."

I gasped because my anger did not feed into courage, and my pride had fled, leaving only fear in its place. "Tell me how to win your stupid trial."

Wrath laughed cruelly again, letting go as quickly as she had reached for me. I staggered to the side, the loss of her anchoring hand throwing me off balance. "I see you, human. I see the fire inside of you. You have no hope in this trial. It is harder to overcome the wrath in humanity than you believe. It drives us to impulsivity."

"Tell me, then," I repeated. I hated how pitiful I sounded.

"What's the challenge?"

Wrath settled back on her heels, her sleek black wings rustling, and she raised herself to her full height. Although she wasn't taller than me, she held command in the way she carried herself, in the intensity of her power, and I shrank back on instinct.

> "Emotions run rampant in the war between sins.
> Wrath feeds envy, and envy fuels wrath,
> In the violence of battle…
> Forbearance is the only way to win."

I wet my parched lips, and shook my head, confused. "What does that even mean?"

Wrath's cruel, rage-filled smile danced across her face. "Welcome to war, human," she crowed. "You're now a dispensable part of my army." My chest felt tight as I remembered what dispensable meant. Wrath nodded to a door to the right of the room. "Dismissed."

"What?" I asked.

Thin-lipped fury turned to me. "I said *dismissed*, soldier."

I was halfway to the door before I, stupidly, turned to speak again. "Why did you meet us like this?"

For a second, the angel appeared startled by the question. A flickering moment where this godlike creature appeared almost human, but it disappeared between one breath and the next, for the angels of sin would never have a shred of humanity.

"I know the faces of all of my soldiers, whether or not they are wanted," she stated, her voice firm. "All their sacrifices deserved to be mourned."

It was a sombre note to finish on, and Wrath said no more when she turned away, dismissing me once again.

I couldn't help but wonder if she mourned the girl I had killed, if she knew Aieke's face with the same sickening details I remember. Sickly, dying, but deserving of my cold, rough attempts at mercy. I could still feel her blood as it had pooled over my fingers.

Did she wonder if Aieke was still alive? I guess not. The lives of humans were miniscule compared to the angels, even those that dared mingle among us like Wrath.

I wasn't sure if I liked it that she had bothered to look us in the eye before the challenge.

A soldier met me on the other side of the door. They stood with their chin raised, spine tall, dark eyes watching me warily.

Outside, I could hear growing noises. When the soldier led me down the hall, I paused at the window and tried to get a glimpse at what was happening. It was too dark to see much more than the soft glow of the lanterns.

"What's going on?" I asked.

"War," the soldier grunted.

It took everything within me not to sigh. "I know that. I mean, right now."

She paused, twisting to glance back at me. Judgement rolled from her body. "War," the soldier slowly repeated, as if I were thicker than the bricks holding the building up. "The next rotation leaves to defend through the night."

My throat contracted as these words settled. "You fight at night?"

"War doesn't end because we want eight hours of sleep."

The bite in her words made me pause. "Have I offended you or something?"

The soldier didn't pause this time. She didn't turn back or offer me that same insolent, wrathful stare. Instead, she grumbled loudly as she paced through the front door and down the tiled streets.

"The lot of you offend me, abandoning your lives, your obligations, to run through these trials. Where's your sense of duty to your homes . . ."

"Maybe I don't have a home."

The lie hurt to say more than I thought it would. I hadn't thought I'd miss my family as much as I did, but it turned out it was easy to take them for granted when they were nearby.

The soldier turned in front of a sprawling one-storey building, her eyes narrowing with scrutiny, her genuine expression covered by the soft leather mask. "Then, I guess you've found one, soldier."

Her knuckles rapped on the wooden door; heavy steps shuffled behind it before the door creaked open.

A tilt of the soldier's head directed me inside, and I stepped into the poorly lit room abuzz with chatter.

"Another one?!" someone groaned from the back of the room. "There's barely enough room as it is!"

"Enough!" the soldier barked, authority ringing in her tone. All whispers of conversation died at her command. "Welcome to the barracks. Find a place to sleep, recruit. Basic training starts at sunrise."

I didn't know what she was talking about, but before I could ask, the soldier was gone, slamming the door shut in her wake.

Whispers picked up within moments, and I felt as invisible as I had.

It didn't matter. I was used to it. Carefully, so I wouldn't trip on any sprawled soldiers, I edged my way further into the room. It was a large hall, wider than it was tall, housing bunk beds. It wouldn't have looked so full if not for the people strewn all over the floor, chatting.

Those with competitor's cuff's stuck to themselves, and those with Wrathling features slid sideways glances at the newcomers.

I made a beeline for one bed, eager for the soft comfort of a mattress, but just as I reached it, a voice rang out.

"Oi!" A woman walked up, dropping her muddied boots beside me with a loud thump. "That's my bed!"

I blinked.

Normally, in a fight-or-flight situation, I was on team flight, but I was riled by Wrath, and part of me wanted to gouge out her eyes for her attitude. A lingering irritation possessed me, a cloud of a bad mood I couldn't shed.

"Does it have your name on it?" I snapped.

The woman shoved me so suddenly and hard that I stumbled backwards.

I slammed into another woman, who let out a shriek. "Uh—"

Before I could consider apologising—not that I would have—that person rammed me towards the first, who swung at my face.

Her knuckles cracked my cheek with a flash of sharp pain. The room spun, and I hit the floor, landing hard on my arse, a gasp sticking to the back of my throat. Prickles of discomfort webbed out from the point of impact, radiating across my face as it started to throb. I willed myself not to cry, even though the bridge of my nose prickled with emotion, my eyes burning.

"Mine." The soldier spat on the floor beside me. "Find somewhere else. As far away from me as you can get. Understand?"

"Eww," someone else complained. "Peliela, don't spit on the floors. That's *disgusting*!"

Nobody came to my rescue.

Soldiers and competitors watched, but not even my friends dared to interrupt as the woman, Peliela, swung herself into the bottom bunk and kicked her legs up on the sheets.

She watched me from the corner of her eye to see if I would fight back.

Tension built in the room, heavy and expectant, and it didn't take a genius to realise these women wanted to see us fall to violence. They wanted a fight.

It took a moment to piece together the fractured remains of my pride, but I pulled myself upright.

The room felt too quiet, and my neck prickled with the heat of attention. I forced myself not to touch my sore cheek, swallowing roughly, turning my back on Peliela to walk away. Surely, walking away was more of an insult.

Other women parted for me to move through in search of somewhere else to sleep, and Peliela's sharp laugh was inescapable. The queen of the barracks mocked me from her bottom bunk.

"Coward."

That word condemned me.

Many of the Wrathling women turned away as I approached, looking for a place to sleep. I paused at the end of Nash's bed, prepared to ask him to let me bunk with him, when Peliela's voice rang out again.

"No sharing, or you'll be out in the kennels!"

It took everything in me not to ask who had died and made her queen. My unsettling intuition told me she could provide a name in answer.

Nash offered me a sympathetic glance, his lips curling down at the corners, before one of the Wrathling women made a bid for his attention again. He would not offer me a safe place.

Glumly, I left him alone.

By the time I found an empty bed, a top bunk in the far corner that squeaked with every movement and no blanket to be seen, I was in an angry, sulky mood. The bed announced every restless shift of my body, and various women screeched to shut up and stop moving.

Closing my eyes, I tried to stay still. I wanted no more confrontation. Maybe I was a coward, but when everyone had seemed thirsty for a fight, maybe my cowardice would keep me alive.

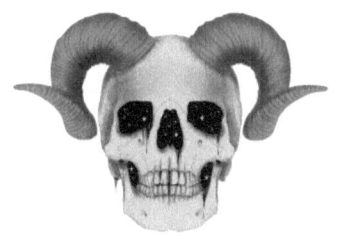

Chapter Nine

A siren blasted through the barracks, high-pitched and screeching. I catapulted into consciousness, dizzy and disorientated, as the last vestiges of sleep clung to me. Pressing my palms against my skull, I clamped them over my ears to block the noise, my head aching.

The door to the barracks whipped open.

General Inaina and the soldier from the night before stepped inside, scoffing at us as they surveyed the room. "Up! Get up! Outside, now!"

Groaning, I felt like I had an hour of sleep, my head spinning. By the time I staggered down the metal ladder on the bed and towards the door, I realised my guess could be accurate. The sun had long sunk behind the hills when I had entered the barracks, with no sign of it rising over the camp any time soon.

We amassed in the streets in our sleepy, fatigued state, no longer divided between Wrathlings and competitors but simply recruits for Wrath's army.

I stood beside a Wrathling woman, rubbing my eyes with the sleeve of my shirt and fighting a yawn.

"What's going on?" I asked stupidly.

"I'm not sure."

She was breathless with fear.

It surprised me. I had assumed they had all been here forever, trained soldiers prepared for anything.

"Who's that?" I pointed to the soldier beside General Inaina.

Blinking, she wrapped her arms around her middle and shrank back as if whispering her name might call her attention to us.

"Major Akua." The major stalked near us, spitting sharp commands and insults to stand straighter, stop yawning, to get it together.

The major seemed harsher on the competitors than the locals, and I recalled her words about our abandoning our duty to our people, something she seemed to take too seriously.

I was so busy watching her I'd stopped paying attention to Genera Inaina. Before I could prepare, the general stood in front of me, her eyes narrowing with assessment.

"Are you paying attention, grunt?" General Inaina hissed.

I blinked. "I . . ."

"Three marks," she commanded. "Get moving!"

"What?" I felt dumbfounded. "Three marks of what?"

"Keep talking, and it'll be four."

Wisely, I clamped my lips shut, but my confusion must have reflected in my face because General Inaina grunted.

"Move!"

'Start running, Little One.' Samael laughed, my discomfort seemingly delightful to him.

His command, I followed blindly, a far easier one than the soldier's.

For Samael, I would do a lot without question.

98

My feet beat the tiled streets, staggering in the middle of the group. The night air was colder than I had expected, but running kept away the chill. It didn't take long before my pace slowed significantly, and I found myself in the way of other runners as I slowed.

"Get out of the way!" one grunted, shoving me aside.

My thighs were burning, my chest tight, and an acrid taste touched the back of my mouth.

Three marks felt like an impossible distance, especially with no real understanding of how far it meant.

Slowing to a stop, I doubled over, bracing my hands on my thighs as I struggled to catch my breath. I sucked in a fast lungful of air, but nothing stopped my head from spinning, and I was so disorientated I barely noticed when another woman skittered past with the general and major riding on horseback, chasing her down.

They loomed over me, intimidating and judgemental, with fury sparkling in their eyes.

"Get moving!" Major Akua swung down from her horse, standing over me. "You complete this run, or you're on scut duty."

"I think I'm going to be sick," I groaned.

I didn't understand the threat, so it missed its mark.

"Puke on my shoes, soldier," she snarled, "and I'll make you eat it for breakfast."

Something rang true in her tone, and I swallowed down the bile.

My legs felt shaky as I straightened, nodding slowly. One of her brows rose as she waited for me to move.

A quiet sob threatened to roll from my lips, but the steel in her eyes indicated she had no patience for it.

I turned on my heel and stared down the path on which the others had disappeared. "Three marks," I muttered. "That's just three things. One, two, three, easy as that."

"Get going, recruit!" Major Akua roared.

I startled, drawing in a final ounce of energy, and staggered into a run again.

It felt like General Inaina and Major Akua were breathing down my neck with every step. It was the only thing that forced me through. Even my head felt light, and the world turned darker at the edges despite the rising sun. Three marks took just over two hours to complete, and I walked most of it.

I was struggling for oxygen, shaky, and incredibly unfit. Adrenaline had carried me through in the past, but that spanned short distances, and this length was my undoing.

By the time I had reached the end of the selected track, where the other recruits lay sprawled across a field, my body shook with fatigue. With my elbows pressed to my knees, I let myself relax, my stomach churning, a shudder rolling through my body, before I retched once, twice.

I turned, unable to stop what was coming.

Vomit splattered all over the major's shoes. She stood over me again, and I swayed. The major's darkened squint swam in front of me.

Before I could collapse into the puddle of bile, however, powerful arms gripped my biceps and held me upright.

Niklaus Heira wavered in my peripheral vision, standing tall, the only thing keeping me on my feet.

"She apologises, ma'am," he grumbled in the most subservient tone I had ever heard from him.

Irritation sparked in my chest that he spoke for me. I wouldn't apologise for it, not after they had pushed me well beyond my limits, but I couldn't find the energy to speak the words.

"You vouch for this little runt?" Major Akua asked, sounding curious.

Niklaus tensed, his hand tightening on my arm to the point of pain.

"Don't," I groaned, stomach flipping again. I pressed my hand to my mouth, mumbling through my fingers. "Nik, don't."

He shot me a dark look, his lips pressing into a thin line.

I struggled against him, trying to stand on my own, but Niklaus held tight. My body shuddered. I was going to vomit again.

"Yes," Niklaus said firmly over my heaving. "I'll vouch for her."

He was a fool—one look at the major's face confirmed it.

"Hmm." Major Akua met Niklaus's green eyes without flinching. "Then, you'll share in her penalty, recruit."

The major and the general swung up onto their horses with ease and looked down at us. They were an intimidating sight, swathed in armour, wrath in their eyes. They stared, as if we were nothing, as if our efforts had been for nothing.

"Walk back to the barracks," General Inaina commanded. "You have an hour and a half."

Cries of indignation rippled around the field at the impossible timeframe. Weary recruits pulled themselves upright, rage burning in their eyes.

"Ninety minutes! To make it back three marks?!" one cried.

"You're just setting us up to fail!" another yelled.

There was no doubt in my mind that, behind those smooth, leather masks, the general smiled with amusement at our pain or maybe at the fire it lit beneath us instead.

"Well, then." The general kicked her heels against the horse's flank. "My advice is that you better run."

Foul-tempered and far too late, we spilled into the brick-and-tile town, staggering with fatigue.

Thirsty and hungry, I was battling the increasing desire to pass out. I'd felt like I was on the verge of darkness for most of the walk.

As I staggered back along the trail, Niklaus had held me upright, using his strength to carry me, the warm, familiar shape of him easy to lean against when depleted.

In the outer camp filled with canvas tents, we found drums of water, and fights broke out as we all tried to get more. It wasn't enough, even as we staggered through the doors to the barracks.

"It's trashed!" someone yelled from inside. "What the devil?!"

Blearily, I latched onto Niklaus, my fingers twisting tight in his shirt.

The barracks were wrecked. Our possessions strewn everywhere, the sheets stripped and tossed aside, half the mattresses flipped aside and shredded.

"That's strange." Finley Nightingale almost sounded like he was laughing. "Could have sworn I made my bed this morning."

Despite myself, despite the fatigue, I snickered. I wasn't the only one.

"You think this is funny, recruits?" Major Akua's voice cracked through the room like a whip. "Clean it up. Only then you can eat."

Recruits groaned. The clean-up effort was slow, and I was no help, leaning against one wall, one palm pressed against my grumbling belly. I felt weak and miserable. It became one of life's small joys when the barracks was back in impeccable order and food became the next order of business. I was hungrier than I was in the Gluttony trials.

Major Akua appeared in the doorway for inspection and announced our work "satisfactory" after stalking the room. They dismissed us to eat, and despite my fatigue, I couldn't move fast enough at the thought of filling my belly, making a beeline for the door.

"Uh, uh, uh," Major Akua mocked as she forcefully caught my arm. She stepped swiftly into Niklaus Heira's path, blocking

102

his way. "Not you two."

Margot hesitated by Niklaus's side, but when he shook his head, she hurried to meet Helina outside. They disappeared with their heads bowed together. I watched them go with a growing sense of dread; I knew that I wouldn't like what Major Akua had in store.

"What now?" Niklaus growled, his impatience clear.

The major's eyes didn't waver, but I imagined behind that mask, she smiled smugly.

It filled me with an intense, sudden rage and left me trembling.

Wrath's influence felt more potent when I was hungry, exhausted, and sad.

"Now, you pay penance for your indiscretions, recruit."

"Because she threw up?" Niklaus's voice was flat. "After running so far."

"Because every action you make in this army has a reaction." Major Akua turned, leading us outside. "They will not always be proportionate, but life is unfair. You should be grateful to learn that lesson early in your training."

It might have been sage advice if I didn't think this sparked vindictive pleasure in her ability to dole out punishments.

The little town was coming to life in the midmorning sun. Soldiers strode through the tiled streets in pairs, and recruits skittered out of their way. General Inaina led everyone else to a large outdoor firepit where food was served. The essence of roasting meat drifted, and my stomach rumbled. If possible, I felt even more miserable than a moment ago. I could have never avoided this punishment because there was no way to finish the run without being sick. It was too far, too much.

Outside the town, beyond the dark brick and red tile, the sounds of war-camp life carried on the wind. Laughter and fights, the clank of metal, and cries of pain. All of it intensified the nausea rolling in my stomach and the regret I felt.

Major Akua led us around Wrath's Hall in silence until we stood beside a small sturdy building between the stables and the latrines. Between the horses and shit, it stank enough to set my teeth on edge. I covered my nose and mouth to ward it off, taking slow, measured breaths.

Major Akua threw open the building door. "Many of our soldiers have donated to your penance. Come and have a look, recruits."

There was nothing I wanted to do less, but I crept forward, nudging past the bulk of Niklaus's body to stare into the dimly lit room. He stared straight over my head, and I could feel his heat as he pressed against me, warm and strong.

Boots filled the room, all of them caked in mud, blood, and worse. The pungency was that of unwashed, sweaty feet, leaving me retching again.

Niklaus and Major Akua scurried away, but nothing was left in my stomach, just bile burning my throat.

"Right," Niklaus said. He swiftly rolled up his sleeves, revealing the brightly coloured ink decorating his forearms. "We clean the boots. Understood."

He was far more accepting of this punishment. It was surprising because, in Ilrea, he was one of us who lived in luxury. He had people who cleaned his home, washed his clothes, and I wouldn't be surprised if he had a servant just to cut up his food. Niklaus Heira was one of the last people I could have been as comfortable scrubbing horse shit from the soles of soldiers' boots.

"Okay." I struggled to pull myself together, as if this didn't affect me. "That's easy enough."

I was lying. There was nothing I wanted to do less, except the run again.

Major Akua chuckled, a dark sound that grated my nerves. She pulled two objects from her pocket and held them out, one for me and one for Niklaus. "You'll need these to get the job done."

I blinked, absorbing the sight of the toothbrushes. "What?"

"You'll be cleaning them with these." Major Akua dropped both brushes, and I had to snatch one from the air, my palm wrapping around the coarse bristles. I hoped it hadn't been in someone's mouth recently. "Water is over at the latrines. Don't forget to get in the treads. I want them sparkling by the time I get back."

A loose rock bounced off the toe of her boot as she strode away.

I felt like I was choking on helplessness. Wrath's army was a place that thrived on fighting, and I wasn't sure how I could survive this place, even with the angel's influence suffocating me, urging me into the fight.

Niklaus stalked to the latrines, disappearing into one of the roughly built squares. He spewed curses before he came back out and ducked into the next and the next. When he returned, he had a plastic blue cup clenched in his hand.

"What's that for?" I asked, hating how high-pitched my voice sounded.

I wasn't a strong woman, but I didn't think I'd ever sounded so weak, except for when I was dying below Envy's castle, feverish and succumbing to final peace—although I like to think that was normal.

"There are no buckets," Niklaus grunted. "Get a move on."

Striding into the building, he cracked his head on the low-hanging lantern. Niklaus swore loudly again, probing the cut blooming with blood above his brow.

The room felt tense, the penance serious, but I giggled at his collision with the light.

"Shut up!" Niklaus barked.

Biting my lip, I couldn't stop laughing. Every time I looked at him, I giggled until I was panting, waving to communicate, my eyes blurring with tears.

Until Niklaus overturned the cup of water on my head.

It sobered me instantly. The cool stream of water running

down my spine turned my snickering into a shriek.

"Niklaus! That better not have come from the toilet!"

"I told you to shut up."

"You didn't have to—"

"All actions have reactions, and they're not always proportionate," Niklaus mocked, parroting Major Akua. One hand holding the swinging lantern, he edged around it and towards the door. "I'm getting more water."

When he returned, I was sitting on the floor, holding a black boot and staring glumly at the crusted blood on the heel.

Niklaus stooped to sit next to me, awkwardly folding his long legs and setting the cup between us.

It became routine. Dunking the toothbrush in the water, scraping the boots to loosen the crusted grime, dipping the brush to clean it off, scrubbing harder until my anger seemed to melt a little, scrubbing more until my fingers ached and the boot looked decent, stacking it against the wall in a line of mismatched sizes, and repeat.

Every time I'd become used to the stench, no longer choking on it, I had to refill the cup. The brief reprieve of fresh air made it worse when I had to come back in. Then, my stomach offered its own commentary, which seemed to be what sparked and lit the end of Niklaus's short fuse.

"Stop that!" He dropped the boot and pointed the bristled end of his brown toothbrush at me.

"Stop being hungry?" I rolled my eyes at him. "Fat chance."

We fell into a disgruntled silence, broken by scraping bristles against leather.

A vein throbbed in Niklaus's forehead every time my gut rumbled, and it didn't take long for him to shatter the peace again.

"Why do you always do this?" he snapped.

I threw down my toothbrush, gritting my teeth. "Do what, exactly?"

"Get yourself in stupid, dangerous situations."

"Cleaning boots is dangerous now?"

"Getting on the wrong side of Major Akua is dangerous," Niklaus argued. The lantern swung, casting shadows over his face. Anger swept across his features. "You make stupid choices, Octavia, and one day, they're going to kill you."

It was the most accurate summary of my life. My teeth ground together so hard that my jaw hurt, frustration welling in my veins. I should have told him off, but I threw the boot at him. It thudded against his chest, and Niklaus blinked, disbelief marring his expression. He caught the boot as it bounced off him.

"You didn't have to vouch for me, Niklaus." I seethed, so angry at him I could explode. "You didn't have to be here, scrubbing boots. I didn't ask you to be here."

"You never ask. You just expect!"

Raising my voice raised, I tried to talk over him. "Not from you. I have zero expectations of you! You're a—"

He returned the boot, and it slammed into me, knocking the air out of my lungs and the words from my mouth.

I jumped to my feet and kicked it away. "Seriously!?"

Niklaus climbed to his feet, too, the bulk of his body taking up too much room in the shed. The lantern swung past his face, taking away from his intimidating stance, making it easier for me to get in his face.

"What is wrong with you?" I spat. Crowding against him, I shoved his chest.

"With me?" he growled. "What about you?! Little Miss Trauma."

"Yeah, you." I shoved him backwards. "You wanted nothing to do with me in Ilrea, Niklaus, *nothing*. I was a plaything for you there, not worth a second look. Then, in these stupid trials, you keep acting like my self-appointed saviour, like it's your responsibility to keep me alive."

"Octavia—" he snarled.

"Newsflash, Nik," I spat, "it's not your job. I don't want you attacking me, kissing me, taunting me. I don't want you carrying me back from the run or standing up to the major for me. I don't even want you thinking about me."

"You threw yourself at me! You wanted me!"

"Years ago!" I protested hotly. It felt like a lifetime ago, when I'd wasted my days in Ilrea, wishing he felt the same passion for me that I had for him. "I don't want you now, you thick prick!"

"You want me," he refuted. "You told me once you'd wait for me."

"Not forever, Nik!" I screamed. "Nobody waits forever!"

He folded his arms, face darkening at the rejection. "If that's what you think."

An edge ground into his tone, an underlying smugness hinting he thought I was lying. It left my blood boiling, my clenched fists shaking.

Right then, I hated him.

"I've found someone better," I told him evenly.

I don't know what prompted me to say it, half a lie, but a darkness crossed Niklaus's face, his jaw tightening, so I continued.

"Someone you can't dream of living up to . . ."

"Who?" he asked, aggressive.

As I paused, my anger faded as I realised the precarious situation that I'd put myself in. I'd made very few connections in these trials—or at least a few who still lived—and, of course, Niklaus would demand a name.

"His name is Sam."

Samael laughed in my ear. *'Oh, Little One. Are you really telling this poor man that he can't compare to the devil?'*

Ignoring him, I focused on Niklaus, stepping back when he stepped forward, closing the space between us.

'You're right, of course. Poor human. He'll never live up,' Samael whispered, distracting me. *'But don't mistake me as yours to claim, Octavia Nox. That's not how this works. I am not yours,*

Little One. You are mine.'

Niklaus moved forward again.

I moved back, my heels catching on a stray boot and throwing me off balance.

His hand shot out, and he gripped my arm, keeping me upright, nails digging into my skin.

I couldn't focus on Samael's whispers, not with the intense way Niklaus looked at me, the way I'd always wanted him to, as if I were the missing puzzle piece to complete his soul. He wrenched me forward, my shoulder twinging in protest, and I staggered into his chest. His arm banded around my waist, anchoring me in place.

"Let go," I demanded through clenched teeth.

"No."

"Nik, I swear to the devil—"

"If he's so much better than me, why isn't he here?" he asked, heated. "Come on, Octavia. Where's Sam? Why isn't he scrubbing boots with you?"

My body flushed red hot, and I gulped, struggling to get away from his warm, hard body.

"He's not stupid enough to throw himself in the firing line."

"Not even for you?" Niklaus asked. "Actions say more than words, love."

Sighing, I slapped his chest.

Niklaus didn't budge but just stared down at me.

"You don't want me."

"Says who?"

"You!" I said, exasperated. "A thousand times before. You implied it, and you made it explicit. I got the message, Nik. You don't want me."

Niklaus held me tight, while I struggled to put space between us, even as I lashed out at him. He towered over me in the small disgusting room, and I shook my head, rejecting him.

"Why did you pull me off the fence in Invidia?" Niklaus

asked finally, the question heavy in the compact room.

"I . . ." My teeth scraped over my lower lip, pinning in an answer I didn't want to reveal. "I don't know."

"Tell me, Octavia."

"I just didn't want to lose someone else," I snapped, half lying as I beat at his chest with my clenched fists. "Is that all right with you? I just didn't want to deal with another death."

He let go of me, and I staggered backwards before landing hard on my arse, the air knocked from my chest. Sitting in the boot pile, I glared up at him.

"You're right," Niklaus said harshly. "I don't want you."

"What?" I gaped.

Hearing him say it left me stunned, and it hurt just a little. I had spent years wanting Niklaus, years, entertaining the fantasy that he would change his mind and want me, too. Even though I knew, deep down, someone like Niklaus—brutal and mercurial— didn't want to end up with someone as desperate as me. I had been a distraction and not a desire. It still hurt to hear it, even though I insisted it was true.

"Screw you, Nik." I kicked out at his shin with my heel as hard as I could, earning a grunt of pain.

"Isn't that what you wanted?" Niklaus growled, shifting out of the way and running into the light again.

I rushed to my feet and ducked towards the door.

"Look, Octavia, I just want you to live."

Pausing, I turned to glare over my shoulder, imagining I could reduce Niklaus Heira to dust with the force of my bitterness. "Why?"

His lips parted, chest lifting with a deep breath, but he said nothing.

The lantern's soft light flickered over his decorated skin, and the hurt welling in my chest intensified.

We were stuck in a moment, both on the precipice of saying something we couldn't take back, finally admitting nothing more than desperation hung between us.

Niklaus Heira was simply in my life but not in the beginning or the end, just an interloper who appeared as needed.

"See . . ." I shook my head. "You don't even know why."

"That's not fair, love."

"Don't call me that."

"Octavia—"

"You and Mikhael both," I told him. He flinched at the mention of his brother. "You have an angel complex, and I get it. They raised you to be the next generation of chancellors, wealthy, favoured, powerful. Leading a little town out of ruin if you could. So, you want to lead us to victory. You want to say I dragged Octavia, kicking and screaming to Eternis. She's here through my leadership and my strength of will. I made sure she survived."

Bitterness burned my tone, and Niklaus said nothing to reject my words.

"You keep '*saving me*,'" I spat, "and it's easier to do if you're dangling yourself in front of me, offering a kiss in Gluttony's trial, making cheeky remarks in Invidia to make me think of how I had you before . . . You can keep me close, keep me out of trouble, and it feeds that complex of yours. You think you're powerful. You think you're necessary for me to survive."

"You wouldn't be alive if it wasn't for me," Niklaus growled. "What's wrong with wanting us both to succeed? Besides, I owe you my life now. Everyone else would have let me die on that gate. Even Mikhael. But you, you pulled me down."

"Really? You think I need you?" I said, scoffing. "I survived Envy's castle on my own, and you don't know what I did in there. I don't need you to save me, Niklaus. I don't want you to save me. I'm going to win this competition on my merit, no matter how many times I fuck up. Do you hear me?"

"Don't be stupid, Octavia." He sniffed.

"Do you hear me?"

The fire in my soul struck the match to burn this bridge and leave Niklaus behind me, and for all my frustration, I still mourned it. I mourned the girl I used to be, infatuated with the concept of rising above to be a chancellor's wife, but since then, I had a chance for more than that, and I wouldn't achieve it by bending to Niklaus's will and allowing him to take to brunt of my success and failure.

"I don't need you, Niklaus Heira. Never have and never will."

He stood tall, arms crossed, face clouded with anger. "Fine."

"Fine," I spat back.

My attention dropped to the boots behind him, with more than half the pile to go, but I couldn't do it. The thought of staying in this tiny room with him left me angry and lightheaded.

So, I scoffed at him, half a cruel smile lifting my lips. "Better get scrubbing, Heira. You have a lot to do."

It was easier than I expected to not look back as I left, even though it felt like some part of me was fracturing. Leaving a version of myself behind in that room, I broke and reset the bare bones of my soul to reshape myself into the person I needed to become. I should have expected it to be painful. I should have expected tears to roll down my cheeks as I hid behind the stables and tried to piece myself back to some semblance of me. They dripped off the edge of my chin as I allowed myself to mourn the Octavia who had viewed the Heira men as the strongest people in her world, to make room for the stronger version of myself, who would succeed alone. I didn't need him, and I would prove it. One day at a time, I would survive Wrath and her army and come out with the strength to face the devil.

I didn't need to impress Niklaus Heira anymore. I had the devil to play with.

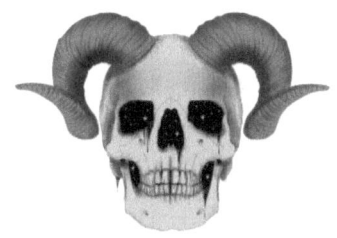

Chapter Ten

Major Akua towered over me, a deep line creasing her forehead. Her braid swung over her shoulder. I had jolted into awareness when she kicked the sole of my boot hard. "Wake up, recruit."

I didn't remember falling asleep behind the stables. Exhaustion had been pulling at me, so inevitable fatigue weighed me down as if my blood had turned to stone.

I'd dreamt of Aieke, of her blood spilling over my hands, warm as I stole her life. I dreamt I had liked it instead of feeling horrified. In my sleep, I had stabbed her repeatedly until it bathed me in the red remnants of her life, and I laughed like the devil himself.

"Huh?" I murmured.

The sun had risen high in the sky, well past midday, and it burned my skin, leaving it red and sore.

Squinting against the bright light, I tried to reconcile my

abrupt awakening and focus instead on Major Akua's aggravated stance.

She did not look happy.

"You think you can finish a task and then wriggle off to sleep, worm?" Major Akua yelled, her voice piercing even through the leather mask. "Who gave you permission to sleep?!"

Jagged rocks jabbed at my skin as I grasped just enough awareness to push myself upright. "Nobody, ma'am," I croaked, mouth dry, brain piecing together the fact that she thought I'd completed the task.

Agitation licked the base of my spine, instantly souring my mood. Niklaus, despite all I had said, had finished the task and said nothing about my disappearing act. He was still feeding his angel complex, still trying to save me. I wanted to punch him for it.

"You're late now," Major Akua hissed. In response, my stomach roared, and the major laughed. "No time for food now, worm. Get moving."

Rushing relief surged through me as I realised no punishments went beyond going hungry, and it was a balm against my flaring agitation.

Forcing myself to nod slowly, I kept my response submissive.

"Yes, ma'am."

I could deal with being hungry, although the way my stomach curled inward and begged for food reminded me of the grit of the Feast of Samael. Desperation and panic I had for food left me with raw worry of never being satiated, that I might die of starvation. I had to firmly remind myself that it wouldn't be forever, just until dinner. A few more hours of fasting would be uncomfortable, but it wouldn't kill me.

Major Akua gestured for me to lead the way back into town, and I strode with purpose beneath the faded red archways and into the tiled paths. A few steps in, I faltered, not knowing where we were going. It forced me to fall a step behind the major, who was hot on her heels as she picked up the pace.

"You missed the tour this morning," she informed me, her voice sharp, as if she believed I'd missed it on purpose. Her punishment had kept me from it, but I wisely said nothing. The major paused in the middle of the town, her boot tapping the tiles underfoot before she pointed at the hall we'd been in last night. "Wrath's Hall—you don't enter unless invited. Barracks is where you all sleep, although we'll split you between the four halls soon enough. There's no lounging about in there during the day. You've seen the stables, latrine, and the wash-ups." She spoke quickly, and I nodded, trying to keep track. She pointed to a small brick building with two stories. "That's the food stores. You eat outside at the campfire. If you don't make it in time for meals, you go without, and you don't whine about it. If you're on kitchen duty, and you steal food, we'll cut off your hands. Understood, worm?" She waited, expectant, until I found my voice.

"Understood, Major."

"Out the south exit is the training grounds." She pointed out the path leading to another red archway and trailing into a dirt track beyond. "Remember that you'll be headed there soon."

"Sure."

"Armour stores." Major Akua pointed out a building beside Wrath's Hall, where familiar people lingered out front. The major started towards them, and I took the cue to follow.

"I don't know what that means," I said before hastily adding, "Major, ma'am."

"It's just Major, worm."

A knot formed in my stomach. I knew this unfortunate nickname would stick.

"Right, Major."

She sighed heavily. It felt like every time I spoke, I irritated her to no end. "It's where you get your weapons, uniforms, any other supplies you need to replace in your kit."

I nodded. "And why are you showing me this, Major?"

"That's the thanks I get, worm?" The bite in her words made me almost flinch. "For giving you the tour, the one you missed?"

"I am thankful," I corrected quickly, stumbling over the words. "It's just . . ."

Major Akua lifted her chin and assessed me. Again, I had the distinct feeling that, behind her mask, she was smiling cruelly, enjoying my discomfort as I squirmed beneath her scrutiny.

"This tour, worm, is so that, the next time you're late, you have no excuses. You know where everything is now, and so you better be on time."

Something ominous lingered in the way she didn't tell me what the consequence would be for running late. Punctuality was a skill I needed to learn if I wanted to stay in her good graces—a difficult task, since her opinion of me was that of a worm.

"Get moving," she barked.

Startled, I scurried over to join the back of the line by the armour stores. Niklaus was there, thankfully ignoring me. He had Margot on one side of him and Helina on the other, not a group I wanted anything to do with. Helina watched me out of the corner of her eye, and Margot was complaining to Niklaus. I planted myself a short distance behind her, close enough to listen in. Not because I cared but mostly because of my nosiness, and a spiteful part of me liked to see Margot Galatea uncomfortable.

"I don't see why I have to do this," Margot said. "I'm not a competitor. There is no cuff on me. Why would Wrath make me join her dirty army?! I'm not fit for war."

It was hard not to grin as I imagined the interaction between Wrath and Margot, the indignation that Envy's former treasure would have felt at being forced to complete a trial she hadn't signed up for. I also envisioned the vindictive pleasure the angel would get, knowing she was breaking down one of Envy's favoured—if she knew. Margot was a message—or would be—when she died. That much was clear.

General Inaina stepped out of the amour stores and beckoned the last of us inside. Niklaus, Helina, Margot, Wrathling women, and I lingered to the side, keeping our distance. The building housed us with ease, supplies packed down one side of the room and the other.

Some soldiers scrutinised us. One walked a quick circle around me before dumping a uniform at my feet. It bounced against my muddy boots.

"Strip," General Inaina commanded, "then dress quickly. This will be your only uniform, so look after it."

Throughout the indignity of these trials, I had lost my sense of modesty. It was all too easy to strip down to my dirty knickers, the cool air from the overhead fans brushing my skin. I didn't bother covering myself the way the Wrathling women did.

They started whispering, flushing as they caught sight of Niklaus unbuttoning his trousers and sliding them down over his muscular, tattooed thighs.

I looked away, resolving not to look at him, focussing on the pile of clothes at my feet. The leggings clung to my body like a second skin sewn of a strange material that breathed and moved with me. A long-sleeved black shirt was tugged over my head, covering the rest of me, the tight sleeves just stretching over the flare of the devil's cuff. A faded red tunic went on next, falling below my butt and removing any semblance of shape from my body.

One soldier approached me, carrying an armful of leather armour. When she spoke, it was in clipped sentences, showing me how to tell the front from the back of the breastplate, how to correctly slide it on and buckle it up, and tugging on each strap until it cinched my body.

It felt so tight that my breathing turned shallow as I wriggled around, trying to get comfortable. When the soldier tapped roughly on the red lion on the breastplate, I could feel the sturdiness in the weight it held; I just couldn't bring myself to believe it would be enough to protect me.

"Arms next," she demanded.

I lifted my left arm, paying close attention as she slipped the sheathing up my forearms and bucked them tight. Unexpectedly, they stayed in place when I moved, taut and uncomfortable, but I had endured worse.

"What next?" I asked.

The soldier knelt on one knee in front of me, slapping her thigh. "Place your foot here."

I did as she asked without question, and she wrapped her hand around my ankle.

My heart rate spiked as the thought that she could pull me down caught me.

She picked up the leather greaves and helped slide them up my leg.

"Left-hand or right-hand dominant?" she asked.

"Uhh, right . . ."

"What hand do you write with?"

My teeth pinched my lip.

I couldn't read, and all I could write was my name. I had to think about the question, staring at my hands as if I had never seen them before, trying to gauge which one I would pick up a pen with.

The soldier sighed, setting my foot down and gesturing for me to put my boots back on.

I did as she asked, and she watched me through narrow eyes. When I straightened, she nodded and turned back to the shelf. She searched until she found a little rubber ball.

"Catch!" the soldier barked.

Instinctively, I raised a hand to catch it before it could slam into my already-bruised face. It slipped from my fingers as I fumbled, dropping to the ground where it bounced twice and rolled away.

The soldier didn't look impressed by my failure, but she

nodded firmly. "You're right-handed."

"Okay," I said stupidly.

I had no idea what difference it made.

She picked two leather straps with buckles, threading small sheaths through them, and then dropped to her knees in front of me again. She strapped them both snugly around my right thigh. It felt strange, and I adjusted my stance, feeling like I was waddling.

The soldier tapped my thigh. "Be still." She slid a small, sharp dagger into each sheath before reaching for the final leather strap, a scabbard holding a sword laced my across my torso, then settled the blade down the length of my spine.

"It's heavy," I commented.

It felt like it was weighing me down, and I knew by the day's end my back would ache just from having the weight strapped to me.

"Yes, it's made of steel. You'll get used to it—quickly." The soldier laughed and twirled her finger. "Turn around."

Her fingers thread through my hair, rough as she tugged the strands back from my face and braided them.

It had grown just past my shoulders and always tickled the back of my neck, just long enough to form a small braid. I hated having my hair tied back, all too conscious of the way my ears stuck out.

The soldier frowned at my ears before roughly plucking out each rough wire piercing and dropping to the ground.

I hissed with pain at the rough treatment. "Hey!"

"Piercings aren't allowed."

I huffed unhappily, watching them bounce off the mats, my ears stinging.

She handed me the final part of the uniform, a worn leather mask affixed over the bridge of my nose and tied in a knot at the back of my head. It felt more suffocating than any other part of the uniform; my lungs seized with panic that I wouldn't be able to breathe through the mask. It stole my facial features, stripping me to nothing more than eyes, armour, and weapons.

They set us in front of a mirror just for a moment to get a glimpse of ourselves.

Other women's features were erased, the features that made us unique. We wore the same uniform, the same braid; there were no odd noses, soft lips, or strong chins, just angry eyes to tell us apart.

Wrathling women appeared almost identical when stripped away. Only the men truly stood out—too tall, too muscular.

My stomach twisted into a complicated knot; I felt like I'd had lost something of myself.

"Good." For the first time, General Inaina sounded pleased. "Now, take it off and put it back on again. Quickly."

They had us repeat the daunting task until our speed picked up. With practice, I could buckle the armour without hesitating in finding the right strap until I felt like I had ingrained it in my soul. My fingers ached from tightening and undoing the straps so many times. They gave us a small medical kit, a rations bag, and a canteen to carry in a leather pack.

General Inaina then paired us off at random. Two Wrathling women, Niklaus and Margot, Helina and the woman to her left, the woman on my right and me.

I turned to face her, but my scrutiny was for nothing; all of her features had been lost to the uniform, and all I could determine was that she was my height. She remained quiet, focussing on the general.

"These are your partners. Get to know them well," General Inaina announced. "This is the one person above all others who will have you back, and you will have theirs. Your success is their success, your failure their failure. You will train together and fight together. Your success in this army relies heavily on your partner and your ability to work together."

Tension loomed in the thick silence. Relief of not being

partnered with Niklaus—or, devil forbid, Helina—washed over me. But the woman to my right was a wildcard, and I had no idea how we would work together, especially when I still had the weight of my conflict with Niklaus on my shoulders. I could feel his attention burning my skin, but I refused to look at him.

"Dismissed," General Inaina said sharply. "Head to the training grounds for testing."

I lingered at the end of the group to avoid Niklaus, and my new partner waited for me without question. She fell into step beside me as we exited and turned to the south.

It was slow moving, adjusting to the weight of the armour and the sword at my back, but my partner never complained, only kept my pace.

Soon, it became apparent I would have to crack the silence.

"What's your name? I'm Octavia."

"Ngaire."

It was a strange name. I'd never heard it before, but I tested it out, and she shook her head with a soft snort.

Ngaire repeated her name slowly, and I tried again and again until she nodded and stated it was close enough.

Butchering her name carried us down the dirt path to a large circle marked out with an enormous length of fraying rope.

Coarse sand covered the inside of the circle. Other recruits sat around the edge of the circle, and tension had been building between some pairs.

Nerves fluttered in my stomach, worried that everyone's fuse would be as short as my own. That we would fall prey to the uncontrollable well of frustration that seemed to have welled up inside of us.

General Inaina arrived on horseback. She swung herself to the ground, her smoke-grey braid pushed over her shoulder. She paced through to the centre of the circle, nonplussed by the sand slipping beneath her boots, and lifted her chin.

"Normally," General Inaina began, not waiting for us to pay

attention, clear in her expectation we would fall silent, "we would all train together as one group, led by two seasoned soldiers, but The Devil's Trials has filled us with excess bodies and excess responsibility. It is more than Major Akua and I care to handle alone. Therefore, General Teulia and Major Noa have graciously offered to aid us in your preparations. We will divide you up between us appropriately."

Two more soldiers marched to stand by her side, tall and proud. They then proceeded to split the entire group into four, shuffling us to each side, until it set us apart.

Ngaire stayed by my side, stoic, compared to my fidgeting and twisting to inspect others, counting the familiar faces.

Niklaus and Margot, of course, I couldn't escape if I tried. When he caught my gaze, he winked.

Nash and Finley seemed to have had the best luck of all of us to be paired.

To my surprise, they had separated Aureen and Kyra, and neither of them looked happy about it. Helina stood by the eldest of the two sisters, arms folded across her chest, face obscured with displeasure, and I wondered which of those two would murder the other first by being in close confines.

"We will split you into different barracks for ease of group training. You'll have a small window of time to move your belongings before the next meal," General Inaina continued, giving us barely any time to adjust. "Now, we test you."

Soldiers swept through, shuffling the three groups away, and I strained to see which of the four—Inaina, Akua, Noa, or Teulia—we would end up with. I was hoping for the smallest of them. General Teulia was tiny and the least intimidating by far. I should have known the devil wouldn't let my luck extend so far, though, and it was Major Akua who stalked towards us, barking orders to remain in place, as the other groups departed.

"Now"—Major Akua clapped her gloved hands together—"we need to find out exactly how much work you need, worms."

There was no disguising the contempt in her stare. "Many of you were already a disappointment in the run, so we'll start with basic fitness."

Nobody spoke, tension building around us.

"Who can manage a sit-up?" Slowly, one of the Wrathling girls raised her hand. "Demonstrate," Major Akua ordered.

Hesitating, the woman rolled onto the balls of her feet before she pulled herself together, unstrapped the heavy sword from her back, and dropped to the ground. The sand kicked up on impact, and when it settled, she was lying on her back with her knees bent. My interest piqued as she settled flat and then curled upwards, reaching with her fingertips until they skimmed the caps of her bent knees. She then rolled back to lie flat.

Major Akua grunted after the fourth time the woman performed the moves and told us all to get on the ground.

It was difficult to remove my sword in the heat, but my back relaxed when the weight was gone. I dropped to the ground, the sand finding its way beneath my armour, as I tried the movement. It looked easy, and my first one was smooth, but ease was relative, and Major Akua sounded amused when she barked orders for us to complete two hundred of them, counting aloud, mocking us who failed early. She taunted us with our failures until fury flashed in more gazes than not. By the time the sun dipped and the shadows rolled in, I'd learned many exercises, like what a push-up was and how to heave sandbags over my head, until my arms felt like they were going to fall off.

Major Akua stalked in front of us, sneering at the way we lay exhausted and broken in the dirt. She took our names and noted our progress.

"Well, worm, not unexpected," Major Akua sneered when she approached me. "Only thirty sit-ups—barely hit half of that for the push-ups—and do you think you surpassed double digits for the overheads? No."

My face flamed; I knew I hadn't done well. My numbers were low compared to a couple of Wrathling women who had excelled to hit a perfect round nearly every time, but even with low repetitions, I was winded and exhausted. My arms and legs felt boneless, and I didn't trust they would hold me upright, my entire body aching with exhaustion. I was weak. I knew I was weak and lying on my back in the makeshift arena, squinting up at the major. I wondered for the first time if mental strength wouldn't be enough to survive this trial.

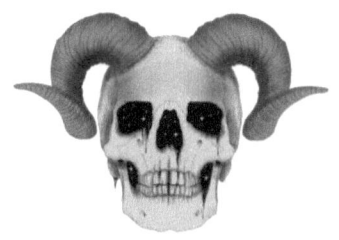

Chapter Eleven

We were split into the smaller barracks, still filled with the metal bunks and still too crowded for comfort, but it was a little easier to breathe when we weren't stacked atop one another. Somehow, though, I'd still ended up on a top bunk with a lumpy mattress after Ngaire had pleaded her case for the bottom bunk.

Peliela was one of the high achievers in our group, scraping third best in the fitness activities, and from the moment we returned from dinner stuffed, full of stew, she let no one forget it.

It was just my luck that she was in my group, and I muttered prayers to Samael she would get eaten by a hellhound.

She stalked back and forth down the corridor of space between the bunks, crowing about her achievements, her voice grating as she grew more and more insufferable.

She only lost the attention when her Wrathling cohort

realised the men had started stripping for bed and that no amount of bragging could overtake the soft giggles rolling off their lips, the whispers from behind their hands.

Niklaus, of course, preened beneath their attention. He flexed his muscles deliberately as he shed layers of armour and weapons, piling them at the end of his bed.

"Fuck off, Heira, and put on a shirt." The words left my lips before I could stop them. "Nobody wants to see you naked."

"Deny it all you want, love. I know you were looking." He laughed, and my face flushed.

"In your dreams!"

He licked his lips slowly. "Definitely."

Heaving a sigh and annoyed, I tried to focus on unbuckling my armour.

Repetitiveness from the morning helped with the muscle memory, but my fingertips ached with protest. I could remove my heavy sword without looking, the absence of its weight leaving me deliriously light for a moment.

I stowed the knives under my pillow, the way Ngaire had done it, although it left me scared of slicing my face open at night.

Without hesitation, I abandoned the rest of the armour piled beside Ngaire's smaller pieces in a haphazard stack at the end of the bunk. We inspected it in silence, and when I peeled away the leather mask, I felt like I could finally breathe again.

"Do you think we have to clean them?" Ngaire questioned hesitantly.

I groaned aloud. "I swear if you've cursed us and Akua comes in with a toothbrush . . ."

"Why a toothbrush?"

I shook my head, not wanting this woman, my partner, to know I was the idiot who had spent the morning scrubbing shoes and picking fights, even if I'd only scrubbed a handful of them. "Just sounds like a cruel punishment. You know what I mean?"

She scrunched her nose, giving me a questioning look. "It

would be."

The bunk bed's frame groaned as I gripped the ladder and hoisted my body up, then rolled onto the bed with a soft moan of pleasure. The mattress was thin and had strange lumps that pressed into my body in horrible places, but after the day I'd had, I could have sworn it was like sleeping on a cloud. I could have sworn I'd never lain on anything so comfortable in my life.

I wanted to ask Ngaire about herself, whisper questions in the darkness, and gain a better understanding of what I was dealing with, but sleep was swift in claiming me, tiredness winning out. My eyelids felt heavy, and before I knew it, I was gone.

'Good night, Little One,' Samael whispered in the last moments of consciousness.

Four hours of sleep was all they allowed us before Major Akua kicked the door open. It bounced off the wall with a crash, setting my heart skittering, my mind sluggish as I tried to wake.

Shifting, I fell off the top bunk and slammed into the floor, the impact waking me properly. It knocked the breath from my lungs and left me wheezing.

Ngaire stepped carefully over my body, rubbing her eyes with the heel of her palms. Her body shielded me from Major Akua's gaze as I struggled to my knees and then onto my feet.

"Get dressed," they barked from across the room.

My legs wobbled with fatigue, but I reached for the armour and slid it into place. It was more of a struggle in the dark, when I was still lethargic with sleep, my fingers pinching the buckles. It felt heavier in the middle of the night, and I wanted to sink beneath the floor, curl into a ball, and sleep for a decade. The weight of the sword was heavy at my back, leaving it aching, the knives slipping down my thighs, until I had to pause and restrap them.

As we filed out into the street, I fought a yawn. Without the blazing sun, the Wrathlands had cooled enough to leave me shivering.

Major Akua watched us closely, expectantly. "What are you waiting for?"

We shuffled, confused.

"Run," she barked.

With a jolt, we followed the same path as the day before, but it felt worse this time around. The armour weighed me down.

I had to stop more than once as I dry heaved, attempting to empty my stomach and suck in deep breaths of air at the same time.

Ngaire paused every time I did, too patient every time we stopped. She waited by my side, carefully out of the firing range, until I was ready to run again, muttering encouragement.

It felt like it took me twice as long to complete the run with the armour on and a body that still ached from the day before. An undeniable rage hit me, as Ngaire barely seemed out of breath when we reached the end of the run, standing tall beside me.

"How . . ." I wheezed.

"How what?"

"How did you do that without feeling like death?" I asked, struggling to get the words out. "Or wanting to vomit up your entire stomach."

Ngaire's dark eyes crinkled at the edges. I imagined that, behind the mask, she was grinning at me. "We prepare for this our entire lives. Even as children. We run and do fitness activities."

I blinked, my head spinning at the thought. "This war has been happening for your entire life?"

"On and off. For my lifetime and my mother's and grandmother's. Envy and Wrath get under each other's skin all the time. We're not always the defence—I've heard that, sometimes, we drive the attack."

"Oh," I said, dumbly.

"Yeah." Ngaire firmly took hold of my arm and helped me upright as Major Akua approached on horseback. "Although they say it's easier to be on the defence than the offence."

That part wasn't what had taken me back. I had imagined that, when the war was over, Mikhael and the other forfeits to Envy would be free to leave, but Ngaire had just revealed that this war was never-ending. They would always remain chained to his petty jealousy and the battle with his sister; they would truly be forfeited for the rest of their lives.

Major Akua peered down at us from her horse, and her attention settled on Margot, who seemed to pull herself together beneath the major's glare; although she still looked winded. She rolled her shoulders, stood tall, one of her white brows raised in challenge. "Let me guess, we're walking back?"

Major Akua scoffed. "No."

"What next, then?" Margot frowned.

Major Akua lifted a hand and pointed to a hill where a large structure peeked from a cluster of trees, dark and imposing in the low light. "Keep going until you reach that."

It took everything to not groan, but I needed no more of Major Akua's attention. Biting my lip, I stood just behind Ngaire and waited until they gave us our marching orders. I didn't like to seek trouble—not really—but it had a habit of finding me all the same. By the time we marched to the base of the hill, I felt like my legs were going to fall off.

Even though we had dressed them same, our faces hidden as they stripped us of our individuality, most of the trial competitors stood out from the Wrathling women because they sprawled in the grass, gasping for breath and grumbling.

In comparison, Wrathling women stood tall, impatience sparking in their eyes. When paired, they moved on quickly further up the hill, leaving us behind to wait.

Ngaire watched me, concern pulling her brows together.

"You really learned to be fit from birth . . ." I muttered.

"Nope." She popped the *p* at the end, humour lacing her tone. "They, at least, waited until we walked."

I blinked, taken aback by her humour.

Ngaire held out her hand, and after a beat of hesitation, I took it, letting her help me off the ground. When I stumbled on fatigued legs, she laughed.

"What?" I asked defensively.

"You're going to keep on your feet better than that, soldier." Her chin jerked towards the structure nearby. "We're just about doomed."

"Why?"

"Welcome to Obstacle Hell." Major Akua startled me with her booming announcement. "This course extends around the base of the mountain. You'll crawl, climb, carry, balance, hang, and jump."

My teeth bit down on my lower lip, gaze flicking to the others in our group, but the leather masks made it impossible to work out their expressions. Did they dread this as much as I did? I already felt ready to collapse; an obstacle course seemed impossible.

A hush had settled across the group, with an almost nervous edge of tension.

Major Akua waved at the first of the structures. "You'll have to pass in your pairs, and I will not return you to camp until the course is complete." We waited for more information, but her chin dipped, gaze knowing as she refused to elaborate. "Well, what are you waiting for?"

Ngaire offered me a sympathetic look, and we approached the first of the obstacles in the middle of the group. Above mud was a suspended layer of thick metal wire, and it seemed to be covered in tiny, spiked bits of wire. The mud smelled like it was mixed with shit, worse than the latrines. I pressed the back of my wrist against my nose to staunch the smell, but it did nothing.

With grim disappointment, I watched the teams ahead of us

complete the task, throwing themselves onto their bellies and crawling beneath the wire it to reach the other side.

We shuffled forward to the edge, and Ngaire let out a slow breath, muttering, "Smells worse than your mother."

"What?!" I gaped at her, but she had already thrown herself onto her belly, using her elbows and knees to propel herself through the mud before I could think of a witty reply. Instead, she left me staring after her, completely dumbfounded.

"Get a move on!" someone complained behind me, shoving me until I almost fell into the wire. I had two seconds to think, two seconds to feel regret, before I dropped into the mud. It slipped and squelched beneath my fingers, sliding beneath gaps in my clothing, and it stank even worse up close. I tried to mimic Ngaire, using my knees and arms to crawl through, but I kept pushing myself too high. The barbs in the wire caught the back of my armour, and the wire tangled with the sword, slowing me down until I could untangle myself. Every now and again, my arms flailed too high, and the barbs bit through the dark fabric of my shirt and sunk into my skin, pulling soft grunts of pain from my lips, small cuts gouging into my skin.

By the time I made it to the end, staggering upright, smeared from head to toe in mud, Ngaire was chuckling. "What was it you said about my mother?" I asked, scraping mud from the back of my neck and flicking it at the ground. It was the only thing I could do, or else I'd cry.

"You heard me," she laughed, leading the way.

The second obstacle was worse, if possible. Rows and rows of sandbags had little signs perched next to them.

I squinted at the strange cluster of letters and sighed with frustration.

Ngaire didn't hesitate. She read the signs and reached for a sandbag. After counting to three beneath her breath, she braced herself and hoisted the bag up off the bench. She grunted as she positioned it over the back of her shoulders and slung it around her neck. Her expectant dark glance made me realise I was supposed to do the same.

The hessian casing on the sandbags was rough beneath my fingertips, and the muscles in my arms and down my back strained and burned as I tried to lift one. It was heavier than I'd expected, and I couldn't get it up to my neck. I dropped the sandbag, and it thumped at my feet. Frustration welled in my stomach until tears prickled in my eyes. It annoyed me I couldn't lift it with the same ease as Ngaire.

"Oh, come on." She scoffed loudly. "I've known twigs with more strength than you."

I glared at her. "Do you have to keep picking on me? We're supposed to be partners."

"Why shouldn't I?"

"It's irritating," I said. "And unhelpful."

"Good," Ngaire muttered.

"What do you mean 'good'?" I asked, gritting my teeth.

"Irritating is a step closer to mad," Ngaire explained, twisting to kick the toe of my boot. She repeated the sharp action until I tried to kick her back. "Mad keeps you moving. Mad keeps you driven."

"Mad will get you dead," I muttered when her next kick caught me solidly in the ankle, sending pain up my leg. "Keep it up, and I'll strangle you."

"How?" Ngaire laughed. "You can't even pick up a sandbag."

"Pfft," I hissed through clenched teeth, irritation shivering through me. "Yes, I can."

"Prove it."

Those were the two worst words in the world. I couldn't back down from them. The same instinct to show off at card table after card table in the past pushed me to do as she said and prove her wrong. The sandbags were heavy, like someone had filled them with stones instead of sand. My arms shook, trembling as I lifted another sandbag from the table. It raised as high as my chin before my strength wobbled and Ngaire stepped in.

She gripped the bag, helping me pull it over my head and settle it on my shoulders. It felt awkward, pushing the edges of my armour against the tender parts of my shoulder, compressing my spine. It took me more than a moment to adjust.

"There!" I crowed. "What now?"

Ngaire stepped away from the table, adjusting her balance in the first few steps, then jerked her chin at the incline path up the mountain. "Now, we hike."

I swore, not bothering to hide it. "I hate this place."

By the time we staggered to the top of the incline, my shirt clung to my damp neck. Sweat rolled down the bridge of my nose. It beaded at my hairline, causing the flyaway strands to stick to my face. For all the moisture I was losing, I was so thirsty, my lips dry, and I had become overly conscious of where my tongue sat in my mouth.

Up, up, up we climbed until my thighs burned and tears pooled in the corners of my eyes. Until I felt faint.

"Here." Ngaire gasped, turning and releasing the sandbag from her shoulders. She sounded as affected by the task as I felt. "Drop it here."

I could have cried with relief when I let go of the sandbag, pressure easing from my spine. Seeing Ngaire sweating brought me grim satisfaction, her chest heaving with her next breath, even though she had slowed herself down for me.

We staggered down the path, our pace slowing to a crawl, until we reached the third element of the obstacle course.

The climb. A large man-made wall of wood loomed above us, smooth enough that I knew my boots wouldn't have any hope of finding grip against it. A few scattered nooks had been strategically placed in the wood for us to find some leverage.

"I'm going to be sick," I announced.

"No, you're not," Ngaire said, quick to deny it. "I'm not

133

being paired with the puker. Let's get some water and get over it."

I didn't know how she could be so sure that we were going to make it over the wall when I could barely make it the four steps to the large barrel filled with water. It was murky, mud and dead bugs floating through it, but I couldn't bring myself to care, not when I was so thirsty. It was sweeter than the river in Gula, fresh on my tongue despite the muck. I scooped it in my hands and greedily drank until my belly ached. Only then did I bother to look at Ngaire, who was scrubbing her palms across her face.

It was the first time I had managed a good look at her face without the cover of darkness. She had delicate features, although my mother would have said her nose and chin were a touch too sharp to be pretty. Her mouth was small; it didn't stretch widely across her face as I'd imagined but was a little plump bow, unintentionally pouty.

Ngaire caught me staring and raised a thick brow.

I dropped my stare back to the water and said nothing, heat flaring right to the tip of my ears.

We were both quick to secure our leather masks back in place. We filled our canteens, and ten minutes later, we were both staring at the wall.

"You first, then?" I asked.

Ngaire had completed the last two first, so there was no reason to believe she wouldn't do it again.

The irritated look she threw in my direction surprised me.

"You're the fit one."

"And that means I should be first into battle?" she asked. "First to risk my life?"

"Well," I said, regarding her point but standing my ground, "nobody's going to be shooting you with arrows while you're on the wall."

"You don't know that!" Ngaire grumbled.

The way she said it raised the hair on the back of my neck, and the cool sweat left me shivering. I wanted to question her

134

certainty, but I couldn't bring myself to seek those truths. Sometimes, ignorance was safer. If I didn't know the truth of what was coming, I couldn't be afraid of it.

Ngaire sighed, so heavily it implied I had placed the weight of the world on her shoulders. She moved towards the wall, her hands grazing the wooden panel. She located each small knot and backed up.

I frowned in confusion.

"What are you—"

Without a word, she launched herself forward, running at the wall with a burst of energy I envied. Ngaire leapt up at the wall. Her feet found one of the small ridges, gaining just enough grip to propel herself upwards, her fingers scrabbling for the top. For a heart-stopping moment, she hung there, fingers pressed into the wood, body flush against the panel, before she pulled herself up. Even I could tell it was an enormous effort, and by the time she was straddling it, her chest was heaving, and she gasped for air.

"I can't do that," I told her with certainty.

Ngaire let out an agitated sigh. "Are you going to say that at every task?"

I frowned. "Only the ones that require physical skill."

"What are you good at, then?" She huffed.

The question caused my heart to race, discomfort a living entity breathing down my neck.

My fingers flexed once, twice before I forced a casual shrug. "Absolutely nothing."

She rolled her eyes. "Look . . . you don't even have to get to the top. Just run, jump, and go for my hand."

It took three tries to manage it, my sword weighing me down, all while another pair overtook us. By the time Ngaire hauled me over the wall, she looked like she wanted to set me on fire.

I grumbled about her rough treatment as we followed the path to a river, where we stopped to drink and refill our canteens again.

The next task should have been easy, leaping from rock to rock to cross one side of a shallow part of the river to the other, the water level so low I could see the bottom. Except the rocks emerging from the glassy water were slippery with moss, and more than once, we both fell beneath the cold depths, sliding and flailing back to the riverbank to try again. It cleaned away the mud, blood, and tearstains on our armour, but with each failed attempt, we grew more and more frustrated. Twice, I had slipped and slammed into Ngaire, sending her into the water, and the last time, she'd cracked her temple on a boulder, blood dripping down the side of her face.

"Knock me down again," Ngaire threatened, "and I'll drown you."

"I'll take you down with me," I bit back.

It was difficult to catch my balance before leaping to the next rock. My shoe slipped, and only the frantic wave of my arms kept me stable, all while my stomach flipped.

"I'd like to see you try," she snipped.

At that moment, I wanted to knock her in, send her plummeting into the rock-lined river again, just to teach her a lesson, but when I jumped after her, intent on knocking her down, Ngaire had already moved to the next stone. It became a game of cat and mouse.

I don't know if she knew I was hunting her across the riverbed, but when I finally caught her, I tackled her onto the shore.

"Oof!" Ngaire groaned as she hit the ground, jerking her elbow back.

It caught me in the ribs, in the small panel where the breastplate buckled but didn't protect. I yelped in pain.

"Bitch!" I hissed. "That hurt!"

"Get off me!" She shoved me, sending me sideways, as I scrambled upright.

I kicked her in the thigh as I moved, feeling a vile, wrathful satisfaction at the flash of pain in her eyes.

No way would we survive training together, let alone a war. We would kill each other first.

The second to last obstacle had been described as hanging. It loomed before us at the next bend of the river. A great metal structure was grounded on each side of the river, stretching across with metal bars connecting the panels like a bent ladder.

We stared at it, unspeaking and bewildered, another pair shoving their way past us.

They climbed up the ladder, inspected it, and one let out a giggle. "Monkey bars!"

Crossing them was a skill they made look easy, reaching for the first bar, holding it tight with both hands. For a moment, the recruit hung dead-straight with her arms stretched above her head, toes pointed towards the deep bend of the river. Then she shifted her hips, wriggling and swinging. When her momentum had built, the woman let one hand go and grasped the next bar, an action she repeated. Left, right, left, right . . . It reminded me of a strange, quick-paced march. She swung across the bars to the other side of the river, her partner close behind. When they dropped to the other side, I was stunned at how easily they'd conquered it.

Ngaire and I shared a look, her leer mirroring my nervousness.

"No quips about my mother this time?" I asked sharply.

The sigh she released was heavy, the slender column of her throat bobbing, and she kept looking at the river. It was deeper than the rock crossing, the water darker, rushing down the side of the mountain. No sign of the bottom.

"Not even jibes about mothers make me like this task," she muttered, wringing her hands.

Ngaire seemed dumbstruck by this task, too caught up in her own mind. I wanted to point out that she needed to go first, just like every other time, but it felt like a bad idea to push her, so I waited her out. I'd waited out opponents at a card table until they folded; I could wait out a Wrathling soldier and her hesitation, too.

Seconds ticked into minutes, into hours, and the day slipped away from us, the light fading. Too many other recruits had passed us by, familiar and unfamiliar, until I finally realised that Ngaire would never go first. Stubbornly, she would starve on this side of the river, on the cusp of failure, then climb onto the monkey bars above the water.

Something about the raging current, deep and dark, left her immobilised.

I moved forward. The first rung of the ladder was strong beneath my foot, but the higher I climbed, the more precarious my balance felt, the wind louder in my ears, pulling strands of hair from my braid. At the top of the ladder, I could just reach the smooth metal bars lining our way across. They were cold under my hands, heart rampaging in my chest, beating wild in protest. Swallowing roughly, I fortified myself to step off the top rung and let myself hang free as everyone before us had. My body felt heavier than it ever had before, pulling at my arms until they burned.

Many things that had once felt impossible in these trials had been survivable. This challenge felt impossible too, as I hung like deadweight, seconds from falling into the water, but I could get through it.

Armour and supplies made me clumsy, my arms trembling. I grit my teeth hard, psyching myself out, before I bucked my hips awkwardly, kicking for momentum. When my body swung forward, I reached for the next bar, my fingers pawing for the metal.

As I struggled, my heart felt like it had lodged into my throat. Fear seized me like ice was slipping down my spine, my nails scratching against the bar until I found my grip. The adrenaline racing through my body didn't settle. Momentum propelled me forward, and I grasped for the next bar to the next to the next until there was nothing left, and my hand swiped through the air.

Without another rung, I fell, my body flushing hot and cold in quick succession. I slammed into the ground, my teeth piercing my lip on impact, filling my mouth with the bitterness of blood.

It took monumental effort to sit upright, dizzy and struggling to breathe. My head spun as I peered across the river at Ngaire. She stood at the water's edge, half perched on the ladder, her face as white as a summer cloud.

My armour was heavy as I dragged myself to my feet. It felt like I had dislodged something vital on impact, but I forced myself forward all the same, reclimbing the ladder on my side of the river, the one I'd had too little sense to climb down and had swung right past.

"Come on," I called, battling to keep my voice coaxing.

Ngaire was almost cruel when pushing me through the obstacles, but I was too tired to try the same tactic and antagonise her across the riverbed.

"It's easier than it looks. Your body is going to want to get across it."

As she gazed at the rushing water, tension coiled through her neck and shoulders, which she rolled in an attempt to relax. "I don't want to drown."

"You won't," I said.

The lie spilled from my lips too easily. I didn't know if Ngaire would fall to her death, lost to the power of the icy river, but I would have said just about anything to get her across the river. If she failed, I failed, and I didn't want to endure Major Akua's wrath.

"Liar!" Ngaire's eyes, stark above the leather mask, narrowed.

The commanders had tried to strip us of our individuality, but there was a lot of Ngaire in the way she studied me, an unexpected fire in her assessment.

I'd heard once that eyes were the windows to the soul, which sounded like a crock of shit, but Ngaire said a lot with hers.

She turned her attention from me and focused on the metal bars. Her body swayed, as if pushed by the wind, and when I thought she would fail, she forced herself forward, leaping from the metal ladder with surprising grace.

Her hands caught the first rung, a loud grunt of exertion echoing around us, but her slender body rolled forward. She kicked her feet forward, caught the next bar, and repeated the movement.

Before I knew it, she was across the river, and I stood dumbly on the top of the ladder, right in her way.

Ngaire's legs wrapped around my waist, her strong thighs squeezing as she let go of the last of the bars and pushed forward. Her momentum sent us both down to the ground again. I cried with pain, but Ngaire landed on top of me, her body cushioning mine.

"Get off!" I groaned. "You've just about killed me."

"You were in the way." She relaxed the death grip from around my middle. "What else was I supposed to do?"

My hands braced against her waist, and I shoved her hard.

Ngaire laughed, so bright I could have believed the task had never scared her. She rolled onto the ground and found her feet quickly, barely hindered by her armour. She held out a hand in offer of help. I'd have been foolish not to accept.

"Crawl, carry, climb, jump, and I think that was hang?" Ngaire ticked the obstacles off on her fingertips while we followed the winding path. "One more obstacle left. Balancing!"

Sweat was dripping down my neck. The sun had crested in the sky while we battled with the hanging challenge, and even though it was rapidly disappearing, calling the cool dark night forward, I felt like I was overheating. My skin flushed red, my hair was soaked, and the distinct odour of sweat lingered around my body. It wasn't the worst I'd ever smelled, but I was conscious of it. Exhausted, stomach growling, muscles shaking, and head spinning, I was ready for the day to be over.

"Just one more task," I repeated, dully. "We can do one more."

Ngaire's dark brow quirked, as if she might smile behind the mask. I said nothing to crush the positive reaction. It might help us through whichever impossible task came next.

The path dipped back down the side of the mountain. My legs trembled less without the climb, and another sturdy, weather-aged structure rose from the ground before us. A thin beam extended down the mountainside, steep and troubling. Other recruits were balancing precariously on top of the beam, and big black horses awaited us at the base of the mountain.

We were so close to the end.

"What's stopping us from walking under it the whole way down?" I asked.

Ngaire jammed her elbow into my side. "See those?" She pointed down the hill, where curling branches grew wildly from the ground, threatening to climb up and overtake the structure.

"Yeah."

"Thornbushes." The plants looked half dead and unthreatening. "They're covered in these thick spikes. If you fell into it or tried to walk through it . . ."

"We'd die?"

Half the elements of these trials could kill us.

Ngaire blinked. "No!"

"Oh." I pulled a face.

Samael laughed smoothly in my ear, and I tried to ignore him.

"It'll just hurt. A lot. Better to go over them."

Ahead of us, one recruit wobbled. Her arms windmilled to keep her balance before she plummeted off the beam. Snapping branches and pained moans echoed up the hill towards us.

I hesitated, not wanting to do either. I didn't have the best balance.

"We could stay here."

Ngaire laughed. "Let's do it. I'm getting hungry."

"Getting hungry?" I spluttered indignantly as she approached the beam and lined herself up. "I've been starved for hours!"

"Well, then." Ngaire didn't look back as she spoke, walking steadily along the beam. "You better hurry."

She disappeared down the beam quickly, her arms thrown out for balance as she worked her way down the sloping piece of wood faster than I could have imagined.

I hurried to follow, but the beam looked to be half the width of my foot. My stomach lurched in the first steps as I struggled not to pitch over to one side, feeling dizzy, even though we weren't too high up. With a quick glance at Ngaire, I imitated her again, throwing my hands haphazardly out to either side for balance. It worked for a while, until the slope of the mountain became steeper, and my tired muscles struggled to keep me upright. More than once, I wobbled, too close to be dropping into the thick, gnarled thorns.

'*Keep going,*' Samael encouraged when I slowed.

Hopelessness crashed through me so heavily that I wondered if it was even worth it. Reaching the bottom of the hill meant another day of training, another day of exhaustion. Maybe I should have let the river sweep me away like Ngaire feared.

'*You've come too far to stop now, Little One.*'

"Along the beam or in these trials?" I whispered, my eyes prickling.

'*Both, Octavia.*' It was strange to hear the devil speak my name instead of his little endearment. '*You should be proud of all your achievements so far. Staying alive is not always an easy feat.*'

He was right, of course. Not only in the trials but in life, I felt like I'd been swimming through mud since I'd grown into an awkward teenager, when the veil of hope carried in childhood had been swept away, and I had realised that my future would consist

142

only of hard work and tired moments. It was always hard to find enough to eat, to keep going, to find peace. I saw my parents as tortured souls, people I didn't want to be. I still hadn't found my peace, not in Ilrea nor in The Devil's Trials. I was a woman haunted by my past and my future. Slowly, I descended the mountain, thinking less about my impending thorny doom and the trials of the future but more about the struggles of life itself.

The end of the task came surprisingly quick. Ngaire waited at the end of the beam, her arms crossed over her slim chest, eyes narrowed as I jumped down, kicking up dirt as I landed.

"Done," I bragged, mustering a false cockiness.

"Late." Major Akua's voice cut through my elation as easily as a hot knife through butter. I set my jaw, determined not to give her a reaction. "Off you go, ladies."

We didn't need to be told twice.

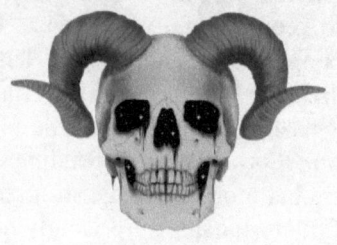

Chapter Twelve

A campfire cook allowed us a second serving of the hot bitterroot stew, even if she hadn't been so gracious as to offer a second piece of bread.

I ate quickly, gluttonous in the way I ran my fingers across the rim of the bowl, sucking droplets of fat and gravy off the end of my fingers in a manner reminiscent of Ophelia.

Often, I had mourned the bright blonde girl in Invidia, wishing she had made it further in these trials. But over the days, I had slowly put her memory to rest instead of continually wishing she were beside me. I couldn't have pictured her here, in the training camps, completely exhausted and begging for a second helping of food. She would have hated it here, in the dust and grime. Maybe it was best she died at home and at the hand of their ruling angel instead of beneath the grit and fury of Wrath, with tear-stained cheeks and none of the extravagances she loved from home.

I dropped my spoon, and it clattered against the tin bowl, leaving a fat piece of stewed carrot sitting in the bottom.

Ngaire glanced over at me. "I thought you were starving?"

I shoved my bowl aside and stretched as I pulled myself upright. "A tithe for the devil."

The same homage we had paid night after night in Gula.

Ngaire paused mid-bite, glancing dubiously down into the remains of her stew.

The devil wasn't as revered here, not as much as their reigning angel.

'Perhaps I need to call you Cheeky One instead,' Samael mused as I walked back to the barracks. *'You know I need no tithe from you.'*

"I know," I whispered. "I lied. It wasn't actually for you."

'Hmm?'

"It was for Ophelia," I explained.

"Who are you talking to?" Ngaire fell into step beside me.

I shook my head. "Just myself. Couldn't remember something."

"Great." She pushed ahead, reaching our bunk bed and shucking off her armour quickly. It hit the floor with a *thunk*, and I caught myself staring as Ngaire stripped from the armour that uniformed us.

Without the weight of leather and chain, she was tiny. Her sweat-soaked undershirt clung to her body, showing she didn't have a spare ounce of fat to waste, her slender frame sturdy with muscle. Ngaire had the Wrathlings' sun-baked skin and dark wavy hair. She massaged her scalp after unwinding it from the tight bun at the back of her neck.

"Stop staring at me," she snapped, removing the mask last.

Blinking, I stared at her strong, pointed chin, her rounded, full rosy lips, all features I hadn't quite imagined would lie beneath the leather mask but seemed to suit the rest of her strong details.

"I, uhhh . . ."

Without a good excuse, I busied myself with removing my armour, stacking it at the end of the bed beside hers. I was self-conscious of stripping away the bulk around my body and showing I wasn't slim. My taut muscles and bony hips grew softness since I'd eaten. My bones were no longer prominent, my face no longer gaunt, and I wasn't strong like my partner.

"You stink," Ngaire commented. She threw a threadbare towel at me, and I barely caught it before it hit my face. "Time to shower."

It was too cold to slip back outside and round the buildings behind Wrath's Hall. Showers were occupied, so we leaned against the outside wall next to a pile of discarded clothing, then waited our turn. From inside the showers, soft giggles and whispers bubbled up around the men, and as one described the colourful inked patterns on Niklaus's skin, I rolled my eyes.

"Ngaire?" I kicked her shoe gently. She looked up as I asked, "Where are all the men?"

"What do you mean?" Her brows drew together with confusion.

"Well . . ." I shrugged awkwardly. "It just seems like the only men here are from the trials. All the Wrathling recruits are women."

The corner of her full lips tugged into a blinding smile, but it disappeared as quickly as it had arrived, a humorous note I didn't understand. "That's because they are. Traditionally, Lady Wrath doesn't accept men into her army."

It didn't seem like a far-fetched idea, given the blunt way the angel met and challenged her recruits, but that didn't mean women wouldn't challenge her back. We had as much spine as men.

"Why not?" I asked bluntly. I knew there were men in the Wrathlands. Without them, there'd be no children, and the cursed triplets from Invidia had a Wrathling-born father who had slipped into Eternis. "I mean, isn't that just losing half your potential strength?"

With the way Ngaire's lips quirked, I thought she might be laughing at me.

My blood flushed hot, offended, even though she hadn't snickered out loud, and I instantly went on the defensive. "I'm not saying you *need* men. It's just . . ."

She shook her head. "Wrath doesn't want them here. She says women are stronger for her and less vulnerable to Lord Envy, and that's that. They stay in the cities. Ira, which is our capital, and the smaller cities like Fearg and Vinha. Littered through the towns, too."

I frowned. "I don't understand."

Ngaire's lips pursed for a moment before she explained. "They prepare women from a young age to join these legions. It's the way of the world. We train throughout our childhood. School is as much fitness and weapons as it is literacy. We're allowed to stay in our homes until we birth a single child. The day they're born, we leave them to come to the frontlines and serve in honour of the Wrathlands."

Struggling to process what she was saying, I gave her the time to continue.

"The men stay behind. They raise our babies in our stead. They forge our weapons and run our cities. Someone needs to keep the country running while we're off at war with Envy. Bake the bread, grow the vegetables and whatnot."

"Wait—"

"What part don't you understand?"

My eyes swept the length of her body, slim, muscular, nothing at all like the mothers I knew. "You've had a baby?"

Ngaire's smile reappeared, but it had a brittle edge. "Yes, a little girl. Eleu would be two months old today."

"And you've just left her behind?" I asked, tense with harsh judgement. "To come and fight on behalf of a stupid angel's

147

grudge?"

"I left her with her father." Ngaire hugged herself tighter, the muscles in her arms tense. "I shouldn't know her well enough to miss her, but I do. She grew inside of me for nine months, and I was her protector that entire time. I only held her for a few quick minutes before they took me to the hospital for assessment and then brought me here."

"Right . . ." I couldn't bring myself to accept it. She said she missed her baby, but the rage of war didn't seem like it was worth it. "What does Eleu mean?"

"Lively," she murmured. A sense of quiet settled between us before she added, "He'll raise her well. I know it. My mother never came home from her service. My dad raised me alone. He was the strength of my entire childhood. If my husband does half the job our fathers did, then my Eleu will be one of the very best women of her generation. That's all I can hope for . . ."

It sounded like she had resigned herself to death on the battlefield and never seeing her child again.

I felt acutely uncomfortable.

There were many differences between the lands of Kaida, each angel of sin ruled their lands in differently, but this Wrathlands tradition set me off kilter. My skin felt strange as discomfort crawled through me, as if it didn't fit right.

The showers freed up, and I followed Ngaire inside. Stepping into the stall, I stripped off quickly, contemplating how it would feel to prepare myself for that, enduring a pregnancy while knowing I'd never meet the child. It would never be my future but just imagining it turned my stomach.

I turned the handle on the wall, and pipes groaned and spluttered above me. Cold water rained down, chilling me through until my skin pebbled and my teeth chattered. It forced me to hurry through scrubbing the layer of dirt and sweat from my skin with the thick bar of soap.

By the time the pipes groaned for the second time, the cold

water shutting off, I'd mulled over the idea again. The towel was rough against my skin, and I wrapped it quickly around my body, stooped to collect my discarded belongings, and came face-to-face with my partner in this trial a moment later. "Are you honestly okay with this?"

Ngaire was silent for a second. "No. But it's just the way it is."

"Why do you think she does it?"

Ngaire looked much younger with her dripping hair and a flush of colour to her cheeks. War raged in her dark eyes, tinged with a sadness I would never forget.

"Because it gives her what she wants."

"What's that?"

"Rage." Ngaire bit down on her full lip, closing her eyes momentarily. "We're torn from the people we grew to love, forced to lose ourselves in this painstaking process, while we grieve them and then they put us in front of an enemy. She sets us on the battlefront with the knowledge of our childhood. We've been told for years that the Envy battalions are at fault. They're the reason we can't see our children. If not for the Envylands, we would be home with the child, and now we'll miss out on watching them grow. If not for them, we'd be spending time with lovers who will now be strangers when we make it back. We'd have other choices and more than one destiny. A life beyond war."

"She uses you."

Ngaire nodded, genuine pain in her expression. "Lady Wrath winds us up and puts us right in front of the enemy so that she can win."

"What a dick."

Ngaire laughed, a hollow agreement.

We stepped outside, other recruits rushing to take our places.

I forced my wet feet back into my boots, shaking the water from my hair and glancing at the shed where I'd fought with Niklaus. With my lips pressed into a sharp line, I chewed on the flesh inside of my cheek.

Maybe it was a mistake to push him away? The only person to care about my welfare as of late.

"Do you want to go back to your husband?" I asked impulsively.

Thoughts of Niklaus shouldn't have prompted the question. He wasn't 'my' anything. I wished I was a world away from him, instead of always too close for comfort. His ridiculous need to protect me grated my last nerve, yet I couldn't stop thinking about him, wondering how he fared.

Considering the sheer time she took to think about it, I could have sworn that Ngaire was going to say no, but she sniffled, suddenly holding back tears. "In a heartbeat—he . . . We weren't one of those couples that got pregnant hard and fast, straight out of school. It took me a long time to have a baby, so long I thought I'd be able to ignore this war completely. Long enough for us to fall in love. I knew him better than anyone else in the world."

She sounded so wistful, so full of longing that I felt envious.

I didn't know what love felt like beyond my childhood, my mother's soft forehead kisses—a required love, not a chosen one. I didn't know what I was missing, but the resentment for the yearning and desire in her voice, I wanted.

"He was—*is*—my person. He will always be my person. I fell asleep next to him every night for five years. I laughed at all the dumb jokes and the stupid moments, and he was there for every milestone, every failure I faced. We cherished every win together. We tried so many new things. We lived our best years as partners. He reassured me when I was envious of the babies my friends left behind, and he held me when I fell pregnant and cried because I knew it meant my end was coming. I cried because it turned out I loved the baby, too, the baby I didn't want to love because I wouldn't get to know them. He held my hand through every excruciating minute of that birth and then he held our daughter . . . He looked at her with so much love, the same way he looked at me."

"Ngaire . . ." I murmured.

"He had the best of me." She sighed, pushing her way into the barracks and crawling into her bunk. She pulled her knees to her chest and rolled towards the wall, blocking me out. "This war will have the worst."

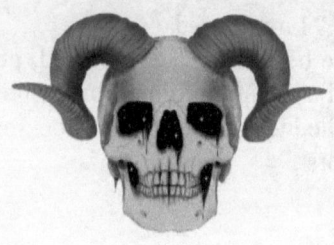

Chapter Thirteen

There was no rest for the wicked. Major Akua worked us from the early hours of the morning until well into the night. The first weeks of our training were all physical, day in and day out. We walked, we ran, we carried, and we lifted until the soft edges to my weight gain dropped, the burning in my muscles dulled, and I wasn't as out of breath.

Slowly but surely, Major Akua was forcing me to become fit. I would never catch up to Ngaire and the other recruits, who had trained their entire lives, but it meant I didn't feel like death at the end of each night, falling into a deep unconsciousness that could barely be called sleep.

The days of training felt never-ending, and Major Akua never listed goals for us so that we could know when we had succeeded. She simply continued to move the target, pushing us further and further past the limits we thought we had. It became routine to rise in the dark morning, pulling the armour against my body tightly. It felt like a second skin, fitting perfectly to my form, making me feel off kilter without it on.

Ngaire and I stumbled into the cold, dark mornings, avoiding the tethered hellhounds and stretching before each run.

Every few days, Nash and Finley joined us, silent with fatigue, and by that time, they found their humour again, cracking jokes.

Finley fell into step beside me as we hauled bricks from one side of the camp to another, extending the structures within.

Major Akua delighted in giving us tasks she considered productive to the army and not just for our own development. Picking up the compact dark bricks and lugging them down the streets reminded me of my elder brothers, the same job they had worked each day. I'd once laughed at them for having this sort of job, and I had to do it for free.

I was the greatest fool of us all.

"Here, Tav." Finley loaded the next brick into my arms and then another and another until my body burned with the strain of it. He was holding another thick dark brick and went to place it in my arms when I shook my head.

"Stop!" I cried. "That's enough!"

"Too much for you?"

With the way his eyes brightened, I knew he was laughing at me instead of with me, a ridiculous thing to do, since I could have dropped the bricks straight on his feet. He would have deserved it.

"I know my limits," I said.

"Do you?"

One of his brows raised with disbelief.

"What's that supposed to mean?" I snapped. I turned to carry the load, or my arms would refuse to cooperate.

I didn't want to deal with one of Major Akua's punishments for dropping the bricks. I'd had enough of those in the past few weeks—although nothing was as bad as the punishment for deserters who met Lady Wrath's disapproval. The energy sent them so wild they could have been beasts, her influence forcing them into fights until they died, leaving remnants of them barely even human.

"I was at the tavern in Zerut, you know." Finley caught up with me easily, carrying only two bricks. I'd noticed Nash carried him through the more physical aspects of the training. Finley preferred to talk than to work. "You don't know when to quit."

The comment grated my nerves, stoking the anger building within me. My fuse, always shorter than it should be, was low here, especially when Wrath was so close, stalking through her hall.

"You didn't seem to mind before," I snarked. "You gamble as well as me."

"Ah, yes . . ." I could hear the laughter in his voice. "We wagered for a kiss back at the feast."

"You wagered for a kiss, which was disgusting, by the way."

"You think kissing you is disgusting?" Finley sounded surprised, then snickered. "How self-aware."

"I think I had been in days of complete frenzy, covered in mud, blood, and eating everything in my way," I corrected, none too gently. "It would have been the worst kiss of your life if you'd won it."

He cackled, and my stomach sank. I wouldn't like his next statement, not with the way his eyes flared mischievously bright.

"Hear that!?" Finley all but bellowed down the stone-paved walkway. He easily drew attention as looks swung in our direction. "Octavia Nox was the worst kiss of my entire life!"

Their gazes burned me alive. I wanted the earth to open and swallow me whole to avoid their attention.

Ahead of us, Niklaus Heira spun around. I didn't want to look at him. I couldn't stop myself from noticing his muscles tighten with rigid anger. He dropped his load of bricks, tattooed hands bunched into fists at his side.

My heart raced as he stormed towards us, all of his attention on Finley. I welcomed the confrontation just as much as I wanted to avoid it. Niklaus's rage directed at Finley, who was having too much fun to realise the trouble he had created, whose eyes glittered with the remnant of his hidden, teasing grin.

I didn't want Finley to meet the hard side of Niklaus's knuckles, so I stepped to the side, placing myself in front of the curly-haired man. He stepped in front of me, not paying attention and tripping over my ankle.

Between breaths, Finley Nightingale had landed on his face.

"Ugh, fuck the devil!" He screamed in pain, the crack of his nose echoing down the street, the sight of him stopping even Niklaus in his tracks.

If I had thought the attention was bad before, it was nothing compared to the looks people gave us in that moment, searing right through me. With an armful of bricks, I wasn't sure what to do about his cries of pain. Finley's flailing fall to the street had eased my vicious anger from at his remark, as if he had been rightfully punished.

Luckily, Nash stopped in front of him, pulling the curly-haired man to his feet and peeling away the leather mask for a better look at the damage.

Blood splattered across Finley's top lip, bright against his teeth, when he flashed a pained grimace.

Nash peered at his nose, his brows furrowed, and I watched, too, as if either of us knew anything about these injuries. The only one of our little groups of Ilreans who would know looked as if he wanted to break Finley's nose a second time.

I wasn't about to ask Niklaus for help, anyway.

Ngaire nudged me to keep moving. "It's definitely broken, boys," she informed them without an ounce of sympathy, hustling me away. "Maybe you should watch where you're walking, Nightingale."

I smiled behind my mask, pleased that Ngaire had my back,

even though a street full of witnesses knew I had tripped him up.

Finley nodded stiffly. "Guess I'll watch my feet."

"And your tongue, I'd expect," Ngaire added, placing a hand on my shoulder and pushing me to move faster.

I didn't hesitate to put space between the incident, more than ready to drop the bricks off.

"Octavia—"

Niklaus tried to get my attention as I shuffled past him. Heat and irritation flushed through my body when he stepped close, too close.

Stubbornly, I kept my eyes trained on my destination and ignored him. I'd only tripped Finley because I didn't want to deal with Niklaus and his hero complex the way he truly believed he should and could stand up for my honour.

It was a laughable concept, truly, because I didn't think I had an ounce of honour left.

Not anymore.

For the next two hours, I spoke only to Ngaire and lugged bricks from one side of the compound to the other, staring at the pile that would become sturdy walls.

When Major Akua returned, sneering at the lack of organisation in our stack of bricks, Finley's face was swollen and bruised, looking haunted, dark blemishes blooming beneath his eyes.

"Dismissed," Major Akua barked, which had fast become my new favourite word.

I was on my feet, brushing brick dust from my hands onto my thighs, more than ready to escape the city and sit around the campfire.

These camps were a different world outside the brick-and-mortar compound, where the soldiers returned from days of battle and collapsed by the fireside. They relaxed, finding a peace that seemed to disappear with proximity to Lady Wrath.

The angel was always too close. When she lived in her hall,

tension weighed down my shoulders, bunching muscles along my spine, and my jaw ached from clenching my teeth too hard. When Wrath was nearby, my words became sharper, a weapon of their own, and I purposefully baited others, just for an excuse to release the tension the angel was creating within me. I became impulsive, and it left me in trouble with Major Akua.

Often, she flew above the compound and campground, shrieking a battle cry above her marching legions, sending them to a front line while knowing full well they may not return, her dark wings sleek as she carved through the air. She went with them, a weapon in her own right, to decimate Envy's army. In Wrath's absence, everyone breathed easier.

She had been in the compound for two days, unseen but felt, and I was keen to leave as quickly as possible.

As we fled the proximity of the angel, Major Akua folded her arms across her chest, lifting her chin. For a small woman, she radiated intimidation.

"You'll report back here in one hour."

A groan echoed from the back of the group, and Major Akua's chin jerked sharply as she looked for the offender. We parted in unison, opening a path from her to the woman who had dared to object.

I glanced over at Ngaire as she marched forward, shoulders set, chin high.

"Time to go," I whispered.

Ngaire nodded, and we fled.

The hour disappeared too quickly, much faster than it seemed to pass when I was carrying bricks. When I returned, belly full and spirit warmed, I was on the cusp of exhaustion, yawning behind the leather mask. I daydreamed only of my bed and a midday nap.

"Pay attention, recruits." Major Akua's voice was a crack of a whip, and we all heeded the command. My shoulders rolled, and I stood straighter, trying to shake off the wistfulness for sleep. "Tonight, your training changes. You will continue with a basic fitness routine each morning, but our focus will vary between physical and psychological elements."

I had no idea what she meant and fought another yawn.

Major Akua appeared to be waiting for one of us to speak, but over the weeks, we had all learned unsolicited input led to unwanted consequences. I wouldn't be the one to tempt her delight of issuing punishments.

The corners of the major's eyes crinkled, as if she might smile, and she nodded firmly. "Come with me."

We moved through the streets, bypassing the tethered hounds and entering Wrath's Hall. A hush fell within the building, the distinct silence before a moment of rage. The Angel of Wrath appeared in the doorway to her office, harsh lines of displeasure etched across her features, her upper lip pulled back in a snarl.

"My lady." Major Akua bowed low.

A beat later, we all hastily followed suit, and I kept my head low. The angel's black, void-like eyes flicked over us, her snarl slipping into a grin and turning as sharp as a knife. When her gaze darted to me, catching the way I watched her assessment from the corner of my eye, I forced my attention back to the polished floor.

"They look fresh?" Lady Wrath commented, a strange observation, since I felt completely ruined from the hard work. "It must be the first night."

Major Akua straightened and nodded sharply. "Yes, my lady."

The way they discussed us caused bile to rise in my throat, my stomach filled with stone instead of meat. Wrath laughed a low and sultry sound, but it grated my raw nerves, sliding beneath my skin until it crawled.

Behind my mask, I bit down on my lip, until warm blood beaded in my mouth, the bitter taste enough to ground me and

158

stop the growing impulse to snap back at them both. My fists trembled.

"Rise, recruits." Wrath's command was almost lazy, accompanied by the wave of her hand, even if her influence was not. The effect of her mere presence left me wound tense, angry for reasons I couldn't begin to comprehend, a pressure weighing on my shoulders until I itched to lash out.

I straightened at her command, and Ngaire stood as stiff as a board beside me. The tiny angel stalked through our group, surveying us, and her glare seemed to light my skin on fire. It felt like a challenge. Beneath her scrutiny, I forced myself to take measured breaths, three seconds in, three seconds out, until she turned her energy towards someone else.

When the angel stood nose-to-nose with Peliela, the tension between them mounted. Wrath sneezed, and Peliela looked like she wanted to commit cold-blooded murder. I snuck a glance at Major Akua, who stood tall, a vein throbbing in her forehead and tension cording along her neck, proving she was as human and susceptible as the rest of us.

"See that they break," Wrath demanded.

"Yes, ma'am."

Wrath was gone before Major Akua had finished answering, but I could still feel her within the building, too close for comfort. "Come this way, recruits."

We descended stone stairs into darkness, tunnelling deep below Wrath Hall. It reminded me of the caves of Gula, which had been filled with bioluminescent mushrooms, pretty but tainted by Mikhael trying to strangle me. Lost to the hallucinations of the monster he had been below ground.

The lower we moved, the more my chest seemed to squeeze, my head spinning. I still hadn't rid myself of the nightmares stemming from that memory. The start of true danger and death, the first time I'd realised I might not survive.

"Make yourselves comfortable," Major Akua said as she

shifted at the base of the stairs, allowing us to move into the room. "You'll be here a while."

With the last of us inside the cramped room, she shut the door. The lock clicked loudly, and they left us in the dark, waiting for our eyes to adjust.

I blinked, just able to make out Margot as she approached the door. She gripped the handle with her slender fingers and pulled as hard as she could. It didn't budge.

Tension in the room thickened, and the woman slammed a fist against the door, knocking hard, a plea unanswered. When she realised it was useless, her shoulders slumped, white lashes laying across her cheeks.

Niklaus pulled her away from the doorway, tucking her beneath his arm.

A sparsely furnished room with a small partition to one side had one shared toilet hidden behind it. The rest of the room was bare except for stretcher turned into uncomfortable-looking blanketless beds that lined the walls. A pile of ration packs sat in the middle of the room, waiting for us. A quick count showed there wasn't enough beds for everyone, inciting a flurry of movement as recruits snatched at the food and hurried to claim beds, leaving half of us empty-handed.

Niklaus and Margot crowded onto a bed together, and I tried not to look at them, a spark of anger igniting my veins.

Finley lay stretched out by the corner, with Nash seated in front of him. When I edged closer, I could hear them bartering over a schedule, with the plan to share their bed. The idea offered me hope, and I turned to find Ngaire, but she stood awkwardly in the middle of the room, a ration pack in each hand, and lines deepening in her forehead. We were both out of luck.

A tilt of my chin beckoned her over, and we dropped to the ground near Nash and Finley. I drew my knees to my chest, wrapping my arms tightly around them for comfort.

"What now?" I asked, watching the others out of the corner

of my eye.

"I do not know," Ngaire admitted. "But I can guarantee it's not going to be good."

I thought of the light in Major Akua's eyes and the locked door, of the tension building between us, wrought of our proximity to the angel.

Ngaire was right, nothing good could come of this change. I leaned against the wall, the bricks cold at my back, and closed my eyes.

"Any advice?" I murmured softly, not for my teammate but for the devil invading my mind. Samael was silent, the absence of his advice so stark that my nose prickled, and tears threatened to build in the corner of my eyes. I shouldn't have relied on Samael to see me through the trials. The strange favour he bestowed on me wouldn't last forever, but I'd become accustomed to his advice.

He left me alone in the dark room of threatening faces, lost to the quiet and trapped by my own thoughts. Sleep threatened to claim me, aided by my general exhaustion, coaxing me until my chin ducked to my chest, and I faded.

An alarm blasted through the room. Bright lights blinked around us, flashing rapidly, rousing me from less than twenty minutes of sleep. A high-pitched wail screeched from the walls, so grating that I pressed my hands over my ears, teeth gritting against the noise. It blared and blared and then simply stopped, the lights turning off and plunging us back into darkness.

Bleary-eyed and confused, we were left in the echoing silence. My pulse raced and head spun, and I glanced to Ngaire, who grimaced, pressing her forehead to her knees.

I waited in tense silence for an attack or some sort of surprise, but nothing came forward. It took a while for the tension to melt away, for us to relax, bit by bit, lulled towards sleep again.

I'd barely dozed off when the alarm screeched again.

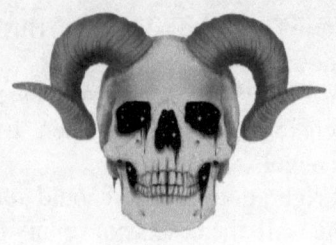

Chapter Fourteen

There was no way to tell how time passed beneath Wrath Hall. I easily lost track of whether it had been minutes or days. Every time sleep claimed the room, an alarm wailed, always a different pitch, tone, or pattern so that we couldn't sleep through it. The lights blinked jarringly, leaving me dizzy and breathless.

Someone was watching—I'd worked out that much, noticing the alarm only sounded when most of us had succumbed to sleep. It sharply forced us all into awareness again. Whether I had spent hours or days in this room, it felt like years without sleep. My entire body suffered a bone-deep ache, a cracking pain searing through my head. My eyeballs felt like they were made of stone, threatening to drop right out of my skull.

My already-raw nerves unravelled, frayed, and burned at the edges. Every time Nash turned to cough into the crook of his elbow, I was on the precipice of exploding in anger, screaming at him to shut up. Each shuffle of movement in the darkened room drew an irritated sigh from my lungs. A sniffle from the corner left my skin itchy with the need for violence. If they sniffled again, I'd spoon out their eye. Exhaustion flowed through me in waves, levels of fatigue, without a single moment of rest. I was disintegrating without sleep, turning flesh and bone into grains of coarse sand.

The alarm sang through the room, a high-pitched whoop, and I groaned, tipping my head back to rest against the wall. It had become hot in the room, the dungeons beneath Wrath's presence, degree by degree, until it suffocated me, leaving me sweltering and fidgety.

Ngaire sat too close for comfort, jammed against my side, and I suddenly hated her very presence. The way she invaded my space made my skin crawl.

My eyelids fluttered shut, too heavy and too tired to stay open, but I had barely a moment's rest before it jerked me back into consciousness, another wail of the alarm sliding under my skin, prickly and agitating. My nails dug into my skin. I bunched my fists tighter, jamming them beneath my thighs. My knuckle popped softly as it blanched, my bones protesting. Fragments of flashing light accentuated everyone's haggard edges, my exhaustion mirroring their faces. I could choke on their frenzy of desperation. We all needed sleep. I didn't understand why they were doing this or what they wanted from me. I didn't know how to make this torture end.

One recruit shuffled towards the bathroom, and we had to listen in the stark quiet to the sound of fluid hitting the porcelain bowl. The smell of concentrated urine permeated through the room. It caused my stomach to roil, and I pressed a white-knuckled fist against my abdomen.

When the alarm blared again, the lights stayed on. It was too harsh and too bright. My eyes burned, and I wished for the darkness while pressing my palms against my eyeballs until bright bursts of colour twinkled behind my lids.

"Sam, how long are we doing this for?" I whispered.

The devil did not respond, always so frustratingly quiet when I felt I needed him the most. "Come on, Samael, help me. I feel like I'm tied up in knots here. I—"

"What's wrong with you?!" someone spat.

When I removed my hands from my eyes, my skin crawled with discomfort, and I found Peliela towering over me.

The bulk of her body left me feeling small. A snarl drew her lips back from her teeth, dark eyes flashing with the heated desire to pick a fight. A moment later, she spat at me, and the glob of saliva landed on my cheek.

The tension in my body responded in kind, my empty ration pack dropping from my fingers as I scrambled to my feet and pushed forward in a desperate attempt to stop her from having the upper hand. The back of my hand swiped my cheek, flinging her spit to the floor.

"What was that?" I asked through grit teeth, daring her to say it again.

The confrontation was inevitable. For some unknown reason, Peliela had hated me ever since the first night in the barracks. She usually made my life hard in small ways, but half-crazed and lacking sleep, I anticipated the time had come for true confrontation.

"You're sitting there." She grumbled loud enough for everyone to hear.

Peliela didn't hesitate. She stepped forward, pushing into me, upper lip drawn back. "Talking to yourself like you've gone completely off the wall. Woman up! You're a soldier in the Wrathlands' infamous army, not the gutter trash you were before. You bring shame to us all with this behaviour."

My blood felt like it had boiled, dousing me in fiery shame at the dose of humiliation. A sharp pain flared in my jaw, tensed.

"Octavia," Ngaire said softly, pulling herself upright.

I ignored the warning in her tone, the obvious hint to proceed cautiously. There was no room for caution for me. My fingers trembled with pure need, and my mind spun with a singular reckless thought. She had insulted me, and I needed revenge. Peliela deserved it. Verbal spars weren't my strength, and I'd never been skilled in a physical fight, but rage-tinged words consumed me all the same. From the corner of my eye, I saw Niklaus stand, edging towards us.

"I'm the shameful one? Between you and me?" I asked, my voice almost high-pitched and hysterical, my laugh hollow and cruel. "You're so half-rate that they put you in with us. Hiding you away amongst the competitors to shield themselves from the shame of a Wrathling being so pathetic. It was the only way they could make you look good."

Peliela's face shuddered, tension clustering the muscles in her neck, veins throbbing in her temple. She moved before I could defend myself and shoved me backwards so hard that I was flung to the camp bed, and my head slammed against the concrete wall. The world spun, a buzzing rattling my ears so loudly I couldn't make out the words she spat in my direction.

Trying to blink away the dangerous black spots in my vision, I foolishly staggered back to my feet, a growl rolling from behind my clenched teeth. Filled with reckless adrenaline, I launched forward and pummelled Peliela with as much force as I could muster.

We went flailing backwards. She lost her footing, and we slumped straight onto the floor, into the wide berth of space encircled by the other recruits. The victory of having moved her in my attacked devoured me with a heady sense of self-confidence, and I laughed, nearly hysterical, as I clenched my fist, drew it back, and swung towards her face, repeatedly. My knuckles met flesh and bone. Pain spiked in my hands as they battered her reinforced breastplate and arms. Shifting, I clobbered the soft, unprotected flesh of her throat.

Peliela tried to claw the side of my face, scratching my skin until she found purchase by gripping my ears. It felt like she was going to tear them from my skull, her nails digging into my flesh, but then she screamed. It wasn't a cry of pain, but a loud, piercing call to war. She used her leverage on my skull to jerk me forward and lurched her head up at the same time.

We met in the middle, smacking together like lightning striking the earth. Her forehead smashed against my face. Blinding pain shot through my skull as my nose shattered, blood gushing hot down my mouth. I gasped for air, my cry of pain stark around us, dizzy, struggling as the blood dripped off the curve of my chin. Letting go of her, I shied away in pain.

Wrath's influence seemed to pulse in the room, encouraging us, and even through the pain, my anger built, heady and overwhelming.

I bared my blood-stained teeth, growling like a hellhound at Peliela, who triumphantly smirked back.

"You bitch!" I spat. Blood and saliva flecked her cheek. "I'll kill you!" I screamed. "I'll kill you!" I scratched her face, determined to dim that smug glimmer in her eyes.

Red lines gouged into her skin, and she hissed curses back at me like a spitting cat.

Then a muscled arm wrapped around my midsection, knocking the momentum right out of me, as someone wrenched me backwards, my feet lifting from the ground.

Peliela was quick, scrambling up after me.

"Hold Peliela!" a familiar voice barked by my ear, his tone laden with unmistakable command.

Other soldiers scurried to do Niklaus Heira's bidding, and I thrashed in his grip, my anger redirecting from Peliela to him. I kicked back with my heels, pawing at any free inch of his skin I could find.

Humiliation from him "rescuing" me burned as hot and stark as my rage.

It was worse than Peliela's insult, better to be known as half mad than weak and in need of a strong man's help.

My fury focused on Niklaus. He tried to stop me from thrashing, banding his other arm firmly across my shoulders. I scrounged to reach for my mask, tugging it down over my chin, and bent forward to sink my teeth into the flesh of his forearm. I bit hard enough to taste the sharp tang of blood. He had his armour off, and the thin black shirt did nothing to stop my sharp teeth.

"Argh! Fuck!" His grip loosened, and I crumpled to the ground. "Octavia!"

"What?"

Spittle made of his blood and mine flew from my mouth. Within seconds, I had whirled on him, Peliela forgotten.

Niklaus was a known enemy. One I could scream at all I wanted.

"I told you I didn't want you anywhere near me?! Why the fuck are you here? Why are you touching me?!"

A growl of frustration rolled from his throat; Niklaus's jaw tightened, and his eyes narrowed. "You'd rather get beaten to a pulp?"

"I'll beat you to a pulp!" I screeched.

"Will you, Octavia?"

The sharpness of his tone stopped me from launching to attacking him, even though my body vibrated with the need to draw blood.

Niklaus stepped closer, and I danced a step backwards. A wide smirk pulled at the edge of his lips, and Niklaus spread his arms, puffing out his chest in challenge. "Go on, love. Beat me up."

"I'll do it," I warned.

My weight shifted to my back foot. I clenched my fists, glaring at him. "I don't need your help. You don't need to rescue me. I don't want you anywhere near me."

The corner of his lips tugged up again, pulling his smile

wider, and I sneered right back.

Anger was a living, breathing entity in my soul. The whisper of rationality pointed to the fault of the angel above us, her influence sinking through the floorboards and beneath the hall to wreath around us, binding us right in capriciousness. I only saw red and wanted blood. It wasn't me; I didn't fall naturally towards violence, but I couldn't fend it off. I couldn't shake the weight in my lungs, the pressure on my chest, the absolute need to act.

My fist swung, and Niklaus danced out of the way. Swing after swing, he laughed at me. He watched each clumsily thrown punch, so intent on my hands that he missed the way I kicked out haphazardly. My foot caught his inside of his knee. Much to my surprise, his leg gave way.

Niklaus crashed to kneel in front of me. A bitter laugh spilled from my lips, drowned out by the voices that egged us on, fuelling my bloodlust. I rushed at him, but he was expecting me. Niklaus caught me around the middle and shoved forward. My back crashed into the ground so hard that my lungs felt like they spasmed beneath my ribcage.

He was on top of me in seconds, his strong, muscled body pressed against my own, his weight pinning me down. His legs wrapped around my middle, hands shackled around my wrists. I wriggled but couldn't move.

"Do you still think you're winning, love?" He laughed.

I spat at him, jerking beneath his iron grip around my wrists, aching to strike out and draw blood again. I would only settle when he was black and blue—or better yet, when he was dead.

Niklaus's breath flushed hot against my neck, his laugh too loud in my ear.

"Get off me!" I screamed, trying to kick him. "Get off me, you coward."

"You sure that's what you want?"

His hips shifted, the intention behind his words all too clear as his body pressed close. This was turning him on, with a crazed, angry glint in his eyes. "Stay close to me, Octavia. I'll keep you safe, love."

"I don't want you . . ." I seethed through grit teeth. "I want to—"

"Enough!" someone barked from the side of the room.

It took three people to pull Niklaus off me, and it pulled me upright as he refused to let go of my wrists, dragging me with him.

Nash was by my side, forcibly peeling his fingers from my skin and wrenching me backwards so that I couldn't rush him again.

"Enough," Ngaire repeated. "No more fighting. That's what they want, you idiots."

Niklaus glared at me over Ngaire's shoulder, baring his teeth in a wide grin.

I flipped him off, and Nash pushed me behind him to stop me from leaping forward.

We retreated into our separate corners, and every time I looked up, he was watching me, the challenge clear in his face. He was enjoying it. The tension in the room doubled as we fell into fretful sleep, woken by sirens and lights until we were strung out, desperate for real rest. My fight with Peliela and Niklaus were not the last in that room. Other competitors beat each other senseless and screamed in one another's faces until the day we felt Wrath leave the compound. When she departed the halls above us, the air no longer felt too thick to breathe properly.

Slumped against the wall, I sucked in oxygen, as if I'd never had it before and couldn't get enough, finally aware of the amount of stress I had been carrying beneath the angel's influence.

When Major Akua unlocked the door and stood in the doorway, she looked over the broken mess we had become and smirked, the corners of her eyes crinkling, obscured by her leather mask.

"Good work, recruits." She nodded firmly and led the mass of weary, broken challengers to our barracks once more.

As we staggered into our beds, ready to sleep for a week, we were quiet, damaged by the experience.

Major Akua nodded again, her parting words a reassurance and a curse. "Broken recruits can be rebuilt into perfect soldiers."

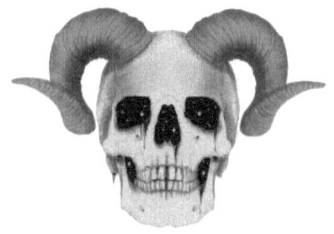

Chapter Fifteen

It took days to pull myself back together. They allowed a luxurious eight hours of sleep in the first week outside the dungeon beneath Wrath Hall, but what we had lost could never be recovered. For the first few days, my body was achy, my thoughts scattered like leaves in the wind, until even the ever-patient Ngaire became frustrated with my inability to hold a full conversation.

It wasn't long before our grace period ended and Major Akua decided that our new focus on our training, morning runs, and periods of rest were not enough for her soldiers to develop. She led us from atop her horse outside of the compound and down the dirt road. We reached the small sandy arena on the outskirts of the war camp.

We hadn't been back here since the day they had divided us into groups.

At her barked command, the soldiers training there packed

up and found better things to do, while we waited, weary and still bone-tired, for Major Akua to dismount and spit her demands at us. The change, despite the promise that it could be gruelling, was something I had welcomed. Too much time to rest had meant too much time with my thoughts, and scenarios I created in my own head haunted me. All while Samael remained quiet.

"Now, recruits, pay attention." Major Akua paced through the midsection of the training grounds, surveying us, as if she had never seen a sorrier group. "Today, we begin weapons training. In Lady Wrath's army, we are all taught the basics of sword fighting, and those with skill will continue to learn archery."

Some recruits rustled at this, appearing more alert at the prospect of rising above others. Peliela was one of them, and I made a mental note to stay out of her way.

Major Akua's boot tapped one of the wooden crates in the arena. "Everyone, lay your swords to the side and collect a wooden blade instead. I won't be trusting you lot anything sharp until I know you won't slice off your own hands . . ."

Derision dripping from her tone was clear, and we scuttled to obey, splitting into our pairs, the splintering wooden blade rough in my hands.

"Someone tell me what the primary purpose of sword fighting is," Major Akua said.

Peliela puffed out her chest, standing tall as she called out her answer. "To cut down the enemy."

"Correct," Major Akua said, nodding. "And who is our enemy?"

It sounded like a trick question. The group seemed to shudder in the silence.

A vein in Major Akua's temple throbbed as the silence lengthened. She seemed unimpressed.

"Envy!" she spat, as if it were the most obvious answer in the world, as if we had all disappointed her by not reciting it readily enough.

"Right," someone murmured in a vaguely familiar tone, but I didn't know his name. "But why's Envy the enemy?"

Major Akua's boots squeaked as she twisted on her heel before marching to stand in front of the man. Her eyes narrowed, as if he were nothing more than a worm to squash beneath her heel. "Your ignorance is fascinating, trial rat." His throat bobbed at her words, but he said nothing to incite more anger. "I'm not here to educate you on basic history. Ask another stupid question, and I'll have you polishing every weapon in camp, twice."

Silence that followed was a deafening agreement.

Major Akua turned back to stand at the head of the group, her razor-sharp sideways glances flicking over the crowd, searching for her next opponent or the victim she wanted more. Her eyes snagged on someone. "You. Come here."

Finley Nightingale's throat bobbed, his chin ducking forward as he shared a bleak look with Nash. After steadying himself, he marched to stand in front of Major Akua, holding himself tall, as if he were a man of privilege instead of a competitor in an impossible trial. "Yes?"

"Yes, *Major*," she corrected.

She smacked his ribs with the edge of her wooden sword in sharp reprimand. Finley flinched, inhaling sharply, and repeated her words in a mumble. Major Akua motioned for Finley to step back. His eyes narrowed warily, but he complied, holding his sword loosely at his side.

"How many angles of attack are there?" Major Akua asked loudly.

"Eight," Peliela answered.

"Name them," she commanded.

"Uhh"—the woman blinked—"straight down, straight up. Diagonal up to the left, diagonal up to the right. Diagonal down left, and right." A pause hung before Peliela nodded to herself, reaffirming her thoughts, then continued. "Horizontally, left and right."

Major Akua nodded, and well before Finley was ready, the armoured major leapt forward, striking as she repeated each of the angles. Her wooden sword cut through the air swiftly. He stumbled back, step after step. She had forced him out of the arena and over the length of rope until his feet hit the crates. Finley lost his balance, crashing to the ground.

"Get up, trial rat," Major Akua demanded.

Finley scrambled to obey. The parts of his face visible above the leather mask a deep shade of red. He held himself tense, waiting.

"What did he do wrong?" the major asked our group.

Ngaire rocked forward onto her toes, and I glanced in her direction, chest aching with anxiety. It took a moment for her to find her courage, and she muttered when she answered.

"He didn't use his sword to defend himself."

"Good," Major Akua said. "And that means . . . ?"

Ngaire's voice strengthened with confidence.

"He'd be dead."

The words seemed to linger in the arena, settling in the blood-splattered dirt.

Wooden swords or not, the stakes of war were real.

"Exactly," Major Akua agreed. "You should find the offensive—and fast. Cut your enemy down at the knees, but you must still be able to hold your own if they have the advantage." She tossed her wooden sword, the dirt rising as it hit the ground, and stepped towards Finley.

He was stiff, tension obvious in the knotted muscle of his neck as Akua touched him. He positioned his arms and sword into five different defensive stances, explaining which angles these stances could protect him against.

"Understood?"

"Understood," Finley replied, his voice strained.

"Back to your partner," she barked, and Finley was beside Nash in an instant. Major Akua stalked leisurely along the line of recruits, her dark eyes surveying us as if we might suddenly prove to be more than we were. "You may begin."

For the twelfth time that day—as always in the past three days of this training—Ngaire had the advantage. She thought and moved faster than I could ever dream to, and it was as if she'd been sword fighting with sticks her entire life.

Half the time, I felt like I'd killed her mother and she sought revenge, with the bloodthirsty way she leapt after me, intent on cutting me down. Her arms swung, precise, where mine were clumsy and slow, the edge of her wooden sword bouncing off my ribs.

"Ouch!" I whined.

She twisted, the hilt of her sword hammering my knee, which buckled on impact. Not for the first time had I landed face down in the dirt, and Ngaire pressed the blunt point of the sword between my shoulder blades.

"You're dead," she announced proudly.

"Again." I sighed heavily.

Painted black and blue with bruises from this new phase of training, I rolled onto my back, and when Ngaire held out a gloved hand to help me up, I took it. My knee twinged as I dared to bear weight after the way she'd hit me. "That one hurt."

"You need to try harder." Ngaire's tone was bland, the statement matter-of-fact, but irritation skittered down my spine at the accusation. "You know, properly."

"I am," I said, irritated by the implication.

She blinked at me, schooling her face into a carefully blank expression as the bell tolled, signalling we could stop for lunch.

"Are you really, Octavia? Or are you just waiting to die?"

Throwing my sword to the ground, I stepped over it to reach for the canteen of water I had discarded earlier that morning. "This isn't me. I wasn't born to fight in wars and wave a sword around."

"You joined The Devil's Trials." Her disbelief was almost palpable. "That's a war of its own. You must have some ambition?"

I offered her a dark look, draining the canteen before I said, "Ambition and desperation aren't the same."

A haunted edge clung to her expression as she sat and drank from her canteen. A light had gone out in her eyes, and that told me Ngaire knew something of desperation, too.

Two weeks later, we had progressed from wood to steel. If I had thought the length of wood was heavy, my arms aching from day after day of lifting, it was nothing compared to the weight of a real sword.

My muscles ached, trembling with exertion, as Ngaire and I crept the blades through a pattern of offensive and defensive positions. The change in weapons had her struggling, her balance thrown off, and her speed had disappeared. With the new weapons, it felt like we were moving through mud, and for the first time, I found my opening to attack her properly.

A laugh rolled from my lips, and I swung with as much force as I could muster, heady with the realisation that I'd finally found my opening.

Ngaire's grip slackened when she saw it coming. She dropped her sword and threw herself backwards to avoid it. My blow fell short, my blade's sharp tip sliding against the leather bracer at her forearm, cutting deep into it.

Her cry of pain startled me, destabilising me. I staggered

176

forward, weighed down by my blade and by the realisation we weren't playing with toy swords anymore. A good swing wouldn't leave a bruise but would remove a limb.

"Shit. Shit, Ngaire, I . . ."

She waved me off, panting. "Don't." Ngaire pressed that same hand to her forearm, where blood had soaked through her sleeve, dripping off the ends of her gloved fingers. "This is the whole point of the training. Envy's army won't take pity on me."

Major Akua stalked over to us. "Why are your blades on the ground?!"

"We . . ." I started, but she had already caught sight of Ngaire and wasn't listening to a word I had to say.

Major Akua's hand curled around Ngaire's wrist and held her arm still as she pulled back the cut section of her sleeve to inspect the damage.

"Sheath your swords properly and go to the medic," she barked, then twisted her dark stare, pinning me in place.

My throat felt like it was closing beneath her inspection, the uncomfortable, crawling anxiety I'd felt in Wrath Hall causing my heart to race.

"Good work, Nox. The first to cut their opponent."

I shivered.

Her approval felt like a thin layer of oil across my skin, grossly uncomfortable. I was wise enough to say nothing, though, holding my mouth shut to stop the words from flowing out. Determined not to slice her open again, I stepped towards Ngaire, picking up her sword and sliding it into the sheath strapped around her waist.

When my cumbersome sword weighed at my waistline, slowing me down in normally effortless movements, I collected our canteens and nodded at Ngaire. I let her lead the way, who was still dripping crimson, back into the camp.

"Sorry," I muttered for the fifth time, feeling guilty after a cry had ripped from Ngaire's throat, drawn by the harsh sting of chemicals pressed against the wound.

"No, you're not," Ngaire panted, her dark brows knitting together, while the medic pressed cloth soaked in a second solution to her gash. "And you shouldn't be, this is . . . this is the whole point."

I couldn't help but cringe. I had never been a pacifist, but the idea of voluntarily cutting others down turned my stomach and twisted it into knots. I would do it—just as I had done many other horrible things throughout my life. But I couldn't believe how prepared for this life Ngaire seemed, how accepting of the consequences she appeared.

With a white bandage hidden beneath the sleeve of a new undershirt, Ngaire strapped her leather bracer around her forearm, grunting softly upon tightening it.

"Should we take the afternoon off?" I asked.

She shot me a look so dark that Samael roused and chuckled in my mind. I tensed at the soft whisper of his laughter, waiting to hear what he had to say, but he divulged nothing, disappearing as quickly as he had appeared. His absence left me shivering, disappointed.

"I miss you, Sam," I whispered, dragging my feet after Ngaire, right back up the dusty road and into the area of blood and sand.

A bead of sweat dropped from the soaked strands of my hair and slithered down my arm, distracting me as Ngaire spun and struck in my direction. I parried, the movement easier than I had expected. A month had passed us by, heavy days of sword drills, as we learned to balance the weight of the weapons until they felt like nothing more than an extension of our arms.

My breath seemed to catch in my chest as her sword clashed against my own, the force of her strength sending me staggering back. I swallowed, exhausted beneath the rays of the harsh midday heat, and forced myself to find enough strength to push her away.

Ngaire laughed, the sound agitating me, sparking at the end of my already short fuse. We were one of three groups in the arena, battling until Major Akua barked at us to stop, or until one party was too injured to continue.

Over the past week, the fights had become more aggressive, the injuries more severe, and any fragments of patience I had had disappeared completely.

It was evidence enough that Wrath was back. She was as poisonous as her brothers and turning us inside out through sheer proximity. Sure enough, when I shifted, lashing out at Ngaire, the angel's wings rustled in my peripheral, and she waited beside Major Akua.

She stood, proud, with her arms folded across her chest. Her sharp eyes studied each of us closely, as if she didn't miss the way our muscles bunched in preparation to move or the way my chest squeezed with fear every time Ngaire almost struck true.

"Enough!" Major Akua barked.

The point of a sword slashed past my face, and I staggered backwards, wrenching myself to the side so quickly that I almost lost my footing.

"What the fuck?"

It wasn't Ngaire who had struck at me. My eyes were on her, watching the deadly edge to her blade. Instead, when I spun, I found Peliela's beetle-like gaze honed on me, and I imagined she was laughing behind the leather mask. She had almost decapitated

179

me.

Where others had dropped their swords, turning to face the Angel of Wrath, bowing their heads, I couldn't tear my eyes from the woman who was becoming a consistent threat in my life. My grip tightened on the hilt of the sword. Sweat dripped down my face, sliding along the bridge of my nose, the salty beads threatening to blind me, but I watched Peliela, waiting for her next move.

"Recruits," Major Akua warned with threat in her voice.

I lifted my sword in challenge, despite my aching arms, and the sides of Peliela's eyes crinkled. She shifted into a familiar fighting stance.

"Recruit—"

A low voice cut off the major's rebuke.

"No," Wrath said, her ethereal voice carrying across the arena. "Let them fight."

Nothing could bode well from the Angel of Wrath wanting to watch us fight.

Feet shuffled, and Ngaire disappeared from my peripheral vision, but when I shifted, I could see her standing beside Niklaus. Wisely, most others fled the arena, not willing to bear witness. Peliela moved, and I forced myself to shift the opposite way, keeping a safe distance between us. The fatigue weighing me down before felt nonexistent, as my body tensed, and I studied her quickly.

Fighting with Ngaire was one thing; we were relatively the same size despite her being built of muscle and years of training, far stronger than I.

Peliela was a different opponent. While also strong, having had trained for her whole life, she was bigger than me. She stood inches taller and thicker with muscle; her movements were slow, and she'd taken a nasty cut to the ribs two days prior, which left her shielding her left side. I had to be faster than her, or I wouldn't survive.

Peliela struck first. A warrior's cry echoed from her throat as she lunged for me; I twisted on instinct, throwing myself down low and hearing the soft whistle of steel through the air. She cut right through where my neck was a moment before. I scrambled to one side, slipping out of her reach, and adjusted my grip on the sword. It quickly became a deadly dance, and Peliela's eyes seemed to glaze in a haze of fury with each missed strike. She lunged again and again. Each time, I slipped out of her reach, encouraging her to strike once more when I laughed, a giddy, nervous sound. The laugh of a fool barely alive.

She struck again; I twisted, but where she had slowed, so had I. The side of her sword bounced off my own, the force of her swing so jarring that I staggered backwards. The laughter died on the edge of my lips as I swiftly lost any advantage beneath the fumble of my feet. She lunged again, and I blocked, falling backwards from the force reverberating down my arms.

The sand was unforgiving when I collided with it, wrenching the air from my lungs on impact, my sword jolted from my grip. Blood filled my mouth, tart on the edge of my tongue, but I barely had time to choke on it. Peliela didn't give me a split second of reprieve; she followed her successful strike with a jab threatening to skewer my heart.

My body ached as I threw myself to the side, rolling across the sand, right over the top of my lost sword. The sharp edge sliced my palm, a stinging pain pulling a cry from my throat. I forced myself to my feet, my bleeding hand wrapped around the hilt of my sword as I dragged myself into position, ready for the next attack.

Wrath shifted in my peripheral vision. She stepped across the frayed rope and into the arena of blood and sand. Fear coursed through me as I tried to work out which of the two were a bigger threat. I was as good as dead if Wrath drew her weapon. The red strands in her hair proved that sin had no mercy for fools, and I was the biggest fool of them all.

One step, then another, and I shuffled back until I could monitor them both. Blood dribbled from my punctured lip and slid down from beneath my leather mask, staining a collar at my throat.

Wrath's sleek wings rustled, her chin lifting, her gaze seemingly drawn to the blood.

"Continue," she demanded of us. With that one word, the binds of her power tightened around me. It was so suffocating I could have believed I had literally been tied tight in the red strings that they used to marker death. "Go on, little fighters. Rage war on one another."

Her voice was a caress sparking my frayed nerves and set me alight; irritation, turned to anger, turned to fury, turned to wrath.

My mind went blissfully blank. There was nothing but me, Peliela, and my growing desire to seek vengeance for the humiliation and pain she had caused me. Nothing but sweat, blood, and sand, a burst of rage-fuelled energy and oncoming death.

We battled until our legs gave way, until our blood dripped down our bodies, and we were moments from determining winner and loser, death triumphant, when the angel gripped the back of my neck with her cool, strong fingers.

'Octavia . . .' Samael whispered, calling through the nothingness in my mind. 'Octavia . . .'

"Enough," Wrath announced.

I caught one look at her face, the blazing satisfaction in her slender features, her force of will cutting through my mindless rage.

For a second, I thought she could see into my soul, hear Samael's whispered plea for me, before she threw me backwards like nothing more than a discarded plaything.

My body screamed as I hit the dirt; all the gashes earned from Peliela felt too real, suddenly acknowledged as too deep, too deadly. Without adrenaline and the blissful ignorance of Wrath's control, I felt them all. A panic not my own flared through my veins as the world narrowed, darkness cascading at the edge of my vision.

'Octavia!' Samael screamed as the world went black.

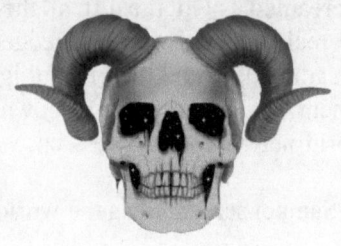

Chapter Sixteen

I woke in the sterile medic's room. The too-strong smell of boiled acrid herbs and wound-cleansing solutions burned my lungs with every breath. The world slowly came into focus, and several people had clustered at the end of my bed.

Ngaire's face pinched into a severe expression that aged her.

Margot stood by her side, staring out the window, tension and worry tight on her face.

Niklaus was close by her side, his tattooed hand resting on her shoulder, as he spoke in a whisper, the words not seeming to reach past the ringing in my ears.

Nash had turned to him, lips moving quickly as he replied.

When he turned away, coughing into the crook of his arm, I dragged my eyes to the last visitor, the only one watching me and aware I was awake.

Finley Nightingale offered me a crooked grin, his dark eyes too serious for the humour across his face. He watched as I blinked rapidly, the haze over my vision clearing, the ringing in my ears dulling.

"What time do you call this, exactly, Octavia Nox?" His voice was muffled but discernible, its humour forced. "We don't sleep in during The Devil's Trials."

Finley's words caught others' attention, and four more sets of eyes zeroed in on me, so fast and attentive that I wanted to cringe back into the uncomfortable mattress.

Beneath their gazes, I realised how bad I felt. The bed itself wasn't uncomfortable, but every muscle felt sore, aching at the protest of being conscious.

"What happened?" I asked. My voice was gravelly, even to my own ears, as if someone had scraped my vocal chords. "I don't remember much."

When I wracked my brain, I could remember the angel stepping into the arena. Whether she was a friend or foe—I couldn't quite recall—I remember the jarring feeling of her need for vengeance and battle and then nothing, lost to her wrath. My memory contained only a black hole of blissful ignorance.

Ngaire sat tentatively on the side of the bed, the mattress compressing beneath her, and she inhaled deeply. "It was insane. You both . . . changed. It was like you were just mindless soldiers fighting it out. You would have battled to your death if she hadn't seemed to get bored with it."

"Who?" I asked, although I thought I already knew the answer.

"Wrath," Ngaire said.

I shuddered. "I don't understand . . ."

"You seemed to disappear." Ngaire splayed her hands, shrugging, as if she couldn't find the words to describe the fight. "It was like looking into your face and seeing Wrath look back at me. It was like she had possessed you both. Drove you into such a berserker rage you would have cut through yourself to win the battle, and you almost did."

185

Silence fell as I tried to process this, struggled to reconcile this account with the black hole in my memory. It took everything in me just to breathe, while panic threatened to crush my lungs and finally kill me.

Eventually, I dragged my attention from my stained sheet to Ngaire's pinched face.

"Did I kill her?" I asked hoarsely, thinking of Peliela.

"No," Nash answered firmly, stepping aside to show me the occupied bed on the other side of the medic room. Peliela looked horrible beneath her own sheet. "But it was close, for both of you. If she'd let you fight much longer, you would have both bled out on the sand."

A sharp pain lanced through my chest. "I—"

"Is she awake?"

The medic marched over with disapproval stark in her expression, the blazing red lion of Wrath on her black tunic.

I wished I could see her face, that she wasn't just another masked soldier.

She took a single look at me and waved the others away. "Leave her be! Out! Now!"

They exchanged looks but didn't protest, filing out of the room at the sharp order.

The medic turned her stern gaze on Ngaire next, who was still perched on the end of the bed, and tapped her foot as she waited for her to leave.

"I'm her partner," Ngaire protested. "Where she goes, I go."

The harsh knit to the medic's brows softened, but she did not back down. "Recruit, back to your barracks. You, and you alone, may return in the morning."

Ngaire sighed but nodded, pulling her leather mask from her pocket and securing it in place, erasing a piece of herself as she, once again, became a faceless soldier. She rose, saluted the medic with a tap to the chest above her heart, and strode out without a goodbye.

The medic turned on me, slowly. She scrutinised me closely before nodding and strode off. A moment later, she returned with a trolley of supplies. She pulled a chair close to the edge of the bed and sat. "Can you sit up, recruit?"

"Is it nighttime?" I asked.

She nodded. "Come on now, recruit. Sit up for me."

A pained groan rolled from the back of my throat as I tensed my muscles and tried to force myself to move; a shuddering breath followed, but the medic's slender, strong hands were there, bracing my shoulders as she helped me upright.

My head spun dangerously, the world tipping sharply at the change in position, and I wanted nothing more than to collapse.

"Breathe slowly."

"It hurts," I whimpered, battling to do as she asked. "So badly."

"I know, recruit."

"My name is Octavia."

"I know. Mine is Heiau."

With time, the spinning calmed.

Heiau propped a pillow behind my back, and I settled into this new position but prayed she wouldn't ask me to move again. I wasn't sure if I could find the energy or the pain tolerance.

She rifled through her equipment and set it out on the bed, rising to pull a bloodred curtain around us, boxing us in, giving the illusion of privacy. I wasn't dumb enough to believe the rest of the room couldn't hear every word.

"Why are you here, Heiau?" I asked to distract myself from the pain ebbing through my body. "Instead of out there, fighting for Wrath."

"Someone has to do it. Healing the sick can be as tough as wielding a sword." She offered a bland smile that told me it wasn't the entire answer to my question. "Let's remove that gown now."

Slowly, I glanced down at my body, at the white gown marked with the red lion. It was a far cry from the leather armour

I had been wearing in the ring. Heiau's cool fingers unfastened the ties behind my neck and back before she slipped the gown down my front. I shivered as the cool air slipped over my skin.

Three deep breaths later, I found the courage to look at myself, the motley bruises of black, green, and blue worse than the previous trials. Tightly wound bandages broke them up, once white but since marred with strike-through from the wounds beneath.

Heiau held a small cup in front of my mouth. "Drink this, recruit."

"What is it?"

She ignored the question, pressing the cup to my lips and waiting patiently for me to follow the order.

Slowly, I wrapped my hands around hers, gulped the bitter liquid, and recoiled against the pillow.

Heiau sighed heavily. "It'll help, I swear. You must take it."

I glanced at her, struck by the rare kindness in her expression.

I had seen little of that since coming to the Wrathlands. It was enough to convince me, and I lifted the cup back to my lips, plugging my nose, and quickly draining it. My stomach churned in rebellion, but a warmth spread rapidly through my veins. After a minute, Heiau reached for me and sliced through the first of the bandages, first along my bicep, across my ribs, peeling one from my back, then drawing back the sheets to unwrap the wound on my thigh.

That was the one I focused on, breathing slowly through my nose at the sight of the angry red gouge, puffy at the edges and leaking a yellow fluid onto the bandages, which stuck to the open wound.

I hated the sight of my flesh torn apart. It left me breathless; I'd never felt so weak.

Heiau explained her process as she did things, but I stopped listening, counting the rough stitches of ugly red thread over my wound that would soon knit into an ugly scar. Mostly, I tried not to pass out.

"Fourteen," I whispered to myself, crying out as she cleaned each wound, the disinfectant stinging. "Fourteen wounds."

"Yes," Heiau answered brusquely. "They're healing nicely, though. It's much better than it was in the first few days. Not the worst of the wounds I've seen from Wrath's frenzy." She frowned as she pressed a new dressing against my ribs, then reached for a bandage to bind them.

"Her frenzy?" I asked, almost not wanting to know.

The hole in my memory could be more of a blessing than I knew.

"Mhm. You two are both very lucky that you're relatively unskilled. When senior soldiers get caught in the thrall and turn on each other on the front—well . . . it's a massacre. Many die just for getting in their way."

The thought turned my stomach, already soured from the herbs.

"Right."

I didn't feel lucky, not when my body ached with a fresh wave of fatigue, my head light and soul tired.

Heiau was quick and efficient as she cleaned the reddened edges of the gouge in my thigh with a solution that burned right through me. She covered it up quickly with a fresh dressing and a bandage to secure it in place.

Closing my eyes, I lost track as she worked on the rest.

"Here, recruit, put this back on." She slid the gown back up my arms, preserving a modesty I hadn't cared about, and tied it loosely at the back of my neck. Heiau settled me back against the pillow, offering a second sweeter drink, which I gulped down like it was the elixir of life.

"Sleep."

I didn't hesitate to obey.

In my dreams, I was back in Pride Palace, the early morning sun filtering through the stained glass above us. I stood in an angel's arms, barefoot, wearing nothing more than the white-and-red medic's gown.

The golden-haired angel whirled me in circles, whispering his secrets in my ear, a handsome smile stretched across his face, his easy humour relaxing me. The medic's gown fluttered around my knees as we spun around and around, but between one spin and the next, Pride transformed.

He melted from the gold-haired, confident Angel of Pride into a man borne of shadows. He was far taller than me, forcing me to look up and meet his gaze. His body was slender but strong. As we danced, he led me around the room with an air of power.

With my face pressed against his black shirt, I found that the absence of the beat of his heart did not alarm me.

Shadows wreathed him, lifting him through the air in the absence of wings, and I felt I would have known him anywhere. A smattering of dark hair lined his sharp jaw, his full lips twisting into a mocking laugh. A laugh I knew all too well.

Shadows obscured most of his face, hiding it from me, but there was no hiding the curve of thick horns protruding from his skull.

A shiver worked through me when he laughed, the brush of shadows and fingertips tracing the knots of my spine in the open back of the gown.

"Samael."

I breathed his name like a prayer.

'Hello, Little One.' The creature of my dreams didn't speak, but his voice drifted through my mind, as it always had. *'You've been hard to reach. I thought you had died.'*

"So did I . . . I should have died."

190

'What kept you alive?'

"Sheer, dumb luck."

He'd always protested that I was simply lucky. Samael spun me away from him, his firm touch disappearing as he sent me spinning, and the world shifted with each twirl. The bright stained glass windows of Pride Palace disappeared, and when I slammed back into his chest, his hands easily found the curve of my waist. We danced beneath pure moonlight, in a grove of darkness, stars glittering around our bodies, as if he had teleported me from one world to another.

"Where are we . . . ?"

'This is the power of dreams, Little One.' He laughed as if I should have known he would never tell me the answer. *'We can be anywhere we want, any time we want. You'll learn all about them in trials to come.'*

"And where are we?" I pressed. "When are we?"

Samael lifted my hand above my head, nudging me to rotate on the spot to music drifting in from nowhere and everywhere all at once.

I was no dancer, but with his gentle coaxing, I felt graceful. I wasn't surprised, though; he had a nasty habit of leaving my questions unanswered.

'I'm glad you lived, Octavia.'

A breath of a scoff rolled from my throat. "I don't know why you would be."

Surrounding shadows seemed to shift, as Samael leaned close, filling my nose with the earthiness of oncoming rain, with undercurrents of salt and smoke. I felt the crackling promise of an oncoming storm, and I wondered where he was while I slept, if the devil himself were dancing alone in the rain. His shadowed face bowed so close that I could have sworn he was real, tangible and in my arms, that I felt his breath on my cheek, the flicker of a forked tongue causing my heart to skitter.

'You need not know why.'

191

He waited a beat, as if to see if I would push for an answer; but even in my dreams, I was exhausted, swaying against him and the comfort of his broad chest.

Samael, the devil, wound his arms tight around my body as we drifted through the shadows before landing on the ground, nestled in the soft grass and staring up at the stars that danced without us.

I blinked at the sky, wondering if Heiau had drugged me. "Samael?"

He didn't answer straight away; a presence beside me—there but not—was close enough that I settled.

'Are you going to ask me to rescue you, Little One?'

I fidgeted with the button on his shirt. "I'd thought about it."

'You don't need rescuing, Octavia. You need only to win by any means necessary.'

"What if I don't make it to the end?" I asked, feeling a thrill of panic. "What if I don't beat this one?"

He made a noise in the back of his throat, soft and derisive. *'If you believe you will win, it will come to pass. Manifestation is a wonderful human concept.'*

Irritation seemed to clamp around me, hot and suffocating.

"You want me to just think positively? Think positive and win. Like these trials aren't a one-way ticket to death, designed to make us struggle?!"

'The trials aren't impossible, Little One. Humanity can win.'

My throat tightened, and I felt overwhelmed. "At what cost, Samael? If I make it to the end, what part of me will be left?"

'That's entirely up to you.'

"You're *so* helpful," I muttered.

The horned devil at my side stretched and sat up, as if he had grown weary of me.

A horrible sense of regret coiled in my belly, and I was left wondering if he would abandon me, like so many others had in the past.

'You should ask the medic, Heiau'—Samael stood, and he disappeared into the shadows, his disembodied voice floating behind him—*'about the Sinning Twins.'*

Without him, I fell into a dreamless sleep.

Most of the day passed before I saw Heiau again. My morning was filled with idle chatter as Ngaire told me about the training I had missed, warning that our days on sword work were coming to an end and that they had picked recruits to work on the archery ranges.

When the medic arrived for her shift, she tended to Peliela first, who had glared darkly at me with such ferociousness that the medic had drawn the bloodred curtains between us.

When Heiau finally came to tend to me, I was almost climbing out of my skin with the desire to speak with her about the Sinning Twins. I had enough restraint to let her get most of the way through my dressings.

"Can I ask you something?" Heiau offered me a sharp look, like she knew nothing good could come of curious questions. "What is it you want?"

"Can you . . ."

I almost couldn't get the words out.

"Can you tell me about the Sinning Twins?"

Surprise flared in her eyes. "Who told you about that?"

"A man in a dream." It would be easier not to lie to her when I had already lied about Samael so much. "What is it?"

Heiau shook her head, her eyes narrowing on the bandage she wound around my arm. "It's a children's story, told mostly in the heart of Ira. You're a child of another sin—you wouldn't have heard it."

"What's it about?"

Heiau stayed silent until she finished bandaging and helped

me redress, then drummed her fingers against her thighs.

I could see the indecision flickering across her face, heavy in the pull of her thick brows.

Finally, she gestured for me to relax against the pillows and nodded firmly. "It's a story of a brother and sister. Twins born on the high night of winter . . ."

The soft pillow threatened to lull my tired body into sleep, but I forced my eyes open and gestured at Heiau to continue, a lazy sweep of my hand that had the medic rolling her eyes. Folding her arms across her body, she settled against the metal chair and dipped her chin. "As children, the twins were as close as two could be. Kolè, the female, was born three minutes before her brother, Jalou, and much like their entry into the world, she seemed to lead him through every trial of life. They were as similar as they were different, and of all their many siblings, none were as close as those twins. Kolè was wild and short of temper, always quick and eager to incite conflict. She was loud and brash, although not well liked. She was a natural-born leader and no matter where they went, people followed in her choices. Jalou was a follower but full of deep desires of his own. He followed his twin through life, at her side whenever needed but always wanted the assurance she had in her next step. He wanted what she had. Often, people would gossip that Jalou felt overshadowed by his sister, always wishing he had been first born and first noticed. Despite this, they were thick as thieves . . ."

Heiau frowned, and as much as I wanted to let her mull in the silence, I asked, "What happened next?"

"It's a common story theme. Something came between them."

"What? What drove them apart?"

She gave me a look indicating it should have been obvious. I blinked, and she shook her head, chuckling. "A woman, of course. Both Kolè and Jalou came to love the same woman. Her name was Nakola, and not much is said of her in the stories, not

194

truly. She's a quiet soul, soft compared to the powerful personalities of both twins. Some retellings say she was the calm in the face of their storms; and both loved her ever so fiercely. Kolè, as the eldest, believed it was her right to lay claim to Nakola, and she was quick to pick fights with her brother if he vied for the woman's attention. Jalou burned with the need to have Nakola for himself, his desires threatening to set him alight, until he resented her sister for wanting what he wanted, fearing she might take the love of his life for himself. It created a divide so deep that they ignited a war. All their friends divided, pitted against one another just for the love of a woman."

A trickle of discomfort and warning worked down my spine, my mind spinning despite the concoctions she had given me for the dressings.

"Nakola, soft soul as she was, refused to choose between the twins. Refused to voice up and state who she wanted. Some said it was because she truly feared both. My grandfather liked to say that it was because, while they loved her, she loved them both in return for different reasons. The twins, however, would not share. It was not in their true nature."

Leaning forward on the pillow, I propped my elbow up. "How did it end?"

Heiau's voice softened with sorrow. "Kolè stole Nakola away for herself in a fit of rage, locked her away where her brother could never have her; it is said to have sent Jalou mad. He was so worked up that he would stop at nothing to find Nakola, desiring what his sister had. It's unknown how he found where she was keeping Nakola, only that he broke in when his sister was distracted and dropped to his knees before the woman, near begging her to pick him, to choose him. Proclaiming a love like sunlight desperately needed to thrive."

I bit my lip. "She said no, didn't she?" I whispered.

"Soft-hearted, peacekeeping Nakola, the balance between Kolè and Jalou stayed firm in her unwillingness to choose. Jalou

195

could not handle her response. He saw it as his sister winning, as Nakola picking Kolè instead, and so he decided she could not have what he could not have . . ."

"What did he do?"

My question was soft, daring, even though the twist in my stomach suggested the answer.

"He took the slender black knife from his belt, decorated with otherworldly green stones, and carved her heart right from her chest. He left her remains for Kolè, pinned with a note that he had Nakola's heart, and his sister may have rotting corpse she deserved. It ignited a war that lasted the rest of their lives."

A lump obstructed my throat.

I'd seen and held a knife like the one in her story. I'd drawn it across a woman's throat, a woman from the Wrathlands, her hair braided with red, her heart dedicated to a war not her own. My heart thumped in my chest dangerously fast, as if it wanted the rest of her way out.

"Kolè is Wrath, and Jalou is Envy, isn't he? You're telling me their history?"

Heiau's face shuddered but not before I saw the truth in her eyes. "It's a bedtime story. Sure, it may be based on the angels we know, but it's merely a fable for children about why we don't give into the sins."

She stood, her chair scraping the floor, before she disappeared behind the curtain.

Drawing my knees slowly to my chest, I held my head in my hands.

All this for a woman, all this death in the name of love.

How utterly typical, almost human.

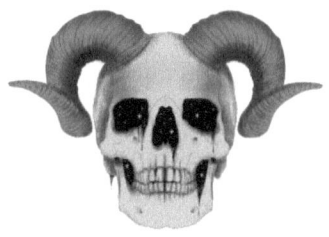

Chapter Seventeen

Four days later, they discharged me from the medic rooms and sent me back to the barracks. I spent an extra day lying in bed, listening to the hustle and bustle of the other recruits as they enjoyed a rare day off since finishing weapon training.

A small part of me felt relieved that I didn't have to do it anymore, even if the weeks of missed lessons left me at a disadvantage. Then there was the growing nerves about what would come next—I had a bad feeling that the worst was yet to come.

Drifting in and out of sleep, I was hopeful Samael would visit me again, but when I woke, I had no memory of the devil. It created a chilling paranoia that I had irritated him when he had visited me in my dreams, enough that he had stayed away forever.

"Major Akua wants you at training tomorrow," Ngaire said softly from the bunk below.

Pretending I was already asleep seemed pointless. She would

just wake me at the crack of dawn to come with her, so I grunted to acknowledge the comment and rolled on my side, drawing my knees to my chest and dreading the coming day.

I was right to dread it.

We rose for the morning run, which was harder after weeks off, my body still healing, my muscles screaming.

Ngaire didn't complain when I fell behind, chattering to keep me distracted, slowing her pace to settle beside me. Side by side, we reached the end of the track and fell into familiar formations to march back.

"Do you know what's coming?" I asked.

So far, Ngaire had seemed prepared for everything, and it stood to reason she would be ready for whatever came next.

She shook her head, chin lifted, and eyes straight ahead.

Major Akua waited at the entrance to town, sitting proud on her horse and looking down her nose at us, a familiar sneer glimmering in her eyes.

I dropped my chin and kept my attention on the toes of my boots, trying to avoid her attention and critique. I had already felt shattered without the mental battle of facing off with the major.

"Follow me, recruits," she said, heels digging into the horse's flank and turning us back the way we had come.

We paraded towards the mountain and its obstacle course.

The morning had almost passed by the time we reached the monkey bars. Beside me, Ngaire had become quiet and tense.

Major Akua cleared her throat loudly, drawing my attention away from my partner. She climbed down from her horse, her armour squeaking in the silence. Wrath's major strode purposefully through the thick of our group, studying us before snagging a recruit by the arm and dragging her forward.

The recruit stumbled to keep up, but she didn't fight. I would have wanted to kick and flail at the rough treatment, but she ducked to her major subserviently like a good little soldier and stood at the edge of the river.

"Today," the major announced, "we begin your endurance training. Today, you will learn if you sink or swim." Without warning, she planted her hand against the recruit's chest and shoved her backwards. A screech of surprise ripped from the woman's lungs. She extended her arm to save herself, but Major Akua stepped to the side, firmly out of reach. The recruit fell heavily, weighed down by leather and steel, splashing into the water. Cold river droplets splattered us. Then she was gone, pulled beneath the surface.

I dared not to move in the silence. Even breathing felt too loud. My stomach churned, and it reminded me of falling headfirst into the sweet river of Gula, inhaling a lungful of the water. It had plagued me with hallucinations, and I couldn't shake the ghostly, gut-wrenching, heart-breaking sorrow.

Unable to help myself, I glanced towards Nash. He looked pale, almost tinged green.

The recruit broke through the glassy surface of the water, gasping desperately for air. Her arms flailed, thrashing to keep herself there.

Ngaire's fingers curled around mine, her grip tight, nails digging into my skin. We watched the recruit struggle to keep her head above water, dipping below the surface twice more. When we had faced this obstacle course, Ngaire had struggled to find the courage and will to hurtle herself across the depths of the river, and she looked just as drawn and pale as she did that day. Lines crinkled at the side of her eyes, the muscles in her neck taut, showing her tension. If the numbness in my fingers from her grip wasn't telling enough.

"You'll go for as long as you can today, and then we'll fish you out," Major Akua explained. "Then, we'll repeat this every day until you have the endurance to keep your head above water for at least an hour."

Shivering, I wondered if they were fast enough to stop us all from drowning or if this was their way of weaning out the weak.

I couldn't see the vengeful spirit of Wrath tolerating the weak for long, and not all of us would be decimated under the guise of being a deserter. Although we'd lost many people that way, people who fled and were then destroyed by her hand all the same, people driven mad by the angels' influence.

Behind us, more soldiers appeared on horses, settling at the back of the group, and it occurred to me they could be about to herd us into the water as a group. I tensed, unsure if I was ready. The recruit used the precious air she'd earned to call for help, a plea screeching across the riverbank. Not even her partner moved a muscle for her aid.

Major Akua turned. She stepped into the shallow bank and made a clicking noise beneath her breath. Her horse shifted, following her into the water, where Major Akua used the beast as an anchor. She held out a hand, and the recruit didn't hesitate to take the major's lifeline.

Major Akua lifted a wet foot and wedged it in the stirrup, clicking her tongue a second time. The beast snorted, twisting in the water, then moved to the shore. They dragged the recruit back and dropped her unceremoniously into the dirt, where she wheezed for air, coughing up water. Then, she curled up in a ball, unmoving and utterly spent.

Major Akua watched her closely, then lifted her dark gaze to the rest of us. "As always, learn from the mistakes of your fellow recruits; panic will only exhaust you faster. You'll do well if you can exert some self-control."

"Why are we doing this?" Niklaus drawled from the back of the group. "We walked across that entire war front to get here. I can tell you there's not a lick of natural water out there. We will not fall into a river during battle." He stared the major down, ignoring Margot as she tugged on his arm. "This is pointless."

Major Akua had stilled. I wondered if she would approach him, exert her power over him, try to intimidate him the same way she had to so many others—or if she knew he wasn't so easily cowed.

Angry hunger flashed in his eyes that matched hers. Niklaus leaned forward, his arms folded firmly across his chest, and waited for the answer.

It felt like he was prepared for the chance to rip her to shreds. It foolishly occurred to me he might want to take her place. I didn't know which would be worse—Major Akua or Major Niklaus Heira. Or maybe I did know. I would have taken Akua over Niklaus any day.

"Because I said so," she replied, speaking with a soft, almost lethal edge. "So, get in the water, recruit."

Shifting, I waited for him to move first, for the tension to break between them, but then her piercing gaze roved over everyone else, and the major barked, "All of you! Now!"

Shuffling, we threw ourselves towards the water's edge.

I dragged Ngaire with me. She was still, pulling back against me, undeniably scared. "Come on," I whispered. "It's just water."

She shook her head. I was knee-deep by the time she dug in her heels properly. Her chest rose and fell faster and faster when her breaths shortened with panic.

"I can't."

"Yes, you can," I said, tugging her arm. "You know you can. Come on, Ngaire. It's just water."

She hadn't let me falter in the previous tasks, hadn't let me give up. She had supported me through every long week of training.

I needed to get her in the water but didn't know how to.

She shook her head, attempting to pull herself free of me, but I held on as tight as I could, my fingers digging into her wrist.

Her free hand pressed against her chest, as if her heart hurt, and Ngaire thrashed against my hold. "NO!"

"It's just water." My gaze darted to the major and the other senior soldiers.

My heart sank when I realised we had attracted their

attention. Nothing good could come from Major Akua's tense stance and the way her dark eyes narrowed on us.

"Ngaire," I hissed, panicked urgency threading my voice. "You need to move. Now."

Major Akua had already started moving towards us, and we hadn't moved even a fraction before she was looming above us. "What's the problem, recruits?"

"Nothing," I blurted.

Ngaire was still pulling against me, pressing all her weight into trying to scramble back up the river bank, her panic blinding her to everything else.

Behind us, other recruits were already in the water, gasping as they tried to keep afloat, their cries for help echoing.

"We're getting in now," I assured Major Akua.

"No," Ngaire said, her voice mournful. As I twisted to capture her other wrist, holding her tight like manacles of flesh and bone, she struggled away, tears pooling in her dark eyes. "I can't swim, I can't swim . . ."

Her words were a stark admission of her shortcomings. It was on the end of my tongue to tell her they wouldn't let us drown, that they needed bodies for their war—only, I didn't know if I truly believed that, if I could force it from my lips.

"You don't need to get in the water," Major Akua said.

Surprise flared through me, followed by a flush of suspicion.

Ngaire's body sagged with pure relief. I let go of her wrists quickly, and she staggered backwards to dry land.

I studied Major Akua, sizing her up, but I couldn't read a thing in her dark eyes, her tells hidden behind that leather mask.

She stared me down. I stood ankle-deep in the water and waited for the inevitable change of her mind.

When I realised—a moment too late—she was waiting to see if I could climb into the water, I shivered.

"Where she goes, I go," I said in what I hoped was the correct sentiment.

202

They had said we would succeed and fail by our partners, and I needed to have Ngaire's back the same way she always had mine.

I dragged myself out of the river. Water filled my boots, my thick, soggy socks squelching with each step. I reached her quickly, throwing myself to sit beside my partner, who sat with her knees drawn to her chest, hugging them, as she seemed to battle the horrors inside her own mind.

"Thank Wrath," she praised beneath her breath. "I couldn't . . ."

"Don't thank her too fast," I said, my stomach knotting. "I think Major Akua has something much worse planned for us now."

I should have known to be weary. I should have trusted my instincts. There was no way Major Akua would let us bow out of a training exercise with such ease, free of punishment or humiliation.

While other recruits had staggered back to the barracks, waterlogged and exhausted, wringing water from their clothes, I fretted.

I couldn't help but pace around our bunk until exhaustion claimed me, too, and I wound up in bed, lost to a deep, dreamless sleep.

They ripped me from my bed, jarringly catapulting me into consciousness. Strong hands secured my limbs. Pressure mounted against my skin as my arms were bound with a rough rope. Then they hauled me from the mattress and dropped me to the floor. It left me winded, whimpering from the pain shooting through my healing body.

"Quiet!"

A booted foot slammed into my stomach, and I grunted,

curling up tight to protect myself. It was hard to see in the darkness, but I counted at least four soldiers. They gripped my arms again, lifting me to my feet. I struggled to catch my balance before they dragged me into the cool night.

A hellhound growled from the street corner, a low and dangerous warning, making the hair on the back of my neck rise.

I didn't have time to focus on it; my captors dragged me forward too fast. I caught sight of Ngaire, who was bound beside me with bright red rope. In the low light, the insignia of Wrath-trained soldiers reflected on their chests, the twist of blue-black hair and red cotton.

Ngaire's voice was sharp and filled with pain as she cried out.

I tried to twist towards her, but one soldier jerked me back. Their gloved fist came flying towards my face—an attack I was too slow or too restrained to dodge—and slammed against the side of my skull.

The world went black.

I blinked as the world came back into focus, while a sharp pain seared through my head.

Slowly, I figured out that they had hung me upside down and tied me to the back of a horse. Blood had rushed to my head, and the edge of the leather saddle dug into my gut.

The horse moved quickly, and the jolting sensation of its gait left me disorientated. By the time it slowed to a halt, I was dizzy and on the verge of vomiting. Firm hands untied the knots keeping me secure to the beast, and when the rope loosened, my battered body flopped to the ground.

I could taste dirt. Small rocks scraped against my skin, and when I tried to soothe my erratic breathing, I realised the rushing sound I could hear wasn't my hyperventilation but the running river. A dangerous shiver worked its way, knot by knot, down my spine.

A soldier appeared, silhouetted by the bright moonlight. She crouched beside me, grasping the rope around my wrists, and dragging me to the water's edge.

My stomach flipped as I searched her face for anything recognisable, anything human, as the soldier crouched and strapped familiar armour around my body. It was in the wrong place, not quite strapped right, with my arms and legs restricted, but still weighing me down. She held the anonymity of uniformity, unapproachable and disinterested in my struggle. This soldier wasn't a soul to whom I could appeal, to plead my case where desperation to live might save me again. But she was a soldier set to do her commanders work, nothing more, nothing less.

Said commander, Major Akua, stepped gracefully into my line of vision, her stance and gait all too familiar. Her foot swung out, her heavy boot catching a solid body, and Ngaire rolled against my side, a cry of pain following the harsh sound of her cracking limbs. Major Akua crouched to look us in the eye, the harsh anger in her face clear, even in the low light.

"Poor little recruits," she mocked loudly. "Poor entitled little worms. You think you can get out of training just because you're afraid of a bit of water?" She sneered, and I knew better than to answer. Instead, I focused on my rising fear, the sense of panic that had me trembling. "One way or another, worms . . . you'll swim." Major Akua straightened, gesturing flippantly to the soldiers.

They reached for us again.

Ngaire thrashed about, but I forced myself to still, gulping deep breaths. I was about to need all the air I could get.

The soldier lifted me off the ground as if I weighed nothing, hoisted me over her shoulder, and waded into the river.

"Swim or drown," Major Akua sneered. "Your choice."

They launched us forward.

A weightless, worriless infinite moment of suspension carried me before I broke through the river's glassy surface.

The water was cold and jarring without the harsh sun to heat it. It was dark as my weight pulled me under, the water rushing up my nose and down my throat.

Even though I'd tried to hold my breath, it found a way in, choking me. I dropped like a stone stuck in time before my brain kicked into gear. Panic flooded through me.

My boots were missing—thankfully, but my armour weighed my legs down, the red rope resisting when I tried to kick my way back up.

Fighting, I kicked until my head broke the surface, and I could suck in a deep lungful of air.

Nothing had ever tasted so good.

It was a split second of reprieve before I went back under. Dark water claimed me, and I thrashed against the sodden weight of my clothes, tugging at the rope at my wrists. It had loosened, just fractionally, when the soldier had used it to drag me down to the riverbank, so I tried to focus on freeing myself, overwhelming panic and a bright spark of anger writhing in my body.

Ngaire thrashed violently nearby, spluttering, crying out with pure hysteria whenever her head broke the surface of the water. It was tempting to turn and to scream back because my anger came with a sense of blame.

It was her fault we were here. If she'd swum earlier that day, in the light and with the safety net, we wouldn't be drowning in the dark.

Water claimed me again. My legs tiring from the effort of kicking against the binds. I pulled my hands one way and another, twisting them and then ripping one of them backwards to free myself from the binds. My wrist hurt, the rope tearing my skin. My chest burned, a desperate plea to get my head above the water again, a flare promising death. Bubbles slipped from my nose, the last vestiges of a held breath.

A soft sense of hopelessness sparked in my heart, rushing forward alongside the thought that I couldn't do it. With the one chance I had to save myself, instead of relying on others, I'd failed.

I'd told Niklaus I could win off my merit, and here I was, stuck beneath the surface.

My hand slipped, jerking backwards and free of the red rope tangled around my cuffed wrist. I used my hands and legs to propel myself up, up, up.

Air had never seemed so precious. With my arms free, it was easier to tread the water and keep my head above water. I took a deep breath and let myself sink long enough to reach for my feet, prising away the rope at my ankles with stiff, sore hands.

Without the terror of being bound, the certainty of sinking, I realised the river wasn't running as it had earlier in the day. It was my fear propelling me downstream.

I tried to remember what, if anything, I'd learned of swimming as a child. When the rain fell in Ilrea, water, garbage, and mud would fill ravage holes, creating small pools. They were putrid but still tempting enough for children who only knew water as rationed out to the thirsty. I could remember my brother, Mason, lanky limbed and floating on his back in the water, even though all common sense said his gigantic head should sink to the bottom. He'd drifted for minutes with his eyes closed as the sky poured more water down on him.

Now, I tried to mimic the child he was. Forcing my head back and my hips forward as if I were back in the barracks and lying on the bed. With my ears beneath the water, my body seemed to stay at the top of the river, buoyant. I calmed a little more. There was something inexplicably peaceful about floating in the moonlight. A moment where I felt joyously free; time could have passed in minutes or hours. It didn't matter, and I didn't care.

Until a hand caught my arm, Ngaire's stress still alive and

thriving, when she clung to me like a lifeline and dragged me beneath the water again with only a half breath of air. Keeping myself afloat was one thing but keeping Ngaire afloat, too, was impossible. Her fluster left her heavy, her rapid movement contradicting everything I tried to get back to the surface again. She curled around me, weighing me down, an anchor to send us to the bottom of the river.

It was anger, pure wrath, that saved my life. It burned bright in my chest, until I struck out, burying my fists against Ngaire's body, striking her until she let go of me. I didn't want to die. I needed to get to the surface. I needed to breathe.

The moment she let go, I kicked wildly for surface and then the riverbank. When the water became shallow, I dragged myself into the muddy banks and up onto my knees, retching at the burning into my chest. I lifted my head and stared into the darkened glassy water for any sight of Ngaire resurfacing.

"Ngaire!" I called. My voice was hoarse and croaky. "Ngaire!"

Her face broke through the surface, desperate for air. She thrashed no more, and I could see the red rope fastening her tight. Her movements had dulled, slowed.

Looking around, I searched for anything I could use to help her. I wanted to save her, but I couldn't throw myself back into the water. All I had was the loosened rope around my arm, and with shaking hands, I unwound it.

"Ngaire!" I called, again, forcing myself to stand, holding the red rope in both hands.

I waited for her to reappear, the flash of her pale face in the dark depths. I had a plan. I would throw her one end of the rope and use the other to tug her back to shore.

"Come on!" I screamed into the night hoarsely.

Her dark head broke the surface, and without hesitation, I threw the rope in her direction, and it landed to her right, bobbing in the water. "Grab it! Take the rope. I'll get you out."

208

Ngaire never took the other end. She slipped back below the water despite my desperate pleas to hold on. Instead, the rough rope began to sink. I dropped to the ground, sobbing, and Ngaire never resurfaced.

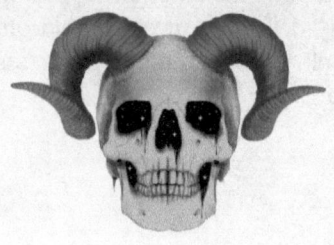

Chapter Eighteen

I lay in the muddy banks of the river, emotionally crippled and numbed to the core by the realisation that I fated anyone who worked with me in these trials to die.

The bright and lovely Ophelia had her heart ripped out of her chest and eaten by an angel. Cunning and sneaky Monika had fallen prey to savage harpies, who had torn her apart and left her for dead. Now Ngaire, too, had succumbed to the risks of being my friend—or in the very least, my associate. I hated she had died in the way she feared, trapped beneath the cold water, unable to draw a breath, struggling for the surface.

I cried and cried until there were no more tears, until all I could do was shiver and stare hopelessly at the bright moon.

'It's not your fault, Little One,' Samael murmured in my ear. *'Death is simply a part of living.'*

Heaving a sigh, I curled into a tighter ball, ignoring him, hating that his advice came too late to save Ngaire. I'd thought when he reappeared, I would be the happiest woman alive, but not even the devil pierced through the cold, lonely reality of my existence.

Soldiers marched through the edge of the water, having finally arrived, no doubt looking for the lost recruit. They crowded over me, demanding to know where Ngaire had gone, but I remained stubbornly silent, my teeth chattering as the cold set in my bones.

Within the hour, I was back in the medic rooms.

Heiau frowned as she leaned over me, calling for more blankets and muttering.

Nobody told me a thing, but soldiers marched a stretcher through the rooms, a white sheet covering the body, water dripping.

They had found her at last.

"Ophelia, Monika, Ngaire," I said beneath my breath, curled up tight on the uncomfortable bed. "Ophelia, Monika, Ngaire . . ."

I repeated the names until I drifted to sleep, three of many deaths through the trials, but the three I felt most responsible for, three names, along with Aieke, my first kill, I would never forget.

I was worse than the creatures of the otherworld. Humans expected them to kill, but I was a woman who dragged others to death thoughtlessly in my pursuit of living. I was the worst.

Soon, I was back in the barracks, my bed needed for more severe injuries. When I walked inside, it felt like everyone stared at me accusingly, the true recruits blaming me for the death of one of their own, the competitors looking curious about what had happened.

Guilt churned heavily in my gut.

When Niklaus tried to intercept me, I cringed away, dodging around him and throwing myself onto the top bunk. I wanted the warmth of his presence, the chance of a hug and reassurance, but I didn't deserve it.

"Stay away from me," I said when Nash appeared at the side

of my bunk, concern bright in his hazel gaze. I stared dully back at him before twisting to face the wall and blocking him out. "Please."

"Tav," he mumbled, his hand brushing my shoulders. "What happened?"

The cold of the previous night would never leave me. I was chilled right through.

I wasn't sure why I answered him.

"You sink or you swim," I said, parroting the words of Major Akua. "I swam, and Ngaire didn't."

Nash squeezed my shoulder. "Octavia . . ."

"Don't," I said harshly. "Just go away, Nash."

He didn't listen. He climbed into the top bunk with me and wrapped his arms around my body, tight and snug. With his head nestled in the crook of my shoulder, the warmth of his body finally settled my shaking. Anyone who didn't know us might think we were lovers entwined in bed, but all I felt for Nash was relief. It had scared me that he'd take the demand and run with it, leaving me alone.

"It's okay to cry," he whispered into my hair. "You lost someone."

"I know."

Tears never flowed. They'd dried up on the riverbank. I stared at the wall and wondered if Nash would be the next person to die, simply because he'd chosen to stay near me. I was poison, and I hated to infect him, but I couldn't bring myself to pull away.

"But I think I killed her . . ." I whispered when I thought he'd fallen asleep, but his body tensed behind me, indicating that he'd heard.

"What do you mean, Tav?"

"I could have . . ."

A frustrated sniffle rolled from my lips. I had floated in that water, basking in a moment of serenity, while Ngaire struggled for air. The partner I was supposed to keep alive was going to enter the war with me, and I had failed her.

"I should have . . ."

"You can't think like that, Octavia," Nash said. "Not with regret and wishful thinking when the moment's passed. Many people are going to die by the end of these trials, and that's not on you. You're not responsible for their lives. We're doing what we can to survive, and you did that last night. Most of us would have done the same thing. You know it."

I shook my head, and Nash sighed softly into my hair as I mumbled, "You don't even know what I did."

"I trust that you did your best."

Nash's statement drew a breathy scoff from my chest, and I rolled in his arms to get a better look at him.

In the low light of the barracks, he looked as haunted as I did, gaunt and broken beneath the mask of optimism he wore to protect himself.

"You're a fool, Nash Wickham."

The corner of his lips quirked. "A fool but alive."

Nash squeezed me in a hug until I relaxed in his grip.

He shifted on the bed. "Get some sleep, Octavia. Tomorrow's a new day."

"Since you're now without a partner," Major Akua said the next morning, "I'll be allocating you to others to train with as I see fit."

An edge scorched her tone, as if I'd put her out by losing my partner and ruined her day.

She turned her attention to everyone else. "There will be no training this morning."

A murmur rippled through the group, and someone asked, "Why?"

When Major Akua responded, her wide, vicious smile was obvious, even with the leather mask fixed across her face, emotion glittering brightly in her eyes. "Lady Wrath has requested to see you."

If I could have felt anything beyond the numb edge of my grief, my stomach would have turned to stone. Instead, I lingered at the back of the group, apathy dragging my feet, as we marched through the dark doorways of Wrath Hall, to where the angel waited for us.

Wrath wore no armour as they waited for us, appearing smaller without the padding of leather and steel.

I couldn't help but see her within the context of Heiau's story. An older sister, seething with so much anger that her rage burned through the world.

She sat on a stool with one knee propped over the other. A hellhound lay next to her, its yellow eyes fixed on us, a snarl reverberating through its body as if waiting for her permission to attack. We shuffled into the room, the angel browsing a stack of letters on her lap.

Wrath's black-and-red hair was twisted into a thick braid that fell over her shoulder. Her slender arms bared in a loose tunic, displaying the metallic red ink that marked her suntanned skin, the shifting image of a lion stark on her right bicep.

If not for the overwhelming amount of power she radiated and the strong, dark wings taut against her back, she could have been any woman in her army. We stood in structured lines, kneeling in front of the angel of sin.

She paused her inspection of the papers, lifting her gaze to us, mouth pursed into an unimpressed line. Her dark eyes were ablaze with simmering rage. She lay the papers against her knee, slowly and purposefully smoothing out the creases as she made us wait, even though my apathy, a flicker of fear, ignited inside of me. I was partnerless, and they had claimed we lived and died by our partners. Would this be my public execution?

Wrath cleared her throat, and we bowed our heads. I kept my gaze on the tiled floor.

The slap of a fist against armour rang out as Major Akua saluted her commander, a strong and silent indicator that we were ready. She received a sharp nod in return.

"Nikaus Heira and Margot Galatea," Wrath called, her voice ringing with authority.

Relief set my veins on fire before irritation chased it away.

What had they done to bring us in front of the angel? I watched Niklaus closely as he straightened, holding out his hand to help Margot up.

"You may approach."

Tension in the room thickened. Our group parted in the middle to make way for the two of them to approach. Niklaus, of course, stepped forward first. His white-knuckled grip on Margot pulled her to move a step behind him, shielding her with the bulk of his body. She had paled in the face of conflict and under Wrath's scrutiny. Where she had once been a demanding, entitled woman, pampered in a dangerous position of privilege, loved by an angel, she looked half scared out of her mind.

I didn't blame her. If she had heard the story of the Sinning Twins, if the tale truly came from history, and if Wrath had heard that she was Envy's prized possession, then Margot had a worse fate coming. She was in a world of danger, with a surefire way for Wrath to hurt her brother, shattering the jewel of his collection.

The angel settled back in her seat, studying the pair closely. When she shifted in position, her hellhound moved, stretching before it crouched on its haunches, those golden eyes fixed on Niklaus.

"Tell me," the angel began, "how have you found your training?"

It felt like a dangerous question, and it lingered in the air.

Niklaus, to his credit, didn't look disturbed. He shifted his weight forward, the muscles in his shoulders tensing, then relaxing as he prepared to answer. When he did, he looked at ease.

"It's been fine."

"Just fine?" Wrath asked.

The temperature in the room rose, the tension so thick I could have cut it with my sword.

Margot cringed back. She tried desperately not to look in Wrath's direction. Once the queen of a castle, almost my tormenter, she looked pathetic.

I felt a vindictive satisfaction.

"Yes," Niklaus confirmed fervently. "We humans define fine as satisfactory or very well. If you prefer those answers, Lady Wrath."

I couldn't believe he'd said that with the sarcastic bite in his tone, the challenge burning through the room.

"Hmm." The angel's lips had thinned further, the glow in her eyes flattening dangerously. "You don't think it's been"—the angel turned over the papers on her knee, her voice high-pitched and mocking—"and I quote . . .'Utterly boring and cruel.' 'A waste of time when I know Envy's leagues will slaughter us.' 'Foolish, if Wrath thinks she can win.'"

Finally, Niklaus reacted. His throat bobbed, and he leaned his weight away from the answers, pressing against Margot, his hand snaking back to grip her wrist. "I don't know where you got those quotes from." His cockiness dulled.

"Don't lie to me, boy," Wrath snapped.

My anger built at Niklaus and Margot, encouraged by the angel's rising rage, her influence prickling against her skin, little sparks intent to catch and create a flame.

"Step out of the way so I might speak to Galatea."

A sour edge lingered in Niklaus's gaze. It reminded me of when were four, and he'd bitten into a lemon, unable to back down from the challenge, dared by his brother to eat the whole thing.

He stayed still, stubbornly shielding Margot from trouble.

She pressed her hand against his arm, in a gentle, placating movement. "It's okay, Nik."

She sounded resigned, as if she'd accepted her oncoming death, should Wrath have learned what she meant to Envy. His body relaxed fractionally, and he stepped to the side.

I understood why. He'd sworn to Mikhael that he would protect Margot, and Niklaus was a man of his word. It irritated me that she had someone so resolutely in her corner, and I simply had death on my hands.

In the few spare seconds Niklaus had given her, Margot pulled herself together, turning into a reflection of the woman she once was. She stood tall and haughty, as if she were wearing one of her finest gowns instead of rough-spun clothing and heavy armour of a recruit. Her chin was lifted, head held high, as she approached the confrontation head on. The only giveaway were the flushed red splotches appearing on her neck and ears.

"Yes, Lady Wrath?"

The three words dripped with an edge as if the angel had impeded on her time by calling us here, as if it were an inconvenience that needed to be dealt with. As if Margot Galatea were queen of a realm.

Wrath bristled. Her fingers curled around the papers, and she stood so abruptly that the stool toppled to the floor.

Within two steps, they were standing so close that Margot must have been able to feel the heat rolling from the angel's body, practically nose-to-nose.

"'Dear Mikhael . . .'" Wrath mocked, and Margot's hands fisted behind her back, her spine ramrod straight. "'I miss you. The training here is so dull; I cannot wait for when you march across the plains to find me again . . .'"

Margot said nothing, but red blotches on her skin spread higher, disappearing beneath her leather mask. Her clenched fists trembled, and for the first time, a pang of sympathy stung me. Nobody could save her in this moment, nothing that could be done.

"'Dear Mikhael . . .'" Wrath began again in her crude

imitation of Margot. She stepped forward, and Margot stepped back. "'I wait patiently for when you cross the borders to slay Wrath's army. The long days of training are foolish when I know, as you do, that Envy's leagues will slaughter us with you commanding them . . .'"

The angel paused, silence sinking between them, as she gave Margot time to explain herself. When the woman remained silent, Wrath crumpled the papers and dropped them to the floor, where they rolled towards the rest of us.

"'Dear Mikhael . . .'" Wrath hissed, her power extending outwards until I flinched, her influence a solid kick to the stomach.

Sweat beaded at my brow, my muscles tense, and my growing anger left me bursting at the seams to lurch forward and throttle someone. It wasn't anger at Margot, though. My stomach burned at the angel's righteousness, at Wrath, for daring to humiliate her like this after I'd stood in front of Mikhael myself and twisted his love for her into a demand to let her be free.

A recruit at the front of the group staggered forward a step, then another as Wrath read out passages. "'I can't wait to see you slide a knife into Wrath's heart, to end this war and free yourself from Envy. We will be together. We will be safe. We will be free. I miss you so much, my sweet.'"

Margot's slender throat bobbed as her treasonous words were announced to the room, but she remained mute beneath her leather mask, rage dancing in her eyes.

Margot Galatea had faced Envy through day and night for a year, while he tried to break her down. She had the strength of will to stand tall in the face of the sin.

"Who is Mikhael?" Wrath asked. When Margot didn't answer, she swiftly pulled a blade from her belt and pressed the sharp edge against the woman's soft throat. Margot stiffened. Wrath turned her blazing gaze on Niklaus instead. "Tell me."

Tension in Niklaus's body was unmistakable, corded into his

muscles.

"He's my brother," he admitted—but only when the first bead of blood pooled at Margot's throat and slipped down her skin. "He forfeited to Envy."

"What does he do for Lord Envy?" Wrath asked.

It was strange, I thought, for one sin to use a title for another, affording a respect that didn't seem to correlate with the war between them.

"He's commanding the front line . . ." Niklaus said tersely. Rage and pain warred in his expression for betraying his brother. Which would be worse betrayal? Selling out what he knew of Mikhael's position or letting Wrath slit his brother's lover's throat? He couldn't win.

Wrath turned her attention back to Margot. "Why did you write to him?"

When Margot answered, her voice was soft. "We were lovers. He was so different before. I wanted him to remember me. I wanted him to free himself of Envy and be *my* Mikhael. I wanted him back. I wanted . . ." Words failed her, and Margot Galatea finally broke eye contact as the first tear coursed down her cheeks. "I wrote to him because I love him."

Wrath had gone still, the knife still clenched in her grip, poised against Margot's jugular.

"Are you going to kill her?" Niklaus asked, moving closer, as if he could intercept the angel before she bled Margot dry.

"Not yet," Wrath stated, dropping the knife to her side. Her wings rustled with agitation. "You're going to do a very special task for me, Margot Galatea. If you refuse, I'll drag you in front of your lover and feed you his still-beating heart."

Margot nodded. "I don't have much of a choice, do I?"

"Good girl." The angel smirked, lifting her crimson eyes to the rest of us, as if she had forgotten we were standing there and emotionally wound taut by the rage she emitted. "Dismissed."

We made it three steps out the door before the first fight broke out.

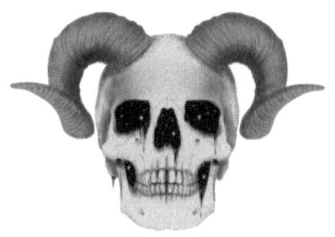

Chapter Nineteen

"What task did she give you?" I asked sharply. I'd cornered Margot in the barracks as soon as she came back, demanding an explanation, panicked because freeing her was for nothing.

"Nothing."

"Nothing never actually means nothing," I pointed out. "Which must mean it's something serious."

"Exactly," Margot sneered, giving me a pointed look. "It means I'm not telling you because it's none of your devil-damned business, Octavia!"

"What's going on?" Niklaus drawled, suddenly standing too close for comfort.

I tensed; I hadn't noticed him. Facing him quickly, I was more at ease with Margot at my back than Niklaus.

"Nothing," I bit out.

"Nothing never means nothing," he mocked, proving he'd

been eavesdropping. He leaned against the bunk, blocking me in. My heart turned to stone as he smirked and asked, "So, Octavia . . . where's Sam?"

"Busy," I said, my mouth turning dry.

I'd thought Niklaus had forgotten about it.

"Interesting," Niklaus murmured, his green gaze alight in a way that told me he wasn't going to let it go. Margot squeezed past us, cruelly leaving me at his mercy. "You lost a partner, and he hasn't stepped up to fill the spot. Slack."

"That would make him a bit of a dick, don't you think?" I asked, folding my arms over my pounding heart. "To abandon his partner just because Ngaire . . ."

The word died in my throat.

"I would have," Niklaus said without a beat of hesitation.

It took everything in me not to laugh.

"Devilshit, Nik."

"Are you calling me a liar, love?"

"Don't call me that," I snapped. "We both know you wouldn't abandon Envy's princess."

Niklaus pressed me in, and nerves fluttered in my belly like the rapid flutter of dragonfly wings. "For you, I would."

"Don't kid yourself." I rolled my eyes. "You wouldn't do that to your brother. I thought we sorted this, Nik. I don't want you, and you don't want me. You're going to stay the hell out of my way."

"If you don't want me." He chuckled. "Why do you keep watching me?"

"I don't!" I blurted before struggling to regain my composure. "Is your ego really that big? You're not special, Nik."

We stared each other down, and he shifted to rake his fingers through his hair. It had grown out long enough he kept brushing it out of his eyes, a tell of how long we had spent here.

"I won't forget, Octavia," he said, gazing at me.

"Forget what?"

222

"That you saved my life," Niklaus whispered, leaning close, his full lips a breath away from my cheek. "You may be done waiting for me, Octavia, but I'll wait for you. I'll wait for the only woman strong enough to save me." His lips grazed my skin, a feather touch of a kiss pulling a shiver from me. "When you're done playing games with Sam, I'll be waiting for you."

The devil's name was like cold water splashed onto my soul, wrenching me from the allure of the moment.

I slid my palms up Niklaus's chest, studying the smirk at the corner of his lips, before I shoved back as hard as I could, forcing a harsh edge as I spoke.

"You'll die waiting, Nik."

Hours later, cold and alone on my bunk, I couldn't help but wonder if Niklaus truly thought that I'd saved him when I could barely save myself. I tried to forget him, put him out of my mind. Niklaus wouldn't get me through these trials. Samael would be my path to success.

As I drifted into a deep sleep, I prayed the devil would dance through my dreams.

"Welcome to the basics of poisons," Major Akua said as we entered a brick building, bypassing a muzzled hellhound at the door. "General Inaina will preside over these lessons." She turned to survey us all, eyes narrowed like a disappointed parent, and shook her head. "If you embarrass me, recruits, I'll have you digging out the latrines."

Major Akua gave me a hard look, as if I were the most obvious culprit, then disappeared.

A cluttered mass of chairs filled the large room, and a long table sat at the head of it.

General Inaina was nowhere to be found, so we clattered about choosing chairs, naturally separating into groups split between trial competitors and natural-born Wrathlings.

For all that we had endured together, we would never be a unit. I sat at the front of the room between Nash and Finley. The curly-haired man sat backwards on his chair, chin resting on his arms, complaining about the mushed grain we'd had for breakfast.

"Finley . . ." I said as the hall door opened and General Inaina appeared.

"We've had the same thing every day for the past six weeks," he continued. "I'm just saying it would be nice if—"

"Fin!" I said.

General Inaina stood in front of us. Her smoky grey hair threaded with red was wound into a thick bun at her nape. With her arms folded and her gaze sharp, she was intimidating.

"What?!" Finley turned, only then realising the general was standing behind him.

"Nobody cares what you think of the food, recruit," General Inaina said. "What I do care about is that you pay attention in this class. Which starts with sitting in your chair properly."

Finley scrambled around in his seat, his cheeks blooming red as he nodded in a quick, submissive gesture. "Yes, General. Sorry, General."

It seemed Finley Nightingale had very quickly learned that the best way to survive in Wrath's army was through submissive compliance.

General Inaina paced around the room, taking the time to study us as we stared back. She paused by two different recruits, barking demands to fix their sloppy uniforms. When she was satisfied, she moved back to the front of the room and lifted a large case onto the table. "I mean what I say about paying attention in this room," General Inaina said with undeniable, firm authority. "We are studying poisons. One moment of inattentiveness, and you could kill yourself or your partner. Today, I'll introduce them all, and over the coming weeks, you'll study until you know them inside out."

Quick murmurs swirled across the room. General Inaina pulled bottles out of the case.

My sights caught on one in particular. It looked suspiciously like the vial I had protected for weeks, the one I had walked across the Envylands to deliver to this woman. My palms turned sweaty, and my breathing felt harder than normal.

Had I carried a poison here? Who was the crone looking to poison?

"Are you paying attention?" General Inaina snapped.

Blinking, I glanced up and realised the full focus of her glare was on me, my attention caught so fully by the possibilities that I'd missed everything she'd said.

"Yes?" I said hesitantly.

"Go on, then . . ." Her brow arched, belying her disbelief. "Answer the question."

"Uhh," I mumbled.

My ears burned with embarrassment.

General Inaina sighed loudly and turned her attention to the rest of the room.

"Can anyone else name a deadly poison?"

Peliela stood quickly, standing tall and at attention. She tapped a salute against her chest. "Belladonna."

"Correct. Anyone else? You need not stand up to answer."

Peliela quickly dropped back into her seat, her head bowed.

"Uh, Hemlock?" someone called.

"Good. Give me more!" General Inaina demanded, only to be met with silence. She shook her head, clicking her tongue. "In this class, we will focus on several core deadly poisons. These are not what you would bring to general battle, as most of our battles are a collision of warm flesh and cold steel. However, some of you will slip further down into enemy territory than you might think possible and will have the chance to poison food and water supplies. Or you may find yourself in a position where you will need to poison yourself. Why might you have to do this?"

Deafening silence reinforced the nervousness in the room. If Ngaire were here, she would have the answer, and it was for her that I raised my hand slowly, mulling over the information she had given me over the past weeks.

"Yes, recruit," General Inaina called on me.

"In case the Envy troops take us," I whispered, hesitant.

"Speak up!" she barked.

"We'd . . . we'd poison ourselves before giving away information."

General Inaina's brief smile crinkled the edges of her eyes. "Very good."

I glowed beneath her fleeting praise.

She turned back to the vials she had laid out, adjusting them carefully.

"We have ten deadly poisons for you to learn. Strychnine, Ricin, Mandrake, Devil's Eyes—also known as Henbane, Opium Poppy, Belladonna, Adder's Tongue, Datura, Salvia Divinorium, and Hemlock."

The potion I'd given the general was called Devil's Eyes.

I leaned forward, watching with mounting interest, but she didn't start with it.

"Ricin." General Inaina picked up a vial, the contents small and nearly transparent. It looked as if it contained nothing more than water. "This highly concentrated dose has no known antidote. If you ingest a good dose of this, you're dead. It'll cause fluid buildup in the lungs, which is a nasty way to die. Victims of ricin poisoning will often experience fevers, nausea, and seizures in the short time before death." She placed the vial back on the table. "In tiny doses and with caution, however, it can be used medicinally."

"Hemlock." She lifted a milky-white potion and swirled it around gently. "Easily identifiable. It smells like hellhound piss and will cause a quick muscle paralysis. Incidentally, however, it can be used as an antidote to our next poison."

"Strychnine." General Inaina flashed a small round vial filled with a pale grey poison. It looked like dirty water in a stoppered bottle. "This poison is the most painful of those we have here today. It will cause full body convulsions, a rapid rise in blood pressure, while the heart rate slows. It has been described as excruciating—of course, few live to recount the experience. As I mentioned, Hemlock, in the right dose, may be used as an antidote for this poison. Questions?"

Nobody spoke.

"Opium Poppy." She looked at the soft brown liquid. "This is chaos in a bottle. Opium poisoning will cause the victim to behave erratically, and often induces a stupor-like state before the organs shut down, inciting death. It's a slower way to go but amusing if you have time to play with your victims." That sentiment and the way the general said it, a catlike gleam in her eyes, left me unsettled and knotting my fingers in my lap to keep from fidgeting. "It hails from the Lustlands, where opium is smoked recreationally."

She moved on quickly. My head was spinning with the rapid-fire information.

"Datura."

This poison was a deep purple, and I could imagine someone not noticing if they slipped it into their drink.

"Also known as The Devil's Trumpet for the shape of the flower it hails from. Traditionally, this can be used as a sleeping aid. You'll see many people in the sinning cities using it for a good night's rest, but in large doses, it becomes a powerful hallucinogenic, and sleep gives way to death."

At the back of the room, someone whispered something about the poison.

General Inaina glared at them sharply, waiting for silence to continue as she held up a stark, bright red concoction. "Adder's Tongue. This poison grants a quick—although painful—death. It is said to feel like your throat and stomach have been set on fire.

Ingestion of Adder's Tongue causes swelling of the throat, loss of the airway, and death some few minutes after."

"Henbane," she said. I leaned forward as she picked up the pale mauve liquid, my interest piquing. "Also known as Devil's Eyes. Don't let the colour deceive you—this poison smells like death itself."

Before anyone could protest, General Inaina prised the stopper free, and the stench of rot wafted through the room.

I had to press my nose into my arm, eyes watering to avoid the smell. My head spun, the world seeming to tilt on its axis.

"The effect of Henbane starts with dizziness and delirium, descends quickly into an unarousable coma, and gives way to death. And that it simply from smelling this potion, let alone ingesting it."

A flurry of unease seemed to spread through the room, recruits staggering from their chairs and flinging themselves out of the room. After a wide-eyed, pointed look at Nash, I followed suit, staggering out to the street, inhaling deep breaths of fresh air to clear my head.

The dizziness seemed to worsen before it cleared, and for a moment, I didn't know which way was up. The sun bore down on me, hot and relentless, making everything worse.

"She's mad," Finley croaked, bent over beside me. His fist pressed against his chest as if he could beat the influence of the poison out of his body. "Absolutely mad."

General Inaina appeared in the doorway, seemingly unaffected by the Henbane. She looked us over as if performing a headcount, then nodded. "Return within two minutes. We still have three more poisons to cover before lunch."

Reluctantly, I followed Nash and Finley back into the room and fell into the same chairs we had abandoned. Despite the now-open windows, I could have sworn I could still smell the poison.

General Inaina didn't wait for us to get comfortable before she continued.

"Salvia Divinorium." The general reached for a pale-blue liquid. Her fingers twisted at the stopper, and we all tensed, causing her eyes to gleam with mirth. "Good to see you're paying attention. This poison will leave you a wreck, giggling, screaming, gasping. You'll be caught in the nightmare of your own muddled mind until your heart goes out. We have an antidote for salvia poisoning, and it must be drunk within the hour of consumption."

"Belladonna." She held up another almost-transparent poison. "Only a tiny drop is necessary, so use it sparingly. This pretty lady induces blurred vision that turns into absolute blindness, confusion, tremors, agitation, and death follows swiftly. While there is an antidote, often, the poison works too swiftly for it to be consumed with any effect. If you ingest Belladonna, very few people could help you."

"Mandrake." The final vial was raised for our inspection; the concoction green to look at, thick when she tilted it to the side. "It tastes sweet. This is an anaesthetic, and it induces a slow paralysation of the victim. First the fingers and tongue go numb, telltale signs, spots in the vision as the limbs fall heavy and drag. Breathing becomes difficult, and the heart slows as the trunk is affected. The victim will crumple, and lie there for well over an hour, unable to breathe properly, unable to call for help as they die. There's an antidote to Mandrake that will reverse all symptoms if applied in time, which we will cover in later lessons."

A shiver worked its way down my spine. The entire morning left a bitter twist in my gut.

General Inaina placed the last potion down on the table and shifted to stand in front of them. She knotted her fingers together and stood in contemplative silence for a moment, letting the information sink in.

"Questions?" After a beat, a hand rose. "Yes, recruit?"

"Some of these poisons, I've heard of them, in cooking and

remedies back home. They can't be that deadly if we use them all the time . . . ?"

Their half statement, half question rang hesitation clear in their voice.

My attention moved swiftly back to the general.

General Inaina nodded, tucking a wisp of her smoke-grey hair out from her face. "Some of these poisons in small amounts can be beneficial—medicinal, even. When we use them to poison others, they're prepared in concentrated doses, much like the sharpened edge of a blade. They're intended to kill."

"Oh, okay . . ."

The general moved back to her case, reaching inside to pull out a fistful of small black pills. "You will all carry one of these with you, somewhere easily accessible. Let me be clear when I say you would rather die than get tortured at the hands of Envy's demonic leagues, and Belladonna will make the process swift."

I thought of the young girl in Wrath armour forgotten beneath Envy's castle, wounded, infected, and left to die, who didn't voice an objection. A quick death was better than the way Aieke had suffered. A quick death would have been better than my fumbling end to her life.

General Inaina glanced at the ticking timepiece on the wall. "Lunch time, recruits. Be back here within the hour."

We collected the small pills, and I tried to catch the general before she disappeared, but she evaded me with ease, leaving me with no answers about the Henbane.

The smell of roasting meat led us away from the tiled town and out towards the thick of tents and soldiers. One of the camp kitchens had set up just outside the town—as per usual—to feed recruits who weren't offsite for training. We gathered by the edge of the makeshift kitchen, watching the appointed cook cleave roasted meat dripping with fat with a heavy knife and dropping it in a giant pot.

"What are we having?" someone asked.

The cook looked up, her face bare of the suffocating leather masks, skin ruddy from the heat of the fire, sweat dripping off the curve of her chin and into the meal. Dark hair clung to her skin.

"Skinned recruit," she answered, laughing at her own joke, as if it were the funniest thing she'd heard all day long. "No, no. Just hellhound gone lame. They make a good soup."

Someone groaned, and the cook scoffed. "Don't knock it 'til you've tried it, recruit."

My glance slid to the courtyard behind us, at the muzzled beasts, a feral glint in their eyes. I hadn't worked out if they were there for our protection or to keep us in line, but I didn't want to get too close, still haunted by the feral beasts that had stalked us in the forest.

"Who cares what's in it?" Finley shoved past me to pick up one of the tin bowls and held it out to the cook, who beamed back at him. "I'm starved!" He broke the tension and the hesitation, recruits piling in after him.

Joining the line and bowl in hand, I waited for my serve. By the time I settled on the ground with a chunk of half stale bread in my other hand, Finley had slurped down most of his soup.

"Is it that good?" Nash asked with a laugh.

"Mhm," Finley said through his mouthful. "It's sweet, like they've put in a heap of the good stuff. Didn't think the hellhound would be this good. You think she'll give me seconds?"

I shovelled a spoonful into my own mouth, nodding with agreement as the overly sweet gravy coated my tongue. I found myself staring down into the mix and sucking it from the edge of the spoon. "Wonder if there're more peas in . . . What are you doing?"

Finley was shaking his hands in a strange way. Clenching his fingers as if they'd gone numb. His face screwed up. "My tongue feels weird."

An unsettled feeling washed through me, my spoon dropping back into the dirt. "What?"

"Yeah," he grunted, "and it's like my fingers don't want to work."

I twisted, spitting my lunch onto the ground beside me, scraping my tongue. "Water," I croaked, snatching for Nash's canteen and drinking quickly.

He'd stopped eating, watching me closely.

"What's going on, Octavia?" he asked as Finley started to hyperventilate, fear flashing in his eyes.

"It's not supposed to be sweet," I said, kicking at the bowl and sending it spilling across the dirt. "It's just hound and gravy. There's nothing sweet in there."

"But . . ." He stared down at his own bowl.

Other recruits began to complain about numbness in their hands.

When he looked up, his face was taut, grim.

"Mandrake. Sweet-tasting paralysis."

"Fuck!" I hissed.

"She didn't tell us what the antidote was . . ." Nash said.

"Who cares?" I pulled myself to my feet. "Finley ate a whole bowl. We need to go to the medics. *Now*."

He jumped to his feet, shaking his own hands, flicking his fingers.

"Are you okay?" I asked cautiously, bracing a hand under Finley's armpit and hauling him upright.

"Yeah," Nash grunted. "I don't know if I'm feeling it, or I'm just paranoid that I'm feeling it. I didn't eat that much, did I?"

"Just . . ." I grunted as Finley found his feet and promptly lost them, his legs bucking beneath him. He staggered to the side, whimpering that he couldn't feel anything, before tumbling towards me. The full force of his deadweight twinged at my knee, and recruits scattered around us, some shouting for help as the

232

poison began to affect them.

Niklaus appeared and pulled me free of Finley, grasping my arms before I could protest and dragging me out from beneath his weight.

"Don't," I said sharply, scrambling to my feet, unwilling to accept his help.

"Don't start with me, Octavia." His face was in mine, too close as he inspected my eyes. Devil knows what for. "How much did you eat?"

"Not much," I said. "Did you eat?"

"Mar and I hadn't been served yet." He nodded at Margot, who watched the crowd of recruits disapprovingly with her lips pursed. "I'll get Finley, you get Nash."

"All right." I nodded, turning to find the blonde man in the throes of a panic attack, his head buried between his knees. "Nash?" I hurried for him as Niklaus braced to lift Finley, dragging him over his shoulders like a sack of grain.

"Listen up!" The command in his voice cut through the panic, wild-eyed recruits stopping in their tracks. "If you haven't eaten, you're fine. Help someone who has. If you can walk, start moving to the medics. Now, if you fall, someone will come back for you."

Silence clung to the aftermath of his demands, and rage flashed across Niklaus's face.

He wasn't a man used to being ignored.

"Go!" he boomed, creating a flurry of action. "Move!"

Recruits scrambled back towards the buildings, and the cook laughed in our wake, clicking her tongue. "Better hurry, or it will really be recruit stew for supper!"

Nash fought me the entire way, swearing that his legs barely worked, nearly suffocating himself in the panic, and when I got him inside, my own hands tingling with loss of sensation, we found General Inaina waiting for us.

She stood at attention, clearly unimpressed. "I spend the

morning teaching you about poisons, and you don't pay enough attention to stop yourself from ingesting it?" she asked, disapproval dripping from every word. "Pathetic, recruits. You should be ashamed."

Her disappointment had my stomach flipping, and I couldn't bring myself to meet her gaze.

I'd wanted to do well in her poisons class. I'd wanted to know the reason for the Henbane, and she looked as if we weren't worth a second more of her time.

"I expect you all back in the hall in twenty minutes."

She marched out, and Heiau appeared from the back rooms, wiping a hand on the front of her medic's tunic, while holding a basket of vials filled with a mud-coloured liquid with the other.

"Don't worry," Heiau said, offering a small smile. "We've literally all been here before. There's very few people who don't eat the soup."

Somehow, that didn't make me feel any better.

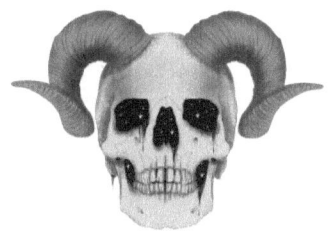

Chapter Twenty

General Inaina put us through an intensive course on each of the poisons until I dreamt of them at night. We learned to taste some of them, the antidotes on hand for quick relief, but only administered after we had experienced the brutal side effects.

It was only on the last day of poisons training that I found a moment with General Inaina, on the pretence that I had no partner and needed someone to train with. She saw right through my excuse, given the unimpressed tension in her face.

"Why?" I asked, picking up the vial of Henbane and rolling it between my fingers. "Did the crone give this to you?"

It was foolish to think that a general in Wrath's army would have answered my questions, but I had to satiate my curiosity.

"What makes you think that's any of your business, recruit?"

I shrugged, a play at nonchalance. "I'm the one that carried it across the Envylands. I think that means I deserve some answers."

"You *deserve* it?" she asked, chuckling darkly. Derision dripped from that word. She stepped close, her voice lowering so they would not overhear us. "I am a decorated general in this army. I have served here since I was sixteen years old and was declared barren. I have defeated countless enemies, poisoned entire camps of those green mongrels, and barely survived. What have you done, recruit, to deserve information from me?"

My fingers clenched the vial. "I stood in front of Gluttony and Envy and survived. Friends died before my eyes. I watched monsters come alive. I learned what it is and how it feels to be so gluttonous and excessive that you might explode, to be so envious that you could tear yourself apart for wanting everything so badly. And now I stand, with my head bowed to an anger that runs through my veins. I've never been a violent person, but Wrath has brought bitterness from my core to the surface of my being, and I still stand in front of you, surviving each day." The emotion rising, prickling at my eyes, was too much for me. "I could have laid down and died a thousand times over since these trials started, and I'm still here, still alive. That, *General,* is what entitles me to know why I risked my life carrying you poison."

"The trials are no borderlands war . . ."

"No. They're *worse* because we're battling ourselves as well as the enemy. All to impress a devil that doesn't really care."

"Why did you join the trials?" she asked. "It was your choice to endure so much."

"Why didn't you?" I countered. "Were you afraid each decade that the devil bid you to play? Too afraid to try."

"Never," she snapped. "Don't think yourself better than those of us who strive for a better life where we are rather than the fantasy of a city that may not exist."

"Then, tell me!" I demanded, gaining unwanted attention.

General Inaina stared at me, her eyes narrowed, the deepening lines in her forehead warning that I might have made myself an enemy for life, one I truly didn't need.

"You're all dismissed!" she said.

Recruits scattered in every direction, more than willing to take the afternoon for themselves.

When the room emptied, General Inaina shook her head. "That means you, too." Stiffly, I strode for the door, my pace too quick. "Wait!"

I paused in the doorway.

"Give it back, recruit."

"Give what back?" Refusing to look at her, I stared at the exit.

"The Devil's Eyes," General Inaina growled. "Or I'll treat you to a taste test."

I heard the *shink* of metal as she unsheathed a weapon, and I considered whether I could get out the door before she ran me through, but I still felt lethargic and worn out from training, swimming, poisoning, and life.

Turning, I jerked the vial in her direction.

If it smashed, we'd both die. A nonpoetic ending to a tough life.

General Inaina was quicker than I gave her credit for, her weapon-worn hands catching the vial with ease. "A piece of advice for the still-alive fool." She tucked the poison away. "Stop making people want to kill you because, one day, we may just do it." She soldiered past me, her shoulder ramming into my own so hard that my body ached from the impact, and I stood alone, in the now-empty hall, no better off than I had been before.

A free afternoon was a rare occurrence in our training.

We scattered before Major Akua could appear and put us to work for looking too idle. A group of competitors ended up together, the same old cluster of Ilrean's—plus some extras, hanging around the balance beam on the side of the hill. The sun sizzled my bare skin as I dropped my mask and rolled back my sleeves.

"Which do you think has been worse?" Helina had appeared out of nowhere, joining us without her partner, and I'd instinctively put space between us. There was nothing left to trust about Helina Archer. "Gluttony, Envy, or Wrath?" It was a heavy question, fracturing the peacefulness I'd felt a moment before.

"They're all as bad as each other," Niklaus said as he pulled his shirt over his head, baring his tattooed chest.

I loathed that I caught myself looking, my gaze flickering to his knowing grin, before I purposefully shut my eyes.

He had the audacity to drop next to me in the grass, his arm brushing mine, sending a jolt of mixed feelings through my body.

"Go away," I murmured.

"Never," he said with a chuckle. "I told you, love, I'll wait forever."

Finley swung himself up onto the beam and then hung down the way children did. His knees hooked over the sturdiest part, his curly hair falling from his face and skin darkening as the blood rushed to his head. "This trial is taking forever. A week in Gula, a month in Invidia, it feels like it's been a year of marching and 'Yes, ma'am,' 'No, ma'am.'"

"Maybe that's the trial," Nash said. "March until we die."

"A bittersweet end," I mumbled.

Heat and the small sense of freedom we had lulled me into relaxing, until sleep claimed me, calling for all the time I'd missed.

This time, Samael sat on a throne of skulls; the emptiness where their eyes had once been seemed to follow every step I took. The darkness that swirled through the room parted to make way for me.

Shadows shrouded him again, his face unseen, although his long body stretched across his throne, presenting idleness.

'Hello, Octavia,' he purred.

His use of my name pulled a shiver from my body. It caught me between breathlessness and alarm. The way he said it, the caress of his voice, resonated within my soul as a predator despite how much I wanted him to say it again.

"Samael," I greeted, wanting to sound as smooth and effortless as he did but lacked the finesse, as per usual. "Where are we? Is this Eternis?"

The thought left me chilled, that Eternis could be a place of darkness and decay instead of the land of our dreams. We might have been chasing a myth across the world, and this was what waited for us?

'No,' Samael refuted, his voice soft in my mind. *'This is another world, a realm they once destined me for, before I found my home here.'*

It took some courage, but I inspected the cavernous space. It was large and earthy, as if we'd burrowed further underground than I could fathom, when I stepped to the side, venturing to look further, brittle bones crunched beneath my feet.

I looked down at the shattered ribcage beneath my heel, the Wrath armour torn to shreds beside it. It was strangely warm, sweat gathering at my hairline.

When a screeching sound echoed from the tunnel, I twisted back to face the devil, hands behind my back. "How do you know what it looks like if you came here instead?"

Samael stretched, almost catlike in the long languid movement.

He rose from the throne and descended the steps until he towered me.

Disappointment fizzled in my belly that I could see only his strong jawline and the curve of his thick horns.

239

'This is a dream, Octavia. You're sleeping. It's your imagination fuelled by my influence. It's merely a projection of what I thought it could be. We could be anywhere . . .'

"Where are you, then?"

'Home.'

"Show me your home, Samael?" I demanded, desperate for any actual sense of him.

I needed something, anything, that would make him more than a figment of my imagination. More than just the voice in my head.

"Show me your face? Please?"

'In time, Little One.'

"Show me something, now!"

I sounded like an angry child.

'I am, Octavia.' Samael sounded far more patient than I deserved. *'If only you'd learn to pay attention.'*

I stepped away from him as I searched his shadow-wreathed body for any sense of him.

He stepped away, arms spread in a gesture that was unmistakable. I shouldn't have been paying attention to him but to the realm he had created for us to meet within.

My throat felt thick. I wanted to keep studying him, but my eyes flickered around us, unable to stop myself from following his prompting, trusting what he told me. Even though it was dangerous to trust the devil.

A growl rolled through the space, rocking the world, and the bones rattled in response. Fear had my heart skittering.

"What was that?"

'That came not from a place of dreams,' the devil warned. *'Wake up, Little One. Trouble has come to you. As per usual.'*

He was fading into the darkness, disappearing before my eyes.

I shook my head, an aggravated huff rolling from the back of my throat. "Doesn't it always."

Trouble may as well have been my middle name.

I woke, filled with fear, opening my eyes to the luminous yellow gaze of a hellhound. It was crouched too close to where I'd fallen asleep, where *we* had all fallen asleep, since Niklaus was snoring next to me, one arm thrown over his eyes and the other resting on my stomach.

The sun had dropped below the hills, throwing us into darkness, and I dragged myself to sit upright.

The hellhound growled as I moved. Pressing a hand against Niklaus's ribs, I nudged him in the side.

He mumbled in his sleep, shifting obliviously to the danger, and wrapped his arm around my side before rolling over.

Before I could stop him, he'd dragged me with him.

A startled shriek pulled from my throat, and the hellhound shifted.

Its powerful muscles flexed before it howled, a soulful, deadly sound. It was enough to wake everyone, and they jerked into consciousness, Niklaus murmuring sleepily in my ear.

"Let go of me," I hissed.

He murmured a sleepy, incoherent reply.

Clenching my fist, I rammed it into his ribs. "Danger."

His body rattled with tension, and in one swift movement, he had rolled me beneath him. He hurtled himself to his feet and placed himself between the hellhound and everyone else.

It took me a second to get oriented, to pull myself upright, by which time the hound had started to pace.

"Don't do it, Nik," Margot warned softly. "You don't have a weapon."

"Toss me my knife, Mar," he demanded. She shuddered, like the nickname offended her delicate sensibilities, and didn't move to follow his command. "Now, Mar, or we're all hellhound lunch."

"Not all of us," Helina Archer whispered. "Just the slowest of us all . . ."

When I turned to glance carefully over my shoulder, she had already fled, Finley edging sideways to follow in her steps.

My gaze swung to Nash, accusing, as I waited to see if he would stay or if he would flee.

He reached out, burying his fist in the soft material of Finley's shirt, anchoring him in place. "We don't leave each other behind anymore, all right?"

He nodded to me, and I inhaled sharply, emotion prickling the bridge of my nose, an acute sense of shame. Deep down, I would abandon them one day for the man in the shadows, for my chance to win, to survive.

"Hand him the knife, Margot," I said, my voice steady.

"But . . ." She was holding the blade, hesitation evident in her stance. Her gaze dropped to the knife as if it might bite her; fear shining in her eyes as she glanced to the hellhound.

"Do it," I snapped. "If he wants to be a hero, let him die like one."

Niklaus's gaze flashed at me, his teeth clenched, jaw tense. He held out one hand, and Margot crept forward, placing the handle in his open palm. His tattooed fingers folded over it, and he tested the weight, his focus back on the predator.

"Now, get out of here!" he demanded.

"What?" I shook my head, but Niklaus didn't look back.

He stepped towards the beast, testing it, and the hellhound growled in warning.

"Get out of here. I'll catch up."

I doubted he'd survive the hound sinking its teeth into his throat.

Margot had crept up behind me, her icy hand catching my wrist. "Let's go . . ." she breathed in my ear. Stubbornly, I shook my head. "Like you said, Octavia, if he wants to be a hero . . ."

Something didn't sit right in the twist of my gut, but I couldn't deny the words I'd spoken.

I glared at Niklaus for being such a fool and let Margot drag me back down to the camp, threading our way between the tents and soldiers.

We stumbled back into the epicentre of the training camp, tiptoeing around the anchored hellhounds in the square and making a beeline for the barracks.

Where we stepped into a place of utter chaos, Major Akua and General Inaina's gazes snapped in our direction, full of lethal, demanding rage.

"Where have you been?" Major Akua hissed, flicking her hand toward the floor.

A recruit lay there with eyes vacant, joints dislocated, her neck sliced open. A crude drawing of the spiralling horns had been painted beside her, inked with her own blood, a sign of the trials, an accusation.

Her blood was on our hands.

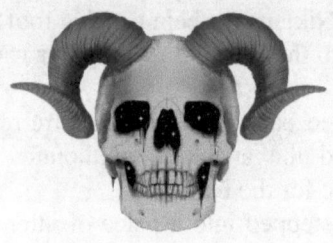

Chapter Twenty-One

Soldiers swarmed through the barracks, Heiau with them, as they removed the body. Major Akua stayed at the side of the room, glaring with open hostility at the lot of us. When the hustle and bustle died down, she loosened a heavy, disappointed sigh. "All the Wrathling recruits may leave. Wait by Wrath Hall." She gave them a beat to move before her furious gaze swung at those of us who remained.

Myself, Nash, Finley, Margot, and two girls whose names I hadn't bothered to learn. Our numbers had thinned. Some challengers hadn't been cut out for the preparations of war, and when they'd tried to flee, Wrath had turned them mindless with rage until they'd torn one another to shreds.

"Where's Heira?" Major Akua asked.

My throat bobbed, and I looked to Margot, but she was staring down at the floor, her pale lips pinched together.

Of course she wouldn't talk and put herself in the line.

I glanced to Nash and Finley next, but neither of them spoke.

With a deep breath, I pulled myself together, the only one willing to say something at the risk of inciting the wrath flaring in her gaze.

"We weren't there. We were up on the hill."

"Silence!" she barked.

They had drawn the evidence in blood, and Major Akua was all too willing to believe it. She watched us closely, eyes zeroing on me.

"Where is he?" she asked again.

"How would I know? I'm not his partner."

It was effectively throwing Margot into the line of fire, and she straightened when she realised what I'd said. Her blue eyes blazed with cold flames. It had worked, and Major Akua marched around the blood to stand in front of Margot. "Where's your partner?" she asked, the question softly lethal, as if Margot didn't want to find out the consequences of refusing to answer.

Margot shifted, lifting her chin with the arrogance of a woman who had known privilege her entire life. She sneered her nose at Major Akua. "He's . . ."

"Here . . ." Niklaus croaked from the doorway.

We all spun as he staggered forward, blood soaking the front of his shirt, his flesh torn, the savage tear of the hellhound's teeth evident in his skin. "At your service," he added bitterly. His eyes rolled back, and Niklaus Heira, a man I'd always seen as a pillar of strength, crumpled to the ground.

Major Akua stalked forward. As she exited, she glared over her shoulder. "Clean up the blood, recruits."

Two days later, we were still all on edge, the mystery of the killer at large, the other groups whispering behind our backs, increasing the tension.

Training hadn't stopped for a minute, the major forcing us into drills each day until they wore us out.

My body ached, exhausted in new ways, as we settled in the makeshift arena, slick with sweat from the morning run. They had partnered me with the wrath-born woman whose partner had been murdered, and she treated me as if I caused her partner's death.

Hostility radiated from her. She abandoned me on the morning run and sat across the arena.

"A piece-of-shit Envy soldier has taken your sword from you. What do you do?" Major Akua asked.

"Run?" someone said. If looks could kill, Major Akua's gaze would have burned them alive. ". . . Or not."

She sighed, and I wondered if she had this much disdain for everyone or if she especially reserved it for us. "You engage in hand-to-hand combat. How many of you know how to spar?"

Scattered hands rose, Niklaus's, one competitor's I didn't know, and most of the Wrath-born recruits'.

Her head bounced as she counted through us and then nodded firmly. "I'll partner you off based on experience." She moved through us, tapping off recruits at the shoulder, pairing them up. When her gloved hand bumped my shoulder, I turned and watched her slap Niklaus's injured shoulder, causing him to inhale sharply.

My stomach felt like it turned to stone, a whole new level of tension coiling in my muscles, as the tattooed man grinned widely and turned to face me, beckoning me towards him.

"Those who know how to spar will teach their partner. I'll correct you as necessary," Major Akua said, stepping out of our way. "Begin!"

I could feel Niklaus studying me, my already burnt skin prickling beneath the weight of his attention. When I looked up at him, his green eyes had turned serious as if training me was the holiest of tasks.

Around us, other recruits flew into motion, launching themselves at each other, but I held back, watching Niklaus warily.

"Come on, love." He flipped his palms up and gestured me forward. "Attack me. You know you want to . . ."

Stubbornly, I stayed in place. When he moved to the side, circling me the same way he'd circled the hellhound a few days prior, I made sure I kept the distance between us.

We orbited one another slowly, each waiting the other out.

For all the enemies I had in these trials, all the obstacles that needed to be overcome, Niklaus Heira could be the most detrimental of all.

I'd wanted him so badly in Ilrea, wanted him to notice me, to want me, but since, I wanted nothing more than to be free of that desire.

The tiny thread of worry I had for him would anchor me, tethering to the earth beside Niklaus Heira, and I'd always be looking over my shoulder to see how he was faring. It was the reason I'd pulled him free of Envy's barbaric punishment, the reason I'd wanted to know if he lived.

Niklaus Heira was a part of my history, of Octavia of Ilrea, but I wasn't that girl anymore.

I was Octavia Nox, survivor of Gluttony and Envy.

I was going to win The Devil's Trials.

Without warning, I lunged for him, my fist clenched, as I aimed to knock the smirk from his lips. Niklaus laughed as he danced out of the way, beckoning me forward again.

Over and over, I lashed out, missing each time. He retaliated, his fist colliding with my ribs hard enough to wind me but nothing more. I faltered mid-step.

"You're holding back," I accused.

Niklaus hesitated. "Yeah."

"Why?"

"You don't know how to fight," he explained. I bristled with agitation. "What's the point in pummelling you?"

"So I'll learn?"

"Trust me, you won't."

"Don't tell me what I will and won't do. You're injured. I have a fair chance," I snapped, flinging another clumsy punch in his direction.

Niklaus kicked at me, and it caught me unprepared. He hooked the back of my ankle, and I slammed into the ground.

Air rushed from my chest. My head spun, and Niklaus was on top of me, his strong thighs locking me in place.

"Surprise," he laughed.

"Get off," I demanded, wriggling beneath him to buck him off.

He made a sharp, almost pained, noise in the back of his throat, one hand capturing my flying fist, the other bracketing around my throat in a way that left my breath hitching in my lungs.

Instinctively, I stilled beneath his touch.

He laughed softly, and the hand at my throat, pinning my free arm easily. Nikaus bent low over me, his face too close to mine, sending my heart rate skyrocketing as he kept me pinned in the sand.

"That's not how it works, love," he murmured against my skin, and I loathed the fact that the weight of him against me was tempting enough to forget where we were. It reminded me that I didn't want to be lonely. "Come on, knock me off."

My hips bucked, but he didn't budge, barely shifting to accommodate the movement. "Niklaus!" I seethed, trying to pull my wrists free.

"You said not to pull my punches." He sounded amused. "So, fight me off, Octavia. I promise it'll be fun."

I thought about flinging my head forward and smashing it into his face, but before I could lurch into action, he swore, pain clear in his voice. He staggered sideways, taking me with him as he held tight to my wrists.

Major Akua's polished black boot flashed in the corner of my eye, the boot that had solidly kicked Niklaus in his injured shoulder. His pain was enough of a distraction that I pulled my hands free.

"This is a war zone, not a game, little boy," the major spat loudly, enough to draw attention.

My face warmed with mortification as I scrambled backwards, as far from Niklaus as I can get.

"Flirt in your own time. After the war." Her dark gaze flickered over him, her disgust plain for all to see. "This is why Wrath doesn't let men in her army." She turned away, glaring at everyone. I dragged myself to my feet as the major snarled. "Did I say you could stop?"

Niklaus sat up, and I approached him cautiously, tiptoeing around the dangerous hellhounds. After bracing myself, I held out a hand, and Niklaus nodded as he reached for it. When he pulled himself up, I swung one last time, using the leverage of our positions and that he didn't expect it to my advantage. My fist slammed into his jaw, which cracked loudly, along with my thumb, crushed where it was tucked beneath my fingers.

He groaned; I screamed with pain, the sound piercing through the arena.

Behind us, Major Akua looked like she wanted to strangle us. "That's it," she spat. "Everyone out of my sight before I kill you all. Except you two."

Unlikely to be an idle threat, recruits disappeared quicker than anyone could have imagined. I was too busy cradling my hand, biting my lip through the jarring pain radiating down my arm to flee, to realise that there were far better places to be than at the end of Major Akua's lit fuse.

She didn't bother approaching, as if we weren't worth her time, merely sneering from behind her mask.

"Get up, recruits, and follow me."

Niklaus groaned loudly, and I watched in horror as he pushed his fingers inside his mouth, holding the inside of his jaw. He used the other hand to brace his chin and wrenched it sideways. I almost saw stars at the crunching sound that echoed from his body, my stomach turning violently. His eyelids fluttered, dark lashes pressed to his cheek, and I was sure he'd pass out, but he didn't. "She needs a medic—"

"So does he!" I cradled my hand to my chest, voice weak with pain. "What the fuck was that? You can't just . . ."

Major Akua shook her head. "You're both fine," she growled, "which is more than you deserve."

That was a matter of opinion, but the only opinion that mattered in the war camps were those of the major and generals that kept order; the recruits had no voices. As foreigners, we didn't matter at all.

She led us back down to the camp, winding out the back, and I wanted to groan. There was no way I could polish boots with the pain radiating in my hand, my dominant hand, at that.

"Stay."

The major's tone was condescending, as if giving an order to a troublesome hound instead of two grown adults. She disappeared, then returned with four buckets and two rusty shovels. "Get digging."

"Digging?" I repeated, confused.

"I told you . . ." Major Akua dropped the shovels at our feet. "If you embarrass me, and you'll be digging out the latrines."

At her words, my eyes slid to the badly constructed rooms. Each looked half primed to fall over and enclosed a deep hole that we'd been squatting over for months now. It smelled as bad as it looked, the stench of marinating piss, blood, and shit. My stomach twisted, threatening to bring up the bile and water within.

"Dig it out?" I parroted back, sounding as thick as the major believed me to be. "And do what with it?"

Major Akua shook her head. "Shovel them out, into the

buckets, and carry them out there." She pointed out to the distance, to the empty plains of the Wrathlands' side of the war front. A dangerous space, given that we didn't know how far from the action we were.

"Bury it somewhere that we don't have to smell it. Nobody wants to sleep in the reek of shit."

My eyes dropped to the bucket, the shovel, then to the latrine. "Just this one?"

I regretted the question as soon as it left my lips. Major Akua's eyes lit up, and I imagined she was smiling behind that suffocating leather mask.

"All of them, recruit. I'll have some rations dropped, make them last. A single bedroll, since you two have proven you like to get so *cosy*."

Her words dripped with derision, and my face heated. Unwilling to look at either of them, I stared at my boots and waited for her to be done. "You'll need to train in your own time. You're not welcome back to the settlement until they're all dug out."

She marched away, leaving Niklaus and me in silence.

My head ached almost as badly as my hand did, pain sharpening when I tried to pick up the shovel. Niklaus was rubbing his jaw, the flickering in his green eyes the biggest indication of his fury.

"What a load of shit."

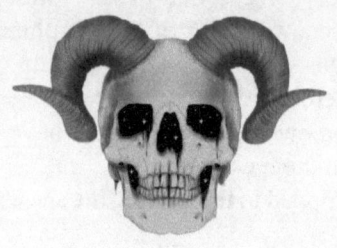

Chapter Twenty-Two

There was no way to stop the retching as the smell turned my stomach. I would never feel clean again after kicking open the door to the first overflowing latrine, realising the enormity of the task. They were deep, and they were full. It was disgusting; I could see why this was one of Major Akua's punishments. I would move Kaida itself to avoid being in this position again.

My stomach twisted, the stench intense and unforgiving, and without warning, I vomited into the bucket until there was nothing left inside of me. A groan rolled from my chest. The bucket hit the floor as I ran outside, desperately seeking fresh air.

It was easier to procrastinate, linger outside until the heat of the sun cooled, leaving most of the work to Niklaus. He was grunting inside the stalls as he worked but didn't whisper a word of complaint.

Some of the other recruits came by, pushing past to relieve

themselves and adding to the task. Peliela lingered outside of the stalls.

"Downgraded to cleaner already, rat?" She laughed, and her friends joined in.

"Piss off," I snapped.

"You look as happy as a piglet in shit," she crowed, and they laughed again. "The latrines are where you belong!"

The grating edge to her presence was almost enough to send me fleeing back into the stall.

In the meantime, Niklaus had filled up his buckets, and shit coated his arms when he came back. He set them down and came back with my abandoned tubs ten minutes later, filled to the brim.

Peliela and her friends skirted away from him, plugging their noses at the smell emanating from his body.

"You need to do at least one," he said. "I'm not doing this all myself."

A bite snapped in his tone as if he blamed me as much as I blamed him. He was stubborn, though—maybe more than I was—and Niklaus would let the fourth bucket sit there until I filled it myself.

It took me twenty minutes to pull myself together, to gasp down a lungful of fresh air and march back into the latrines, breathing through my pursed lips and shovelling as fast as I could.

When I finished, Niklaus was at the waterspout, pumping the handle and washing the waste off his arms. I hurried to set the bucket down and join him, scrubbing at my skin with the slippery bar of soap.

With the pails full, we had nothing else to do but carry them into the war zone, an idea that filled me with trepidation. I didn't know how close the battle had moved to us while we had been training, and I was worried we would march right into a blood bath.

A soldier delivered a pack of supplies while I was working, and true to Major Akua's word, only one rolled sleeping bag was attached.

Niklaus slung it across his back with ease. "If we don't start walking, it's going to get too dark . . ."

He'd already picked up two of the buckets.

Pain in my hand ricocheted up my arm as I picked up my containers, my throat hissing. I tried my best to ignore it, biting down on my complaints, and I followed Niklaus down the path, away from the safety of camp. But by the time darkness had fallen, I was whimpering from the unrelenting stinging.

Niklaus's sigh was heavy. "Put the buckets down."

There was no hesitation when I did as he asked, setting them down and moving away quickly—not that it did anything for the smell inside my nose.

Niklaus shifted, his tall form a shadow beneath the starlight. "We'll leave them here and find somewhere safe to sleep."

"Okay, good idea," I agreed, following his lead.

We moved far enough from the buckets that I didn't feel so disgusting, and he dropped the pack into the dirt. Dropping to sit, I cradled my sore hand, gingerly pressing against my thumb to assess the damage.

I didn't move as Niklaus bustled around, leaving me behind but always coming back within a few minutes. He tossed sticks in a small pile between us, rummaging through the bag and dumping supplies all over the place until he found a small box of matches. Three strikes later, we had flames, and I was grateful for the soft heat.

None of the rations were worth cooking, mostly dried strips of meat and stale bread, but the crackling fire was enough to take the edge off the cool night. Just enough to give us light to see each other. He sat next to me, the shadows dancing across his face, and took my injured hand with surprising gentleness.

Niklaus probed my swollen thumb with his strong fingers until a hiss of discomfort rolled from my lips.

He frowned. "I think it's broken."

"Yeah. I could have told you that."

"I don't know how to fix it," he admitted. He pulled a rag from inside the pack, tearing it into strips and then pressing my thumb backwards in a blinding moment of agony. He bound it tightly against a small stick, keeping it straight. "There we go."

"What's that supposed to do?" I asked, my hand awkward beneath the binding, my thumb stuck back.

"Stability." He shrugged and tore open a wrapped packet of dried meat. "You're not supposed to tuck your thumb in when you throw a punch, you know."

I offered him a dark look, wishing I could burn him alive with it. "Obviously, I know that now." I raised my undamaged hand and curled my fingers to make a fist, my thumb feeling awkward, stuck out to the side.

"How should I set it, then?"

It didn't feel right no matter where I rested it. I didn't think I was cut out for physical combat, but training wasn't optional, and I didn't want to break all of my fingers along the way.

Niklaus took my hand and repositioned my thumb. "Like this, over your fingers, drive forward with your knuckles so you don't smash it." He tapped my knuckles.

"I know what knuckles are," I snapped, pulling my hand back, and relaxing my fist. "You don't need to show me everything."

Staring at me, his green eyes practically glowed beneath the flames.

My chest felt tight, waiting for him to unload the tension that had been coiling between us all day.

To my surprise, he just sighed and nodded. "All right, Octavia."

"Okay," I echoed.

Silence lapsed between us. In the distance, battle, the clash of steel, was too close for comfort. The quiet became too heavy. I felt restless, and so I broke it.

"Do you miss home?"

Niklaus turned his head slowly, his gaze searing me through. "Yes."

"Oh?" My surprise couldn't have been plainer. "Why?"

Somehow, I thought Niklaus would be all for the adventure and the challenge of the trials. I'd thought he'd wanted to escape our little town and the suffocating idleness within it.

"I miss my family," he said finally. He flexed his hands, cracking his knuckles one by one. "Mikhael, mostly."

I thought about it, considering the way the brothers had treated each other when passing through the Envy camps. It was strange to think that he missed his mirror image, when, half the time, I tried not to think of my siblings, who probably had been happier without me.

"Is this the longest you've ever been apart?"

Niklaus jerked a nod, his face shuddering.

We'd been in training for this war for months. The days had melted into each other, passing in a blur of exhaustion. I didn't know how long it had been since we'd left Mikhael behind.

"I don't want to talk about it," he said bluntly. "We should get some sleep. We'll get up at first light and bury the first load." He stretched and stood, finding the sleeping bag to roll it out a decent distance from the fire. "Octavia?" Niklaus asked expectantly, but I was stuck sitting by the fire.

"There's only one."

I stated the obvious, my hushed tone too loud in the night.

I didn't think sharing a bedroll was the best idea.

"And?"

"Can't you sleep on the ground?"

"Not a chance, love," Niklaus said. "You can sleep on the dirt or cuddle up to me, but I'm not giving this up." He shucked off his leathers, unbuckling the clasps and letting it fall to the ground. As he stripped them away, I inhaled sharply, purposefully turning to look back at the fire.

256

"You can watch if you want, love."

"You wish," I said, reaching for the buckles of my heavy breastplate.

It was difficult to remove with my strapped thumb, and I fumbled with the buckles until Niklaus appeared at my back.

He crouched behind me, body heat warming me. Before I could protest, he sat, stretching his legs on either side of me as he unbuckled the first of my bracers, peeling it from my arm and tossing it aside. He reached for the other one.

"Nik," I cautioned.

"Octavia," he murmured against my neck.

His lips drew a shiver from my body, and I closed my eyes. I'd missed feeling close to someone. "You don't want to sleep in this . . ."

He'd removed the other bracer, reaching for the buckles on my breastplate and loosening them easily.

Air between us grew thicker, and I relaxed back against the warmth of his chest, feeling secure as his arms wrapped around me, and he eased the breastplate over my head, his hands skimming my sides.

"Nik," I said again, his name a half caution, half plea.

I wasn't sure what I wanted from him. To forget him, break the attachment between us, or sink fully into the sense of security he provided, the familiarity. It felt good to have someone close, to have someone care.

'I care, Little One.'

Samael's voice was like being doused with a bucket of ice water.

My entire body tensed, flooded with a hot flush of shame. Irrationally, I felt as if I'd betrayed his trust, a being I'd never met made of whispers and intrigue instead of flesh and blood, a godlike creature who had never made promises to care for me before.

Niklaus paused halfway through, unbuckling the greaves

around my calves. "What's wrong, Octavia?"

"Let go of me," I said breathlessly.

Niklaus instantly released me, lifting his hands, palms up as I skittered out from between his legs and almost falling over the armour as it slipped to my ankles.

"Nik!"

This time, his name was a scolding.

"Nothing would have happened, Octavia. I was just teasing you." He shook his head, standing. His hands braced behind his skull as he stretched. "No offence, but when I want in your pants, it's not going to after shovelling buckets of literal shit." His gaze shimmered, his amusement plain as day.

I stiffened, kicking off the graves he'd loosened but keeping my knives strapped to my thighs.

"Nothing's ever going to happen," I told him firmly. "Never again, Nik."

He shook his head. "I don't believe that."

"Believe what you want," I whispered, swallowing roughly.

It didn't matter that my body wanted him. Samael was the better choice. I would win if the devil cared for me. "Delusions don't come true."

Niklaus's lips pressed into a thin line, his face falling, the humour draining. "Go to bed, Octavia." He walked away from the bedroll, leaving it for me.

"Where are you going?" I called after him, inexplicably worried he would leave me here alone.

Niklaus glanced back over his shoulder, his expression flat. "To take a piss. Why? Do you want to give me a hand?"

"Devils, you're an asshole."

He kept walking. "So, you keep telling me, Octavia."

After he disappeared into the night, I glanced up at the soft light of the stars, searching for the answers I needed to survive.

"Am I wrong to trust you, Samael?" I asked, but there was no hint of the devil in my mind, no whisper of his voice. It was all the answer I needed, but I ignored my feelings of doubt. I shook my head and climbed into the bedroll before falling asleep so fast I barely felt it when Niklaus climbed in with me. His body draped over mine, the heat of him warming me as I dreamt of a devil that wore his face.

It took us a week to finish emptying the latrines.

After a week of nights with Niklaus, I realised what little we had to talk about, despite all the history we shared and days of warring feelings, torn between the man who kept me safe and warm and night and the voice in my head. It murmured stories until I fell asleep, manipulating my dreams until he invaded all of them.

When the job was done, we marched back to the barracks and stopped only to shower, where I scrubbed at my skin until it was red and irritated. I'd never felt so relieved to see other people, the mill of training continuing, as if we had never left.

"Nash!" I slammed into him, squeezing my arms around his body. He convulsed slightly, coughing into my shoulder.

"Devils, Octavia, you stink."

I frowned. "I've washed!"

"You definitely need to shower again," Finley piped up, curly head appearing from the top bunk. "How's your hand?"

It had stopped hurting, although I wasn't sure if that was good or bad. The linen wrapping had become stained, but I hadn't been willing to take it off, nervous that my thumb might be dying beneath the binds of it. "I'm not sure."

"Come on," Nash said, wrapping an arm around my shoulders and steering me back out the door. "Let's see the medic."

It took all my self-control to not glance back to Niklaus, even though I was acutely aware of where he stood.

Tension from the nights on the plains had disappeared, the moment having slipped between my broken fingers as easily as sand.

Heiau directed me to sit on the bed and unwrapping the dirty linen from my hand. She pressed against my thumb deftly with her strong fingers. "Why didn't you come in sooner?"

"Couldn't," I said quietly. "Akua gave me latrine duty."

One of her dark brows rose, but she didn't comment. "Can you feel this?" She squeezed my thumb.

"Yeah, but it feels funny, sort of dull." She nodded, letting go of my hand.

"Show me how you move your thumb around?" Heiau continued.

I did as she asked, but the joint felt weird, stiff from lack of use. I couldn't move it as far or rotate it with ease. Heiau frowned, clicking her tongue like a mother to an errant child. "There's not much I can do since you let it heal that way, but at least you can still use it."

I stared at my hand; it felt strange to be disappointed at the damage. It could have been a lot worse, but I still hated it, blaming Major Akua for the loss.

Nash sat with me, letting me wallow, until the doors to the medic room burst open, and Margot Galatea stumbled inside, her pale skin painted with blood.

"Help me." She gasped, her blue eyes wide and startlingly clear as she looked down at the blood coating her hands and smeared up her arms. "There's been another murder."

All hell seemed to break loose, the medics scurrying to action. They had forgotten us, sitting on the bed, as they disappeared out the door, leaving her drenched in blood and rocking back and forth on the balls of her feet.

I rose from the bed, approaching her carefully. "Margot."

She didn't seem to snap out of her state, her eyes fluttering from side to side. I touched her shoulder, and she startled.

"You didn't kill someone . . . Did you?"

She looked up, her eyes blank, teeth pinching her lower lip as she rocked and rocked. I moved and whispered, "Is this what Envy asked you to do?"

The haze in her gaze cleared, a sharp clarity beyond anything I'd seen before in Margot Galatea's eyes, stark enough that I wondered if her day-to-day personality wasn't all for show. There could have been an intelligent woman beneath the show she put on for others.

"No," she told me, eerily calm and firm. "I just found the body. I tried to stop the bleeding but . . . but . . ."

Nash had come up behind us. "What happened, Mar?"

She glanced to him and sighed heavily. "Same as last time. She had her throat slit, one side to the other, so deep I could practically see inside it." A shudder worked down her spine. "I fell over her body, face-first into a pool of her blood. I can . . . I can still taste it." She scrubbed her lips, then, with the back of her hand, smeared the blood further.

Nash found a cup and water for Margot to rinse out her mouth, following up with wet bandages, dabbing at the blood smeared across her face. She smiled gratefully, taking them off him and scrubbing at her skin harder, until the wet white linen came away pink. The rest of it streaked against her skin, and when she dropped the rag, it left her looking flushed.

"Do you think—"

Thudding boots on the tiles approached, and we turned as one to see General Inaina marching into the room. Her mask was missing, revealing the heavy lines of age pulling at her skin.

Startlingly, she didn't look as I had imagined beneath the leather mask, the soft shape of her ace leaving me stunned.

"You three," General Inaina said, looking grim, "come with me."

STEPHANIE GLUCK

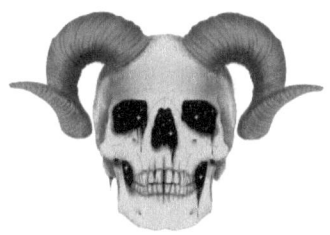

Chapter Twenty-Three

They led us across the courtyard, a loose hellhound nipping at our heels, until we reached Wrath Hall, where we joined the rest of the competitors for an audience with Lady Wrath. The angel had flown straight off the battlefield, still covered in muck, grime, and blood. The rage of war radiated off her as she stalked back and forth, her dark wings rustling with agitation.

"Recruits killing each other in two different cohorts," she hissed, turning her dark gaze on us, glaring until the weight of her anger left me breathless.

Swallowing roughly, I clutched the knife by my thigh as the wound-up feeling tugged at my nerves, giving way to the heady impulsiveness I always felt around Wrath.

"As if I don't have better things to do! As if I don't have a war to win!" the angel roared. She turned and flung her own knife, and it spun through the air, whistling overhead before it pierced the door.

"Who's responsible for this?!" she all but roared, at the edge of her own berserker rage.

As a group we said nothing, and Wrath let out a bellow so otherworldly that, for all her efforts to appear and battle alongside her human cohort, she could never be known as anything but an angel.

A sin amongst women, pure magic and rage.

"I should turn the lot of you against each other and let you tear one another to shreds! Nothing more than the pathetic scraps debasing human nature," the angel hissed, her eyes glowing wildly.

I didn't know what debasing meant, but some recruits stiffened. Her gaze flicked to General Inaina, who stood at attention.

My knuckles popped softly as I curled my hands into fists, my head pounding with such growing, ever consuming rage that I could barely see straight as it turned me inside out.

"My lady?" General Inaina asked, waiting for the command.

The Angel of Wrath studied us one last time, disdain clear on her face, lip curled up to bare her jagged teeth. "Speed up their training. These recruits will eat, drink, and sleep their way to the battlefield. Keep them locked below Wrath Hall with the hounds at night. I want them ready and at psychological training within the month. They'll break, and someone will die for their impertinence."

"Consider it done, my lady."

Wrath glared at us, waiting for any sign of dissent, any reason to lash out.

The pounding in my head matched the beat of my heart, rapid and dangerous, like I was going to explode. A bead of sweat dripped down my back, trailing to my tailbone; that would be the end of me.

I'd descend into the red sheen of madness invading my mind,

and the world would rain in blood.

Wrath's sneer widened, flashing more teeth, as if she could feel how close we were to the edge, and she was waiting or for us to succumb to the lure of her power.

On my right, someone crashed to their knees, their hands shaking at the effort to remain still. The angels' laugh echoed in my ears, like clanging bells calling me to action. I surged forward with several others, my hand reaching for the knife belted to my thigh. I could incite violence—I knew that much.

They'd trained me to stab the enemy, and despite my reluctance, they'd trained me well.

We descended on the angel, and she spread her arms, laughing as she fed on our building wrath. She glowed with the energy she had pulled from us, the chaos she created. Her giant black wings snapped out, spread wide, and she no longer looked small compared to her brothers. She was as tall and powerful as Envy, as monstrous as Gluttony and as tempting as Pride.

I pulled my arm back, wrist loosening as I prepared to throw my weapon.

I would draw blood from an angel and not rest until I had carved the names of our dead into her skin, penance, and punishment for what we had endured and who we had lost, for everything the angels had done to us . . .

"Enough!" Wrath cackled.

Anger drained from my body, the world fading to black.

I awoke bound in red rope and secured to an iron circle, which was attached to the stone wall.

I sat in a nest of competitors, overwhelmed by the stench of urine and wet hound.

The glowing, yellow eyes of the hellhounds were everywhere. They were bound and furious, just as we were.

Tension crackled in the air, a feeling of danger that we all acknowledged. The low light offered only a glimpse of shadowed angry faces in the darkness, the torment of my fellow competitors.

We barely slept, watching one another, watching the hounds, wondering which would kill us first.

They had us training from the crack of dawn until long after nightfall, while we moved through drills and movements until they became mindless and fluid with repetition. They fed only us because we couldn't train without energy, and each night, they removed our weapons, binding us tight and sending us below the hall. More competitors were thrown in with us each day until the space was full, crammed together with the beasts as they snapped and snarled at us for invading their space, for daring to go near the pups in the corner.

Within days, they had separated us entirely from the Wrathling-born recruits. It had forced every remaining competitor into the rigorous training schedule until we were fighting like we were born for it.

With time, I'd become more muscle than skin and bone. I could run, I could fight half-decently, I knew a little about poisons, and I was bubbling with never-ending rage.

Wrath was honing me, all of us, into weapons, but I was also burning out, lying beneath the hall at night, agitated by everyone in sight and prey to the influence of the angel in the halls above us. It wouldn't be long until we cracked into pieces and tore one another to shreds.

I didn't know how the Wrathling citizens did it, lived in places influenced by that angel, endured the constant ache of anger that left my muscles tensed and jaw grit, until fatigue overwhelmed everything.

"Surely," someone grumbled in the dark. "Surely, we're almost done with this one. It feels like we've been here half a lifetime. I'm done with it."

They weren't wrong; I didn't know long it had been since we

266

left Invidia, but my braided hair fell to midback, my only true marker it had been a long time.

"What do you think is next?" someone else said.

Voices perked up everywhere, talking over one another. They grew louder, drawing agitated growls from the hounds.

"Stop it!"

Niklaus's command was a whipcrack through the room. People stilled. "Stop focussing on the next challenge, or you won't survive this one."

He sounded annoyed, as if he couldn't care less if they lived or died, but in the low light, I could see the hard glint in his eye, the flicker of sin-induced madness shining.

Niklaus and a handful of others were thriving in the energy that dwelt below the hall, revelling in the violence of our training. I couldn't deny that Wrath was his sin to bear. He was quick to temper, quicker still to rile others and the fastest to draw blood.

A lazy smirk tugged at his mouth when he caught my gaze.

Pointedly, I broke eye contact, turning my body to block him out but not before I saw the outrage flashing across his face.

"Does anyone actually know how we pass?" Helina asked, sounding like the girl I'd known in Ilrea, a bossy know-it-all who wanted to share what she'd learned with the masses but knew they wouldn't want to listen. She was always in search of more information.

Aureen Willett scoffed. "Do you?"

Helina didn't answer, giving Aureen a sour look. "What was the clue?"

"Emotions run rampant in the war between sins," Margot said, her prim, proper voice echoing. "Wrath feeds into envy, and envy fuels wrath. Forbearance becomes the only way to win."

"What does that mean?" I asked. "Forbearance?"

I'd been hoping for a repeat of the Feast of Samael, when a word triggered knowledge that saved us all, but my question met silence. I couldn't help but wonder if the answer lie across plains of savagery and gore, sitting in the black-and-green scale-patterned tents, commanding armies while we waited for the war. Would we fail without Mikhael's presence?

The conversation died when the walls shook with the power of the angels, Wrath's influence rolling in waves until every thought in my mind evaporated and I saw red. Hot red spray of blood as it splashed down my front. The competitor in front of me slumping lifeless to the floor. Attacked by one of our own, a man who shook with rage, their eyes as crimson as the angel's colours.

Mindless rage twisted across his face, a vein throbbing in his temple, his fists trembling as he contorted and struck again and again and again.

I spat the blood from my mouth, pressing myself against the wall, even as my own rage tempted me to attack him back. I tensed, ready to spring on him, but Niklaus got there first, snarling as he tackled the man to the floor. His tattooed fists flew as he rained punches against the man's flesh until bone cracked beneath his knuckles and blood misted in the air.

'Calm down,' Samael demanded.

"But . . ." I gasped.

My entire body shook. I could taste the need for blood and retribution. The need to hurt someone. I wanted the release of building rage that would come with attacking.

'Calm, Little One,' he repeated, softer. *'You must have the patience to withstand it.'*

"But . . ." I said in a whimper, "it feels like . . ."

'Like what?'

Suddenly, I could almost feel him invading my mind, a warring presence to the influence of Wrath.

'Tell me how you feel.'

"I feel like I'm suffocating in my hatred. I want to crawl from my skin," I said, nearly panting the words.

It took everything to hold myself back, watching the mindless violence unfold in front of me. "It's a fire in my veins, burning me up, I want . . . revenge."

'Vengeance for what, Little One? What have these competitors done?'

"They survived," I sobbed. I resented everyone, even myself, for living in the place of the people I had lost. "I feel like I've died three times over. When better people should have survived instead, I lived."

'Don't you deserve to survive, Octavia?'

"I . . ."

Wasn't that the ultimate question? Hot tears rolled down my cheeks, and my body trembled.

'What makes you unworthy of life?'

Before I could answer, Wrath's influence eased, and the surrounding haze dropped. Samael's presence disappeared, leaving me chilled.

I slumped back against the cold stone, my heart rate beginning to slow as I took in the damage.

Someone cried out, "The angel did that on purpose. Devils. She wants to kill us."

"Pull it together," Niklaus demanded, a lethal edge to his voice.

When he stood, blood smeared across his skin, no remorse in his eyes. "We've survived worse than this. For some of us, Gluttony was worse than Wrath. I'm sure we all remember that unfathomable, ravenous excess, the overwhelming lack of control. Others crumbled beneath Envy, twisted into unimaginable knots, devoured by the thought of what we want but can't have." His eyes flicked to me, and my stomach curled into one of those knots. "We survived then, and we'll survive now."

He circled the room, stepping over the dead and injured, green eyes blazing beneath our attention. Niklaus Heira was made for this, a man born to lead not a village, not a war but a revolution.

"Wrath wanted soldiers, and that's what she got. We're

strong now, stronger than we've ever been. She's shaped us into weapons, but for all that, they still think we're the worst of humanity. Trial rats, they call us, and doesn't that make you angry?"

A murmur swept through us, a rustle of agitated and indignant agreement.

"And?" Aureen dared say. "What's your point, Heira? We're still stuck below ground, angry and afraid. We're no closer to conquering this sin."

Niklaus turned and stared into the face of her unwavering resolve. "We go to war. Not for the sins but to the sins. They've turned us into weapons, so it's high time we draw blood."

"Let me get this straight . . ." Aureen stood, shielding Kyra with her body as she stared down the blood-soaked man. "You want us to attack Wrath?"

He shook his head, eyes bright with a tinge of heady madness. "I want us to kill Wrath."

The sentiment lingered in the silence, heavy and treasonous.

I half expected someone to laugh in the face of his idea, but from the corner of my eye, others nodded.

"She won't ever let us go, will she . . ." someone cried from across the room. "I bet forbearance means death! Either she dies or we do!"

Agreement rumbled through the room, and Niklaus appeared to become larger than life, emboldened by their support, by the bloodthirsty looks on their faces.

"Kill the angel!" he screamed.

"Kill the angel!" competitors echoed back.

My skin crawled with trepidation. Instinct warned me this was the worst path we could take, that inciting a war with the Angel of Wrath was a sure fate of death.

"How will we do it?" someone asked. Their attention swung to Niklaus.

He'd put himself in a position of leadership, and he couldn't back down. He barely moved beneath the weight of their questioning.

"On the battlefield," he said, nodding.

His little ragtag army whispered with agreement. When he turned to face me, I deliberately avoided catching his eye. "The angel fights with her army. She can't stay away from the rage and bloodshed. We'll kill during battle. She'll be just another casualty."

It was no plan, but if you didn't look hard at the unimportant details, it was believable, and it was enough.

Competitors cheered again. One other person looked as worried as I felt.

Margot Galatea had her bottom lip pinched between her teeth, white brows furrowed, and her ivory cheeks flushed. Her blue eyes were wild with the look of a woman who didn't want to die.

War was coming, and where war went, death followed.

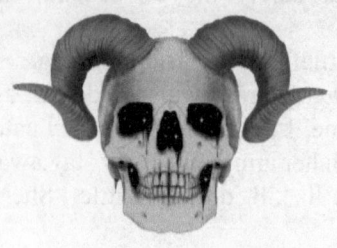

Chapter Twenty-Four

A newfound invigoration bloomed within the group. We came together with a purpose, and it made Major Akua's training slightly more tolerable. There was an end goal in sight, and at night, the competitors whispered plans and told stories of how it would feel to defeat an angel.

They empowered one another, riling themselves up and whispering plans deep into the night. It gave many of them a will to live, but I kept myself away, still unsettled by the idea.

One night, a hellhound howled for hours until she birthed a mewling litter of pups. Pitiful, they looked to be half blind, but we gave their snarling mother a wide berth. It left me tired and grumpy about starting the new day.

We poured out into the cool air, released from our bindings and grateful for the reprieve. I paced the tiled streets, keeping my distance from the beasts.

Major Akua swept around us one way, while General Inaina

moved in the opposite direction, their measured steps herding us into a tighter group. I tensed as someone jolted against my shoulder.

"Follow us," Major Akua commanded.

I walked beside Nash as we entered another of the dark brick buildings, skirting around a smashed roof tile on the way inside. It housed a long dark hallway with plain black doors lining either side and felt cold and clinical like the medic's rooms.

Major Akua cleared her throat, her arms folded across her chest, gaze dark and disapproving. "What happens if that Envy scum captures you?"

A wary silence followed the question. It felt like a trap, and I wasn't sure if there was any appropriate answer.

Aureen was brave enough to find her voice. She pushed her way forward and stood at the front of the group, taking the brunt of the major's attention. "We take the poison pills," she said. It was a topic she had discussed the night before.

We'd have to use the poison should Wrath influence us to stop us from slaughtering one another. "We die before they pull anything out of us."

"What if you can't get a hold of the pill?" Major Akua pressed, nodding her affirmation at the answer. "If you drop it? Or it's taken from you?"

We met her question with an apprehensive silence. I shifted my weight, discomfort a living beast breathing down my neck, lighting all my flight instincts on fire. I was sure I wouldn't like what was coming next.

Major Akua advanced on us, but it was General Inaina who spoke from behind, in a voice laced with undeniable passion. "You survive! They'll torture you for any drop of information you have, but you stay strong and hold out. That's how you win."

A chill slipped in the air; the doors lining the hall creaked as they slid open. "We'll take twelve of you at once. Everyone else can do drills outside," Major Akua announced, ushering the first of us forward, one for each door.

They sent me outside to do drills, and I didn't know what was worse: going first or wondering what was happening while you stretched in the street. They didn't call for the next group until long after mid-meal, when we were weary and half delirious from the burn of the sun.

Before I knew it, they ushered me into a cold room with only a chair in sight. The general tied me to the chair and left. I struggled to adjust as the light went out, plunging me into darkness.

Water dripped from somewhere in the room, and the longer they left me sitting there, the more the sound seemed to pound through my skull.

Drip, drip, drip.

Lights flashed, a face appearing in front of me, sending my heart skittering. I twisted in my chair, but the darkness consumed everything, leaving me blind. I wasn't alone in the room, though. Fear had my skin crawling as I waited for them to reveal themselves. The repetitive sound felt like it was beating into my skull.

Drip, drip, drip.

"Are you paying attention?" someone said.

They were so close that their hot breath slid across my cheek, and I jerked sideways, the chair shifting beneath my weight. It swung, a moment of weightlessness, a moment of infinity, before I crashed to the ground. The wind knocked from my body, and I struggled to breathe. The water droplets grew louder.

Drip, drip, drip.

"What do you want?" I whispered into the darkness. A soft grunt of exertion rolled out before they pulled me upright again, my head spinning with the unexpected movement.

"I said, are you paying attention?"

The voice was jarringly familiar. Something about it left me shivering, so ominously aware that I didn't want to be in a room with this person. "Tell me what you know!"

Lights flickered, fast and bright enough that spots danced in front of my eyes. They blinked again and again until my head spun.

"I know nothing!"

A hand wove into my hair, threading through the twists of my loose braid and anchoring tight. The strands came loose, sharp pain lancing across my scalp. They wrenched my head back, dragging me backwards by my hair, until the chair balanced on its hind two legs, where I teetered, caught between pain, and braced myself for the impact that was sure to come. My fists clenched.

"Tell me!" they hissed. "Tell me about the secret task?"

"I don't know." I gasped, my body flushing hot and cold as I thought of the vial I had carried into the camps.

Was that what they wanted? For me to spill secrets about General Inaina and the crone? Fear seized me as their boot struck the chair leg, the impact reverberating through my entire body. A chunk of my hair tore free, and my head was slammed into the concrete. Lights flashed, and a familiar face danced in my vision before the darkness came rushing in.

Unconsciousness was a sweet relief.

Samael beckoned me back into consciousness with soft murmured words about surviving. I'd found they had thrown me into the cellars beneath Wrath Hall. Finding my wits just in time for Major Akua and General Inaina to collect me and deposit me back on the chair. It was the last place I wanted to be, and I kicked and yelled the entire way, powerful soldiers holding me down as the red drop secured my arms around my back, biting into my skin.

The darkness didn't relent, and when my interrogator came close, they pulled me free of the chair and pushed my head into a trough of water until my lungs burned for air.

The memory of Ngaire falling beneath the river's surface and never coming up haunted me, constricting everything within me, tying me up tight with panic. I sucked in a mouthful of water, and when they allowed me air, I coughed and spluttered it up. "Peliela!" I gasped, having identified the familiar face, hacking up as much water as I could. "Please!"

She pushed me under again. Water rushed up my nose, in my mouth, and down my throat until I choked on it. The need for air was great, yet so far away, that the world blackened at the edges.

Peliela lifted me out of the water and shoved me to the floor. My entire body spasmed, gasping for precious oxygen, like a fish pulled from the river and discarded on the banks. Not worthy of a quick death.

"I don't know any secrets," I said in half a sob as I rolled to my side, pressing my cheek to the cold floor as I tried to pull myself up onto my knees. "Nobody tells me anything."

In the few moments I'd had before Peliela had arrived, I had decided I wouldn't sell out the general or the crone. Telling their secrets might get the pain to stop, but it wouldn't keep me alive. Wrath would see my actions as treason, and I would die at her hand for it. I could survive this pain, this torture to keep myself alive.

"Tell me the secret of Margot Galatea's task," Peliela demanded, moving into my field of vision. Her boot connected with my ribs, my bones cracking. "Tell me!"

"I . . ." I cried, tears springing to my eyes and slipping free. "I don't . . . know what she's doing."

She kicked and kicked until agony fissured out from my abdomen in a fit of blinding pain. Mercifully, I fainted, slumping onto the cold, wet concrete.

Every breath hurt my broken ribs, and every time my lungs

expanded, my body screamed. The next day, she punched me until blood coated her split knuckles. She asked the same question over and over, while I sobbed denials.

I knew nothing. I had nothing to tell her, even if I wanted to spill secrets. Margot hardly considered me a friend, and I knew nothing of the burden Wrath had placed on her in this war.

"I'm telling you," I said, mouth filled with blood dribbling down my chin. I struggled to spit it out. "I don't know."

"What happened in Wrath's offices?" Peliela hissed.

The change in question was so unforeseen that she may as well have blinded me with another punch. "When she was given the task."

"Uhh." I hesitated, taken aback. "What?"

"Tell me!" She swung again.

A pitiful groan rolled from my throat. My entire body hurt so badly I couldn't think straight.

Peliela scoffed, her expression blindingly dark. The angel could have possessed her in that moment, Wrath's influence shining in her eyes. She hooked her foot on the base of the chair and pushed me backwards. I clattered to the ground, devastatingly conscious as she marched out and left me behind.

I lay there, forgotten as the night passed, unable to move. I was bound to the chair without an inch of wiggle room. Red rope cut into my wrists, leaving imprints that would colour into bruises. She left me with blood pooling and gathering in the back of my throat from the cuts in my mouth until I had to turn my head and try to cough it up to save myself from choking. It was difficult to sleep, as I wondered if I did know anything about Margot's secret task or if it was all made up for this moment. It wouldn't have surprised me if there was no task at all and that Wrath had simply let us think there was to bait us for interrogation. I wondered if other competitors spilled lies in place of secrets, and as I lay in the cold, wet room, listening to dripping water, I wondered if I should betray, too.

Morning took ages to come, and it brought with it Peliela, looking determined as ever.

She stood in front of me without her leathers. Her shirt with the worn red lion painted on the front was the only indication to the fiery side of red and not envious green. Her hand fisted in the front of my shirt, her muscles tensing as she pulled me upright.

The change in my balance left me nauseous, and I barely held it together long enough to raise my chin and glare at her before spitting blood and saliva onto the toe of her boot.

"Good morning," I said, voice croakily. When I licked my lips, I realised there was blood crusted around my mouth.

Peliela folded her arms across her chest. "Going to tell me what I want to know?"

"I can't tell you what I don't know."

She scowled. Her knuckles popped and cracked as she flexed her fingers.

I was tired, dirty, and sore—and devils was I thirsty. Desperation made me bold.

"Going to dunk me again, Pel?" I said, my voice gravelly. "I could use the drink."

"Quiet," she hissed.

"Why?" I croaked. "You're only going to hurt me, anyway. Silent or loud."

"You're not wrong. Maybe for the first time in your life."

She circled me, slowly prowling like the lion emblem she wore, but I was too tired to tense up, too sore to be scared. I had no idea how I was going to pass this part of our training, what secrets she thought I knew or could tell. I didn't know how to prove I was as clueless as I claimed.

"You know something."

"Tell me. Why would one of us know anything? We're competitors, here for the trial, not for the war."

"That's exactly why," Peliela said, settling behind me. "You lot are unimportant. You're not looking for victory. You see

278

things others don't." She paused. "You know more than you think."

"No," I denied. "I don't."

"Yes, you do." She sounded so sure, her fingers brushing mine, pressing into my palm until I flexed my hand. Her grip tightened around my fingers, holding them still, when I instinctively tried to curl them into a fist. "Today . . . you'll sing for me, trial rat."

She slid the first thin shard of glass beneath my fingernail; and true to her prediction, I screamed a melody over and over until my lungs felt raw, until I wept for darkness. She slid one beneath each nail until blood dripped from my hands to the floor.

By the time she finished, I was broken, physically and psychologically. My body had given out earlier and earlier between the pain and the sheer exhaustion, until I wanted death more than anything, just for the reprieve.

She left me in the darkness again, the dripping spigot keeping me awake.

I closed my swollen eyes and bowed my pounding head. "Sam?" I whispered. "Samael?"

At first, he didn't answer me, then my name was a whisper, *'Octavia.'*

"Tell me something," I said, feeling pitiful and lonelier than I'd had ever been.

'What sort of something?' Samael sounded intrigued, and I took that as a good sign, enough that I pushed my luck.

"Tell me something about you." I almost begged. "Anything."

He hummed in my ear, a soft sound curling my toes in my boots. Maybe the only part of me that didn't ache.

'I am the father of lies.'

"What does that mean?"

'Lies are my native tongue, and I speak fluently,' Samael elaborated, his voice like honey. *'I can tell when someone else*

lies. They're speaking my language.'

Mulling over this information, I was grateful for the distraction. I thought of all the times I'd lied since starting this competition, too many to count.

Had he known every time?

When I tried to think back, I could only recall the moments I'd told him the truth, since I was damned to the devil all the same.

"Are you lying to me now?"

His answering chuckle was sensuous. *'You'll never know.'*

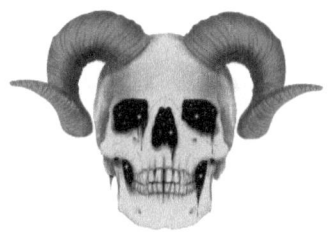

Chapter Twenty-Five

Deep below Wrath Hall, they allowed a day of rest. Unbound, I was recovering from broken bones and a tattered psyche. I hated my forced gratefulness towards Major Akua and General Inaina for letting me rest. Our numbers had dwindled drastically, where many of the trial competitors withstood the torment of the physical training, building muscle and learning routine. The last weeks of damage had been too much.

I didn't blame them, not when I curled in the corner, weary and stiff, sure I had mended the wrong way.

Everything hurt.

During the night, a soft squeaking had irritated me, grating my nerves and forcing myself to my feet to find the source. It was a hellhound, which looked too small, too thin. Instead of their naturally pointed ears, it had soft, floppy ears, like pieces of rich, plush cloth. Its feet and head looked too big for its body, and it had rolls of skin that didn't quite fit its frame, like it was struggling to grow into it.

Large mournful eyes replaced the usually wrathful scrutiny of a hellhound. It tugged on my heartstrings, even as I crept forward with the sick intention of silencing the hound forever.

It had separated from the rest of them. The mother was on the far side of the room, growling at anyone who dared come near her pups. It must have abandoned this one to fend for itself. It cried a pitiful squeak, sounding more like a rat than a beast of the devil. On that thought, I paused, my hands reaching towards the hound.

I'd thought of it as a rat, the same way citizens in Invidia had called me a rat, who would scurry in the gutters for a better chance at life.

I sighed heavily and edged forward. "Hey, hey . . . shhh."

When I picked it up, the creature yelped but didn't move to nip, rolls of dark fur incredibly velvety. It was heavier than it looked, the hound snuggling into the crook of my elbow. I stroked the fur at the back of its neck, debating whether I should put it out of its misery, but it curled close, silencing as its trembling stopped, and I realised I'd never be able to take its life.

'You're too soft-hearted, Little One,' Samael said.

It sounded like a gentle reprimand, as if the devil did not approve. I carried the beast back to my corner, settling down and dumping it into my lap.

"If only that were a sin to beat," I murmured, rubbing the hound behind the ears.

"Tav," Nash called. I glanced up. He approached and sat beside me. "What are you doing?"

I looked into those big yellow eyes, and I reached for my pack of rations, tearing open the bundle of dried meat to offer the canine. "Saving one of us."

The mutt ate as if starved, without coming up for air, and when the food was gone, it cried for more. Hushing it gently, I scratched the back of its ears.

Nash leaned away, coughing into his elbow, a stark, wet sound.

"Are you okay?"

"Yeah." He brushed me off quickly. "Just the damp down here." Nash leaned close, his body warm and comforting, and I tried not to flinch at the sight of his face in the low light.

Most of his skin was a mottled black and blue, one giant bruise, his nose off centre where it had been smashed.

"Are you really going to keep that thing?"

The hound had settled in my arms, having drifted to sleep, faintly snoring.

It was a bad idea. When I formed attachments to human beings, they died. I felt like a reaper, and I wondered if I'd be dooming this hound to the same fate. It would have died anyway, I reasoned, alone in the cold and dark.

"Why not?" I asked. "At least 'til she's on her own two . . . err, four, feet."

His look foretold a thousand reasons why not, but he didn't voice one of them.

Nash sighed and curled up, closing his eyes. "What will you call it?"

It was a question that haunted me for days, until the pup had taken to following me around the chamber, always tripping over her too-big feet.

"Ira. I'm going to call her Ira."

Finley Nightingale snorted. "After the city of Wrath? That's the least wrathful hellhound I've ever seen."

Ira whined at my heels, begging for attention. She was velveteen and gentle. Finley was right, I'd never seen a less wrathful creature. I'd seen no one less affected by the angel above us. Her influence wore on our nerves, winding us tight, humans and hounds alike, but this creature resisted it all.

"That's the beauty of it," I said.

283

The pup followed me as, for the first time in days, we ventured aboveground. In bright sunlight, we looked far worse, our swollen, discoloured bodies on stark display.

"Devils, Tav, you're a mess!" Nash cried, elbowing my ribs.

I sucked in a sharp breath at pain shooting from that point, unwilling to show him just how much it hurt.

"Says you . . ."

Someone tapped me on the shoulder, and I turned to find Finley beaming at me, even though his left eye was swollen shut.

"What do you want?"

"Your pup is eating the garbage," he told me, surprisingly straight-faced.

"What?!" I twisted to look where he pointed.

Sure enough, the little beast had rooted through the garbage and was rolling around in it.

"Ira! No!" I cried.

The hellhound rolled onto her belly, standing to shake her head, her ears flapping, jowls wobbling with the force of the movement, and behind me, someone laughed.

We ventured into the main camp, settling around a crackling fire and listening to the soldiers' stories.

It was easy to lose myself to their determined relaxation. They were making the most of every moment.

When a pack of cards appeared from one of their packs, I turned eagerly into the game, twisting away from my cohort to focus on the flip of the cards. I fished a few coins from within my pockets and eagerly placed my bet, entranced by the familiar game. Time slipped away with ease as the cards flipped over, and elation overwhelmed me as I won but was devastated when I lost again.

When Nash tapped me on the shoulder, bringing me into his conversation, it was difficult to pull myself away, to push away the fantasies of staying in these camps forever. Cosy by the fire, running my own game of cards, and making money as the house.

It felt a world away from war.

I tuned into the conversation, leaning against Nash and scratching behind Ira's floppy ears.

Crude humour of the soldiers lifted my spirits, a feeling dimming when Major Akua approached.

"Trial competitors," she said. "Rise."

Nash looked concerned, sharing a quick look with Finley.

Along with the troops, we scrambled to fix the leather masks over our faces, maintaining proper attire in front of the major.

After a beat of hesitation, Niklaus rose, standing tall despite the healing cuts sliced into his body. They had healed badly and looked as if they would thicken into horrible scars.

Slowly, we followed suit, rising behind him, standing as a small battalion.

"Yes, Major?" Niklaus said, drawing her attention to himself.

She studied us for a moment, the crackle of the flames too loud in the silence of her approach. "You have done well," Major Akua admitted. "Far better than I anticipated. I thought you would all be soft-willed and that you would crumble beneath structure and routine. However, you've proven that you have the patience and the will to survive."

I shifted my weight, distinctly uncomfortable in the face of unexpected praise. Ira sat on my feet, heavy and warm, a reassuring presence.

In the past week, eating most of my meals, she'd grown a little fatter and a lot more comfortable.

"Thank you, Major," Niklaus said with confidence, stepping forward and identifying himself as the leader of our group. He looked around.

We had started this trial with over two hundred people, and less than half remained. We'd watched members tear each other into shreds, covered in blood and gore, before killing themselves out of guilt when the rage abated. Heaviness weighed on our shoulders at the constant losses.

"What happens next?" Aureen asked. "Are we going to war?"

It was the question everyone wanted the answer to. Were we about to join the leagues of tired, dirt covered soldiers on the war front?

The major's eyes cut across to her, but Aureen didn't wither beneath her stare.

"Not yet."

Although relieved we wouldn't see the front of battle that day, I wasn't ready, not when inhaling too deeply hurt and sleep had been scarce. "Head to the medic's room. You meet with Lady Wrath in a week."

I wanted nothing less than to stand before the angel again, too close to her suffocating magic. Others looked excited at the prospect, and it reminded me that Niklaus had united them on the foolish path of killing an angel. Where they fantasised about tearing off her wings and claiming feathers for trophies, the idea left a knot in my stomach, sure killing a deadly sin would have immeasurable consequences.

"Understood," Niklaus said, and I realised I'd missed part of the conversation.

I glanced to Nash, but he was staring at his feet, rolling a piece of white chalk between his fingertips, his lips pursed. "What time, Major?"

"As soon as you finish your meal," she said. "Do not make Heiau wait."

Major Akua didn't linger to say goodbye or to chatter with us but marched back towards the buildings, whistling sharply to beckon her hellhound to follow, the muzzled animal slinking low by her side. I nudged Ira off my boots and collapsed back down into the dirt, watching the way Nash's nail dug into the side of the chalk, scattering white dust.

"Are you ready for war? I'm not."

"No," he mumbled. "I think it's all right to be afraid of war, don't you? We're more likely to die out there. I'll never see Alby again. All this is for nothing if I don't win. I'll have just lost time with him."

"What's he like?" I asked, curious about the man for whom Nash would sacrifice everything, the man so captivating that he would risk the pain and trouble of The Devil's Trials to save him.

I didn't think I had anyone in my life like that, that'd risk everything for, except myself.

"Alby is . . . He's colour in a black-and-white world," Nash said, a soft smile pulling at the edge of his lips. "He's the sort who could find the positive in the absolute worst situation. He has this dark sense of humour, and most of his jokes go right over my head, but he's patient when I don't know it. It suits him, though, you know? He's got dark hair that never sits in the right spot, dark eyes that see too much. His mouth looks suited to a scowl, even though he smiles more than he should." Nash tossed the piece of chalk in the air and caught it. "If he was a colour, he'd be the burnt orange of the rising sun, the glowing promise of a new day."

"Do you love him?"

Nash nodded. "I'd die for him, wouldn't I?"

That simple question, I guessed, was answer enough. My eyes slid to Niklaus, who was watching me. Our gazes connected, and I swallowed roughly, quickly breaking eye contact.

I'd wanted him once. I'd saved his life, and he told me he'd wait for as long as it took, but I wouldn't die for him. I wouldn't die for anyone. I wanted the immortality that Samael offered an endless lifetime to truly live, even if I had no plans for the moments and years it would give me.

I watched Niklaus from beneath my lashes, my fingers buried in Ira's fur to keep my hands busy.

He gawked at me.

My throat was thick. I wasn't entirely sure what to do with him and what had changed. In losing his brother, he had latched onto me, less a tormentor but a determined saviour. Though I couldn't afford to deem him as anything more than a weight dragging me down.

Deliberately avoiding meeting his eye again, I turned my head.

Niklaus cleared his throat, his spoon clinking against the tin bowl to get our attention. "Come on." He tossed his bowl in the dirt and stretched as he rose again. "You heard the major. Let's not keep the medic waiting."

He strode off, Margot on his arm, confident we would follow, and we did.

The medic's room still carried the sharp smell of burnt herbs and cleaning products. It was whitewashed, cold, and sterile. The beds crisply made, and too few for all of us, so we hovered in the walkway until Heiau appeared, wiping her hands on the front of her tunic.

"Right," she said, no nonsense and firm. "Let's get you ready for battle."

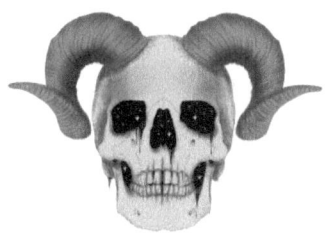

Chapter Twenty-Six

The Angel of Wrath made us wait, tense as we stood tall in our armour.

With heavy swords belted at our waists, we knelt on her office's stone floor with our heads bowed and waited until she deigned to arrive. It was a power play.

My knees ached from the pressure of the stones, a sharp ache in my neck, and for every moment she left us, my resentment grew.

The doors blew open, banging against the wall, and Wrath stalked inside. I sneaked a quick look in her direction.

Her long hair was twisted into braids and wound around her head, the red strands a contrast. It became a halo of death, a crown of her kills.

Her eyes glowed, bright and unrelenting, but she held her power back. Where I had expected to tremble with barely suppressed rage, I was numb.

Wrath gave us a break from the unrelenting tension of her influence, and that scared me more than anything else.

"Rise," she commanded.

We followed the command in eery unison, standing at attention before one of the seven deadly sins. A curl rose to her upper lip as she studied us, as if we would never measure up to what she wanted from her army. Her dark wings rustled and pulled in tight against her body.

"You have completed your training to join my army. Do you know how long you've been here?"

"Six months?" someone guessed. "I think."

"Near over a human year," Lady Wrath corrected.

Shivers rolled through me. I'd lost count of the days when the exhaustion melted one into the other, when periods of broken, blacked-out injury had left me with week-sized holes in my life.

A year meant I'd missed a birthday, and it meant I'd left Ilrea roughly fourteen months ago, long enough for my family to forget me. Weight dropped on my soul. I should have put my family out of my mind, but a part of me mourned the idea of being forgotten.

"You've trained long and hard. How do you feel?" Wrath continued.

We met her with an apprehensive silence. None of the other sins had spoken to us so openly, and after watching her berserker rage shred our fellow competitors, she was no more merciful than Envy or Gluttony.

Niklaus stepped forward, positioning himself at the head of the group. Aureen stepped to stand on his right side. I didn't know if they were brave or foolish.

"Stronger," Niklaus said. "We've grown."

Wrath nodded, the flash of a quick smile more like exposing bared teeth.

My body tensed, alert and aware of oncoming danger. Something wasn't sitting right.

"Indeed," Wrath said. "Tell me, competitors of The Devil's

Trials, do you have what it takes to complete this trial?"

Niklaus's green eyes seemed to glow, brewing madness in the light filtering through the windows.

"We do," he said without a hint of doubt. "We've survived so far, haven't we?"

The angel's dark brows rose in surprise at his tone as his falsified respect dropped away.

Niklaus stood taller, chin lifted as he stared her down, daring her to make a move against him.

"Do you know how to complete it?" she asked, a cruel smile pulling at the edge of her lips.

It was as if she knew we were just as lost as we had been on day one, hardened by her training but still hopeless. We were at her mercy, no matter how many weapons we had.

Wrath clicked her tongue, a sharp sound echoing in the room. She settled within her chair, hooking one booted foot over her knee, staring us down. "Emotions run rampant in the war between sins. Wrath feeds into envy, and envy fuels wrath. Forbearance becomes the only way to win," she recited, staring Niklaus down, the corner of her mouth curving upwards just enough I thought she seemed amused by his daring. "Tell me, human, what does that mean?"

There was no mistake she was speaking to Niklaus and him alone. A fire sparked in her eyes as she asked, and he matched her energy.

His jaw clenched, teeth bared, a feral look flashing in his eyes, as if he knew the angel's secrets and weaknesses, as if it would be him to slide a knife into her heart.

We stood behind him and his little misfit army, but as part of her command, we waited to see which of them would win.

He was foolish and impulsive, and Wrath would flay him alive, but his throat bobbed, a slow movement that shifted the colourful pictures tattooed into his skin. His tongue darted across his lips, wetting them.

"I don't know," he admitted finally, unwilling to look away from the angel.

Wrath laughed in our faces, the sound bouncing off the walls, the derisive edge in it creating a layer of anger beyond anything her powers could have induced. Armour creaked, steel cutting through the air as weapons unsheathed. Wrath's amusement only seemed to grow.

"How do you win something you do not understand?" she asked, lifting a gloved hand and waving towards the side door. It creaked open, and a cloaked figure stood inside. "Are you all simply lucky? No! Fools who don't know how to quit, I think, is more accurate."

"We're determined to win," Niklaus grit out.

"You're all idiots!" Wrath declared. "Who will be shredded in the trials to come. Mark my words."

"But not this one," Niklaus said evenly, having caught onto her words. "In the trials to come, maybe, but we've passed this one. We've done everything you asked of us."

Wrath stared him down, anger glinting in her eyes. "Hmm."

She waved again, and the cloaked figure lifted her hands to knock back her hood.

Starkly familiar and a welcome sight, Cyn's soft tattooed swirls felt out of place in the rough war camp of Wrath, a sure sign of the end of a trial.

"We're done?" a voice cried, filled with relief.

Their sword clanked against the stone as a woman fell to her knees, scrubbing her hands over her face. "Finally!"

Wrath's answering smile reminded me of the hellhounds, utterly vicious.

"Not quite." She stood, gesturing towards Cyn again, who stepped back silently. "You have technically passed. Forbearance, your patience, is the countenance to Wrath. That is what Luce wants from you, but you have not yet fulfilled *my requirements* to pass."

I frowned.

Who was Luce?

Her words made no sense to me, and my head spun as I tried to sort out my thoughts. I hadn't realised they could do that, that the sins weren't bound to release us to continue through the trials when we met the passing requirements.

My heart thundered in my chest, terror enveloping me and stealing the breath from my lungs. We could be forfeited to Wrath and her army for as long as she wanted. I might never find my way to Eternis. I would never dance with Samael outside of my dreams.

"What . . ." I said, finding my voice in the stunned silence. "What do we need to do to . . . uhhh, meet your requirements of passing?"

Her gaze glowed. She stood tall, a proud, vengeful angel primed for a battle. "Fight on my battlefield. Kill in the name of Wrath," she said. "Come back, earn your reds. Cyn will stamp you, and you may move on."

Her attention turned to Margot Galatea, pinning her in place.

Margot didn't flinch, but her hands trembled. "You know what *you* need to do for me to release you."

I shifted, uneasy with this turn of events. All eyes seemed to be on Margot, waiting for her response, but she merely tipped her chin in soft acknowledgement.

Wrath nodded firmly. "Prepare to march out in the morning. I will see you on the battlefield."

She left us in stunned silence, Cyn following in her wake.

Major Akua cleared her throat from the side of the room. She stepped in front of us, placing herself higher than Niklaus as if to remind him of his true ranking, then peeled her mask away from her face.

A startling difference to her appearance proved against what I had expected. There were deep scars carved into the flesh of her cheeks, letters etched into her cheeks, healed into thick, uneven tissue, marring her otherwise slender face. She had a small soft mouth.

"It's spells ENVY," Nash whispered.

I thought she would hide it away, having given us the glimpse of her face, but Major Akua crumpled the mask in her fist and lifted her chin proudly.

"War," she rasped. "War is nothing like your training. It's a thousand times worse. It's hard, dirty, and painful. You will battle, and your opponents won't pull their punches. They don't care if you live or die. Their methods for torture are brutal, many who they capture don't survive. I was lucky enough to come away with only physical and mental scarring." Her lips pursed, and she drew a deep, fortifying breath. "You may think I've been hard on you this past year, just as recruits have before you—and more will thereafter—but I promise you, I have tried only to keep you alive in an angel's war. A war that is none of our business, but we are condemned to fight."

My breathing came too quickly, the remnants of panic lacing through it. "Are you fighting with us?"

Major Akua's lips twitched, as if she wasn't surprised to find me speaking up, and I wasn't sure if I liked that, since I'd never been the bold one. I'd paled in comparison to my brothers, been invisible standing next to Helina, but Major Akua had seen me from the very beginning of our training. I'd never been able to hide.

"No. A new league of recruits will march in from the city and surrounding towns after you vacate to the war tents tonight, and I will take responsibility for them as I did for you. I will prepare them as best I can." She paused, as if she expected us to thank her, but I couldn't find the words. From the silence, I guessed I wasn't alone in the sentiment. "You must pick a leader from your own ranks."

Aureen and Niklaus stepped forward. "Me!" they said in unison, before turning to pin one another beneath challenging, furious gazes.

"Wrath command is always a woman," Aureen argued quickly. "It should be me."

"I'm the one who's stepped up this far!" Niklaus spat back. "You've just followed in my shadow, Willett. Nobody will follow you!"

"*Enough,*" Major Akua boomed, and they stopped instantly, still glaring at one another. "The battalion itself must pick. Stand three paces apart." They did as she said, and she lifted her focus to the rest of us. "Pick a side, soldiers."

I realised we were no longer recruits but soldiers, no longer her problem. The change in title symbolised a significant change in rank. Our group split, Kyra, and many women moved to Aureen's side.

Margot, Helina, and many men rushed to Niklaus's side.

Nash wavered for a moment and then moved to stand behind Niklaus. Finley trailed after him, drawing a scoff and a hiss from Aureen.

"Traitor!" she spat at him.

A handful of us stayed in the middle, caught under their attention, the attention of both proposed leaders searing through my armour and burning against my skin. With no wrong choice, the position of leader meant nothing to me. We weren't the group following command.

"Octavia," Niklaus said, drawing my attention to him. One of his brows raised, head tilted to the side in a command to move to his side, where he thought I belonged.

My face scrunched up behind the mask at his presumption, teeth set on edge, but when I looked at Aureen, all I could think about was the callous way she had disregarded Monika as she died. Leaving her to drift into the ether, unwilling to stay for her last moments. Nothing in that choice led me to believe she would stand for me as a leader, that she would care if I died because of her directives. She was cold and callous—and wanted to win. It

295

was enough to send me to stand tense behind Niklaus.

"Good girl," he said, loudly enough that Helina laughed.

I shot him a dark look, promising pain. "Shut up."

Major Akua twisted when the last of the soldiers had picked a side, her lips moving as she counted beneath her breath, tallying the numbers on each team. When she was done, she nodded and twisted to face us.

"Congratulations, Major Heira." Her hand clapped against Niklaus's shoulder. "You're now the leader of Lucifer's Battalion, Regiment of Wrath's army." She grinned, stretching the words carved into her face with the movement. "Claim your tents tonight. You march out at dawn."

"Who's Lucifer?" I asked when she had left.

'That would be me.' The devil laughed in my ear. *'Welcome to my army, Little One.'*

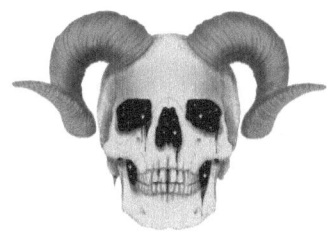

Chapter Twenty-Seven

The camps were no upgrade from the training barracks. When we spilled out into the sprawling mass of canvas tents and tired soldiers, we weren't immediately welcomed. A tired general grunted at us to claim the tents of the dead if we could and make ourselves fit for the night. We ended up cooped up together, with too little room for too many people.

Niklaus kept us together, the Ilreans, plus Finley and Margot. He forced us into the small space together, too close for comfort.

I huddled in one corner, cradling Ira in my arms despite Finley's protests that I could have dropped her and run. I couldn't bring myself to abandon her, the hellhound growing pudgy as too many soldiers fed her, but she still had sad, haunted eyes and a desperate need to cling by my side. I couldn't bring her with me when we marched out; it would be too dangerous, but I could keep her protected in the meantime.

"Margot," Niklaus said, when we had relaxed as much as we

could, "what task did Wrath give you?"

She stilled, her pale skin looking sickly as she refused to meet his eye. "Nothing."

"Tell us," he pressed, frowning. "I can't protect you if I don't know what you're doing."

"I don't need protecting!" Margot protested.

As he clenched his teeth, I watched as rage flew across his face. "I told Mikhael that I'd look after you," he said. "That's a promise I intend to keep. Whether you like it."

She turned to face him, her blue eyes wide and pleading, a definite change of tactic from a moment before. "Take me to him tomorrow, then."

"What?" Nash gasped. "You want to go to the Envy camps?"

"No!" Niklaus declared after giving her request a moment of thought. "The plan remains the same. We march to war; we kill the angel, and some Envy bastards along the way to make sure we can move on from this insanity."

"Nik!" Margot protested. "It's important! I need to see him."

"It's not up for discussion." He spoke over her, tone firm. "It's too dangerous."

Her face shuddered, smoothing out with annoyance. "I'll go without you."

"I'd like to see you try," he said, scoffing.

"He'll die if we don't find him." Those were the magic words, and she knew it. Niklaus went still, the full force of his deadly green gaze settling on Margot.

"What are you talking about?"

She pressed her lips together tightly, refusing to answer.

"Margot," Niklaus warned, "tell me."

Her eyes flicked to the rest of us, a pointed look.

A growl rolled from the back of Niklaus's throat, and he lurched to his feet, snatching her arm and dragging her out of the tent with him. I tried to listen in on their conversation, but other noises in the camp drowned their whispers out.

When Niklaus returned, he was the image of fury, tense with rage pent up in the small tent with us. Luckily, he seemed to realise it, exiting as fast as he'd returned.

"Tomorrow, we're finding Mikhael," he announced as he exited, words stilted, a furious glare thrown in Margot's direction. "It's our first objective."

When he disappeared, Nash nudged me in the ribs. "Go after him."

"Why me?" I asked, scoffing.

He gave me a pointed look. "He doesn't call me *'love'* now, does he?"

With a sigh, I bundled Ira into his arms. "Fine."

She squirmed in his grip, whining that she couldn't come with me, but I rubbed her belly until she settled, steeling myself for a conversation I didn't want to have, and followed Niklaus out into the night.

"Niklaus!" I called. He didn't slow, striding forward, his long legs carrying him fast enough that I had to jog to catch up. "Niklaus, wait!"

I chased him down the path, winding around the canvas tents, my boots slipping on the gravel. It wasn't until we were free of the camp itself, standing in the open red-dirt plains that he spun to face me, tense and haunted.

"What do you want?" he spat. It took everything I had not to flinch, reminding myself that this angry man was more than the Niklaus Heira I knew.

"Just making sure you're okay."

"Done with your precious Sam already?" he asked, stepping forward and forcing me back a step. His tone was so harsh that it left my neck prickling with warning. "I thought I'd be waiting longer for you to come back to me. Is the idea that we could die tomorrow, slaying an angel, so you want a piece of me before we go?"

I shook my head in sharp denial. "Nik!"

His smile turned cruel. "Or are you just here for some fun behind Sam's back? Are you here for one last quickie, an orgasm before death?"

A sharp laugh pulled from my throat, a retort spilling out before I could stop it. "If I wanted pleasure, I wouldn't come to you." I rolled my eyes. "I'd be more satisfied taking matters into my own hands."

His eyes narrowed, a cruel smile twisting into a bitter smirk. "Go on, show me how you do that."

"Asshole," I snapped.

He scoffed, eyes darkening as he advanced another step.

"What's going on with you?" I asked before he could retort. A muscle twitched in his cheek. At first, I thought he wouldn't answer me, his fists clenched, jaw tense. But after a moment, he let out a slow breath.

"Margot's task," he muttered.

My interest spiked, and I fought the tinge of excitement. I'd wanted to know since the day it had been allocated. I wanted to know what use Margot Galatea and her letters had for this war. "She needs to find Mikhael, convince him to take her back to the camps, and drop Henbane into their water supplies."

I stilled, thinking of the vial I had carried across these lands, the one Margot had stashed away somewhere in preparation to kill an army.

"Why Henbane?" I asked.

"It'll look like an inside job," he said. "Apparently, it grows at the base of harpies' nests, so they'll think it was treason from within. Wrath wants them fighting one another to get the upper hand."

"What if Margot doesn't do it?"

Niklaus met my eye, looking haunted. "Wrath is going to

hunt down Mikhael. She says what we've seen of her power is only a drop, and she'll use it to turn Mikhael inside out, into a mindless beast with a blade, and use it to drive a sword through our hearts."

I shivered. "Do you think she can?"

"Do you really want to find out if she can't?"

He would never risk his brother. Mikhael was more important to him than anyone else in the world.

I thought about this, about the conflict warring in Niklaus's eyes.

Truth settled in the idea that we had seen nothing of the angels and their power. The trials were hard, but we could succeed. If we couldn't make it to Eternis, there would be no point in trying. These creatures, gods from another world, had slaughtered civilisation once, turned us into sinful creatures until we'd thinned our own population and receded into oppressed pockets of humanity.

They had true power, and we hadn't seen it yet.

"So," I began, "tomorrow, you're going looking for Mikhael?"

He nodded tersely.

"What if they think he poisoned them? What if Envy kills him, anyway?"

Shadows flickered in Niklaus's eyes, unable to sit still, his agitation growing as he clenched and flexed his fingers.

"One extra day is better than none," he said. "I owe him that much."

"Why?"

I would never understand the bond's strength between the brothers, but I still wanted to know, craved to know what it was like to be so connected to someone for whom you would risk everything. I'd saved Niklaus, as he'd said, but I hadn't thought I was risking my life, not when I'd been sure he would die, anyway.

Niklaus didn't answer, leaving my question lingering in the

air as he walked away, as if he had had enough of questions, of me, of life itself.

Well before the sun rose, I buckled my armour, tightening it around my body as my last line of defence. My sword sheathed at my back, where it pulled heavy but reassuring, and I joined the rest.

We looked simultaneously better and worse than we had a year ago. We were stronger, with a look of determination, instead of wearing the fragmented shadows of our fractured psyche. But we were still no real army. It showed in the way we stood, sectioned into little groups, each one out for themselves. While we had learned to obey commands, learned to fight, built resilience, we didn't trust each other yet, and I thought we never would.

"All right, *General Heira*." Aureen's tone dripped with disdain as she announced Niklaus's title. "What's the plan?"

Nodding slowly, he positioned himself in the middle of the group with his sword strapped down his back, mask clenched in his fist. Niklaus stood tall and proud, as if he'd earned this position, as if he deserved it.

It left me unnerved, after some consideration, that Niklaus was the general of our battalion, while his brother commanded the Envy troops.

"We march out shortly. Split into small effective groups as we meet the Envy troops. Make your kills and retreat," he commanded firmly. "You've already won this trial. It's time to get out and move on."

"What about killing the angel?" someone hissed. "What about our revenge?!"

Niklaus swung around, his green eyes pinning them to the spot, and to his credit, the soldier didn't wilt beneath the ferocity of the look. "If you have an opening and the desire to take your chances, do it. Kill the angel and avenge us all." He seemed to grow taller, mesmerising as his anger grew, almost crackling in the air. "But I won't blame you, any of you, if you want to move on to the next sin."

It almost sounded convincing, and I shivered. A murmur swept through the group, friends turning to one another, whispering. I didn't know what my plan was for marching into war. I would stick close to Nash, and I wouldn't be taking my shot at Wrath, but, otherwise, I just had to find the strength to kill in battle. It wouldn't be the first time I had murdered someone, but that didn't mean it wasn't difficult. It was the one thing we truly hadn't trained for, the one thing Nash admitted late the prior night that haunted him. He didn't know if he could take a life.

It was there that I had an advantage, remembering the way Aieke's blood had flowed from her neck, how it had felt to press the knife hard enough to her skin to flay her open, muscle and more. I had taken a life, and while I liked to think of it as merciful, it might have been an inherently selfish act. I just had to prepare myself to do it again.

"Ready?" Niklaus asked, cutting through my thoughts.

Soldiers nodded, shifting to pick up their packs, rations, and filled canteens.

When we stood with our gear, ready to move, he grinned broadly, securing his leather mask over his nose and mouth until it was only his eyes glowing with determined rage. "The Devil's Battalion!" he cried, a call to war.

We roared it back!

The amount of walking overshadowed war. I'd forgotten how long it had taken us to cross the plains and find the border between Envylands and the Wrathlands. We walked for over a day, camping in the space between the base and battle, rotating a watch team of four studying to darkness for threats.

Nash's body curled around my own, heavy and warm, but even after sleep claimed him, I couldn't stop my brain from turning, the thoughts a constant flow of distraction that left me lying beneath Nash's draped arm, staring at the way the stars glittered above us.

"Samael," I whispered into the night. "Or Lucifer. Which do you prefer?"

His presence was not as discomforting as it had once been, although the strange feeling of invasion crept in that something wasn't quite right. *'Whichever you would prefer to call me, Little One. I answer to many names.'*

"Can you do something for me?" I asked, daring to request a favour from the devil himself, although I could return nothing.

He'd already lain claim to my soul as a part of these trials, and if I was brave enough to admit it, he was etching himself slowly into other parts of me as well. I sought him out more often than I wanted. I turned to him for knowledge and comfort. The devil had become invaluable to me, tattooed onto a small piece of my heart.

'What is it you want? I can't strike a bargain until I know.'

"I want you to tell me if I'm lying when I tell you something."

'And what will you give me in return, Octavia?'

He murmured my name like a caress, the sound of it causing my breath to catch in my throat. I pressed my lips together, considering what I offered.

'What do you have to tempt the devil?'

"What is it you want from me?"

He chuckled, a soft, toe-curling sound filled with sensuality and promise.

It caused my heart to beat faster.

'What a dangerous question.'

"But you won't tell me . . ." I mused. "You don't know what you want?"

'Oh, Octavia,' he whispered. *'I know exactly what I want from you, Little One. You're just not ready to hear it.'*

"Oh."

'Oh,' he repeated, sounding amused. *'I will be your truth-sayer, but you will owe me, and I will collect when we meet in Eternis.'*

His statement gave me hope that the devil thought I would make it as far as Eternis, to see him in the flesh. That I would survive long enough from him to extract what I owed, but it also left me weary, reminding me of Niklaus and the way he had extracted nameless favours from me in the past.

I'd been fortunate that he'd used it to embed a memory on my skin, in coloured ink. I'd been fortunate that he thought I'd saved his life, and old debts seemed to be erased.

"Okay," I said before I could second-guess his bargain. "Are you ready?"

'Always.'

"I am ready to kill someone to survive this war," I stated, a clear rhetoric that had been rolling through my head for hours on end, hoping if I repeated it often enough, I would believe it.

Humming a soothing tune, the devil considered my words. *'Truth.'*

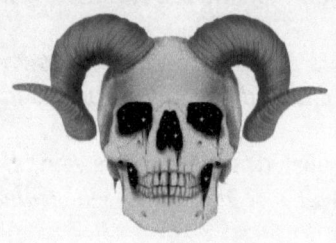

Chapter Twenty-Eight

B attle was pure chaos, a mess of red-and-green soldiers, their swords clashing loudly. Our group had dissolved into small pockets, and soldiers fell on either side of me.

I charged forward, focused only on staying close to Nash and Finley, my blood thrumming in my ears, a marching beat to keep moving and stay alive.

The boys had learned over the past year how to work together and watching them fight was almost like watching Nash sketch. A fascinating art, as they became a fluid movement of bodies, their swords an extension of themselves. They blocked and parried, pushing their way forward, following their leader as he surged forward.

Niklaus had his hands woven into the hair of an Envy soldier, their head wrenched back, the sharp edge of his blade pressed against the soft flesh of the soldier's throat.

"Where's your general? Where's Mikhael Heira?" He

demanded, roaring the words. The soldier refused to answer, stubbornly silent, and Niklaus's knife carved him open, proving that, no matter the side of the war, we all bled red.

He moved to the next man, and the next, savagely leaving a trail of bodies in his wake, until one of them screamed the answers he desired, setting our path and still losing his life. Niklaus dropped him to the ground, stepping over his lifeless body, and striding in the direction he'd pointed.

"Octavia," Nash called, turning to find where I staggered forward, his eyes flashing with a dangerous command, "stay close."

We forged our way forward, following Niklaus's lead. He was determined, single-minded in his goal to find his brother. Above us, a piercing screech stilled the battle for a moment, the impact of two angels slamming into one another, sending us all off kilter. The earth trembled beneath my feet, sending me staggering off balance as shockwaves ricocheted up my legs.

"Die, bitch!" an Envy soldier screeched.

He took advantage of the situation and launched himself at me. I dropped back a step, raising my sword to block the attack. The sound of clashing metal close to my face was so loud it momentarily deafened me, the reverberations shaking my body. Breathless with but adrenaline flooding through me, I shoved him backwards. He staggered, and I adjusted my grip on the hilt of the sword, still amazed I'd learned to balance the weight of it. That I knew how to wield it in such a dangerous way.

He launched into another attack, and I dodged, ducking beneath steel as it whistled through the air. My breath caught in my chest, that I had been too close, and I was aware of he had almost caught the side of my skull with his blade.

Springing up, I slashed at him, the edge of my blade finding purchase in his arm. He grunted with pain and slashed out, forcing me backwards.

"Goodes, come here!" he called over my head.

307

I frowned, confused, and allowed only a split second of warning before someone lunged at me from behind. A scream of fear and frustration poured from my throat. I twisted, swinging blindly, but I couldn't work out how to focus on both threats at once. Most of our training had been one to one. The man at my front slashed his blade, and I shifted back. He struck again and again, and it took too long for me to realise he was herding me backwards. Right into the line of fire.

His comrade swung, their blade catching my thigh, and I pitched sideways, pain shooting through my leg.

"Fuck!" I screamed, blood dripping down my leg.

They advanced on me, and I shook my head hard, trying to focus on the threat instead of the pain, struggling to contain the anger in my body that felt like it might explode from me at any minute. It caught me in a turmoil of emotions.

The angels were manipulating us, even as they battled in the sky. I was envious that they'd struck me down, drawn blood, and I was angry at myself for letting them get too close. Angry at them for winning.

Rage and envy combined propelled me forward; I launched myself off the ground, using my strong leg, and jabbed at one man. He flinched back as I drew blood, and it left me filled with heady exhilaration, as if I'd gained the upper hand.

I wouldn't make the same mistake twice, though, and I twisted towards his partner, striking out roughly to force him backwards. He caught his balance, shifting back one step, but I didn't have to focus on him for long. A blade slid against his side, cutting deep along his ribs.

He twisted, his attacker already hacking at him again and again, using the element of surprise to cut him down until the dirt dripped with his blood, and he sank to his knees. Wild-eyed, with blood-soaked curls flying everywhere and dirt smeared across his face, Finley Nightingale had turned lethal.

I'd already turned back to my main adversary, watching as

he spat on the ground, his teeth bared in a feral grin. I feinted to the left and striking when he moved predictably. We fell into a dance, a pattern of deadly moves. As we circled, Finley, in my peripheral vision, made a swift, sharp move, and the Envy soldier fell on the ground, pain gurgling in the back of his throat.

"Wickham, Nightingale, Nox!" Niklaus roared from the midst of the battlefield. "Come on!"

It seemed he wasn't leaving us behind. I turned back to the Envy soldier, my breath heaving in my chest, my leg searing with pain.

"What's your name?" I asked.

He was limping, and I'd managed a few good strikes.

Finley and Nash appeared on either side of me, swords at the ready, their presence solid and welcoming.

I repeated my question, and the soldier spat a mouthful at my feet. Rage boiled in my belly, my blood running hot. Without a thought, I pulled the dagger from the sheath in my thigh and flung it at the soldier. It spun through the air, lodging in the soft tissue just above his collarbone.

He groaned, an agonising sound I thought would remember forever, then ripped it from his body. His mistake—blood bubbled and rushed from the wound, too fast to be staunched. His breathing came heavy, his fingers slacking on the hilt of his sword.

He wheezed out a word, unintelligible, before he crumpled to the ground. I swallowed heavily, watching his dead body for any sign of movement. Maybe Samael was a truth-sayer after all. In three quick steps, I'd approached my nameless kill, crouching to glance into his lifeless eyes, before I retrieved my dagger from the ground, wiping it on his tunic and sheathing it where it belonged.

Nash and Finley waited for me, and when I turned, the curly-haired man was securing his flyaway hair in a tight knot at the back of his head.

"I'm done," he said, gesturing to the man he'd killed with a wave.

A haunted look took over his brown eyes, as if he couldn't unsee the face of death.

"Done?" I asked.

"I've passed. I'll see you back at camp." He touched Nash's shoulder, whose eyes crinkled at the corners, giving away the quick smile hidden beneath his mask. "Don't be too long," Finley warned and turned his back on the battle, beginning his march to new challenges.

"Tav," Nash said, tearing my attention from where I watched Finley go. "Are you going?" He nodded at the dead man, and I sucked in a sharp breath. I was free, too, although I hadn't completely realised it. I glanced back at him and shook my head.

"Not without you."

Relief glittered in his eyes, and he nodded. "Let's go, then."

We cut through the crowd, following the path Niklaus carved for us, seeking the comrade we had once left behind.

It didn't take long to get caught in the throes of battle again, but I quickly learned how Nash moved, how his height hindered him. He wasn't ducking under sharp attacks. He wasn't moving away as fast as me, but I found I could cut into the small spaces while he kept our enemies preoccupied as the threat they wanted to slay, and I could deliver a deadly blow.

The hilt of my sword crashed into the back of the soldier's skull with a sickening crunch. He waved and then fell; I could see a fragment of his brain pulsing beneath the damage I'd delivered. The sight turned my stomach, but it proved he was still alive.

"Kill him," I told Nash, my voice hard and bitter. Blood covered my hands, so many deaths on my mental list and most without a name, but I'd killed them all, and Nash Wickham had yet to deliver on the last requirement of the wrath trial. "Kill him, and we can leave."

He wavered on his feet; lurching forward, sword raised. For a split second, he was ready, an avenging angel of death, and then he caught himself. Horror flickered in his eyes, and he dropped his sword, the thud of metal in the dirt loud. "I can't."

"Yes, you can." It made me sick to pressure him into it, but I wouldn't leave Nash behind in this trial, not as a forfeit to Wrath, losing to endless days on this war front that would destroy him too quickly. "One death. One kill, and we can leave. Screw Niklaus, screw Mikhael. Kill him, and we're gone."

His hands trembled, and he didn't try to hide it. Beneath a smattering of blood, the colour drained from his face. He shook his head, a look of defeat about him. "I really can't, Tav," he said as the man spasmed on the ground between us. "I'm not a killer. That's not who I am."

"And you think I am?" I asked, the question raw with unexpected emotion.

"No," Nash denied quickly. "You're just stronger than me."

My laugh was hollow. "I'm not strong, Nash," I told him bluntly. "I'm broken." I was built of fragmented shards of my former self that would never fit together properly again.

I stalked forward and hesitated in front of him. "Nash, come here."

He did as I asked, stiff with hesitation. I raised my sword and took his hand, wrapping his fingers tightly around the hilt and pinning them in place with mine.

"No, Tav."

His voice was thick, and my heart squeezed, like I was betraying him, violating him, but I held tight, not allowing him to move, even as he struggled to pull away. "I can't do this . . . Please don't."

"We'll do it together," I whispered and jerked forward, my hand clenching his fingers and steel as I applied all the pressure I could, forcing sword through flesh, blood, and bone.

Nash let out an agonising cry of pain, as if I'd sliced through him instead of our enemy. When I loosened my grip, he staggered backwards, staring at me as if I'd torn him in two. My heart was cracking open at the betrayal in his eyes.

"I'm sorry," I said. "I won't let you die here."

Somehow, in the past fourteen months, I'd grown a slight conscience, just enough that I wanted to see my friend live. He trembled, but when I moved forward, Nash skittered backwards. "Go back to camp, Nash."

"Are you coming?" There was undeniable nervousness in his question, proving he wasn't sure he wanted me to say yes.

I bit down on my lip and shook my head.

"No, I'm going to find Nik."

It was hard not to think of him telling me he had to wait for me. I had to deal with the problem that was Niklaus Heira before I was truly done. His infatuation, the debt he thought he owed me, it would need to die on this battlefield.

"Yeah, I'll see you at the next challenge. Go now, Nash," I prompted in a murmur. "The longer you stay, the more likely you will have to do it. Or you'll die."

Neither option was preferable.

He moved away, and emotion slammed into me like someone had struck me. He stepped out of my peripheral vision, and my chest felt tight.

"Bye, Tav," he whispered and then he was gone, running across the battlefield to his freedom, while I turned to chase Niklaus.

As we approached the dark soldiers of Envy, tension lingered between us.

Niklaus, flanked by Margot and me, stood across from

Mikhael, who stood surrounded by his scaled soldiers. It stretched between us, and we waited for the pain of the recoil when it shattered.

Mikhael was the first to act, removing his helmet, built of black metal and styled after the hood of a cobra; it gleamed under the midday sun. Free of it, he looked alarmingly like the man I'd known. Tall, too handsome for his own good and passive in the way he gazed at us. Rage did not overwhelm him in the way his brother was, not quick to temper or violence. He waited, and he weighed in with what he truly believed to be the right decision. That was why they had picked Mikhael to be the next chancellor. He was strategic and diplomatic.

All men had their weakness, however, and his attention snagged on the woman to Niklaus's right, flaring with unmistakable envy to see her with us. Margot Galatea would forever be his weakness, and Wrath would have been a fool not to use her for it.

"Margot," he murmured. "You're beautiful."

I wasn't sure that was true. Blood smattered across her skin, and she looked exhausted beyond belief. She stepped forward slowly, causing the soldiers on either side of Mikhael to tense, their hands shifting to the hilt of the swords, but Margot laid her sword in the dirt and stepped over it. She peeled her gloves from her fingers and lifted her lily-white hands into the air, as if to prove she meant no harm.

"Mikhael," she breathed, boldly taking another step, moving to unsecure the mask from the back of her head, then dropping the leather to the ground. Her pale lips cracked with dryness, her skin reddened from constant exposure to the harsh, scorching sun of the Wrathlands, her expression unbelievably sad. "I've missed you."

"Margot," he said, her name a word of pure emotion, as if he hadn't meant to speak at all. "You said you'd see me after the war, not in it." She edged closer, and he raised a hand, forcing her to stop. "What's happening?"

She directed the question at Niklaus, whose grip on my wrist tightened until my bones seemed to creak in protest. When he let me approach his brother, it was my chance to run, but my legs couldn't. I was too consumed by the desire to know what would happen next, if Niklaus would send Margot into the Envy camps to destroy them all, play his part in Wrath's plan.

"I'm not safe here," Margot said quickly, drawing their attention. "Wrath knows who I am."

"To me?" Mikhael asked.

"And to Envy," she said. "She's going to kill me, Mikhael."

I didn't need Samael in my mind to know that was a lie.

If the angel knew Margot was one of Envy's precious favoured jewels, stolen away for her near translucent, colourless skin, her hair of ivory—a jewel Mikhael had stolen—then Wrath would have taken her apart, piece by piece and delivered her to her brother in fragments, just for the fun of it.

The words had their desired effect, though, the normally passive Mikhael recoiling from the idea of Wrath destroying the love of his life.

It was not people like Margot who were strong-willed, beautiful, and unique, I realised. But the idea of love, that was the ultimate weakness of humanity. In that moment, I vowed to never truly love, to never open myself up to be destroyed in such a way.

"You need to come with me," Mikhael said abruptly. "We'll look after you where Nik has failed." His brother stiffened, clearly offended. "I'll free you again, Margot."

She played her part beautifully, eyes widening with a fraction of fear, hesitating to move forward when she had been bold before. "What about Envy?"

Mikhael closed the space between them, so fast and unexpected that Margot staggered back, and when he wrapped his arms around her, pulling her close, fingers threading into the pale braid at the back of her skull, we could hear his murmured words on the wind.

"I'll protect you from everything, Margot, from the monsters of the day and the night. Of waking and sleep. You mean more to me than him, to the duty of this position. I live and die for your happiness."

"I love you," she whispered back, melting into his embrace. Her face pressed to his chest without complaint of the scales beneath her soft cheek.

Mikhael squeezed her, his attention lifting to find and pin Niklaus in place, his eyes narrowed. "How are you going to explain her disappearance?"

Niklaus couldn't hide his implication that he had failed the one task his brother had asked of him. Tension in his brother increased, his muscles bunched, his jaw clenched so hard I was sure he wouldn't be able to answer.

"Easy," he said flatly. Niklaus stepped forward, too close to them. Mikhael tensed, reaching for a blade at his hip, but his brother had already wrapped Margot's long white braid around his fist, jerking her head back roughly and slicing at the strands at her nape. Mikhael embrace had secured her in place well enough for him to do it. "Margot's a shit fighter. One clumsy move, and Envy scum ran her through, a stab to the chest, unsalvageable. But this"—he held up her roughly chopped braid, her hair cut unevenly from her scalp—"this is the proof I bring the angel of her death. Margot's too vain to part with her hair if she still lived and breathed."

He wasn't wrong. Her blue eyes had filled with tears, her cracked lips trembling, even though it was only hair, and it would grow back.

Mikhael said nothing, digesting the actions of his brother, then nodded firmly, holding his precious Margot close. "Go, then," he commanded. "Find the angel, brother, and hope to the devil that she believes you."

Niklaus studied them closely and sighed, sounding resigned.

"Anything for you, Mik. Always. Take care of her, yeah?"

He stepped to my side, and we watched as Mikhael whisked her away, promising the death of hundreds if Margot could find the courage or stupidity to do as they had asked her, but if Wrath thought she was dead as Niklaus planned, maybe she need not do it at all.

Whispers would travel across the lands, as they always did. It would reach Wrath and Envy. Everyone would think the angel's pretty toy was broken, never to be thought of again.

Niklaus—if he could lie well—would do as his brother had always asked. He had found the perfect way to protect Margot, because with her fake death came the opportunity for anonymity in rebirth. She could be anything and anyone she wanted, and even though I'd passed the trial of Envy, proved myself better than his sinful ways, I was envious of that.

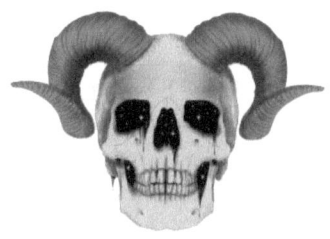

Chapter Twenty-Nine

"Let's find Wrath."

I should have taken my chances when Mikhael marched away, to flee back to the Wrathlands' camps and finally end the trial for myself, but something about the tempestuous rage in Niklaus's expression anchored me by his side.

A sick curiosity that left me wanting to see him lie to the face of an angel, to see him claim this small win for the downtrodden competitors.

He was a man of destruction as we carved a path through the battle. Niklaus twisted and spun, slashing out at enemies in green, and taking lives as if it were nothing. He stepped over their bodies so quickly that they may as well have never existed. Niklaus moved with a single-minded determination towards where the angels battled, where they screeched at each other in an ancient language not meant for our ears, the land buckling beneath their power.

Niklaus's energy increased with every confrontation, every kill, as if he were absorbing energy from Wrath herself, until, angel aside, he was the living, breathing entity of rage, embodying it in his every movement, and I stumbled in his wake.

Soldiers had given the warring angels a wide berth, the terrain cracking open and hard to navigate, but Niklaus didn't flinch, leading me over the rocks until we were too close to the sins for comfort. Their energy crackled in my chest, like inhaling the hot, arid air.

Wrath was a bullet in the sky, tiny and compact. She drove towards her brother, relentlessly attacking him, her dark braid flying as she spun, cutting the air with a dagger carved of the very jewel that Envy had claimed nobody else owned. They wielded blades of akelda as they tried to harm one another, and my heart sunk as I realised we might have all once held a piece of a gem that could harm an angel.

Envy hadn't lost his edge in the year since I'd laid eyes on him. He looked as young and haughty as ever, a breathtaking prince in the place of a king, full of sleek entitlement and vapid desire. He had eyes only for his sister, for the blades she gripped, and he laughed loudly as they battled, the noise striking envy into my heart. He was the sole one of us to be having fun on the battlefield, finding joy in the moment as human soldiers died for their feud.

Every time they clashed, it was a roll of thunder through the air, my ears ringing, the ground shaking, until the world teetered on the precarious edge of a blade. They had decimated us once, flattening our society to rebuild in their image. There was nothing to say they wouldn't do it again.

"Wrath!" Niklaus roared her name. Despite the cacophony of battle and the angel's preoccupation, he pushed through, standing with Margot's braid clenched tight in his fist. "I demand an audience with the angels!"

Anger shook his words.

It was just enough to capture their attention, and they turned in our direction.

In that moment, I wanted nothing more than to crawl beneath the displaced rocks and hide from the scrutiny of angels, godlike creatures who could destroy us with a mere thought. The weight of their gazes left me feeling miniscule and helpless, and I was sure my heart and mind would give out. Niklaus Heira had a spine of steel and stood at attention, waiting for them. I should have run when I had the chance; but with Envy's scrutiny settled on me, there was nowhere to flee. I could only hope my leather mask and the gore of battle was enough to hide me from him.

They dove towards the ground, rocks shaking as they landed. There was an unspoken truce as Envy and Wrath turned to face us, their disgust clear in the curl of their lips and the glimmer in their eyes—who were we to interrupt the battling of gods?

Envy studied me as they strode forward, his wings pulling in tight. Something lit behind his eyes, intrigue, and I stepped behind Niklaus, using him as a shield from the angel who liked to break humans into tiny little pieces. Wrath sheathed her akelda-laced blades, distracting him, and he sniffed as if we were an inconvenience.

"Deal with them, sister," he drawled. "I'm bored already."

Wrath's gaze heated—whether at our audacity or at her brother's command, I didn't know.

"What do you want?" she hissed.

Niklaus glanced between them. His throat bobbed, and he stood taller. He didn't back down, lifting his chin and removing his mas. It dropped to his feet, and his entire face contorted in a leer of excited rage.

"There once was a woman named Margot Galatea," he announced, and Envy went precariously still, poised like a snake about to strike. His green eyes glowed with recognition of his jewel's name. "A woman so pale you could almost see through her, born bleached of the array of colour in humanity. A woman who we hid amongst Wrath's ranks."

"My Margot?" he hissed, turning to his sister. His chest puffed with emotion, his inky black wings rustled with agitation, and he unsheathed a familiar knife. The very one I'd used to kill Aieke. My stomach twisted into a complicated knot. "You stole my Margot, sister?!"

"I stole nothing," Wrath hissed back. She pulled herself to her full height, reaching for a blade of her own. They circled one another slowly.

"You heard him, in your ranks!" Envy cried. "You had her this entire time!"

"She came to me," Wrath bellowed indignantly. "I did not steal a woman from you. If I had, I would have taken the pleasure of annihilating her on your behalf."

Their blades raised, but Niklaus's flat voice cut across the plains, halting them. "She's dead."

False emotion sprang in those words, a welling anger within hollow words, as if he felt betrayed by the loss of life, as if it had crushed him, and he had reforged himself from the pain. If I hadn't known that Margot was alive and well, even I might have believed him.

Angels stilled, and Niklaus lifted the woman's braid for them to see, his fist shaking with barely suppressed rage. He strode forward, leaving me behind, his rage almost palpable. "You sent her on a foolish mission to return home, to poison the Envy camps, and now she's *dead*."

He threw the lock of hair at the angels, and it landed at Envy's feet, sullied by the dirt and loss of life it represented. I didn't expect them to care, not for one human life, when they'd destroyed so many already; but it was a catalyst, an explosive moment.

Everyone moved quickly. Envy ducked to catch the braid of white hair, devastation clear on his face. If I hadn't seen the way his treasures cracked beneath his too-tight grip, I would have thought he actually cared. Wrath lifted her foot, kicking her brother firmly in the chest. It sent him flying backwards, as she took any advantage she had. Envy slammed into the ground, the earth cracking open as he collided with it.

Niklaus took his opportunity and struck; he was nothing but anger, mortal flesh, and steel. He used what he had—the element of surprise—and stabbed through Wrath's left wing, dragging his weight down and shredding through it.

The angel screamed, a sound of nightmares, at her first true taste of pain. Her wail pierced the wild plains. My ears rang, my hearing dulled, and my heart hammered with sickening, too-slow beats. Her power exploded outwards, wrath so strong, so forceful it was a physical blow affecting all the soldiers nearby. Too close, Niklaus, and I took the brunt of it, the power knocking us off our feet and sending us flying backwards.

I landed on another soldier, bouncing off him and rolling through the dirt as my momentum slowed. My teeth pierced my tongue, filling my mouth with blood. My head spun, the world turning sideways as I tried to stagger upright. I couldn't make sense of which way was right, my body leaning to the left as the world tilted. A piercing pain rolled through my head.

Four paces away, Niklaus Heira was groaning, forcing himself upright. In a moment of what could only be called insanity, I dragged myself over to him, reaching for his arm and forcing him to his feet.

"You dick. Why would you stab her?" I asked, my voice raw and mind muddled. I twisted in the mass of displaced bodies and dizzy soldiers, trying to work out where we needed to go, but the deadly plains felt too open and exposed.

"That was the plan." He gasped, holding his head. Blood dripped from one of his ears. "The plan was to kill the angel."

"We'd already won," I hissed. "We were free. She's never going to let you live now, Nik." In the distance, Wrath had pulled the blade free of her wing, still screeching at the pain, as her brother laughed on. "She'll hunt you down. Death will be a blessing compared to her rage."

When he lifted his head, finally looking at me, his eyes were clearer than I'd seen for months. For the first time in and long time, he looked more like himself, and my heart sank to realise how affected Niklaus had been by this angel.

Wrath was his sin to battle. He had been self-aware enough to know that, but, still, we had let her influence wind tight around his soul, leaving him angry, vengeful, bloodthirsty. He'd been wilder these past months than he ever had, consumed by his impulsive rage. He would have never left this battlefield without taking his chance.

"You're an idiot."

"I know." He nodded, wincing at the movement. Genuine fear flickered in his eyes the first time I'd ever seen it. "You need to kill me before she gets to me, Octavia."

"What?" I cried. "No, Nik! I'm not killing you."

"Please," he whispered, a word I thought I'd never hear him say. "Kill me, love. Show me mercy, don't leave me to the temper of that angel. It's a better death at your hand."

"I . . ." My throat seemed to close, bitter tears welling in my eyes. "No. You can run away, hide from her. She'll get bored— the war will call her back. You can get away."

He lifted his wrist, flashing the iridescent cuff we all wore, the tracker that let the angels know when we invaded their cities, that the devil used to keep track of us. "The devil would find me. He'd send me back to her to pay my forfeit."

"He wouldn't hand you over," I told Niklaus, although I wasn't sure I believed it. Samael had shown nothing but disdain when Nik was close to me.

"Of course he would," Niklaus said bitterly. "The devil is the worst of them all."

He drew himself upright, opening his arms and lifting his

322

chin, a man who had accepted his fate, dire as it might be.

"Nik," I warned.

"Do it, Octavia," he demanded. "Kill me. Make it quick."

My fingers tightened around my sword, eyes darting back to the angels, where Wrath was straightening, scanning the surrounding soldiers. It wouldn't be long before she found us, found him. I shifted my weight, finding better balance, and raised my sword.

"Nik?" I murmured.

"Yes?"

"You said you'd wait for me." I shook my muddled head. "You said you'd wait as long as it takes."

"In the afterlife, then," he said, forcing a smirk that felt out of place. "Or the next life."

"Did you love me?" I asked.

His smirk fell away, expression dead serious. "No."

"Good," I said and swung the blade.

It cut through the air, slicing into his flesh. I pressed all of my weight into the strike, my arms shaking as I forced the sharp edge all the way through.

Niklaus groaned, a sound of sharp pain, and dropped to his knees, his green eyes welling up, although I pretended not to see.

"What the fuck did you do, Octavia?" he cried, his hand landing at my feet, his blood soaking my sword.

My eyes snagged on his freed limb, stomach twisting at the jaggedly torn flesh and bone, blood pooling over the iridescent cuff. His other hand, still safely attached, clutched the bleeding stump of his arm where I'd amputated him.

"I saved your life," I said, firmly. "*Again*."

"What?" he croaked.

"Now, when they track you for your sins, Nik, they're going to find body parts on a battlefield," I said, nudging his hand with the toe of my boot. "It was that or your head. But as much as I've wanted to cut you down to size, I will not be the reason you die.

Not here, not now."

"I'd rather you kill me than Wrath," he said, voice hoarse, almost begging for the sweet relief of death.

Shaking my head, I stood firm in my decision, one that I was strong enough to live with.

When he stood, I reached for one of our discarded packs, tearing it open to find a spare shirt. Grabbing his arm, I wound it around his wound so tightly that he winced. It was the only way I knew to staunch the flow of blood, which spilled from his arm and coated my fingers.

"What's that for?" he asked.

"Stability," I said, echoing his flippant tone from when I'd broken my thumb. "You need to run now, Nik," I said, glancing over my shoulder to the angel, who roared wildly, her power shaking the earth beneath our feet. "Get far, far away."

He leaned forward, pressing his weight against me and holding the back of my neck, and it took everything in me not to fight from his grip, even as my skin crawled with fear.

Niklaus pressed his sweat-soaked forehead to mine, holding my eye for a beat too long. I took a second to stare into those familiar green eyes.

"I could have learned to love you," he said.

"No," I laughed, and it felt as cold as it sounded. "You couldn't have. We would have destroyed each other. It would have been intense, as hot as a forest fire, but we would have burned up within it."

"I won't forget this, love!"

"Don't call me that," I said, rolling my eyes, placing the palms of my hands against his chest, pushing him back until he let go of me. "You need to go now, Nik."

"I'll meet you in Eternis."

"Don't . . ." I said. "Don't be an idiot."

"I know I said I don't love you," he continued. "But I'll still wait for you."

"Please don't," I repeated. "Don't wait for me. Don't die for me. You shouldn't *live for me*, Nik. You have the same opportunity as Margot. You can be anyone you want to be, so take this chance and live the fullest life you can. Have what I can't have. Do that for me."

His green gaze blazed bright, confusion creasing between his brows. "But I owe you."

"No, you don't," I said and backed away from him, ending the conversation so that he could leave and flee to the safety I'd tried to provide. My fingers flexed around the cool steel of my sword, and I slid it carefully into the sheath at my back, reaching for the smaller daggers strapped to my thighs instead.

I offered him one last look, one last moment to mourn the people we had been in what felt like a past life, before the devil had entered our lives, and we had learned that we all sinners at heart.

"Octavia . . ."

"All our debts are hereby settled, Niklaus Heira," I told him. "It's time for you to *live*."

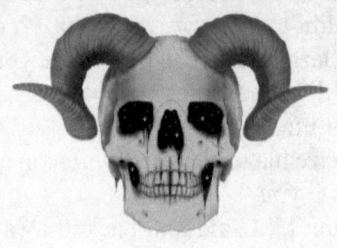

Chapter Thirty

It took a long time to return to camp. I walked right through the night, unwilling to sleep alone and without supplies, and by the time I reached the worn tents and red lion flags, I was half delirious with thirst and completely shattered from the fatigue. My priority should have been to find Cyn and get the hell out of this trial, but I staggered to our tent in search of water, gulping down the too-still, warm liquid in the canteens and then crumpling down onto the bedrolls, tiredness claiming me before I had a chance to even think about my next move. Ira had wriggled around and curled against my side, a soft, warm body, a reassuring presence. I held her close and succumbed to desperately needed sleep.

An intense disorientation came with sleeping for too long. My body was stiff from the lack of a proper bed and lying on the armour and weapons still strapped to my body. My muscles ached as I stretched, protesting the movement, my lids feeling heavy.

There wasn't time for that, however, and I staggered to my feet, finding my balance and searching the camp for three very important things: food, water, and Cyn.

As I left the tent, the little hellhound stayed close by my heels, her eyes big and mistrusting, as if she thought I would leave her again if she let me get too far away.

Food was easy to find. I followed the smell of smoke and roasting meat, then found a large fire with a beast strung over the top, dripping fat into the crackling flames. The cook surveyed me from where she sat, sighed heavily, and pulled herself to her feet.

"Rough days on the front, soldier?" she asked.

I could only nod, realising there were no accurate words for the senseless death beyond these camps. The war fought for no worthwhile reason.

The cook scooped up a tin bowl, shuffling to the fire and peeling cooked meat from the beast's bones. She held it out to me.

I wolfed it down, remembering at the last moment to share it with the pup, blowing on pieces of meat and dropping them to the ground for her to gobble down. The heated fat burned my lips, charred on the outside and tender within, possibly the best meal I'd had outside of the Gluttony trial.

"Sit, sit," she said, gesturing to the logs alongside the other soldiers, and I took my place along with the cup of brew she handed over. It was tart on the edge of my tongue, too strong for my liking, but I couldn't complain, gulping it down quickly.

"So," said a soldier from across the firepit, "what's your count?"

"My count?" I asked.

"How many did you kill, girl?" she asked, leaning forward to give me a glimpse of the red strands of thread bundled in her hand.

My stomach twisted, my hands shaking despite how tightly I gripped the tin cup. It replayed in my memory, the feeling of the first time my sword had pierced flesh, the way hot blood smelled as it sprayed all over my body, and how difficult it had really been, mentally and physically, to cleave Niklaus's hand from his body. I trembled, unable to stop.

"Too many," I whispered, staring deep into my drink as a shudder rolled down my spine. I wasn't a woman with a shining conscience and a penchant to always do the right thing. I had filled my life with dubious and selfish choices, but even I couldn't ignore the enormity of the lives lost in this foolish war. "I honestly don't know."

"Ahh." Her voice filled with soft and reluctant understanding. The soldier stood behind me and clapped a heavy hand against my shoulder. "We'll braid in three, then. It's probably not enough, but at least it won't be overwhelming the first time you catch sight of yourself. Hold still."

It hurt as she pulled strands of my hair from the braid down my back and started at my scalp, twisting the threads and my hair together so tightly I knew the only way to undo them would be to cut it out. The soldier dropped the first one when it was finished, and it swung in my peripheral vision, a flash of wrath red.

Nausea rolled in my belly, my stomach clenching around the meal within. My fingers buried in the soft rolls of fur at Ira's neck, scratching, until she leaned heavily against me for more. It felt impossible, but I found a small sense of comfort in her joy.

"Why do you do this?" I asked the soldier quietly. "Why braid trophies into your hair?"

Her hands stilled for a second before she resumed her task.

"They're not trophies. They're reminders."

"Reminders?" I winced when she tugged too hard at my scalp, moving onto the final piece with single-minded efficiency. "Of what?"

"That we are lucky to live when others do not. When they died by our hand, we ended their lives, and we'll repent to the devil for it when we die," she said. When she finished with the final braid, she tapped my head. "For all the angels in Kaida, all the sins we have to face, the only true unforgivable sin in life is death."

Her words sat with me until the flames in the pit turned to smouldering coal. They were stark and discomforting, but growth came with acknowledging uncomfortable truths.

We didn't move forward if we stayed within the invisible boundaries of our comfort zone. That thought propelled me to my feet; I'd been here, in the Wrath camps, for too long. A year of my life stolen away to this trial, and it was time to move on.

"Where's the tattooist?" I asked, the words raw.

The cook lifted her hand, her fat coated knife pointing the way. "They set up at the black tent on the end of the path. You'll know it when you see it because nobody's lingering about that cursed one."

It didn't occur to me to thank her, not for the meal, the space to reflect, or the directions to my future. I left her behind without another word.

As I approached the tent, Kyra Willett stepped out, her brown eyes haunted, pretty mouth pulled into a taut line. An angry red mark stood stark against her oaken skin. The roaring lion of Wrath, an insignia that could never be removed.

Although they claimed we had won, found the courage to face these sins, and survived, I thought we would be haunted by them for the rest of our lives—and if we won The Devil's Trials, that would be an extraordinary long time.

"Kyra, what's the next trial?" I asked, but she shouldered past me without answering, her head bowed, fists clenched by her side. A single strand of red stark in her swinging ponytail.

It doubled the intensity of the nerves flitting in my stomach, the lump of apprehension growing in my throat. A broken edge to Kyra, marking the loss of her innocence, indicating the end of a chapter in these trials.

There was no delaying the inevitable. I nearly tripped over the hellhound as I pushed my way into the tent, meeting Cyn's eye and bracing myself for the flash of their pointed teeth.

I slid into the chair, and they studied me, making no effort to hurry in their assessment. "You've come a long way from Ilrea, Octavia."

My teeth scraped my lower lip, biting down on the desire to snap back before admitting, "I'm not the person I used to be . . ."

"No," Cyn acknowledged. "You never will be again, but that's a good thing. Growth is inevitable."

"If you say so."

It felt like irreparable damage turned into coping mechanisms, like my life was no better or worse than it had been before, like I hadn't had time to mourn the woman I once was.

Cyn took my hand, pulling it across the table, and pinning it against the hard wooden surface.

Drawing in a deep breath, I closed my eyes, picturing the image of Samael dancing in my dreams, the devil that had captured my interest, wise idea or not, bracing myself to be marked. The brand pressed against my flesh, a searing pain, and it was over as quickly as it began.

"We're done," Cyn advised. They let go of my hand, and I pulled it back to study the third insignia on my wrist.

When I glanced up, they had gone still. Their bald head tilted to the side, eyes narrowed, lips pursed, the shadows and light highlighting the patterns on their skin. Danger highlighted the way they held themself, like an animal aware of a predator, and it cause the hair on the back of my neck to stand on end.

"You need to go outside."

"What about the next challenge?" I asked, stupidly. "I have no idea where I'm going."

"You'll find out very, very soon, Octavia." Cyn's eyes widened, and they jerked their chin towards the door. "Now, go. Someone is waiting for you, and it is not someone who likes to wait."

If I had been more observant, rather than irritated that they didn't give me the information I wanted, I might have noticed the apprehensive silence that had fallen across the camp before I stepped outside. Tension in Cyn reflected in the very atmosphere. Or even my own intuition coiling, the whisper of my fight-or-flight instinct, which had grown more akin to the first response in the past year.

Sunshine blinded me as I stepped outside, and I raised my palm to shield myself from it, squinting until I could bear the harsh glare.

Ira whined softly, squeaking noises of fear. Everything else was silent. Whispers and rumblings of camp had died away. It didn't take long to find the source of the silence.

A tall dominating presence loomed over the campsite, his arms folded across his golden chest as he waited.

"Lord Pride," I rasped his name.

The golden-haired angel's luminous eyes brightened further. "You remember me."

He was out of place on this battlefield, a tall golden god standing in a field of dark-haired women, sullied by battle.

Pride looked exactly as I remembered him, strongly muscled, his face devastatingly handsome despite the off-centre slope of his nose, a sharp shin. His blonde hair curled a little longer at the nape of his neck. A smug smile played at the corner of his full lips, and he exuded the same cataclysmic power that had stolen the breath from my lungs once before. He preened beneath my inspection, reminding me I should answer him before he lost his patience.

"Of course," I said, swallowing quickly, tempering the desire to reach for a blade. "You would be difficult to forget, even if you were not an angel."

"Unforgettable." He chuckled, his silky grey wings rustling at his back. "I like that."

There was no way to work out if he were here as a threat, and I remained tense even as he moved too close, towering over me. I had been told, once before, that dancing with Pride was inviting trouble and only now did I see how true that could be. Possessiveness glimmered in his bright eyes, a sharp edge to his smile. It promised he knew secrets.

I forced myself to speak.

"What brings you to these war camps?"

"You."

It was a simple answer that sent a shiver of trepidation down my spine.

"Me?" I asked, breathlessly. Anxiety wound tight around my ribcage, binding my lungs from a full breath of air. "What would you want from me . . . My lord?"

Almost too late, I remembered to be respectful and polite to save my own life, to smile at him. Surviving angels often came down to appease them, and I'd had an experience with Pride like no other human in these trials. One he'd described as intimate—a word that now left me chilled. Three angels later, I knew that beneath the focus of an angel was not a grand place to be.

Cyn's words rang true. I was so far from the girl I had been, enamoured by the promise of golden-haired sin, I was a strong woman determined to survive, and Pride represented only another hurdle in my life.

His wings stretched, strong and powerful, sweeping around us and caging us in with the illusion of privacy, just as they had once before. My rapid-beating heart felt like it was crawling up my throat so I might choke on it, all my instincts screaming in danger.

It took every ounce of my will to keep my expression calm, to lift my head and let myself smile, like I was still the young woman who had danced with him in a corset of gold bone, hiding behind the face of a skull.

Pride seemed to remember it, too, his tanned hand lifting, fingers brushing to tear away the leather mask. His thumb rubbing at my lower lip as my face was revealed. His touch felt strange, compared to those of human men, too soft and uncalloused, too unburdened.

I fought not to shiver. "My lord?"

"It is good to truly see your face," he mused, and my heart sank at the edge to his tone, the hint of amusement and intrigue. "The mask was beautiful, but you . . ."

"I am not beautiful," I denied quickly.

"No," he agreed. Surprisingly, it hurt to have a golden god acknowledge I was not a beautiful woman; I had never needed to be one. "But there is something about you that's intriguing, mortal."

To be intriguing to the one of the seven deadly sins was the last thing I wanted.

"That's why you're here?" I asked, trying to relax and force a smile, rocking onto the balls of my feet. "To tell me that I intrigue you? That could have come in a letter."

"Actually," Pride said, his tone having sharpened, his smile shifting to a more wolfish look, "I'm here to collect."

Those words struck fear into my heart. I wanted to run, but his wings caged me in, pinned as the sole recipient of his focus.

Nobody was there to save me, only the hellhound pup shivering behind my calves, cowered in the face of sin.

"Oh," I said lamely.

No smart remarks flung about when my lungs felt fit to burst under the weight of my anxiety.

"You promised you would return to Glorae and to me."

"I guess I did," I whispered. Ira whined louder, and I stooped to bundle her up, then cradled her tightly in my arms.

The angel's eyes flicked over the small beast, a glimmer of disgust flaring in his eyes, but he didn't comment. "I just didn't realise I'd be getting a personal escort. Is pride the next trial, or were you sick of waiting, my lord?"

"Come with me." Pride held out his golden hand, the tilt of his lips almost daring me to deny him.

Drawing a deep breath, I slid my hand into the angel's firm grip, allowing Pride to pull me against him, his arms locking me in place.

His powerful wings stretched, his body tensing, and we shot into the air, my eyes squeezed closed, face buried into Ira's soft fur.

I had no choice but to allow him to whisk me away.

Rule number five stated: you may not refuse a direct order from an angel of sin.

Acknowledgements

Writing is always a very solitary activity, there's minutes, upon hours, upon days of staring at a screen and pure imagination; but like all great things, it does in-fact take a village.

As always, my husband Rhys takes the brunt of the life-load when I'm absorbed in a book, and I can't thank him enough for putting up with me as I wrote and edited alongside planning a wedding and moving states. There are no words for how grateful I am for him. Also thank you for once again listening to plot holes about a plot you don't know.

My brother-in-law Dylan was a major help for this book, who patiently answered my annoying questions about what it was like to be part of an army. I did learn a lot, even if I twisted it all up with a lot of creative licence – but hey, it is a fantasy book.

The group at Second Cup Writers Café who sat in sprints with me and excused my miserable attempts at socialisation while I edited.

Café Central in Darwin - who not only kept me caffeinated with their double shots but let me sit in their space for hours upon hours so I could write without the distractions at home. Aussie's, if you're ever in the NT, do yourselves a favour and go get a brew.

Lastly, my friends, family, and readers. Thank you for being excited about this book, for hyping me up, for pre-ordering, for reading. If you're as far as the acknowledgements page, you're the MVP!

About the Author

Stephanie Gluck writes on the traditional lands of the Larrakia people and pays her respects to Elders past, present and emerging. Thank you for allowing me to find my creativity on your land.

I wish I could say that I was a changeling deposited in the world by faeries and that's why my imagination runs rampant, but in all honesty, despite my over-active imagination making me believe I was related to the queen of England at age seven I am just your average person, with a penchant for telling stories.

I'm a nurse, I bake cakes that I then don't want to eat, I cannot keep a plant alive to save my life. I love my dog, possibly more than my husband, but he's okay with that and I have so many stories I want to share.

You can keep up to date with what's coming next via my website or socials.

Website: www.stephaniegluck.com
Instagram: @stephaniegluckbooks
Tiktok: @Authorstephaniegluck

About the Author